Waltz with Destiny, the fourth b[...] Destiny series, grabbed me by the heart and wouldn't let go. Every word captured my attention as the relationship between Esther Meir and Eric Erhardt unfolded on the brink of World War II. And I loved the suspenseful and well-crafted twists, turns, and vivid war scenes. They left me reading nonstop while biting my nails. Catherine's lovely prose, sense of humor, and historical accuracy deliver an unmistakable wow factor. I highly recommend this book to anyone who enjoys romance and/or history.

— DEB GARDNER ALLARD AKA Taylor Jaxon,
author of *Before the Apocalypse.*

Catherine paints a vivid picture of American in wartime in *Waltz with Destiny*. The author wove her father's eye-witness account of the Italian front during World War II into the story, showing readers a deep viewpoint of life on the battlefield. The love story of Eric and Esther is full of faith and old fashion values. The battle scenes are realistic, and the home front scenes are believable. The characters make mistakes we can all relate too. A wonderful history-comes-alive story.

— CINDY ERVIN HUFF, multi-award-winning author

Fans of historical romance will want Brakefield's *Waltz with Destiny*. This final book of her Destiny series once again delivers romance, but not romance neatly tied up with a bow, for Brakefield's characters must live through the gritty realities of World War 2 and other challenges of those years before they can find their destiny.

— RICK BARRY, author of *The Methuselah Project*

Waltz with Destiny

CATHERINE ULRICH BRAKEFIELD

ST JOSEPH, MISSOURI USA

"The wind blows…and you…cannot tell where it comes from and where it goes. So is every one who is born of the Spirit." John 3:8 NKJV

I can still feel the awe, standing beneath the massive white cross at Kolekole Pass marking the pathway the Japanese bombers flew on their way to Pearl Harbor. I can remember seeing the atrocities of the Viet Nam Era spread across my television screen; and, New York's gleaming towers crumble beneath the terrorist attack of September 11.

To the everyday saint—this book is dedicated to you.

"Here is the patience of the saints; here *are* those who keep the commandments of God and the faith of Jesus." Revelation 14:12 NKJV

Cast of Characters

Esther Meir	Daughter of Ruby McConnell Meir
Eric Erhardt	Son of Frances and Anna
William Meir	Brother to Esther and son of Ruby
Ruby McConnell Meir	Mother of Esther & William
Dot McCoy	Friend of Esther. Jewish by birth
First Lieutenant Russell	Eric's lieutenant
Sergeant Rusk	Eric's sergeant
Captain Kimble	Eric's captain

Acknowledgments

I came across a picture at a flea market. The wooden frame was ragged, the glass broken, the picture faded and stained. Yet, the artist's strokes portrayed a scene that I had to possess.

It was a picture of a valley. The sunrise peeked beneath sooty clouds. Below were the bombed and charred remains of trees and a church. Only its walls remained.

A gold cross rested upon its steeple. In the middle of the portrait was Jesus dressed in a flowing white robe, His arms outstretched. His concerned face was haloed and it illuminated the glow of the sunrise.

At Jesus' feet knelt an American soldier, his head bowed and his hands clasped tightly in prayer. In the clouds you could see the busts of George Washington, General John (Blackjack) Pershing, General Eisenhower, and General MacArthur. I removed the frame and found out it was a Ralph Pallen Coleman print, titled *Onward Christian Soldiers*. That painting remained in my imagination throughout the creation of the Destiny saga.

It is bittersweet to be writing this acknowledgement for the fourth book, *Waltz with Destiny*. I feel I should be busy writing the fifth book. Only, sadly, I don't know how that book will end.

The Destiny saga is more than a sweeping romance or the unvoiced history of the United States. It is a testimony of our loving Savior's arms guiding humankind toward a goal that was bigger than any person imagined, larger than the Gatlans, McConnells, Erhardts or, for that matter, our country dreamt possible in the early 1800s.

This Destiny saga is a story about my family, your family, and every immigrant who came to our shores seeking—not to change the American dream, but to embrace its values, morals, and God!

Yes, our triune God. Congress introduced the bill to add the phrase "Under God" to the Pledge of Allegiance and Eisenhower signed the act into law on June 14, 1954, Flag Day! As the Reverend George Docherty said, "To omit the words 'under God' in the Pledge of Allegiance is to omit the definitive factor in the American way of life."

And it is this American way of life we must cherish, fight for, and never relinquish.

Through the determination, patience, and expertise of my publisher, *Tamara Clymer*, and editor, *Debra L. Butterfield*, this conclusion of the Destiny saga, which began in the spring of 2017, now climaxes a dramatic close in 2019 with *Waltz with Destiny*.

Cyle Young, thank you for encouragement. Many blessings and heartfelt thanks to *my husband*, Edward Brakefield, whose inspiration gave me the fuel I needed to reach a satisfactory ending.

My heart sings with my appreciation for *Debra Gardner Allard*. Your God-given talent for the blue pencil and love for *Waltz with Destiny* is my encouragement! *Rick Barry*, thank you for your professional expertise and committing yourself to following this epic series through to its conclusion. Thank you, *Kathleen Rouser*, for your honest reviews and beautiful blogs; *Elaine Stock*, for your inspirational words I always keep close to my heart. *Cindy Ervin Huff*, for your thought-provoking wit.

Without the journal entries, battle dates, yellowed pages of magazines, and newspapers *my dad* left behind for me, I would have been unable to piece together this remarkable journey of American heroism displayed by our valiant infantryman. And without the knowledge I gleaned from the *34th Infantry Division Association* in Johnston, IA, I would have missed the rich knowledge I gleaned from traveling with my dad and his regiment to Gettysburg.

Thank you Historian of the Gold Star Military Museum, *Michael J. Musel, LTC (Ret.) IA ARNG* for helping to clear up some parts of my story. For becoming my friend through reading *Waltz with Destiny*.

To *my grandchildren*, Zander and Logan Warstler, Annabelle and Willow Brakefield, cherish your Christian heritage and remember what it cost our ancestors to keep.

To *Joycelyn, Stephanie, Jeanne, Susanne, Laura*, and all *my faithful group of readers*. You gave me renewed encouragement with your exuberance for this Destiny saga. Your enthusiasm is contagious, as is your honesty; you cannot believe how you encouraged me when you said, "When will the next book be out?" Thank you. From the bottom of my heart!

But most of all, to our God and His son, Jesus Christ, is the glory. The picture I found in that flea market was no chance meeting; Jesus has no chance meetings with us. Be it in our home, office, on the football field of our pleasures, or the battlefield of our regrets, Jesus hears our prayers.

During President Trump's 2019 State of the Union Address, concentration camp survivor Joshua Kaufman stated, "American soldiers proved that God existed. They came from the sky—came from heaven…"

Pray with me that the United States of America will remain a beacon of hope for the oppressed and prove God exists. That America will remain as…one nation under God, indivisible…until our Lord and Savior returns to gather us up with Him for His final victory!

Preface

When the men and women of World War II marched off to war, they didn't know what lay ahead. They only knew that upon their young and inexperienced shoulders rested the plight of the free world.

From the corridors of the Great Depression, new heroes from the Old West sprang up, thundering across the talking movie screen to the pounding hoof beats of The Sons of the Pioneers, Gene Autry, Roy Rogers, and Gabby Hayes.

The offspring of the Great Depression, who had peddled papers and sold apples on street corners, awakened to a new era. Across the nation, they gaily glided into the eloquent ballrooms that mirrored the starlight and splendors of the Aztecs.

The American dream awakened our youth to education, jobs, and prosperity. But across the ocean Hitler was awakening his youth to the idea of a Master Race.

So it was that during the twilight of August 1941 a changing wind began to blow against America's shorelines. Before the autumn moon could chill the summer breezes, many knew the stench of death.

As the lash of Hitler's Third Reich fell upon Europe, the world looked to America, looked to our happy and fun-loving boys and shook their heads.

Compared to their notable fathers of World War I, these boys were like lions are to kittens. These kids couldn't deliver the world from

Hitler's new world order. Not these playboys in their baggy zoot suits, not these "Mama Boys" still wet behind the ears. They were no match for Japan's kamikaze or Hitler's Nazis. They were too innocent, too young, and too inexperienced for the task.

As far as Japan was concerned, America had produced a carefree generation that couldn't rescue themselves from a windstorm, let alone the world from a dictatorship.

Guys like Eric Erhardt remember those days vividly. "The outside world all thought Americans were too soft, and not much more than playboys, and we wouldn't be able to fight—man, did we show them!"

Chapter 1

Steam rose from the overworked press machine at Gill's Dry Cleaners like a haunting refrain from last night's newsreel. "Mother, Britain was blanketed with German Luftwaffe Heavies lighting the night skies with bombs. People were running for their lives—"

"Esther," Ruby Meir said, "Nothing comes from worrying over what you can't change. Only our good Lord knows what lies ahead, and that's the way it's been since God formed this old earth." Her face glistened in the dim light spilling through a dirty window pane. "There's a rainbow with our name on it here in Detroit. It's a city for young people and what you young'uns need before this war sweeps into your lives." She picked up where she'd left off singing "Faith of our Fathers."

Esther Meir replaced a man's dress shirt with another. Mother had traded comfort for commitment to give Esther and her brother a chance to make something better of their lives. Her mother's words mingled with the noise of the machine.

"*Faith of our fathers, holy faith!*" Mother lived up to her name. Being a widow didn't halt her love affair with God's Word. No matter if life handed her a bag of rocks, her faith changed them into rubies. "*We will be true to thee till death!*"

What of herself? Her name was taken from the Bible, the book of Esther. Her grandfather told Aunt Collina that, at times, he felt he was fighting the devil himself during those Civil War battles.

That newsreel caption was the real McCoy. War knew no boundaries.

Well, Grandfather came out unscathed. He named his estate Shushan and claimed Esther 9:2 over America's enemies for generations to come. *And no man could withstand them; for the fear of them fell upon all people.*

How did Grandfather know we'd face a foe like Hitler some day? Mother's words from the hymn were muffled by the noise of the machine. Its vapors stung her eyes.

Memories flooded her thoughts, rising with the steam around her. Aunt Collina saved Shushan from a vindictive lawyer who plotted to steal Grandmother's land and send her family to the poor house.

Esther grabbed a child's dress out of the pile. Did she possess that kind of fortitude?

"Ow!" The webbing of a torn tutu pricked the rough edges of her fingers, drawing blood. She sucked it clean.

Hitler's Third Reich had plummeted Europe deep into his clutches. Mother, Grandfather, and Aunt Collina had the stamina to battle evil. Did she? "Oh, it's hot in here. Can I open that window?"

"I already tried. It's nailed shut."

How can Mother stand this heat? Esther wiped her forehead with the sleeve of her blouse. "You want to hear a killer diller?"

Ruby stopped her sewing. Her face glistened with perspiration.

"Mother, I don't care about Europe, and I'm not prepared to battle the horrors of war if it should come to America—and I have more important things to do than go to a ball!" She clasped the worn skirt to her bosom. "There's no way I'll piece this fabric back together to press it." Will I live up to the McConnell legacy? Or will I tear apart like this cloth?

"Give it to me; I'll sew a stitch here." Mother's gentle hands swiped away a wet strand of Esther's hair from her forehead. Her knowing glance spoke volumes. "You'll do fine. It's after five. I've pressed your gown. Now go and get dressed."

"You need me to stay here to help you."

"I'm done. Go on now."

"I hope the wallpaper's red; that way I'll blend into the décor."

Humiliating memories ruffled through her thoughts like that irreparable cloth. "Are you forgetting about my two left feet? When the guys see I can't dance, I'll become an ornament and spend the evening plastered to some wall."

"When you meet the right man, you'll have no trouble following. " Ruby chuckled. "You'll see."

A ray of sunlight filtered through the steamy window. It sparkled like a star on a Christmas tree. Esther couldn't see the pane's dinginess for the sunlight streaming over her face.

∽

Esther watched as around and around the couples danced. Their laughter rose and fell in response to the waves of notes from Glenn Miller's orchestra. Their steps were in perfect rhythm as if for one purpose, one desire.

She stepped away from the Vanity's balcony, her gaze traveling to the multi-paned windows flanked with draping sheers. They offered the dancers a peek of the stars outside, while crystal chandeliers cast a golden glow on the Mayan ceiling inside.

If she was dreaming, she hoped to never wake up. She stared into one of the glinted full-length mirrors adorning each side of the three promenades. A man smiled back, his eyes resting on hers.

"Oh!" She whirled around to find herself inches from the stranger. He had to be at least six-foot-four. Thick jet-black hair waved around a strong, masculine face. But his eyes caught her interest—intelligent, attentive, holding within their hazel depths a mischievous twinkle.

"Be careful. Some men here will take advantage of a beautiful woman."

"Do men staring into a mirror count?"

"Only if they stare back." A lighthearted laugh escaped. "Has anyone ever told you your eyes sparkle and get as big as saucers when you blush?"

Who is he?

His black tuxedo with shiny satin lapels emphasized broad shoulders and slender waist. An amused glint crinkled the corners of his eyes.

"I'm Eric Erhardt, a junior draftsman at Wood Industries. I'm taking night courses at Lawrence Institute, and I plan to own my own engineering firm someday. And you are?"

And besides being irresistibly handsome, the man was a mind reader. "Esther Meir."

His eyes didn't leave her face. It was unnerving. "So, Esther Meir, what do you do besides looking like a porcelain priestess in this palace of the Aztecs?"

If he knew, he wouldn't be calling her a priestess. Three hours ago she was sweating like a field hand. The palms of her hands still felt clammy. Hope he doesn't ask me to shake his. "My brother, William, and I are attending college. I attend night courses at the Detroit Business Institute. William is a junior accountant at Ford Motor. He goes to night school at the University of Detroit. He earned a scholarship."

"U of D. What's he studying?"

"Accounting. He made the Dean's List and won an all-expense-paid vacation to a dude ranch. He's taking me and my friend along."

"Really?" Eric chuckled deeply. "So, you're, eighteen, nineteen?"

She felt like leaving him talking to the mirror behind her, only she was wondering his age, too. "I'm nineteen."

"That makes you a year younger than me."

His eyes bore down on her like a hawk hunting a chicken. Ridiculous. Here they were immersed in the splendors of geometric stones, gleaming bronzes, and ivory pilasters, a scene fit for King Solomon himself, and he was looking at her like she was his next meal.

"What's your opinion of the Vanity? Some say Charles Agree made a mistake designing it after an Aztec theme."

She'd read about Agree in the paper. "The Mayan Revival theme sort of embodies America's hopes—prosperity and purpose."

Eric's voice dropped an octave. "You fit this palace mystique. I can't pinpoint why exactly. Maybe it's your gown." His gaze traveled downward. "It fits you perfectly, as if it was made for you. I especially like the way that gown gathers at your…um…waist and…Well, it drapes your…everything well. Say, there's something on—" His hand brushed her bare shoulder. His palm lingered there a second too long.

She slapped his hand off her shoulder. "Are all northerners as brazen as you?" He better be happy it wasn't his face.

"Northerner? I thought I heard an accent. You're not from Detroit?"

"I'm from MacDuff County, Kentucky."

"You needn't get in a lather. I thought I might have known you." He shrugged. "But I've never been to Kentucky." A look of polished suaveness bathed his face. "I like meeting a girl on the up and up." His warm hand cupped her elbow, guiding her toward the balcony.

"So you're not just new to the Vanity. You're new to our big city ways. Guess it's up to me to educate you."

A wrought-iron railing separated the onlookers from the dancers below. "The Vanity is one of three ballrooms in Detroit. Each one shows its beauty differently." He closed the gap between them. "Like a beautiful gal."

His breath tickled her ear. Resisting the urge to step back, she craned her neck up. "Does that line work on most uneducated women?"

He sent her an audacious smile, displaying a dimple symmetrically placed on each cheek. "Usually."

She'd never met a guy so insultingly frank. Yet, his smile was infectious and she found herself smiling back.

The sound of the trombone broke through their conversation as the rise and fall of a Glenn Miller intonation of clarinet, horns, and strings echoed about the ballroom. In a flood of blues, reds, and golden full-length gowns against the black tuxedos, couples made their way down from the promenade and onto the gleaming maple floor.

"Eric. Down here."

Alert as a bird dog on a new scent, Eric turned toward a woman's voice on the dance floor below. A tall, attractive woman, her champagne-colored hair rolled in an upsweep, stood on the edge of the ballroom floor. "Glenn Miller's going to play our song."

Eric's eyes swept Esther like a warm summer breeze, lingering on her upturned face. "I promised my friend if she could get Glenn Miller to play 'In the Mood,' I'd dance with her."

19

Did regret cause him to hesitate before leaving her side?

"Esther." Dot McCoy yanked her out of her reverie. "I'd like you to meet my neighbors, Robert and Mary Rizzo. Robert's leaving Monday for England to join the Eagle Squadrons."

Mary stared at her wedding ring, twirling it around her finger.

"Mary is in the family way. Isn't that wonderful?" Dot said.

"I'll be back, though, before Mary has the baby; that's if—"

"America doesn't declare war first," Mary said.

"Oh, now, don't believe what Senator Wheeler said on the radio last night." A shake of Dot's head started her thick auburn curls bobbing across her brow.

"Which part?" Robert kissed Mary's forehead. "The part that Europe wants more tanks and planes and American lives? Or the part that American Jewish filmmakers are 'Hollywood Hitlers' and unpatriotic because their films encourage involvement in Europe's war? I got an earful. No offense, Dot."

"No offense taken, Robert. Our Jewish roots are embedded deep in American soil. I've stopped worrying about what some senator says."

"That's a relief. Mary and I couldn't have better neighbors, and we think highly of you and your parents." Robert kissed Mary's ring hand. "Come on, darling, dance with me. I don't want our last evening at the Vanity to be sad. And I'll bring back souvenirs for you and our baby."

Esther watched the couple as they made their way to the dance floor.

A gust of cool wind from the full-length windows sent the sheers flying madly into the room, breathing the coming autumn. Mary rested her head on Robert's shoulder, waltzing below Esther to the enchanting melody of "The White Cliffs of Dover."

Esther shivered, but not from the sudden chill sweeping the room. She wished it were. Mary's child would miss her father terribly if he didn't return.

"Poor kids." Dot wrapped her fingers around the railing.

"You're afraid, too, that Robert won't—"

"You're the Christian, so you'd best pray a lot, kiddo. Europe hasn't seen the worst of it. Americans haven't a clue."

Dot should know. Some of her Jewish relatives still lived in Berlin. According to the newsreel, British Prime Minister Winston Churchill broadcast that "scores of thousands of executions of civilians are being perpetrated by German troops."

Never able to stay serious for long, Dot turned her attention on her. "Your dress is darling, even though it is homemade. In this light, it's scarlet, right?" Dot snapped her fingers. "I've been wondering why you remind me of that person in *Gone with the Wind*, you know, that Scarlett girl. Your hair's even the same shade as hers. And you wear it down, like she did, except without those funny little bow things."

"I didn't have time after work to—"

"Looks perfect for you." Dot glanced out at the ballroom. "Oh, look, there's William. That blonde he's dancing with is out of step. It's a two-step, not a jitterbug. Well, William's having a good time. All I need is to find you your Rhett Butler." Dot waved. "Well, look at that; I've found him. You're perfect for each other."

Esther glanced over the banister. Right into Eric's upturned face. He smiled back.

"I bet you haven't anyone like Erhardt in Kentucky," Dot whispered. "He's tall as an oak, with shoulders as broad as a football field. Per-fect." Dot stressed the two syllables like smacking her lips over a particularly scrumptious pastry.

A nervous titter escaped Esther's lips. Never could she imagine that she and this Eric guy would lock eyes at that particular moment.

"Eric's the handsomest unattached male in Detroit. When he takes you into his embrace," Dot hugged her arms, skimming her hands down her shoulders, "it's like nothing you've ever experienced."

When the last notes of Glenn Miller's trombone ended, he held up his hand to the applause of the dancers. "The next dance is for our beautiful ladies. The Robbers' Dance will now begin." With a flourish, the orchestra began "Chattanooga Choo Choo."

Dot squeezed Esther's arm. "Isn't this swell? I love being flirted with. I'm planning not to get serious about anyone for a couple of years at least."

"How else would we figure out what kind of man we'll want to marry?"

21

Dot followed Robert and Mary jitterbugging about the dance floor. "Marriage is the lifelong bond between a man and woman. We need to know what we're getting ourselves and our future children into."

"If America is thrust into Europe's war, falling in love could be heart-wrenching, Dot."

"Tragic."

"I pray Jesus will guide me to His choice for my husband-to-be."

Dot slapped the railing with her palm. "Oh, jeepers creepers, that Jesus stuff again. Esther, when are you going to stop leaning on that crutch?" Dot tugged at her arm. "Come on, we've got to hurry."

"What is a Robbers' Dance?"

Dot looked surprised. "You steal a dance with the man of your choice."

"You ask the man for a dance?"

"Don't give me that high-hat look. It's perfectly proper." Her blue eyes twinkled. "Then again, with your goods…what I wouldn't give for a figure like yours."

Esther dug in, pulling back. "You go. I'll have more fun watching from here."

"Come on, it's not unladylike. Surely, you've been to Sadie Hawkins dances in Kentucky. You didn't just milk cows down on that farm."

Esther laughed. "Thanks for the invite. You go; I'll wait here."

The soft, poetic notes of a waltz sent the couples dipping and swaying around the dance floor. Eric guided his partner, and her flowing taffeta gown feathered as gently as a bird in flight around her slender legs. The woman glided effortlessly to Eric's lead as if she were on ice skates.

"I wish I could dance like them." Esther muttered. And I wish I could forget that terrible night I tried.

Chapter 2

Eric's eyes scanned the balcony for the petite brunette dressed in the shimmering red gown. Yes, she was there. Her friend wasn't.

He would love to take Esther Meir for a twirl. What a doll. But, no, she wasn't the type to ask a guy for a dance. As he led his current dance partner across the floor, he glanced up at her, enjoying the sight of her swaying to the beat of the music. He smiled. He could teach her a few steps of his own.

The music came to a breathless halt, and the musicians filtered into the crowd for a break. The women in line to dance with him, rushed forward.

"Eric!" Mary Beth's doe eyes gazed into his. "I claim your next dance."

"No, you already danced with him, it's my turn," said Sally Dodges.

He held up his hands. "Ladies, please—"

"Ahh ha ha!"

Esther? Above the chatter of the dancers, the clear melody of a woman's laughter echoed across the ballroom floor. He scanned the promenade. Yep, it was high time for him to give that shy wallflower a spin. Eric hurried toward the petite beauty that had the laugh of a lark.

*

Esther made a mad dash for the powder room, weaving in and out of the chuckling onlookers like a rooky football player. How humiliating. It was going to be rather hard to find the one as Mother hoped if she continued to look like the fool.

"Well, Little Red Riding Hood, does your mama know you're out and about tonight, amidst us wolves?" A man with a receding hairline blocked her escape.

Then from out of nowhere, Eric appeared.

"Beat it." Eric frowned down at the blatant loudmouth. The man slinked into the crowd without another word.

She lifted her upturned chin. She didn't need Eric to defend her. She squared her shoulders and rose to as tall as her five-three allowed.

Eric's smile grew wider, displaying even white teeth. What looked like a beginning mustache sprouted above his full upper lip. She'd missed that the first time, most likely because of those insane dimples of his.

Dot, out of breath, elbowed her way to Esther's side. "Hi, Eric. Gee, I wanted to introduce you to my friend." She looked at Esther and raised a questioning eyebrow. "Eric and I have known each other since high school." Dot's eager spontaneity fueled the burning flames Esther saw mirrored in his eyes. "Eric, meet Esther Meir. She's a jewel. She and I attend the Detroit Business Institute."

The band, now off their break, struck up a familiar tune.

Eric's eyes crinkled at the corners, pretending to have just met her. "May I have the honor of the next dance, Esther?"

Her heart responded to the melody of his voice. Her hand melted in his, a strong, yet gentle grip.

With the first notes of the saxophones, her shoes tripped over his patent leather wingtips. She groaned. "I apologize." She stumbled again. "I haven't been to too many dances, and—" Oh, sure, he's dying to know that she was the proud recipient of two left feet. She might have laughed, that is, if she wasn't so near crying. "I can't dance. Can you drop me off at the nearest corner?" That's what her last partner had done to the heehaws of everyone in the dance hall back in Emerald, Kentucky.

Eric acted as if she hadn't spoken. He took a firmer hold on her upper back and pivoted her into an elementary box step. "One, two, three, listen to the music."

He refused to give up. Well, then, that's too bad for his patent leather wing tips.

"It's easy." Eric's arm drew her towards him, his smile captivating her thoughts. "Relax and allow me to do the steering."

The notes of the mesmerizing "Moonlight Serenade" floated around them. Eric took ever-widening strides. Soon they were in the current with the others, flowing around the ballroom.

"So, you're from Kentucky. You like horses?"

"Yes." Right, get my mind off my feet.

"Good. I should have guessed you were a high hat, born in the aristocratic Bluegrass Region."

Esther snorted. "I was born in a little nine-by-ten house on the prairies of Colorado. We moved back to the family's farm just before Father died."

Eric missed a step. "I knew you were more than just a beautiful face."

His compassion washed over her like cooling rain on a sultry summer eve. She was two-months-old when her father died. The emptiness came later. Eric's eyes told her he understood. There's a side of him he hides behind his flirtatious demeanor. Why?

"With time, you'll get the hang of following me anywhere."

"You think I'm that easy?" Mother's words echoed in her thoughts. When you meet the right man, you'll have no trouble following. You'll know you and he were meant to be.

"Any man with eyes can see that the way into your heart won't be by flippancy."

He released her. The blood rushed to her cheeks when she realized the music had stopped.

ↄ

"Why, Robert? Why join the Eagle Squadron?" Eric whispered.

"We'll be in Europe's war soon enough." Eric motioned Robert to follow him and Esther toward a corner of the mezzanine unoccupied by the dancers taking a refreshment break.

"I'm going to learn British war techniques and pass that knowledge to our pilots."

"Since Roosevelt cut off Japan's oil supply, war could be inevitable," Esther said. "But Roosevelt did it so Japan would run out of fuel and the war would have to end. Wasn't that what Roosevelt was quoted saying?"

A deep chuckle escaped Eric's lips. *She's a peach and smart, too.* "So, what do you do for fun besides talking about battle strategies at a ball?"

Esther brushed a curl off her shoulder and gazed at him. "My Uncle Franklin got me interested in comparing biblical knowledge to current events. Uncle says we're on the brink of another world war, and this one will have catastrophic consequences."

Mary turned from a previous conversation and stepped closer. "How so? I mean, is this war in Europe in the Bible?"

"Yes. Wars have to come before Christ's return. A world dictator will appear in the latter days. Uncle also says that in the latter days Israel will become a nation again."

"The Jews can't return to Jerusalem; it's already occupied by the Palestinians. Too bad, but the Jews have lost Israel forever," Robert said.

Esther shook her head. "Uncle says nothing is impossible with God."

"That sounds on the up and up." Eric turned to Robert and Mary. "This is Esther's first time at the Vanity. With practice, I think we'd make a good-looking couple."

Esther turned a shade of red Eric had never seen on a woman before.

"Well, we need to beat it, right, Mary?" Robert winked at Eric.

Mary's lips pursed with humor. "Eric's harmless, Esther. He pretends to be a ferocious wolf, but he's a sweet frolicking puppy in disguise."

"Thanks, Mary." Eric placed a forefinger between his tie and neck, then chose another direction for conversation, something a little less lovey-dovey. "I didn't tell you about the Vanity's ballroom floor. It's built on springs. It's meant to give you a bounce when you dance." He sent Esther his most audacious smile.

"I didn't notice. I was preoccupied trying not to scuff up your shoes."

She wasn't falling for his charms as easily as he'd thought. The smell of her roses and gardenias perfume engulfed his senses. She stepped away and turned toward the ballroom. Her shoulder brushed his lapel, sending a tremor of delight to his taut nerves.

"How many people will the floor hold?"

"Oh, a thousand, easy," he whispered softly in her ear.

With a sudden inhale, Esther stepped away and turned to face him. "How many times a week do you dance here? Do you always come stag?"

"You think I'm nothing but a flirt."

"You do give a girl that impression."

Good. He wouldn't want her to know how much he liked her. "Usually, I come stag. Oh, and don't worry about my wing tips. They're always moving in when they should remain stationary. I meant it, Esther, you have the potential of becoming a good dancer. You've got rhythm. Everything else is practice."

A man dressed in a bright blue plaid jacket and baggy pants to match walked by. "What kind of suit is that?"

The man lifted his hand in Eric's direction. Eric returned the greeting. "That's called a zoot suit. It's gaining popularity, much to the dismay of some Japanese and Europeans who think it's a reflection of American's inability to become good soldiers."

"Because you enjoy kicking up your heels and having a good time?" Esther said. "How irritating."

"The word my dad used was *outrageous*."

e⊃

The notes of a clarinet broke through their conversation. The percussion of trombones, saxophones, and trumpets joined the clarinet. Like the shine on a newly polished gem, the exclamations of the onlookers were magnified, mesmerized by the orchestra's haunting refrains.

Esther sighed. "I've heard of the Big Band sound, but words don't do this music justice." Carried into another place, another world, she swayed to the music. "When I first came to Michigan and saw Lake St. Clair, I walked the beach in the moonlight. It was shining on the waters, dancing like diamonds on the waves. The water created a symphony all its own, almost magical—like this. I pray God ends this terrible war soon."

"That war's miles away from our shoreline, but you and I know it'll come. Drawing us into it like the tide, like it drew Robert." Eric stared, not seeing the ballroom, but the blackness beyond the shining crystal chandlers and glass windows.

Was he worried about being drafted? "Japan can't fight without oil, and Roosevelt has forbidden the sale of it," Esther said.

Eric's gaze lingered on her upturned face. "They'll get their oil from some other country. I hope Roosevelt has put the military on alert. We hit them where it hurt. They've got to be mad as hornets. You know why I think we did it?"

"To stop the bloodshed."

Eric's eyes turned hard as steel. A cold shiver crept up her spine.

"We wanted to show Japan that we didn't need their money, because as Teddy Roosevelt once said, 'Americans have too much audacity.'" He stared out across the sea of dancers, his voice low and foreboding. "What's worse, we can't turn our backs on a good fight. Deep down, we know Hitler and Japan won't be satisfied until they've drawn us into their squabble, and we won't be satisfied until we blow them off the map."

Esther squeezed her eyes shut to block out the stark reality of his words. "No. President Roosevelt is determined to stay out of the war."

"Hitler wants world dominance. And we playboys like our gals safe and the battle fought away from our shores." He touched her arm lightly. His eyes softened. "As long as we've got our good right arms and breath in our lungs—"

"Said the wolf to Little Red Riding Hood," Esther said, attempting to lighten the mood. Eric appeared to have the same idea.

He drew his lips back over his teeth in a fiendish leer and rubbed his hands together. He stopped. A sudden thought punctuating his advances. "Say, didn't you say your brother and you won a vacation at Rock-a-Bye Dude Ranch?"

"William, Dot, and I—You knew it was at Rock-a-Bye. I didn't say."

"Over the Labor Day week?"

"Yes? How did you—"

"I have my ways, Red Riding Hood. I have my ways."

Chapter 3

Esther couldn't see her bedspread for the rain coat, umbrella, sheets, and towels. She glanced at the suitcase that dwindled in capacity with every armload of paraphernalia. "Mother, I don't have a place for all this."

"Well, those rooms never have enough towels, and Michigan's weather is as changeable as a man's actions. Speaking of which, have you heard from that nice young man you met at the Vanity? The one that taught you some dance steps?"

Esther was befuddled as to what to say. Tommy Dorsey's music filtered through the Zenith, so she hummed a couple of bars, then said, "I never expected to hear from him." She kept her face buried in her suitcase. "I told you Eric is nothing but a big flirt."

"Your father was quite the gay blade himself. So was Buck Briggs."

Eric's eyes twinkled before Esther like a prologue to a romantic flick. She hurried to her closet so her mother wouldn't see the crimson blush sweeping her face.

"You going to wear that riding outfit your aunt Collina gave you?"

"I wouldn't think of leaving it." Esther removed it from the closet, lifted the coat to her nose and inhaled. Even now after being dry cleaned, she smelled the lingering fragrance of her thoroughbred mare—the one they had to sell for their bus fare to Detroit.

All she had left of her horse was this outfit and her memories. She stroked the velvet collar, its texture reminding her of the mare's coat.

31

"Leave it." William's ash-blond head peeked around Esther's half-open bedroom door. "Let go of the past so you can embrace the present. That's my motto."

"Never."

"Why not?" He grimace.d "We're going to a dude ranch, not a fox hunt."

"Stop with the faces. I'm not going to buy a new riding outfit when I already have one."

Mother clasped her hands together. "I declare. A dude ranch. What will they think of next?"

"We interrupt our program to bring you this important news," the radio announcer blared. "Since France's surrender on June 22, 1940, Germany has blasted London nightly. The London Blitz, however, has not dampened the British spirit. Reports estimate nearly 190,000 tons of bombs have been dropped on London, yet the people continue to refuse Hitler's offer to negotiate. How long can the British Parliament hold out? We have gotten word that more American pilots are volunteering for the Eagle Squadron to aid Great Britain's Royal Air Force against the attacks of the German Luftwaffe. Please stay tuned for foreign correspondent Huntley Haverstock."

A far-away look filled Mother's eyes. Was she remembering the men she loved who had died? First, Stephen, her husband and Esther's father, then Buck Briggs stepped into her life.

"Robert Rizzo left for England five days ago," Esther blurted.

"With Japan and Italy part of the Axis, war is inescapable," William said.

Mother rested a hand on William's broad shoulder. "Don't borrow on tomorrow's troubles; the day's is sufficient."

"This is Huntley Haverstock live from London. The lights are out everywhere except in America. It's death coming to London. It's too late to do anything here. Hang onto your light, fellow Americans! Keep those lights burning. Cover them with steel, ring them with guns, build a canopy of battleships and bombing planes around them. It's the only light left in the world!"

Like a cocoon envelops a fragile butterfly, William embraced his mother, stifling her sobs. "We'll push the Axis back where they belong. They started it, and we're going to finish it."

"I've lost so many of my brave men—"

"Oh…" Esther covered her lips with her hand. Eric had that same resolute look when he'd said Americans have too much audacity to bow to dictators. Her pulse quickened, remembering the sensation of his arm caressing her waist and the smell of his aftershave. He had come uninvited into her dreams nightly. Well, this was not the time to fall in love, and this vacation was what she needed to get Eric Erhardt out of her mind forever.

e⁓

The forests etched jagged mountain-like peaks against a sapphire-blue sky. Ages old one- and two-story unpainted wooden buildings complemented the backdrop of white birch trees, jade pines, and the aqua blue of Lake Michigan.

Esther's boots thumped a rhythmic beat on the wooden sidewalk of Rock-a-Bye Dude Ranch. She angled her head so she could see the top of the wooden church belfry. "This life-size replica of an Old West town makes me feel as if I'd stepped back in time."

An ice-cream parlor with red-checkered tablecloths, general store, stagecoach depot, and leather and blacksmith shop completed the buildings. The sidewalk led to the church, complete with a big brass bell in its belfry.

"Hey, girls." William jogged toward them. "How do you like the new me?"

"Not bad, for a Southern boy," Dot said.

William's perky smile matched Dot's, complementing his sunny disposition. His six-foot height and strapping build fit the cowboy mystique. His chestnut brown ten-gallon hat blended with his shirt and boots, not too ornate.

He encircled Dot's shoulders. "Call me Will while I'm here, okay?"

William had adapted to this Western lifestyle as he had the big city ways of the Detroiters. He had danced Dot around at the Vanity a couple times in playful exuberance.

Dot confided to Esther later that she thought William was swell, but she wasn't going to take his flirtatious innuendos seriously. Esther hoped, for William's sake, that was all they were.

She'd better heed Dot's words. A half-dozen other guys had called, but not Eric. There was something about him that she couldn't forget. Remembering how she scuffed up his shoes, she attributed his change of attitude to her left feet. He was performing his good deed that night, telling her she had the potential of being an excellent dancer. Mother was right: a man's actions were as changeable as the weather, and not even men knew where the wind would carry them next.

"Come on, Sis, put on some glad rags."

William's words jarred her thoughts back to reality.

Esther bent closer and whispered. "I can't spend money I don't have. Your outfit would be a month's wages for Mother and I combined." Esther didn't begrudge William his good fortune of landing a part-time job with Ford Motor. After all, he had the weekend chores of landscaping Uncle Gill's big two-acre estate.

A man outfitted like the movie star Gene Autry, complete with ten-gallon hat, tasseled white-embroidered shirt, and white-stitched leather boots, walked past her. A set of ivory-handled six-shooters dangled from each hip.

"Is he the guy who was bragging over breakfast about how he can hit any target at a gallop?" Dot looked over at the fake Gene Autry.

"That's him." William glanced at his watch. "Come on, we need to head to the stables."

A cowboy in a sweat-stained ten-gallon hat cocked to one side of his head approached them. Two-day's growth of whiskers covered his chin, and thumbs hooked in his front belt loops of his dusty Levis added to his unkempt look.

"Conrad Schmidt's the name." His eyes, two slits beneath his hairy brows, squinted into Esther's. "I don't know where you thought you were goin', missy, but it weren't to no fox hunt."

"Tragic." Esther placed her helmet under her arm and straightened her canary-colored vest. "Do you have a hunt saddle?"

"Well, one I know of, if'n I can find it."

"One is all I'll need. Thank you."

Twenty minutes later, Conrad walked through the gathering riders waiting for their mounts, holding the reins of a big seventeen-hand high bay gelding. The horse pranced around him, creating clouds of dust out of the dry dirt. He jerked on the bay's mouth in time to stop the horse from rearing up. "Here's your horse and hunt saddle."

"Are you sure, Sis?" William eyed the horse. "You want this horse?"

"Fireball. That's his name."

"Hold up, Conrad," Eric hollered as he approached the waiting riders. The cowboy scowled. "I was looking for you."

"You didn't look too hard. I've been up since dawn, saddling horses. Just went to change into a clean shirt."

"Eric?" Dot said. "What are you doing here?"

Eric swept his hat into his hand and smiled. "Dot, aren't you a doll. You enjoying yourself?"

"Did you get a free vacation, too?"

"Kind of, only mine's a working one." He bent over and kissed Dot's cheek. "Jack, the owner of Rock-a-Bye, called me, said he needed help this week. He'd given away free vacations to scholastic high-achievers."

"Guess I should thank him," William said.

"So, you're one of the college guys?" Eric gave him a measured glance and extended his hand.

Esther smiled, visualizing William and Eric becoming fast friends.

A tall blonde dressed in midnight blue with a baby-blue scarf around her neck elbowed her way past Esther. "Eric, Sally Dodges. Remember me?" Sally kissed Eric's cheek.

"How could I forget you, Toots?" Eric planted a kiss on her waiting lips.

On second thought, it's better if William and Eric don't become friends. If they did, she'd have to be nice to Eric, and she'd rather forget she ever met him.

"Esther?"

Eric elbowed his way toward her. She looked up, or attempted to. Her over-sized helmet had fallen across her forehead. She shoved it up with the tip of her thumb and nodded a hello.

Eric swept a strand of dark hair off his brow, as if to gain a better view of her. Esther's heart did a somersault.

"Nice outfit, Esther, but inappropriate for here."

She blinked. Is that all he had to say? At the Vanity he'd acted like there was something between them, then a week elapsed and nothing. Here he greets Dot and, and—that blonde bombshell with a kiss, and he treated her like a kid sister. How could she have allowed herself to feel something for this arrogant—

"Conrad, take Fireball back to the stable and bring out Snowball. Use the hunt saddle."

Snickers from the other riders greeted her ears. Eric's grin intensified her chagrin. She rocked back on her heels, feeling as if Eric had slapped her across the face. "Fireball will do fine. Give me his reins."

"Snowball will suit you better. He's been ridden English before." Eric's eyes swept her face like a hot Kentucky breeze in July. "Fireball hasn't." Eric bent low, his breath tickling her ear, goose bumps popping out over her neck as he whispered, "I wouldn't want to see your pretty face in the dirt, so do me a favor, Toots, and take Snowball."

Toots, was it? Ooooh. The audacity. Mr. Eric Smarty Breeches, that's what he is. Ooooh. What a, a—ego. She'd not give him the satisfaction of knowing how upset he made her. "So, you think me an incapable rider before you give me a chance to prove myself?"

"I don't know anything about your riding ability, but I do know Fireball." He lowered his voice and spoke slowly, as if conversing with an obstinate child. "Tackling a brute like Fireball in the tough terrain of the ranch, now that's a different story."

"Hey, Eric," someone yelled. "Quit flirting and get back to work."

Eric slapped his leg. "Look, sweetheart, quit arguing with me."

She blinked. This was a side of Eric she hadn't seen. The overpowering male dominant, a side she didn't like. She'd show him. "Mind your potatoes. My welfare is not your concern." Turning on her heels, she grasped Fireball's reins and in one fluid motion was astride. Walking the gelding around Eric, she smiled down at him. For once, Eric had to look up to her.

"You don't know what you're in for, Esther."

❧

Rock-a-Bye's large cattle herd grazed off to the left as they rode by.

John, whom they nicknamed Gene Autry, and Buster, rode ahead of Dot, William, and Esther. John and Buster looked to be in their late twenties and had assumed the leadership role of their group.

"Soon the boss man will be taking that herd to Wolf Lake to wait for the cattle auction." Conrad's gray-tinged whiskers gave his age away to be fortyish. He turned in his saddle, his eyes sweeping Dot. He smiled. "I'm going to give you tinhorns a treat and take you up to Shadow Lake."

Dot didn't look impressed. Esther turned her thoughts on the marshmallow-white clouds decorating the sapphire sky as the forest of trees bordering the meadow swayed in perfect rhythm to the breezes off Lake Michigan. "The wind blows where it wishes…but you cannot tell where it comes from and where it goes," she muttered as the aroma of snapdragons, pine needles, and horses wafted past her nose.

Jesus' words to Nicodemus explained being born of the Spirit. She hadn't acted very Christian, letting loose of her temper on Eric like that. He probably thought she was an out-of-control hot head. God, forgive me. Please help me not to do that again.

Thum-thump, thum-thump. Eric might have been right. Fireball was a lot of horse. Fireball's hooves drummed out a war beat that sent the dust flying around her, his choppy canter rolling her like a boat on a roaring sea. His mouth felt like she was trying to pull an iron door shut without a handle.

They stopped to rest the horses, which found the grass an inviting meal. The clear water of Shadow Lake lapped a sandy beach. Conrad led his horse toward the lake to drink. He withdrew a bag from his saddlebags, pulled out a piece of rolled ham and popped it into his mouth, sucking on the meat like a lollipop. "Anyone like some?" He held out the bag, soiled at the edges, to Dot.

"No, thank you."

"You're Jewish, ain't ya?"

"What if I am?"

"It's because of you Jews Germany started this war." Conrad's eyes ran up and down Dot like a stage light. "Germany's getting a bad name, trying to protect their citizens from freeloaders like your kin."

Dot's blue eyes sparkled with indignation. "My relatives are not freeloaders. They're doctors, lawyers, and teachers. But because of Hitler's Nuremberg Law, they were stripped of their rights to be German citizens and couldn't teach or practice medicine."

"Feisty, aren't you? Well, little missy, I like 'em feisty." Conrad walked to his saddle and took out his canteen. He opened the lid, leaned his head back and gulped, then smacked his lips. "Wow, that's got a punch to it. Sorry, only have one canteen. If anyone wants a sip, though, you're welcome to it." He looked at Esther. "You look like you need some, with all that dust on your face. I'm sure your mouth's gotta be as dry as the Sahara." His beady eyes shined into hers.

"No thank you, Conrad." She'd rather feel the grit on her face than the dirty feeling she got from his look.

Conrad touched the sleeve of Dot's shirt and allowed his hand to linger there. "Do your friends call you Dottie?"

She jerked her arm away. "Get your meat hooks off of me."

His lopsided grin displayed yellow teeth, with one gaping hole in the front. He lifted his half-eaten piece of ham to her lips. "Go on, taste it."

Dot turned her face away. "I thought you didn't like Jews."

"I don't. I'll make you the exception."

Dot pulled Snowball away and walked to a grassy spot near William.

"High and mighty, aren't ya? That Hitler fella's got my vote. Jews are a bunch of freeloaders." Conrad snatched his rope from his saddlebag. "Tie your horse up by that nearby tree, Dottie. I'll show you some roping tricks."

William moved closer to Dot. Esther glanced at Conrad. A cold shiver crawled its way up her spine.

Fireball snorted.

"Could be he smells bear. We got lotsa black bear here," Conrad said.

"A bear?" Dot clung to Snowball's bridle like it was a life preserver.

"Oh, is that all?" Esther said. "Come on, big fellow, I'll protect you from that little bear. Let's get a drink of water." Fireball's ears pricked forward. He took a step. Soon he was enjoying the cool spring water of Shadow Lake. Dot and William, Buster and John followed.

"Want to explore? Dot says it's all right with her," William asked Esther.

"Sure."

"Fine with me. Buster and I are in," John said.

"Okay, Gene Autry, mount up."

෴

Eric stood up in his stirrups and scanned the meadows, looking for a petite brunette on a blood-red bay. No sign of them. "Where could Conrad have taken them?" He urged his horse into a lope, crossing the meadows and heading up a gentle hill. As he topped the hill, he looked down. They'd have to come this way to reach the ranch.

This had been his longest week in history. He couldn't count the times he'd picked up the telephone and set the earpiece back on its cradle, telling himself he'd see her at Rock-a-Bye. What had gotten into him? He must be sun struck or something. He couldn't keep the smile from forming on his lips, remembering how ridiculously cute Esther looked when her helmet fell over her eyes and how adorable she was when she got mad. He shook his head. "What I need is a cold shower." He was going to look pretty silly sitting up here when they rode by. Anyways, the last thing he wanted was to get tangled up with Esther or any dame right now.

෴

Esther looked around. "Conrad's gone. Anyone have a compass?"

"No. But I've got an idea which direction the lodge is. Follow me." John waved his gloved hand. He placed his other hand on the top of his hat as he galloped up the hill, his fringed chaps flying in the breeze.

"Nothing looks familiar," William said.

"I'll send out a distress signal." John drew his six-shooter from his holster and fired three shots into the air. In that split second, his horse reared, flipped John off like a pancake, and took off, reins flying on either side of his thundering hooves.

"As if we weren't distressed enough," Dot said.

"At least now we know the direction of the barn." Esther pointed to the galloping horse. Fireball whinnied and started to prance. "Easy, boy." She reached over her saddle and patted his neck.

John slapped the dust off his breeches, and Buster offered a hand up on his horse. Buster's horse bucked.

That was all Fireball needed. His head and front feet bobbed up and down like a cork. "Easy, boy, easy." He shook his head at Esther as if to say no. Fireball's hooves slapped the air in a full rear, and when he came back down, he bucked. Before Esther could gather her reins, he was galloping off after the other horse.

"Jump," William yelled. "Jump!"

Fireball stretched into a run. The cattle in front ran in all directions.

"Whoa, boy." She pulled back hard on the reins. The ranch buildings, Esther estimated about a mile ahead, etched brown jagged peaks on the horizon. She pulled on her left rein, hoping to turn him into a circle to slow him.

From nowhere, a horse and rider sped toward her. Esther's helmet slipped over her eyes. Quickly she unsnapped her chinstrap and over the pounding hooves of her steed, she heard the thump of her helmet as it bounced like a basketball in the grass behind her.

The rider leaned over his saddle, whipping his horse with his reins. "Grab hold." The rider urged his mount closer so their stirrups touched, then reached around her waist, pulling her from her seat. "Take hold of my neck. Now!"

"Eric?" She clung to his neck like a drowning woman. He swung

40

her into the saddle in front of him and slowed his horse to a walk, cradling her, wrapping his strong right arm around her. His beard stubble grazed her cheek, his lips brushed her forehead, and she closed her eyes, drinking in the moment.

She wanted to cry and sing all in the same breath and smother his cheeks with her kisses, so thankful to be rescued and ecstatic knowing he had watched to make sure she was safe. Her feelings left her speechless. But who needed to talk at a time like this? She cuddled deeper into his chest.

"You'd enjoy your stay at Rock-a-Bye a lot better if you'd listen to me." His deep baritone brimmed with humor.

Was he laughing at her? She sat straighter. "Fireball is a barn stormer—and I'm not the first he's done this to, am I?"

Eric's grinned. "You're about the fourth. Though I got to confess, saving you is pure delight. You hardly weigh more than a sack of oats."

Esther gasped. He was laughing. "Uh, where's the sympathy?"

"Sympathy?" Eric looked at her questioningly.

"Yes, sympathy. You impossible man. You knew Fireball had a mouth of steel and loved to take the bit, didn't you? So you waited for me—"

"I warned you, remember?"

"So, you waited. Admit it, you waited, knowing that if he got the chance, he'd run me back to the barn."

Eric snickered. "Let's say I had a good idea that's the way it would end up. Why are you so hot under the collar at me?" He drew her close. "Stop wiggling. We're nice and cozy like this."

"Don't touch me. Did you set it up for Conrad to leave us in the middle of the wilderness, too?"

"What? He better not have left you tenderfeet out there."

She pulled on Eric's wrist and tried to loosen his grip on her waist.

His hand held firm. He gave a low whistle. "Will you look at that?"

Staff and guests had congregated at the gate. They were pointing at—her!

"Sis."

Eric stuck a wad of chewing gum in his mouth, then started his horse back into its ground-covering walk. William and Dot trotted closer. Dot's eyes were mirror bright. "You all right?"

Esther nodded. "How about you?"

"Shook up, but Snowball did beautifully, didn't even shy when John shot off his six-shooter."

"He what?" Eric looked first at William, then at Buster and John riding behind him.

William nodded toward the two riding double. "Ask Gene Autry."

"Didn't you have better sense than to pull a stunt like that?"

John shrugged.

"Well, the boss won't like it. Heads will roll tonight, probably mine for letting a tinhorn like you loose." Eric looked at John.

They walked beneath the gated entranceway, the imprints of double horseshoes burned into the wood beneath the letters Rock-a-Bye Ranch.

William trotted up alongside Eric. "That was some riding."

"Thanks." Eric popped his gum.

"I was really beat up about you, this time, Sis." William looked at Eric. "Maybe you can teach her to listen to good advice. She brushes mine off."

Esther crossed her arms. "I handled Fireball fine until—"

"What?" Eric reined his horse. "Fireball nearly had you in the stall with him." His brows formed half moons above his teasing eyes.

"What are you staring at?"

"I doubt Fireball's accommodations would suit you. Want to give mine a try?"

Esther slapped him hard across his absurd dimples.

Eric coughed.

"What's the matter? Swallow your gum? Good." Refusing Eric's arm to dismount, she attempted to slide off his horse. Miscalculating the distance, she landed hard on her derrière.

"All in a day's work, Miss Esther," he mimicked in a southern drawl. He kicked his horse into a half rear, raised his hat to her in a gallant salute, then cantered into the center of the hooting crowd of onlookers.

"Why you, you...rogue."

Chapter 4

"These stupid things that are happening to me, well, it's not me," Esther said over her shoulder as she stood at the bathroom sink. The rustic bathroom she and Dot shared with the adjoining bedroom was nothing more than a closet. She scrubbed at a dirt smudge across her left cheek.

"I haven't a clue how you're going to get yourself out of this one." Dot continued to brush her auburn locks that trailed down her back in loose curls. "What's so bad about being chased by a good-looking guy like Eric?"

"He just happened along. It's not like he—"

The clanging cowbell ringing that dinner was in fifteen minutes interrupted her words like the blaring alarm in a boxing match.

Dot put on her hat then said to Esther's reflection in the vanity mirror, "Do you dislike Eric like you pretend?"

Esther gnawed on her lip. "No."

"You gave that impression to a lot of people. Present company included. Eric went out of his way to save you, and you threw his good intentions in his face. The icing on the cake was when you slapped him."

"But he had the audacity to ask me an indecent—"

"Eric is all guy." Dot smiled. "He's the real McCoy. He was joking."

"Some joke." Esther laid the washrag on the sink. "And everyone saw me fall on my...humiliating." Glancing in the mirror, all she could see was Eric's teasing face staring back into hers. "I acted like some spoiled brat, hitting my hand in the dirt. I guess everyone was waiting for me to kick my heels, too. What am I going to do?"

"You can't go to chow dressed like that. This is a dude ranch not a hunt field. I think it's time to mend fences." Dot's matter-of-fact attitude had a calming effect on Esther's turbulent emotions.

"I brought one pair of Levis."

"You can use my boots. I bought new ones today. And I bought another hat and cowboy shirt, so you can wear my other ones." Concern swept Dot's countenance. She dumped the contents of her purse onto the dresser. "Did you see my wallet?"

"No. Could you have left it in the general store?"

"I might have. I'll check with them tomorrow. They're closed now."

Esther changed into Dot's royal blue and white blouse etched with tiny pearl-like snaps on the upper breast pockets and front. She ran a finger down the beautiful white stitching across the shoulder that dipped toward the chest and then back. Lastly, she placed Dot's cowboy hat on her head. The hat's large blue band matched the blouse.

Dot frowned at Esther. "You look scared. What about?"

She gulped. "Me? Scared? Why, no I—"

"That Eric won't have anything to do with you, right?"

Esther's heart fluttered like a trapped bird.

"Well, walk up to him and say, 'Eric, thank you for rescuing me.'"

"In front of everyone?"

"Why not? You slapped him in front of everyone."

Esther fumbled through the paraphernalia of makeup and hair ribbons on the dresser for her lipstick. "I fell on my fanny in front of the staff and tourists. They applauded him like he was some movie star." Finding her lipstick, she stared at it as if it provided a solution to her problem. "If Eric was a gentleman, he'd apologize to me. How was I to know he was kidding?"

"It won't do for Eric to know how crazy you are about him. Between us," Dot lowered her voice, "I think he's nuts about you, too." Grabbing their jackets, Dot tossed Esther hers, then opened the door. "Come on, Annie Oakley, let's go get our guys."

৵

Esther heaped her plate with the hickory-smoked barbecue and soaked in the aroma before taking a spoonful of potato salad. She picked out a steaming, buttered corn-on-the-cob, ladled some baked beans onto her plate, then reached for her bowl of coleslaw and cornbread.

"I can't remember when I felt this hungry." Dot's plate brimmed with food.

"Me too." She chose milk over the lemonade and looked for William. He motioned to two places on the log near the blazing campfire. John and Buster suddenly cut in front of them.

Legs sprawled like a young calf's, John looped his thumbs in his belt. "Sorry about scaring your horse."

He's seen one too many Western movies. "That's all right, John." Esther grinned back. "After all, you got the worst of it."

"Come to think of it, I did, didn't I? I'm glad I didn't break anything."

"Too bad," Dot muttered.

"Excuse me?" John looked at Dot with his little calf eyes.

"I can't believe you applesauce-brained cowpokes brought a loaded gun," Dot said.

"Why don't you tell them what you really think?" William whispered, grabbing her plate.

John and Buster followed. Before John could sit on the log next to the girls, William elbowed himself in front. "You two find someplace else to sit. I've got this log reserved."

"But we're sidekicks. We're supposed to stay together."

"Look-a-here partner, we'll ruin your chances with the ladies." William spoke just above a whisper, steering them away. "Esther there is spoken for. You know what I mean." William nodded toward Eric, who was filling his plate at the chuck wagon.

Her brother wasn't helping the situation. The last thing she wanted was to draw Eric into this.

Eric smiled and nodded back. His glance swerved to John, then Buster. A look black as thunder swept his countenance and left no question as to his feelings toward them.

"You don't want to mess with that big guy, if you know what I mean," William said.

"Who is he, a blocker for the Detroit Lions?" Buster stepped back. "What about Dot? She's downright gorgeous when she gets riled."

"She's spoken for, too. Look over yonder. You gents have drawn a queen of hearts. That redhead and her friend have been eyeing you since you clanged your spurs into Rock-a-Bye." William gave John and Buster a nudge in their direction.

"You on the up and up? I thought they were eyeing you. Thanks."

Leave it to William to find a way out of a touchy situation.

𝓮𝄔

Eric joined William and began to eat, but he kept his eyes on the ornately dressed man with the six-shooters.

"Think it's safe for John to be carrying guns?" William asked.

"Jack's from Texas. Firearms are no big deal with him. But we'll ask him. He owns the place."

Jack stood four feet away from the chuck wagon, chomping down on a piece of cornbread. Nearly equal in height with Eric, he was leaner in body weight. Eric didn't know for sure, but he thought Jack was near sixty. His face was a map of well-earned wrinkles. His lopsided grin saw the humor of any situation. He'd never allow a little thing like loss of cattle or money get in the way of his zest for living life the way the good Lord saw fit.

Plates in hand, they walked over to Jack. "Can't you confiscate those shooters?" Eric asked, motioning his head toward John.

"Says he's a trick rider and he performed in some circus," Jack said.

"Some trick. He got himself thrown," William said.

"If Esther had gotten hurt, you'd have one less store-bought cowboy to worry about. I figured John had blanks and not real bullets," Eric said.

"They're blanks." Jack glanced at William. "John's nothing but a store-bought cowboy. No offense."

William glanced down at his shiny new boots. "None taken."

Jack dusted off his hand and reached out to shake William's. "Nice to meet ya." He turned to Eric. "You're doing a bang-up job with the cowgirls. Most are swooning, and those that aren't are about to. Yeah, the Old West has come alive. I should gather a heap more guests next year."

Eric sopped up the barbecue juice with his cornbread. He glanced at Esther sitting by the campfire. He wasn't doing so well with one cowgirl.

"That's the brunette?" Jack nodded toward Esther. "The one you rescued?"

"That's the one, my beautiful and headstrong sister. She kept that big bay under control until John's horse bolted away. Then Buster's horse bucked a little too close to Fireball's side and that caused him to rear."

Jack lowered his voice. "Conrad knew that bay isn't for guests. He won't be giving your sister or anyone else trouble. I saw to that."

Eric gulped down his mouthful of barbecue. "What do you mean?"

"I fired him." Jack reached for another piece of cornbread. "He's ornery as a passel of hornets, so if he comes around you or the ladies, you let me know."

"You think Conrad might try to harm Esther and Dot?"

"He threatened to. I confiscated this before he delivered it." Jack held out a piece of paper.

Eric took the paper and read the scrawled words. "You and that Southern gal's time on this earth are short. I'll be sending you both to hell soon!"

"He's been off his nut since he joined the fascist movement," Jack said.

"He's a Nazi sympathizer?" William said. "Like that Lindbergh fella?"

"Conrad's loco enough to carry out his threats," Eric said.

Jack pocketed Conrad's note. "To be on the safe side, I think Esther and Dot should accompany us on the trail ride."

Eric glanced at Esther. He shoved his spoon in his barbecue and scowled. "I've had about all I can take of the jeering I got from the bunkhouse staff. I can imagine what they will think about that idea. I did what any man would do."

"Not any man could have done what you did." Jack chuckled.

Will nodded. "Don't let Esther's indifference fool you, Eric. She's grateful you rescued her."

The backdrop of a star-draped night caused the fire's glow to illuminate her face to a rosy hue, and strands of her wavy hair rested on each shoulder. She laughed, its melody stabbing Eric's heart. He blinked. From the glow of the fire, he could make out her lips and her iridescent smile. He sounded like a lovesick Romeo. He'd be serenading her next. He shook his head to rid himself of that thought.

Esther glanced his way. He smiled. She turned her back to him. It was downright humiliating, chasing a gal that wanted no part of him.

Jack gazed at the women around the campfire. "All these girls is mighty pretty, but, Will, your sister is the best of the bunch. She's spirited, and don't fall for your flattery, Eric. That kind makes the best wife. Not that you're ready to settle down yet. She's not going to set her cap for any gent that happens along. Yeah, she's worth the chase, but if you don't fancy yourself up to the pursuit…"

Esther gave a shy look in their direction. Jack put a hand to the brim of his hat and nodded. Esther smiled back. "If I was twenty or so years younger and single, I'd show you how to go about winning her."

Maybe she's warming up to me. Eric tipped the brim of his hat. Esther looked away.

Jack cleared his throat. "You got some fence mending to do."

"Probably inviting her to my bunk wasn't such a good idea."

"I'd say that was a definite no." Jack set his plate down and rubbed his hands together. "Now that I've fired Conrad, I've got a position open. Interested in being head trail boss?"

"Conrad's been here since you started the ranch."

"Since the early thirties. But when that Hitler guy started his rampage, I've seen and heard some things I don't care for." Reaching into his pocket, Jack handed a wallet to Will. "Can you return this to Dot McCoy? I believe she came with you."

"But how did you—"

"Conrad. Tell that gal to put her membership to the Jewish Council in a safe place. Not in her wallet. The way people feel over this war, you can't trust your own relatives anymore. I believe Conrad's a member of the Bund movement headed by its popinjay leader Bundesführer Fritz Kuhn. Desperate times produce desperate people. I have a hunch that gal may be affiliated with the Jewish underground." He turned back to Eric. "How about it? You want to be my number one foreman?"

"I have a job as a draftsman at an engineering firm in Detroit. But I am interested in buying a horse. I plan to find a stable close to where I live and board him there."

"That could be arranged. Now, I'm short-staffed this week. I'm in a jam at the swimming pool. My lifeguard called in sick."

e⊃

Esther shifted her place on the log to make room for her brother.

He sat beside her and groaned. "I know this cowboy thing is all the rage. But right now I could use a soft cushiony chair for my throbbing backside. Incidentally, how's yours?"

"Not your problem, brother dear."

He took a mammoth bite of beef. "Mmm, about the only thing worth savoring on this riding excursion is the outdoor cooking." Taking a swallow of milk, he poked his head toward Buster twirling one of John's six-shooters in front of Sally Dodges, who sat on the log opposite them. "I guess being from Kentucky doesn't prepare you for the flamboyance of seeing a piece of the Wild West in Michigan."

A dreamy look came into Dot's eyes. "I wouldn't have minded living in that era."

"Are you forgetting what happened to Sis? What if your handsome hero missed and you ended up landing on your derrière in the dust?"

"I'd rather eat a little dust than live in my cobwebs of daydreams."

"Well, there's Gene Autry."

The man leaned over a redhead in tight breeches and frilled jacket.

"I want someone who can sweep me off my horse," Dot said.

The tall redhead turned her flirtatious eyes to Eric. She had his attention all right. "Well, you better hope he's watching when you're on that runaway horse and not busy chasing someone else." Esther motioned toward the woman who looked all legs.

Her brother let out a low wolf whistle. "Lollapalooza. Where has she been hiding?"

"Really? I'll dye my hair fire-engine red and wear a pair of breeches two sizes too small." Dot frowned at him. "And maybe I'll warrant a 'Wow' someday."

"Are you going to dye your freckles, too?"

Dot jabbed him with her elbow.

"Didn't I rescue you from Conrad's advances, all that juicy ham?"

"Oh?"

Esther bit her lip, watching Will's sudden confusion.

He leaned closer to Dot. "And by the way, Conrad's threat isn't over." Will had captured Dot's attention. "He dislikes Jews and Southern belles who are uppity, and you, Dot, caused him to lose his job."

"What is it that people don't like about me? Is it because I won't take their insults?" Dot asked.

He reached into his pocket and handed Dot her wallet.

Dot gasped. "My—how—"

He put a hand on her arm and whispered. "Conrad stole it."

Dot looked through the pockets. A puzzled looked swept her face as she drew out a card. "He didn't take any money, but look what he did to my Jewish membership card."

"A swastika." William covered the card and her wallet with his hand, his eyes fixed on the people gathered at the campfire. "Jack says to hide that card, but not in your wallet."

"I think I've had enough excitement for one day." Esther popped the remaining cornbread into her mouth and stood.

"I feel violated. I know I'm exaggerating, but I do." Dot brushed off her jeans.

Will touched a freckle on Dot's nose. "Do yourself a favor and get to your room. I want to check it out before you ladies retire."

"What's on the agenda for tomorrow? I don't feel like riding." Dot fidgeted with her napkin.

Esther and Will exchanged looks. There was something Dot was keeping from her and William, but what?

"How about lounging by the pool? I hear they have a high dive and springboard to die for."

"Couldn't you have chosen a different word, Esther?" Dot swiped at her Levis with the back of her hand. "Die isn't a word one should use lightly these days."

Chapter 5

is, watch." William waved at her from on top of the springboard, looking from her to the luscious redhead lounging five feet away.

Esther shrugged. She had tried to strike up a conversation with Will's newest attraction, but Luscious was busy getting beautiful. Making new friends wasn't on her schedule of beauty treatments.

The concern over Conrad and the Third Reich had dissipated into the shadows, and swimmers laughed and frolicked like the sunbeams that danced across the expanse of blue pool waters.

Luscious reached for her small case of cosmetics. Here was Esther's chance. "Nice weather, isn't it?"

"Uh-huh." Luscious tilted her bottle of baby oil mixed with iodine into her palm, applying the lotion to her skin.

"There's my brother on the springboard. He does a great swan dive."

"Uh-huh." Not bothering to look, she layered her rose petal-colored lipstick on her full lips, combed her pink tipped fingernails through her silky-smooth strands of hair, and smiled at herself in her compact mirror. Then she plopped a purple and crimson mask over her eyes and lay down on her chaise with her arms draped over the sides.

"Watch!" Will yelled.

Everyone looked up, except Luscious. Springing off the diving board, he bowed his legs in a heart-shape impression of his emotions, creating a huge splash.

"Hey, mister, do ya mind?" An adolescent got up from his seat alongside the pool and plopped onto a chaise next to Luscious.

Luscious raised her head, peeked out momentarily from her eye mask and then returned her head to her tiny pillow.

Like a puppy looking for a new owner, Will spotted Dot at the wooden gate that separated the beach and pool from the ranch.

Cradled in her arms were a towel, beach bag, and cooler that she refused to drop while trying to open the gate. Will sprung out of the pool with one mighty thrust of his arms. "Here, let me help you with that."

"Don't bother."

"What's wrong?"

"What was that dive all about?"

"I was trying something new. Anyways, why should you care?"

"Swell. Why are you asking my opinion?" Dot looked toward the redhead. "Trying something or someone new? Anyways, I've given men up, totally. They're too confusing."

"Then what would you do?" He gripped her load of paraphernalia.

She dropped down on the chaise lounge next to Esther and buried her head in the folds of her towel. "Give me time. I'll think of something."

He patted her arm.

"You're getting me wet."

"Getting wet—or all wet? You told me in no uncertain words last night you didn't care who I pursued. Looks like you do care." He shook his head.

"If I wanted a shower, I'd have taken one," Dot said.

"Got some water in my ear. Sis, come on. You're not going to lie around the pool all day, are you?"

"Actually, that thought had crossed my mind." Esther yawned and lowered her chair back to a horizontal position.

Will gazed over at Luscious, who was oblivious to his existence. "You think she's angry about last night?"

"I know I would be. After all, you had your chance, and you didn't take it." Dot placed a large sun hat on her head.

He plopped down on the end of Dot's chaise. "Sis, why don't you go swimming? Come on. Do your jackknife. Dot's never seen you dive. She's a real good diver, Dot." He moved Esther's legs to one side and switched seats, then put a finger into his left ear. "It's amazing what a thimble full of water can do to your well-being when placed directly into one's ear."

"It doesn't help that you're hearing impaired in that ear," Esther said.

"Really? What happened?" Dot looked up from her novel.

"From a mastoid infection." Will chuckled. "Well, look who's climbing into the lifeguard's seat."

"Why don't you tell us, so we don't have to look up?" Dot's freckled nose poked in between the pages of her book.

"I concur." Esther rolled onto her stomach and nuzzled her head on the soft folds of her terry towel before closing her eyes.

"Mr. Hero himself."

"Eric?" Dot's book hit the concrete with a thump.

"Eric's one of the trail bosses," Esther said.

"True, but last night Jack asked Eric to fill in for the lifeguard."

"This could be the opportune time to mend some fences," Dot said.

"Definitely no. Go ahead, Dot; it's your turn with Mr. Ego."

Will rose. In that same instant, Esther turned, upending her chaise. She landed hard on the concrete deck. "Ouch. That hurts."

"I don't think you'll get rid of him that easily. Besides, he's in a better mood than yesterday. Downright jolly, I'd say." Will looked for his seat. "Sis, what are you doing down there?"

"Gee, William, where have you been?" Dot started to rise, then flopped back on her chaise, grinning up at the tall man making his way toward Esther.

"I fell and bumped my elbow. It's bleeding." A shadow fell over her.

Eric squatted down. "Let me have a look at that."

Esther jumped up. "I'm fine. Where's my robe?"

Eric slowly picked up her robe. His smile hadn't left his face. Nor his eyes her body. "Why cover such a—I mean—"

She snatched her robe from him.

"Yes, well," he cleared his throat, "you could use a little sun."

"I can't say the same for you, Eric," Dot said. "What do you do? Work out with barbells every morning in the sunshine to get that kind of tan and build?"

"I swim at the YMCA." He set down his first aid kit, opened the lid, and reached in for some salve and a bandage, then encircled Esther's arm with his hand.

"This may sting a little." His voice was low and as soothing as his touch. "There. You'll be good as new in no time. Don't want you not enjoying the amenities of Rock-a-Bye Ranch."

"Thank you." Esther wrapped her robe about her and sat back down.

"I'll get back to my chair."

"Swell." Esther reached for Dot's book, opened it to the middle, and acted as if she was absorbed in the story. His shadow lingered. When the warmth of the sun's rays touched her skin, she peeked over the pages. "Good, he's leaving."

Will looked at Dot and winked. "So, are you planning on working on your tan with your robe on?"

"I like the way I look."

"Evidently, so does Eric." Dot giggled.

"Why don't you admit it, Sis? You're attracted to him."

"Would it matter?" Esther said. "We're not compatible. We're both head-strong, and he's egotistical. Why create a relationship doomed to fail?"

"You should've heard the teasing Eric endured last night over you."

"He did?" Esther stole a look toward the lifeguard chair. "I don't believe you."

"How about, 'You must have waited half a day for her to ride by. Was she worth it? Heard she can't stand you.' And plenty of hee-haws."

"You would have responded the same way. It's all about one's pride." Esther gave Dot her book, then stood and took off her robe, hoping the spurt of heat she felt washing over her body was due to the sunlight.

"And what does the Good Book say about pride? You're always preaching to me. It's time you take your own medicine." William waved a finger before her upturned nose. "'Pride goeth before destruction and an haughty spirit before a fall.'"

"And you sure did, right smack down on your derrière." Dot covered her glee in the pages of her book.

"Do you have to mention that now?" Esther glanced toward the tall lifeguard chair.

"Eric wants to reconcile as much as you do."

Luscious smiled and waved at Eric, trying to snare his attention. He waved back. "He's as infatuated with her as you are, brother dear."

"What? Yeah, and he has the better profile, sitting there like some Greek Colossus."

Dot angled her head. "Yeah, definitely a better profile and physique than yours."

"So I might as well get rid of my competition and make my sister happy all in one swoop."

Dot swiped him with her novel. She looked at Eric, then at Will, her eyes sparkling. "You're right."

"Thanks. I'm getting it from all angles today."

Dot waved his comment away with a sweep of her hand. "Esther needs to get in the water so Eric can rescue her." She smiled at William. "Well, Mr. Brain, think of something."

He glanced toward Luscious who had fixed her gaze on Eric.

"Quit drooling on me." Dot wiped imaginary saliva from her knee.

"Hush. The Brain is at work and needs total silence."

She and Esther crushed their towels to their mouths to stifle their laughter.

"Esther, you could do your jackknife and pretend you got a mouthful of water and go down. Eric will dive in and swim you up to safety."

Dot cupped her arms around her leg. "Hmm, that's sounds dreamy."

Will gawked at her. "Really? You'd rather have Eric's arms around you instead of mine?"

Dot sent Esther a quick wink.

So, Dot did like her brother, or was she playing with him? Keeping up with Dot and William's tennis game of love was confusing enough without her and Eric's drama. "The last thing I want Eric to do is wrap his arms around me."

"Why not?"

"That's not the way I want anyone, especially him, to show his desire for me."

"Esther, if you don't want our help, say so."

"I do not want—nor ever will want—your help with my love life."

"Hmm, Dot, you think Esther really doesn't want our help?"

"Kind of sounds like that." Throwing down her book, Dot whispered, "Now, what are we going to do for excitement? Rescue Luscious? Heaven knows, she needs rescuing from her totally seductive existence."

"Well, that's a thought. I'm not too proud. Why don't you help me with my love life?" William watched Dot's response.

Esther shook her head. It was so obvious to her that her brother was hoping for some emotional response out of Dot so he could determine her feelings for him.

Dot turned to Esther while speaking to Will. "You need to get your fill of Luscious.

"So you can see how phony she is, Will. She had John eating out of her hand last night. Now she's ready to shrug him off for Eric. She's so full of herself."

Pointing at the vacated chaise and Luscious's bobbing bathing cap in the shallow end of the pool, he motioned for Esther and Dot to draw closer.

"What do you have in mind?" Dot said.

"I'll do the lethal dive. Only, you dive first, Esther, and stir up the water a little. The more waves the better. I'll take careful note as to Luscious's location. With all the waves, I might be able to do a little rescuing myself."

Esther put on her bathing cap. "Come on, Dot, you're in this, too." She motioned for Dot to get in.

Esther mounted the steps to the springboard. William was behind her on the ladder. Walking to the end of the board, she paused to see where Dot was in the pool. With a small motion of her left hand, she signaled Dot to move a little to the left, away from where she intended to hit the water. From the corner of her eye, she'd noticed the man on the high dive. He motioned her to proceed.

Was Eric watching? Concentrate, Esther! She took a deep breath. One. She bounced in perfect rhythm to her mental timing. Two. Three. Airborne. She bent down to touch her toes and swung her legs up, entering the water in a perfect vertical position.

She knew she had a perfect entry because she'd plunged the ten feet to the bottom and touched the drain. Pushing off with her feet, arms crossed over her head, she burst to the surface when a solid mass hit her. She reeled to the bottom, somersaulting out of control.

⁀ᴐ

Her lungs ached for air. Someone grabbed her. Then she felt herself pulled from her watery grave.

Gasping and coughing, she was pulled onto the deck and rolled onto her back. Eric leaned in close to her, and she clutched his arm, gasping, unable to speak. A man bent over, dripping water on her. "I'm really sorry. I didn't mean to dive on you like that."

Esther blinked. The guy from the high dive. She tried again to speak but coughed. Eric bent his head toward hers. She coughed.

"Stand back, please." Eric shoved the onlookers away. He placed her over his knee and patted her back. A mixture of water and saliva drained from her mouth.

He moved her on her side. More saliva and some breakfast erupted from her mouth. Disgusting. She was so embarrassed. He whispered in her ear, his voice soft and reassuring, "You're going to be okay."

She blinked away the drops of water that shrouded her lashes like frothy lace. She nodded her head and coughed again. Her vision cleared. She now lay on her back.

Eric's eyes gazed into hers—watchful, attentive eyes noting her every expression. "You recognize me?"

Esther nodded and coughed again.

"Who's this?" he said, pointing to her brother.

"William, my brother."

Eric reached for a towel and wiped her mouth. His eyes spoke his concern. His touch was warm, soothing on her cold skin. She closed her eyes as another wave of coughs brought up more water.

"Oh, don't look at me, I must—"

"You're a doll; you've never looked lovelier to me." He bent closer, his lips inches from hers.

"Ahh…" She closed her eyes, waiting breathlessly. Whisked upon her feet, her robe thrust around her shoulders—startled, she gasped.

Eric headed for his chair, his whistle poised beneath his lips, his deep chuckles filling the gaps between splashing and murmurs.

The terry robe felt damp to her hot flesh.

"Sis, does saying 'I'm sorry' help?"

"This wasn't your fault," she said, eyeing the lifeguard's chair.

"Well, yes and no. I motioned the high diver not to jump, but he thought I was telling him it was okay. So you see, it's sort of my fault."

Esther picked up her towel and swatted at him. "It's okay. Really. I can't figure how he could have knocked the wind out of me like—"

"Who? The diver or Eric?"

Esther swatted him again.

The noisy onlookers hummed around their chaise loungers like an assortment of bees on a sultry summer afternoon. "We've gathered quite a group of spectators." He raised his muscular arms. "She's fine. Thanks." Not-so-subtly, he nodded in the direction of Luscious and whispered, "She feels for you. She said she wishes it happened to her and not you. So humiliating, regurgitating like that in front of—"

Eric, perched on his lofty chair like a crowing rooster, grinned down at her.

Esther tied her robe more snugly and slapped on her sun hat in a haphazard attempt to cover her dripping hair.

Dot gathered her belongings. "It wasn't as glamorous as I imagined. In fact, it was gross. All that water. I didn't think anyone could swallow so much in such a small amount of time."

Esther silenced her with a stony look.

"All is not lost." Will glanced toward Luscious. "Carla understands;

it happened to her." He leaned closer. "We're planning to meet for ice cream. I think she wants to cry on my shoulder about her experience."

Esther's eyes stormed their way to her brother's. Dripping wet, Esther forced her wet feet into her slings. Her heels only half on, she limped her way through the throng of well-wishers.

"Eric's watching." Dot waved. "Thanks, Eric."

Esther ignored her. Dot hurried to keep up. "Gee, he's handsome. And those muscles. He carried you with no problem. But I still can't understand it."

"Understand what?" Will said.

"Was it as evident to you as it was to me that he was planning to kiss Esther?"

"Yep. And he—"

"I'm not won over by muscles and a—"

"Kiss." Dot placed a hand to her chest. "I can think of a happily-ever-after fairy tale where—"

"Don't say it."

William and Dot think Eric kissed me. Esther turned to shower Eric with her most hateful look. "The nerve of that man."

Chapter 6

*Y*ou tell us not to worry about Conrad, but, William, why does Eric want Dot and me on that trail ride if not to protect us?" Esther dumped a drawer full of apparel on her bed and dug through them. "I will admit it's better for my morale to ride with you and keep busy than stay here and be gawked at."

Dot continued to comb her hair as if that took all her attention.

"We're moving Jack's cattle from the Little Manistee to Wolf Lake for winter."

"That's about a hundred miles!"

"The snows off Lake Michigan get deep, and Jack wants to keep his herd fat for spring sale when the price of beef is high. Pack light. A staffer will meet us at Wolf Lake with our car and suitcases. From there we'll head for home Sunday morning."

Esther shoved her non-riding clothes into her suitcase, slammed down the top, and sat down on the lid, fastening the clasp.

"We'll be riding hard for four days, eating chuck wagon food like beans and jerky, and sleeping on the ground, all with absolutely no modern conveniences," Will said.

"This'll be the real McCoy." An adventure she knew she'd cherish for years. "We'll be traveling like real cowboys."

Will seized Dot's hairbrush, slapped it down on the dresser, and turned her. Staring down into her face, he said, "Is there any reason you know why Conrad would want to kill the two of you?"

"No." Dot's face conveyed no emotion.

Esther looked at her brother, then at Dot. Shangri-La had a villain—and Dot was hiding something.

"See you at dinner." The door slammed shut behind her brother.

"Dot, out with it." Dot could pull that innocent stuff on William, but Esther wasn't buying it.

"How should I know what Conrad's problem is. If he is a Nazi sympathizer, then it follows he'd want me dead. He knows I'm Jewish, and he knows about my membership with the Jewish Council. The man you adore—even if you won't admit it—has sworn he will protect us from Conrad. Eric cares about you."

Esther plopped down on the bed. *She's serious.*

"I can tell by your Mona-Lisa smile that you're pleased." Dot began packing her toiletries.

"He cares all right. He likes humiliating me. It gives his ego a boost. But this trail ride—that's all pie and applesauce!"

"Esther, you're a one-of-a-kind woman, so you require a one-of-a kind man." Dot walked over and sat down. "You are a loyal friend, a loving sister, and a truly honest Christian who loves an adventure. I'm never worried when I'm with you because you're the real McCoy, even if it means having to use the back of a tree as my outdoor privy."

Esther laughed. Now, that was a picture she didn't care to see.

ↄ

Esther's brother planted a kiss on Luscious' cheek before mounting his horse while Dot looked on. John, alias Gene Autry, saluted his girl. Then the tall blonde, Sally "Bombshell" Dodges, handed Eric her scarf. Eric tied that around his neck. He lifted her off her booted feet to plant a loud kiss on her ruby-red lips.

"Hmm," Dot said. "Nice shade of lipstick. It'll go well with the scarf."

Esther laughed. Dot joined in.

Eric frowned.

Esther lifted her chin and sat a little straighter in the saddle as they rode out beneath the gate. So he's fallen for Blondie. Nothin' to get in a lather about. Esther loved riding and being outdoors. She'd have a marvelous time, with or without Eric's approval. In spite of Conrad.

As the ranch dipped out of sight, Eric rode up and handed her a long rope-looking thing. "Take this, and if one of the cows should happen to wander, coax it in with this."

"What is it?"

"A lariat."

He galloped off, leaving her with one of Jack's trusted hands. She wished she could rope and hog-tie Eric and leave him in the dust of her horse's flying hooves.

_ಉ_

Esther waved to Dot, stationed on the opposite side of the herd. Dot cantered over. "I could use a rest from this saddle."

"I wish I'd worn a pair of broken-in boots."

"Are they pinching your toes?" Dot said.

"How'd you know? And I'm not used to these western saddles." The saddle was high in the front and back and kept her legs positioned in one spot. She tried wiggling her legs. No help.

Out of the west, a band of black clouds filled the horizon. The wind picked up, too, kicking up the sand and sending the wild grass whipping through the hills. Two horsemen etched the horizon, the setting sun shrouding their shoulders. They galloped down the hill toward them, pulling to a halt a mere foot away. Her heart skipped a beat when one of them turned out to be Eric. The other was her brother.

"A storm's brewing I didn't expect. Look, I'll take your positions. You and Dot can head to camp; William will show you the way."

"I don't mind getting wet." Esther scanned the rear of the herd. Sandy and another rider were working the cattle.

"Well, that explains why you remind me of a cute little mermaid." Eric's plastered frown creased upwards, as his eyes twinkled into hers.

Not exactly the comment she'd imagined, though it was an

improvement over his detached countenance earlier. "You're shorthanded, and we didn't come along to be an ornament; we came to work. I can stay and help you."

Eric leaned across his saddle, sweeping her face like a man holding a full house might his opponents. "You sure? You'd be alone with me."

"Why should I be afraid to be alone with you?"

"Can't blame you if you were, after that pool incident. I apologize for the way things turned out, but I had a job to do."

"What part of your job description authorized you to—"

"I never kissed a mermaid before; the urge got the better of me. But I restrained myself, so, Toots, I say we—"

"I'm not your toots or anyone else's!"

❧

Sparks from the fire lit up the night sky. The only noise, the sound of knives and forks scraping tin plates.

"I never thought a can of beans could taste so good," Esther's brother muttered between mouthfuls.

"Pass the cornbread." Dot's cheeks bulged like a squirrel's as she pointed her finger to the pan.

Esther gulped down her milk, sopped up her beef gravy with her cornbread, and spooned the soggy mess into her mouth. "I feel like a real cowboy, complete with saddle sores." Stretching out her legs, she wiggled her toes through her socks. "Isn't this great?"

Eric came around the corner of the chuck wagon and stopped. "Esther, let me have a look at your feet. You've got some spots of blood on your socks." He knelt beside her.

"They're fine."

"Then you won't mind if I have a look at them." Before she could protest again, Eric had peeled off her socks. He examined each foot, his touch ticklish. He checked the two red-oozing blisters on both sides of her toes. "I've got some salve that will heal that almost overnight." He stood and held out a hand to her. "Come with me."

Esther picked up her socks and boots and followed him, stumbling over the pine needles and stones. "Ow, ouch, ooh."

He patted the tailgate of the wagon. "Sit up here."

"Up there?" The chuck wagon was a replica of the Conestoga, the wagon used during the western expansion, and the lip of the wagon came to her chest. The rear wheels themselves were six feet in diameter, clearly no easy step up for her.

Eric clutched her around the waist and lifted her into the air, his face so close his breath stirred her hair. He wiped the bottom of her feet and applied a poultice to each blister and wrapped her toes with gauze.

He drew out her hunt boots. "I thought you might need these."

"Oh." She hugged them. "Thanks. They're not much to look at, but they feel great on my feet, sort of like an old leather glove." Impulsively, she hugged his neck. "You are sweet when you want to be."

"Attaboy," muttered a cowboy who happened by.

Eric ignored him. "I brought you a hunt saddle, too."

She wanted to fit in. "Won't the guys think I'm high-hatting them? What do you think I should do?"

"You care?" His eyes met hers. "Try the western saddle tomorrow. There's a trick I often use on the stirrups that softens them to mold your leg. I'll try it on your saddle over night. Where's your sleeping roll?"

"William got it down. It's over yonder." Esther jerked her thumb.

"Let's get you bedded down."

She didn't know when her feet touched the dirt. The wind rustling the poplars nearby whispered a melody all their own. Was it a love song? She wasn't sure.

෴

The sun passed over the rolling hills and played hide and seek between the pine trees the next morning as Esther rolled up her blankets. Sleep had been blissfully interrupted with the birds chirping and sunlight peeking into her dreams.

Cook stirred the embers of last night's campfire and fed more tree limbs into the fire pit before placing a pan of bacon and a pot of coffee on the fire. He whistled a familiar cowboy tune. Esther hugged her legs. She felt overwhelmed with joy at being a part of this roundup.

She nudged Dot. "Wake up; it's going to be a beautiful day. 'The heavens declare the glory of God; and the firmament sheweth his handywork.'"

Dot rolled over. "I can't believe I slept on this rock-hard ground." She groaned and rolled back, blinked at Esther, then put a hand over her eyes. "I've got muscles I didn't know could feel sore."

"Doesn't that java smell delicious?"

A breeze stirring the scarlet and gold leaves of the maple trees also carried the delightful aroma of coffee wafting past their noses. The sound of bacon sizzling in the cast-iron skillets mingled with the harsher sound of egg shells being broken, alerting them to the morning's menu of flapjacks cooking on an open fire as the wood crackled and popped in the crisp open air.

"Come to think of it…" Dot sniffed the air. "I am a little hungry."

Cook clanged his skillet, and cowboys clambered up from where the horses were picketed last evening. Breakfast was ready.

Jack walked forward. "Okay. Let's get us a little breakfast and be on our way. We're teasing daylight poking around here. But before we begin, I'd like us to bow our heads and thank our Good Lord for blowing that storm away. Now let us ask Him to bless our food and the day's work which lies ahead of us. Today's prayer is from Joshua 7:13. Joshua didn't know, but there was sin in his camp that caused him to lose the battle against the Amorites. I have found sin at my ranch. I feel the Holy Spirit directing me to this verse today, replacing Israel with America: 'O America; thou canst not stand before thine enemies until ye take away the accursed thing from among you…' Now, I want us all to examine our conscience and make sure you are right with our Lord. I shall close with 1 Timothy 6:18 and 19, 'That they be rich in good works, ready to distribute, willing to communicate; Laying up in store for themselves a good foundation against the time to come, that they may lay hold on eternal life.'"

Later as the afternoon sun touched the tree tops of the western sky, Eric, not more than twenty feet away from her, rode off to coax a wandering heifer back to the herd. Esther inhaled, reveling in the scents of animal flesh, morning dew, and pine needles. The yellow and scarlet leaves of the maple trees seemed alive as they glistened in the sunlight. She always felt closer to God on the back of a horse. Jack's morning prayer heightened that feeling.

Without warning, the wind swooped down, stripping the leaves from the branches. She shivered. Joshua had lost the battle against the Amorites. Had Jack had a premonition of foreboding to come?

*

After three days of riding together, Eric's and her differences had melted like ice on a spring day, allowing the warm sunlight to shine on their commonalities.

Dot enjoyed William's attentions; Esther could tell. "Lord," she prayed, "it would be wonderful if they fell in love."

"Praying on horseback? There's got to be a cowboy code of rules about that one." Eric rode in next to her.

"You haven't done that yourself?"

His dimples played back and forth across his clean-shaven cheeks. Quite a contrast to the sandpaper cheeks of yesterday. "Actually, I'm not a praying man. Do you think it might help me stay on the straight and narrow?"

"It's the only way to talk to God." The breezes off Lake Michigan caressed the loose tendrils of hair peeking beneath her cowboy hat. "When I feel the wind, I often think of Him and I find myself praying."

"The wind? How's that?"

"John 3 verse 8, my paraphrase: The wind blows where it wants to, and you hear the sound of it, but can't tell where it comes from and where it goes. So is everyone who is born of the Spirit."

"I try to go to church every Sunday. How about you?" Eric's playful tone had slipped away.

She and Eric had some things in common, but did they have the ones that really counted? "My family has always been very biblical. They believe in reading their Bible every day, not just on Sunday."

"I knew you were different. I didn't know why until now. You know what you believe in and why. That's a good combination." Eric fumbled with his reins. "What's with the Bible? I know it's important to Jack, too."

"God gave us the Bible to obey for spiritual freedom. 'Now the Lord is that Spirit: and where the Spirit of the Lord is, there is liberty.'"

"And what about this Holy Spirit you and Jack talk about?"

"Jesus knew we'd need His Holy Spirit to guide our decisions and for our protection. As Ephesians 2:18 states: 'For through him we both have access by one Spirit unto the Father.'"

Eric's sudden discomfort spoke more than words. He wasn't ridiculing her beliefs, but he seemed worried over something.

"We'll talk more about this later." He grimaced. "William and I drew the short straws. We've been picked to ride ahead and make sure the corral is ready for the herd."

"You worried about Conrad?"

"No one's seen him." Eric removed his hat and wiped his forehead with the tall blonde's red scarf. "Can you and Dot stay out of trouble till we return?"

"We'll be fine."

"I feel responsible for you."

That wasn't the emotion she'd hoped for, eyeing the scarf. Was his only interest in her pure responsibility? Recalling her mother's advice of not mixing her dating field with her mission field, she prayed fervently for God's wisdom. "Dot and I will do our part and not cause trouble."

As Eric galloped away, Esther's heart sank. When had their relationship gone from suitor to big brother?

⁀

William and Eric left the next morning, promising to be back by nightfall. Esther felt Eric's absence during their noontime meal most.

"Look, Dot." In the cool shade of the forest bordering the meadows, she'd spotted an apple tree.

Esther dismounted and tied her horse to a nearby tree, then picked a few apples and placed them in her saddle bags. Biting into one, she motioned to Dot. "These are juicy. Have a taste." She handed an apple to Dot. "Wouldn't they make a good dessert for dinner this evening? A little bit of cinnamon and sugar and they would be delicious."

"Anything would be better than day-old biscuits mushed in warm milk. Cook has no imagination."

"You mean no sweet tooth, don't you?"

Dot laughed. "It would be a nice going-away gift if we made the dessert this evening." She dismounted and tied her horse up with Esther's.

They picked silently, placing the fruit in their upturned hats. "What was that? I heard something—"

A flock of black birds cawed and flew out of a nearby tree. "What do you think got them riled?" Dot said.

Esther shivered as the warm, happy day grew ominous. She felt someone looking at her. There he was, crouching low. "Run, Dot!" She was clear of the tree—

"Esther!"

"Get back here. Or Dottie is a dead woman," yelled a male voice.

Esther stopped and turned to find Dot caught in Conrad's grip, his gun pointing at her forehead. Esther took a step forward. She cradled an apple in her palm. "Conrad, what do you hope to gain?"

He holstered the gun. His ragged teeth twisted into a grin. "Pleasure."

Esther rolled back her arm and threw the apple at his face.

Chapter 7

*G*et up!"

Esther felt the toe of Conrad's boot kicking her bruised rib. As the fog in her head cleared, she realized her arms were bound behind her back.

"I said, get up!"

She stumbled to her feet, breathing in the stench of dirt, dust, and mold.

"You won't get away with this." Dot rolled over on the dirt floor of the cabin and sat up. "Eric and Will are on their way back."

Conrad scowled at Dot. "Well, they won't find you, least not alive." He pushed Esther toward an oblong table with four wooden chairs. "Sit." His boots made small dust clouds in the dingy room as he pulled Dot up and pushed her toward the table and forced her onto a chair. He untied the ropes that bound her arms.

When he bent over Esther and untied her ropes, she nearly gagged at the sour wine stench of his breath. "Don't get any notion of escapin'. You cost me enough trouble when my horse spooked because of you."

He shoved his dirty hand into his pocket and drew out some paper. Rubbing his arm across the dusty table, he laid down the papers and a stub of a pencil. He pulled his gun from the waist of his pants and pointed at them each in turn. "Don't try nothin' and do what I tell ya."

He shoved a snapshot toward Esther and Dot. A picture of two hollow-eyed boys around four and five years old stared back, a big gold star sewn across their dark uniforms. Their paper-thin arms were locked into each other's grasp as if that was the only thing they had left in the world, themselves. The other paper was a letter on fancy company letterhead.

Comrade Schmidt. You must prove your loyalty to us by performing an act worthy of our führer, Herr Hitler.

Esther scanned the letterhead. She'd never heard of an American company named Weimar Watch.

"When Hitler starts his world order, people will bow when I walk past." Conrad laughed like a hyena.

Esther looked away. The devil himself couldn't look any more evil. Conrad was as crazy as that madman Hitler.

He slapped her. "Don't turn your head away when I speak to ya. And you address me as Herr Schmidt." He shoved a blank paper toward her and handed her the pencil. "Write down your full name."

Pencil poised, she glanced at Dot. She nodded slowly. Esther bit down on her bottom lip and wrote.

"Good. Say that Conrad Schmidt is going to kill me. Do it I say!"

She bent over her paper and silently prayed. *Jesus, I claim Isaiah 54:17, no weapon formed against me shall prosper. And I claim Psalm 91, You will give Your angels charge over me, and You will deliver me!*

"Good." He turned to Dot. "Okay, it's your turn, Dottie."

Esther slid the paper and pencil toward her.

Dot was as cool as a cucumber. *She's got a plan brewing. But what? Concentrate. Watch Dot. Watch for an opportunity to get that gun. After all, God expects me to do my part.*

Dot wrote her name. She gave Conrad a cheeky smile.

"Don't forget to put down that you're a Jew. Hitler hates Jews."

"Want me to finish the letter, Herr Schmidt?" Dot said.

Conrad scratched his whiskered chin with his revolver. "Put in I plan to kill both of you as a testimony to my cleverness and exp—"

"Expertise?"

"Yeah, and any other fancy words you can think of. Then put down I plan to bomb the arsenal and auto factories in Detroit. And don't forget to say I got a list of Jews to be smuggled by the Berlin Underground, thanks to my Dottie."

Dot sucked in a breath.

How many people like Conrad were in the States? Esther was so naïve.

Dot's pencil scratches filled the silence of the cramped cabin. Dot finished, looked up, and smiled brightly. "Herr Schmidt, if it meets your satisfaction, I will write, 'Comrade Schmidt will use torture techniques designed by Führer Hitler.' But I won't put down that we had passionate sex. That'll be our little secret. I understand from many of the people I rescue in the underground that the German soldiers rape the women they capture."

Conrad gurgled deep in his throat as part of one dark lip stole upward in a haughty grin. "Yeah, I plan on keeping that our little secret."

Dot pushed away from the table and fell down on her knees, wrapping her arms around Conrad's legs. "Herr Schmidt, the Nazis want to exterminate Jews, not Southerners. Let Esther go, and I'll show you a time you'll never forget. Promise."

She released his legs and crossed her heart slowly, lingering on the loose buttons of her blouse, then folded her hands as if in prayer. "You'll not forget me, ever!" Dot leaned her head back, pursed her lips, and batted her long sooty lashes as her large sapphire eyes gazed into his.

Conrad leaned toward her, legs spread. His dirty fingers shook as he touched her. His yellow teeth gleamed in the half-light from the burlap-covered windows. His eyes glowed with desire. "You're ripe for plucking." He set his gun down on the table, unbuckled his belt, and reached for her.

Esther seized the gun and hit him over the head.

"Ow…" Dazed, he turned. "Why you…" As he started toward her, his pants dropped to his ankles.

She hadn't hit him hard enough. Jesus help me. She couldn't fire the gun. She might hit Dot. So she did the next best thing. She kicked him as hard as she could in the groin.

He doubled over with pain. His knees buckled. He growled. She kicked him in the leg. He stretched out his dirty hand in a half-hearted attempt to take her down with him.

Her heart slamming in her rib cage, she kicked him again in the groin, then hit him on the head. Conrad's body fell limp.

Dot took the gun from Esther's shaking hands and bent over Conrad. He lay face down in the dirt. She straddled him like a horse, the gun aimed at his head. "Find something to tie him up with."

Esther grabbed the rope Conrad had used on them. "Did I kill him?"

Dot leaned over. "No. Still breathing. Too bad." She turned. "Take the gun and aim it at his head."

Esther complied. Then Dot slid her hands into his pockets. She removed a snapshot, looked at it, and then pocketed the photo into her Levis. Burying her hand into his pockets again, she drew out what looked like a list of names. "Come on. Let's tie his hands and feet. I'll gag him."

Esther leaned over; a stab of pain ran across her back. She groaned.

"What's wrong?"

"My ribs."

Dot stepped next to her and gently lifted her shirt. "Esther, you're bruised bad from when Conrad hit you earlier. Throwing that apple at him was brave, but riled him for sure."

Esther smiled. "Wait until you see your black eye."

"A little makeup will fix that." Dot pocketed the note Conrad had made them write and the bond paper with the bold scrolled letterhead. Dot tied and gagged Conrad while Esther held the gun toward his head. The job done, Dot stood and dusted off her hands. "Okay, let's go."

An hour later, Esther collapsed against the trunk of an elm tree, unable to take another step. "Dot, I—I can't go any farther. Leave me. I can hide while you find help."

"Never. Look, we'll rest. Everything beyond this point is downhill."

Esther swallowed. Her mouth was dry. Sweat stung her eyes and clouded her vision. She tried to take a deep breath, but her bruised ribs kept her from drawing enough oxygen to power her muscles. She had to go on for Dot's sake. Esther concentrated on putting one foot in front of the other.

They picked a spot to rest near an oak that hid them well. A noise.

Burrowing down into last year's leaves, Dot peeked around the trunk of the massive oak.

Esther looked out, and then rested back on the tree. "It probably was some animal."

"Right." Dot wiped her forehead with the sleeve of her blouse. "Don't worry. God is with us."

Esther blinked back her tears. "You feel it, too?"

"Whatever happens, remember, I wouldn't change a minute. This was preordained by God."

Esther's tears dripped onto Dot's arm. "Preordained? If I hadn't gotten you into this adventure, you wouldn't be running for your life. Was this God's will or my selfishness?" Lord, help me find my way. I have been living for worldly pleasures. Please, help me to live for You.

Dot looked toward the sky. Esther followed her gaze. Cotton-white clouds meandered through its blue depths.

"God opened my eyes through your adventure. Being a Jew doesn't give me a visa into the kingdom of God. When I knelt before Conrad in that cabin, I prayed. I prayed like I never did before. But I didn't say one of my Jewish prayers—I prayed that if God would save us, I would read the whole Bible—the New Testament included—and seek out the truth about Jesus Christ. In that split second, you walloped Conrad." Dot shook her head. "I have so much to ask forgiveness for, Esther. My given name is Deborah."

Esther's eyes widened. This was the first time Dot had spoken about her heritage.

"She was a prophetess and judged Israel during the time the Jews were serving Baal. She was a godly woman, Esther. I wasn't. So I told everyone to call me Dot instead. I said my name was Dorothy." Dot swallowed, looking down at her hands. A tear ran down one dirt-stained cheek. The only sound was the poplar trees gently rustling their colorful leaves overhead.

"Like my namesake, I judged, too, only I judged everyone to my standards. Then when Hitler became chancellor for Germany and my relatives wrote what he was doing, I took a hard look at myself." Dot touched Esther's wet cheek. "When you said in steno class your name is Esther, I assumed you were Jewish. I guess there was a little bit of me that wanted you to belong to my heritage."

"My father named me that just before he died." Esther smiled. To continue the legacy of Shushan. "'How can I endure to see the evil that shall come unto my people?' The McConnell women all appear to have a destiny to uphold. Mom said Dad quoted John 4:22 and 23 for me. 'Salvation is of the Jews. But the hour cometh, and now is, when the true worshippers shall worship the Father in spirit and in truth.' I wanted to bring you to the Savior, Jesus Christ."

"I am grateful that you didn't quit on me." Dot sobbed for a moment. "What are we going to do? Hitler is out to annihilate the Jewish race. He wants to dominate the world."

After what Dot had confessed, there was no way Esther was going to quit on bringing Dot to Jesus or give up finding someone to rescue them from Conrad. A stronger gust of wind swept the trees; the chattering of their swaying limbs mirrored the thumping urgency in her bosom. "We've got to alert the authorities about Conrad. But first and foremost, we have to ask Christ's help."

Esther took Dot's hand. "As Joshua 7:13 states, sin must be driven out, and we must sanctify ourselves before we can stand before our enemy. Lord, we admit we are sinners and need your forgiveness. Thank you for sending Jesus to suffer the punishment deserved for our sin. Come into my life—"

"And mine, Jesus," Dot said.

"Help us to live a life that pleases You. Amen."

"Ok, now what should we do?" Dot said.

"Let's climb down this hill and see where it brings us."

Something moved among the trees behind them. Esther jumped to her feet. "Hurry, Dot."

"Maybe it's the angels of God."

"I hope so." They scampered like scared mice over the twigs and rocks. Esther's heart felt like it would burst. Please God, please don't let it be Conrad.

e⁀

Vultures circled in the sky overhead. Eric whistled low.

"Isn't that where Sandy said he picked up Esther's and Dot's horses?" William said. "Do you think that maybe it's—"

"No, it's a mile south." Eric took out his compass, checking his direction. "Probably some dead animal, but we'd better take a look." They loped down the hill to where the vultures circled the sky, reaching the forest edge.

William circled his horse near a trail. "Say, how do you know so much about compasses and camping?"

"From the Boy Scouts. I can't remember a time when I couldn't read a compass or know south from north. My training started at six years old as cub scout." Eric dismounted and tied his horse to a nearby tree before walking into the woods. Coming from the bright sunlight, he had to allow his eyes to adjust to the shadows. William followed.

Eric held his finger to his lips. If they were quiet, they could hear a wounded animal or person before seeing them. Nothing. He looked up and watched the circling birds and motioned William forward.

A groan came from a thin-needled pine tree. Conrad lay semiconscious. His head and back rested on an oak tree, his cotton shirtsleeve discolored with brown blood stains. Eric noticed the dark red blood on his arm and applied a tourniquet. He slapped him on one side of his stumbled cheek.

"Wa–water," Conrad muttered.

"I'll get our canteens." William ran toward their horses.

Eric ripped away Conrad's blood-soaked shirtsleeve. Four deep gashes marked his arm.

William offered his canteen to the thirsty man.

Eric glanced down at Conrad's prostrate form. "What happened?"

"Got hurt," he muttered between gulps.

"Easy with that." Eric pulled the canteen out of Conrad's grip. "You know better than to take too much at one time. How did you get hurt?"

"A bear."

William bent over Conrad. "We thought you left for Cadillac?"

Conrad wet his lips. "Nah, I was out hunting." He cast his eyes downward.

Conrad was hiding something. But what?

"I haven't ate anything today. You got any whiskey in those saddle bags? Might be I could think a whole lot sharper if I had something in my belly."

"I brought some whiskey with me, purely for medicinal purposes," William said.

Conrad tried to rise. A series of curses followed. "I could use a little taste of that whiskey."

Eric hooked a hand under Conrad's armpit and pulled him up.

Conrad's sleeve was torn to shreds; his arm had already turned black and blue from his shoulder to his elbow. Those deep gashes could have come from a black bear and continued to ooze blood.

"William, signal for the riders."

William walked toward the clearing, pulled out the whistle that hung from a piece of twine around his neck, and blew three loud blasts.

"This is going to sting." Eric gripped Conrad's arm and poured some of the whiskey onto the open wound. The man fought him, trying to pull his hand away, but Eric persevered. He dabbed the blood away with some gauze, then wrapped the arm with another length of the material. "That will do until we get you to camp."

"Conrad, during your hunting, did you see an apple tree around here?"

"Been trying to find it. Doing my best to find the girls and my horse."

"Oh? How did you know Esther and Dot were missing?"

"My arm, it hurts somethin' awful. Don't know if I can stand the pain. Could use a drink to help with the pain."

Eric motioned to William. "Give me a hand."

"Ow, my leg. Be careful. It's hurt bad, too."

"Your leg, where?"

Eric bent down to determine if he needed to apply a tourniquet.

"No. My groin got hurt something bad."

"What were you doing when that bear attacked you, using the

privy?" William chortled.

"No, smarty college boy, I weren't."

Eric seized Conrad under his shoulder. "Let's get to the clearing."

The sun made its lazy descent in the western sky.

Conrad wiped his mouth with the back of his good hand and looked up nervously toward the approaching riders. "You didn't say the boss man was with ya."

Conrad visibly shook. Was it from pain or fear? He knew more than he was saying. Question was, how to get him to tell them what he knew?

Chapter 8

The steep hill had not been as easy to traverse as Esther thought. Going down the other side of the hill wasn't simple either.

"There's that noise again. What could it be?" Dot said.

That rustling sound seemed closer.

"Let's get out of here."

They ran toward a large maple for cover and then skidded down the side of a small hill, falling halfway down on their backsides before reaching the bottom.

"Ouch!" Esther rubbed her rump. Her bruised ribs sent a stab of pain through her lungs. The rustling noise had stopped. "Are you all right, Dot?"

Dot groaned and rolled to a sitting position. "My leg. I think I sprained my ankle. You think that noise was Conrad?"

"I think it was some animal. Most likely a deer." A lone wolf howled in the distance. She shivered. The looming trees cast dark shadows and blocked the sun's rays, making it hard for her to see clearly. Dry leaves rustled like discarded newspaper beneath her body. She slid to Dot.

Esther ran her fingers and thumbs along Dot's leg. "I don't feel any bones loose. Here, let me help you up." The odor of rotting wood and worms assaulted her nostrils.

"Get me a branch or something. You can't lift me…That'll do."

A shaft of sunlight between two birch trees gave Esther a shred of hope. "This way." She and Dot hurried toward the light and the clearing. There was no sign of the fruit tree, cattle, or riders. Only a meadow dotted with wild flowers and knee-high grass and the dark forest on each side. Nothing but wilderness. "This can't be the same meadow." Esther looked around. "Nothing looks familiar."

Dot sank to the ground. "God, what do You want of us?" She lay there, sobs wracking her body. "I'm too tired to go on."

Esther stroked Dot's matted hair. Now was not the time to succumb to self-pity. "We've come this far. I'll not give up now."

ↄ

"What'd you find?" Jack said.

"Conrad." Eric shoved the cowboy forward.

Jack sat back in his saddle and pulled his big-brimmed cowboy hat off his forehead. "Do tell. Conrad, I figured you'd be halfway to Cadillac by now, looking for work." A half smirk swallowed his grin. "You wouldn't be following us, would you?"

"He led us to think you asked him to help in the search," Eric said. The pieces of this jigsaw puzzle were beginning to fit.

"Nah." Jack leaned over in his saddle and gave his palomino a pat on the neck. Saddle leather creaked in the silence. His eyes swept Conrad's body and landed on his face.

Conrad slid sideways, turning his head. "I got nothin' to say."

"Come on, Conrad, my man," Jack said. "Climb aboard."

Conrad lifted his left leg to climb up and dropped it like a wounded coyote. "No, I ain't. I'm too bad hurt."

"I'm not asking you to do anything but sit. Eric and William, give him a leg up."

"No. I'm hurt, I tell you. Ain't no way I can straddle that horse in the condition my—"

"Finish it. Or I strip you down myself."

Conrad shifted his gaze. "I—hurt my privates."

Jack leaned on his saddle horn, resting his left elbow. With his right, he hushed the five other cowboys' guffaws. "Conrad, you're full of surprises." Jack's eyes grew hard as steel. "One of you men that aren't too skittish, jump down and check him out."

Conrad turned to bolt.

Eric grabbed him.

"Strip him down, boys."

"No, I'll tell you the truth, so help me—"

"Oh, you'll tell us the truth, and without using our good Lord's name in vain. And I'm sure, before we're through with you, it will be the gospel truth." Jack leaned over, leveling his eyes to Conrad's. "And you'll be awfully glad we're Christian men before this day is done."

Eric and William didn't tarry to see Conrad get his just desserts. They loaded another saddlebag with grub and tied four bed rolls to their saddles. Eric glanced over his shoulder. Conrad was cussing up a storm.

They mounted their horses and galloped along the tree line, seeking the apple tree where this escapade began. After thirty minutes or so of hard riding, they paused to let the horses catch their breath. The wind made gentle swaying motions across the wild grass. Eric smiled. "You know, your sister told me about that passage in John."

William looked up to where Eric was pointing and took a drink from his canteen. "You mean John 3:8, the wind blows where it wishes?"

"Yeah, that one. I prefer to keep my religion in church. But Christ will make a believer out of me if we find Esther and Dot unharmed."

"You think Conrad kidnapped them?"

"Yeah." Eric kept his eyes straight ahead. "They could still be in danger. Conrad is a tough cowboy. He wouldn't have made it through the night alive though, not with the wolves."

William looked toward the heavens. "We need all the help we can get."

"We got that. Now come on and ride."

"We haven't asked the only One who knows where they are." Removing his hat, William bowed his head.

Eric shook his head. "Now, why didn't I think of that?"

"Lord, we come before You humbled and humiliated. We forgot to include You in our search, and we're asking You to show us where my sister and Dot are. We need to find them tonight, Lord, if it pleases Thee. We claim Psalm 91:10 and 14, no evil shall befall you…I will deliver you, and Psalm 34:19, 'Many are the afflictions of the righteous: but the LORD delivereth him out of them all.' We ask this in Jesus' mighty name."

"Let's ride over to that hilltop. We can see for miles from there," Eric said. They cantered to the hilltop and Eric reined up his horse. He scanned the tree line. The meadows lay like a green-hued patchwork quilt designating the areas of light grass, shadows from the looming ten-foot trees, and thick knee-high jade-green patches of grassland. Nothing moved but the grass prompted by the wind. Not even a deer. "Let's head north." The sun peeked beams of light along the horizon. He was hopeful the clear skies would give them a few more minutes of sunlight, just enough to see Esther and Dot resting, eating apples to their hearts' content beneath that tree.

Then, out of the corner of his eye, Eric saw a shaft of sunlight resting on a fruit-bearing tree. "There it is!"

Eric and William galloped across the meadow, dismounted, and walked toward the tree. Eric looked for any signs that the girls had been there. "Most of the apples are still on the tree."

William's boot hit something. Bending down, he picked up Esther's hat. Then found her saddlebag. "Conrad must have assaulted them here."

Tying up their horses, they walked into the woods, looking for signs, but in the shadowed interior, Eric couldn't see a hand in front of his face. Walking out into the clearing, he reached for an apple and took a bite. "They could be hurt. By the looks of Conrad, there was a fight—"

"Or dead." William pounded the seat of his saddle.

"No. They escaped. Conrad was looking for them."

"Or his horse?"

"Nope. He could have stolen one of ours." Eric threw the apple down. "They probably lost their way trying to get back. We'll camp up on the hill for the night, out in the open."

"We can't just wait. We've got to keep looking."

"Not in the dark, we can't." Eric pointed to thick forest. "We'll end up dead if we try to look for them in there. We'll build a fire and hope they're alive, see the fire, and come to us."

❧

Esther and Dot walked back into the woods and headed north. Hungry, thirsty, and tired, they stopped to rest and fell into an exhausted slumber. Esther awoke, shivering from the sudden change in temperature. The shadows were playing tricks with her eyes. She kept seeing shiny eyes staring at her. The forest was alive with night animals in search of food.

"I'm not going to be something's supper." Esther shook Dot awake. "Get up. We've got to get to a clearing. It isn't safe here."

Dot grabbed the stick she used as a walking cane and reached for Esther's arm. The tops of the trees swayed in the breeze. The branches bowed to the left. "Come on, Dot. The meadow is this way." She wasn't sure; it was just a hunch.

Their breath sent tiny puffs of steam into the air. Dot started to shake and Esther rubbed her arm. "We make a pretty pair, Dot, with your leg and my ribs. It'll be a miracle if we get out of this without being shredded to pieces by some animal. How's your foot?"

"It hurts, but I don't dare take my boot off. I'll never get it back on again. And I feel woozy, too. How about you?"

"Me too, and thirsty. We can make it with a little food and some water." Esther stopped. "Dot, we need to pray."

"We did, remember?"

"It can't hurt to pray again." They both bowed their heads.

Esther pushed the words past the lump in her throat. "Jesus, help us please. We need water and food, but mostly we need to be rescued before nightfall. Send your angels and give them charge over us, like it says in Psalm 91."

"Right, and send Conrad somewhere where we'll never have to see him again as long as we live."

"But, Miss Dottie, I can't believe you'd feel that a way about your lover boy Conrad," Esther replied in her best southern drawl.

"Yuck." Dot spat in the dirt. "I get a whiff of him on my clothes sometimes, and I can still feel his dirty hands on me." She shivered.

The moon shone a jagged pathway through three maples. Esther pointed. "I can't believe it. Look. It's our apple tree!"

Esther plucked an apple, bit into it, and sucked out the juice, then bit again. Dot cupped as many apples as she could hold in her arms, sat down at the base of the tree, and ate.

Darkness shrouded their shoulders. A lone wolf howled. This wolf cry sounded closer. Another wolf took up the howl…An eerie silence followed. Esther listened, then walked out from beneath the tree. A light flickered in the distance. "Dot, look." She pointed toward the tiny sliver of light.

Dot's excited voice joined hers. "It looks like someone's campfire. Oh, Esther, do you think it's Conrad?"

"No. He wouldn't go out in the open. Come on. We can make it."

"Are you sure?"

"I'm sure." Esther went on the left side of her friend and placed her arm beneath hers. Thank you, Jesus; at least this side of my rib cage doesn't hurt.

"But what if it's Conrad?" Dot held back. "He's not going to fall for my antics again."

"Dot, we have his gun, and I'm sure it's not Conrad because we prayed for God's intervention. Come on."

The glow from the campfire grew brighter with every step, as did the full moon now set high above the treetops. A low growl a few yards behind them broke the silence. The grass waved with their movements as pairs of eyes gleamed back at them in the moonlight. Esther and Dot scurried toward a small knoll where the grass was just two inches high and waited. A half dozen wolves crouched, their heads lowered, watching them.

Esther raised her arms and swished the air. Dot raised her stick and followed her example.

"Get!" Dot mimicked her. "Get!"

"Remember King David. He was a little boy, and he killed that giant with a single pebble. Nothing is impossible for God."

"Well, no offense to God, but the next time I go picking apples in the northern wilds, I'm bringing a knife, a pack of matches, and my gun. Here, take it." Dot held out the gun to Esther and glanced up toward the fire. "Our choices are letting the wolves eat us or Conrad murder us. You came closer to the bull's-eye more often than I did at the camp's shooting range."

Esther took the gun and cocked the trigger.

"Aim straight, Esther, but leave one bullet for Conrad."

She held her breath, aimed, and fired. One wolf yelped and fell. They backed up slowly, watching the pack. One wolf pounced on the wounded animal, the others followed, tearing the not-yet-dead wolf to shreds.

The muffled noises of horses galloping through the tall grass met Esther's and Dot's ears. A shot rang out. A wolf yelped and the others took off, their bushy tails glowing white in the moonlight.

Eric jumped from his horse and reached for Esther.

"Ow." Esther stifled her cry as his arm came into contact with her bruised ribs. Tears of joy stung her eyes, engulfed within the ecstasy and safety of Eric's arms.

He kissed her forehead and her cheeks. "It feels so wonderful to have you in my arms again."

"How did you know it was us?" Esther's tears wet his shirt.

"A lot had to do with prayer." William caressed Dot to his big chest.

"And God's grace." Eric said. "That moon was shining a spotlight on you and those wolves."

"Come on, we've got a bed roll for you and some fresh coffee, beans, and biscuits," William said.

Eric gently lifted Esther into the saddle, then sat behind the saddle on his horse's rump and waited while William helped Dot onto his horse. Together they walked back into camp. Eric slid off the back of his horse, then lowered her to the ground. He guided her to a log and blanket and handed her a cup of coffee.

"You can't believe what happened." Dot wrapped both hands around her tin cup.

"I think we can." William laid a blanket around her shoulders. "We found Conrad. With a badly cut arm from a black bear and strangely painful testicles."

"You can thank your sister for that." Dot smiled.

"Sis?"

Dot nodded. "Conrad liked me best, so Esther got jealous and kicked him there."

"That's right." Esther laughed. "Conrad liked 'his Dottie.' I just don't know what came over me."

The men looked at the girls and laughed.

"I must admit, in a pinch we do make a pretty good pair," Esther said between her laughter.

"I sat on him, big deal." Dot grinned. "Well, I might have used my fist on his face a couple of times, but Esther saved us from being raped and murdered."

William looked at Dot and back at Esther, his face distorted in a mixture of pride and horror. "I can't believe this. He was planning to kill you, for what reason?"

"Look at this." Dot reached into her pants pocket and produced the paper telling of Conrad's intentions.

Eric and William read the note and sat silent for some time.

"These photos are what Conrad took from my wallet."

Eric and William bent over them. Eric spoke first. "These kids look as if they haven't had a square meal for months."

"What's that pinned to their shirt?" William said.

"A star of David." Dot pointed. "German Jews have to wear that on their clothing day and night. It signifies they are Jews and no longer German citizens. No one is permitted to feed them or give them sanction or else, they too, will be arrested and deported to prison by the Nazis."

"Where are the children's parents?" William said.

Dot shrugged. "Dead or in the Nazi prison camps." Dot handed him another photo.

"A snapshot of some rally—is that Hitler?" Eric asked.

"Yes. One of my relatives smuggled it out of Germany when he came to America. It's a picture of the Nuremberg Rally; it's always held at night. Thousands of Nazis carrying torches march to a stage where Hitler stands like a sort of god. Everyone chants, 'Heil Hitler to thee.' Read the back of the photo."

William bent closer to the campfire. "Blazing flames hold us together into eternity...those who are dedicated to Germany."

"That's part of the oath they say. With Hitler's Nuremberg Law, he took away citizenship for every Jew. They became subjects of the Reich and unable to work in their professions." Dot rose and limped toward the fire. "My relatives coming over through the underground say Hitler's planning to wipe the Jewish population off the face of the earth."

"In order to do that...he'd have to conquer the world," Eric said.

"I didn't think much about it when my professor talked about Hitler being a man 'beyond his time,'" William said, "and that a united Europe is needed for financial growth and prosperity."

"Hitler's vendetta is not just about the Jewish race." Dot poured herself more coffee. "Esther can tell you better than I." Dot sipped her coffee, then said, "Hitler has a loyal network of followers throughout Europe and here in the United States. Go ahead, Esther."

Esther sucked in a deep breath. Her heart beat its own war drum within her chest. What she was about to say was true. Would Eric and William believe her?

"Hitler's hatred toward the Jewish race is satanic. He hates Jews because of Jesus. Jesus was a Jew, and He conquered the grave and sin. Jesus foretold that in the later days, there would be wars—"

"He wants to reign like some kind of god?" Eric said.

"You mean like a sort of anti-Christ?" Williams's face was engulfed in a series of shadows.

Eric glanced down at the photo. "This Hitler thing is more serious than Americans realize. How many other Nazis—and now with the recent oil-embargo on Japan, Japanese sympathizers—are here? Are they planning espionage maneuvers against Americans as we speak?"

Chapter 9

Esther and William agreed not to tell Mother about the kidnapping. A month of investigation by the authorities on Conrad and his allegiance to the Nazi underground had ended.

Breathing the crisp autumn air, Esther dragged her fingers on the waist-high stone wall that lined Fort Street. Tall massive churches with slender steeples reached heavenward and bells chimed the musical strains of "Amazing Grace" this Sunday morning.

Esther's prayers for Eric and Dot spiraled into the celestial blue sky. They walked behind her, laughing and joking with her mother and brother as they approached the church they planned to visit.

The kidnapping began Esther's pilgrimage for her friends who didn't have a personal relationship with Jesus. William said she'd become too uptight about the "Conrad caper," as he put it. Said she could lose Eric if she turned into a religious fanatic. A killjoy.

She thought it funny at her brother's choice of words. Kill-joy? What a pun. That was exactly what she was trying to avoid. She sighed. In the beginning of her relationships with Eric and Dot, it didn't matter what her friends believed—now, it mattered too much to stop. Last night's Bible reading of James 4:14 pricked her conscience. *For what is your life? It is even a vapour, that appeareth for a little time, and then vanisheth away.* God's kingdom is the only certainty of life.

Jesus, let this preacher be filled with the Holy Spirit and give him a message Eric and Dot can't ignore. Ignite them with Your grace, Lord. .

Her mother paused before the Gothic style stone church. Esther and Eric, William and Dot waited, looking up at the old church that rose two hundred feet above the street.

Stained-glass windows of blue, red, pink, and white sparkled in the bright sunlight. Large geometric stone walls laced with moss stood a towering three stories before them. Her mother glanced at the letter and then back at the address. "Well, this is it. It's a little older, and the street has changed since we were here in '33."

The church's decorative brass and iron casing lining the double oak doors and windows was grander than any Esther was used to back home in Kentucky.

A whiff of hazel wood and cedar greeted her nostrils when Eric opened the door. Their steps echoed in the foyer of the high-ceiled interior. Above the altar hung a large portrait of Jesus.

"Impressive, isn't it?"

Esther and Dot looked up toward the voice. A man with sandy-blond hair smiled down at them from the balcony. "Wait there and I'll give you a tour."

A voice from behind Esther made her turn.

"My brother's harmless." A petite blonde smiled back at them. "Pleased to meet you. I'm Betty Jones." She quirked her chin at the man in the balcony. "We're twins."

Adorned in a sky-blue hat and a slim-fitting mid-calf dress with satin lapels and matching baby-blue buttons, Betty's dress proved the epitome of fashion. Her fawn-colored seamed nylons and leopard-colored shoes with matching handbag completed her ensemble.

"Hi." Eric and William spoke in unison, gazing at her long enough to nod and smile.

Breathing heavily from the flights of stairs he'd traveled, the man from the balcony extended his arm. "My name is Ralph Jones."

Betty and her brother looked to be in their twenties.

Eric walked over and extended his arm to Betty. "Eric Erhardt." His lopsided grin swept his handsome face.

"Dot McCoy." Dot smiled at Ralph and then Betty.

Dot was equally attractive with her jet beads and black crepe dress with a polka-dot sash. Dot's hand went to her sassy black-and-white hat perched to one side of her shoulder-length hair.

Esther glanced down at her cotton dress, which Mother had altered with shoulder pads and a wide patent-leather belt to appear modern. She felt decidedly underdressed. Well, she'd get a better paying job soon. She and William would graduate from college next month, and she had an interview with a law and insurance office Monday morning. Her first paycheck would go to moving Mother, William, and herself to a place they could call their own. "I'm Esther, and this is my mother, Ruby Meir, and my brother, William."

"Pleased to make your acquaintance." Her mother extended her gloved hand first to Ralph and then to Betty.

"May I take your coats?"

Her mother slipped out of her coat. "Is this still Pastor Jim's church?"

Betty's brows arched above her wide baby blues like a question mark. "How long ago was it that you visited us?"

"April of '33. That was the month we left for Kentucky," Ruby said.

"I don't remember you." Ralph said to Esther. "I was nine then, but I always remembered the pretty girls."

The Depression years were just another era piled onto the Meirs' years of lack, that is, until Buck Briggs entered her mother's world and hope filled the cavity left by Father.

"My parents weren't regular church goers during the Depression. Too busy trying to make enough money to eat, and embarrassed because they didn't have much money for the offering plate," Ralph said.

"I guess as long as we can remember, its shadow will nip at our heels. That's why Uncle Franklin sold his house and we moved to Kentucky. That's where my sister and I were from originally," Ruby explained.

"The winters were awful cold here. Dad sometimes had to decide between being warm or being fed," Ralph said.

"You must be near my age. Did you have a paper route?" Eric said. "No."

"Well, then, did you sell apples on the street corners of Detroit?"

"Our parents wouldn't allow us," Betty replied. "Did you?"

"I sold newspapers." Eric stretched a little taller. "And apples, too, when I could get them. Pa and Ma needed my help. Had a large family to feed and bills to pay."

"Shouldn't we be getting to our seats?" Her mother nodded her head toward the couples entering the sanctuary.

Betty glanced up from her wristwatch. "Have about five minutes. We'd better find our seats."

"Why spoil a beautiful morning?" Ralph whispered.

"A lot of the young people here don't care for Pastor Jim's fire and damnation sermons," Betty explained in a hushed tone.

The echoing footsteps of the worshipers on the marble floor and the pipe organ's marching refrains of "Onward Christian Soldiers" had them rushing to find a seat.

"Don't expect a lollipop sermon all sugared over with everything nice and you won't be disappointed." Ralph stepped aside to let Esther go into the pew first.

"What's going on here?" William looked around at the congregation of bent shoulders and snow-top heads. "Ralph and Betty are the only ones here our ages. Mother, can't we go to a church for young people? What are Dot and Eric going to think? They'll never want to come to church with us again."

"Church is not a social club. Uncle Franklin and Aunt Collina wrote me to visit him. Guess they thought you two needed a dose of reality."

"Oh, I see." William crossed his arms and rested back on the velvet-covered seat. "It's going to be one of those history lessons again."

"No." Ruby gave William a no-nonsense look. "You don't see, least not yet. It's goin' to be a survival lesson."

Esther's attention swerved toward the pastor who had stepped up to the podium. With hair as white as snow and a beard to match, Pastor Jim resembled Father Time or perhaps St. Nicholas here for a visit. But that was where the similarity ended.

Pastor Jim's heavy-layered syllables reverberated around the four walls of the church, peppering his words with infectious emotion.

"Our European neighbors are fighting for their homeland as we sit comfortably in our seats, a fight that might any time cross the seas to our own shore. Our government has prohibited American companies from doing business with German, Italian, and Japanese firms, and because of our sympathy to China and the Chinese, our relationship with Japan is as tense as a bow string. What should we do? Remain neutral? Accept Nazism? Or should we ready our souls for the great undertaking that may come to our shores any day now? A war that will ask for our sons, daughters, and sweethearts?"

Pastor Jim looked down at Esther from his lofty pulpit. Esther held her breath.

"What do we pray, daughter? Do we pray that our omnipotent Father spares us from the horrors of war? Or for our all-knowing Savior to prepare us for the battle ahead?"

His piercing glance scanned his small congregation. "Jesus warned us that wars would come before He returned. 'Little children, it is the last time: and as ye have heard that the antichrist shall come, even now there are many antichrists; whereby we know that it is the last time.'"

Leaning over, he paused. When he continued he spoke in low tones. "Shall our hearts grow faint with fear—or fearless? We know the grave has been conquered by the cross. Our Almighty God has cut a covenant with us in His only begotten Son. Do you have a personal relationship with our Lord and Savior Christ Jesus? Life is too fleeting to think you may have tomorrow to decide. Make the decision that will change the course of all your tomorrows—today."

℅

After the service, Esther paused on the steps of the church. Sun spots danced across her eyes, the bright sunlight making it hard to see, as her thoughts reeled like a Ferris wheel, around and around, from the pastor's sermon.

"I like Pastor Jim and his church," William said.

"But there's not too many there your age."

"A wise woman once told me that church isn't a social club, and she's right." William smiled and hugged his mother's shoulders. "Dot, would you like to come back with us next Sunday?"

"Yes. I need to get a Bible with both the Old and New Testaments. There's a lot I don't understand."

"Take mine for now," Esther said.

"Are you sure?"

"Positive."

Eric hadn't said a word since they left the church. She looked at him questioningly. "What did you think of the pastor?"

He spoke slowly, feeling his way. "He's like my pastor in many ways."

"Would you like to go with us to Wednesday night service?"

"I prefer seeing God once a week."

Esther's mother glanced down at her watch, "My, look at the time. Esther, we'll have to hurry. Cousin Gill likes his Sunday dinner promptly at 2:00, and we still have to clean their bedroom and the den before they get home."

"Mother, it's noon," William complained. "Besides, it's our Sunday, too. I have to prepare for two interviews tomorrow and my CPA exam."

"Esther and I don't expect you to help. We can manage nicely."

William opened his mouth to answer. Esther shook her head. He shrugged off her arm. "Esther has two job interviews tomorrow. How is she going to prepare for her exams next week if she has to work as maid and cook this afternoon?"

Aghast, Dot said, "Your cousin makes you cook and clean for them?"

"I don't mind. Mother does the cooking; I do the cleaning."

"I assumed you were guests of your relatives," Eric said.

"Land sakes, children." Ruby faced them, her small gloved hands resting on her hips like a sergeant observing her troops. Her little straw hat with the posy sat over her forehead in a tipsy way, half concealing her eyes, thanks to her fast pace down the sidewalk.

"Never in my born days have I nor my children taken a morsel of bread we haven't earned. The good Lord saw fit to keep us beholden to our kin, and so we are."

She turned and walked faster than before. Her shoulders were bent double against the warm autumn breezes. Focused on getting back to the house before Cousin Gill arrived, she didn't seem to notice the colorful leaves on the trees, feel the warmth of the sun, or smell the fragrance of the mums along the way. That's not like Mother.

Eric halted Esther. William and Dot followed Mother. "Say, I could lend you some money so you don't have to take your cousin's crumbs of kindness. He's treating your family like servants."

She wanted to scream. What did he think my life was like without a father? If not for Aunt Collina and Uncle Franklin, we would have been homeless. They were the only ones who treated us like family. But they're in Kentucky and I'm here, going to school and scraping a living as best I can.

"Look. The Meirs don't accept handouts. We're doing fine on our own. A little work doesn't hurt anyone."

"Right. But even God says Sunday should be a day of rest!"

He doesn't get it. There was no place to go but Cousin Gill's. "I'm really busy these next couple of weeks and—"

"You mean you want me to take a powder? Fine with me. You're not the only doll in my little black book." She watched him leave. Jesus, if you're listening, please, oh please find me a good-paying job. Esther walked faster until the only sound she heard was her pounding heels on the pavement. She had two interviews tomorrow afternoon. Lord, please let one of them be a job right for me.

Chapter 10

Esther opened the door to the Special Services Department. A whiff of fresh paint, varnish, and roses wafted through the room as she stepped across the threshold. "Good morning. I'm here to see Mr. Bowden about the secretarial job." She touched one of the dozen red roses lying on the woman's desk.

The receptionist smiled, reaching out to caress one bud. Her manicured fingernails colored in vibrant red matched her lipstick and the flowers. "These lovely flowers wrapped in tissue paper were waiting for me this morning. I told my husband the fumes from the paint gave me a headache, so he had these sent around."

"They match your outfit perfectly."

Her blonde curls bobbed across her forehead as she nodded. "I know. Red's my favorite color. And to think my husband always forgets our anniversary and my birthday. I absolutely forgive him." She glanced at her scheduling book, pointing a finger to Esther's name. "Miss Meir? Mr. Bowden's been waiting for you. Come right in."

The tall oak door swung open to reveal two overstuffed tapestry chairs and a sofa commanding one corner of the room. A mammoth mahogany desk dominated the room like an orchestra leader his musicians, with a picture of George Washington at Valley Forge on the wall behind. The man sitting behind the desk encompassed the folds of the tall black leather chair with his equally large form.

He stood and extended his hand. His mouth wavered from its

downward sweep into a lopsided smile. "It's a pleasure to meet you, Miss Meir. I have your grades from the Detroit Business Institute in front of me and have just finished studying them. Your timing couldn't be more perfect."

Releasing her gloved hand, he motioned for her to take the straight-backed chair on the opposite side of his desk. "I see you did quite well in stenography and typing, finishing at the top of your class. You like using the Dictaphone?"

Esther set her pocketbook in her lap and clasped her hands. "I could use more practice. But if you check my test scores, I did make 85 percent on my final."

"And your telephone skills? There will be times I shall ask you to reply to my messages. And when you understand the way I write, to respond in writing to my clients."

"I can fulfill your requirements, Mr. Bowden. I have been told that I make a good first impression."

Mr. Bowden leaned back on his leather chair, removed his glasses, and chewed on the ear piece as he studied her.

Esther swallowed. Good first impression? I can't believe I said that.

"A good phone voice is what I require for this job and, of course, confidentiality of the utmost. My office is not directly affiliated with the Special Services, but we are in the same building and perform the court cases. You will never see any officials or inspectors. We are, more or less, the legal arm of the department."

Esther, relieved, said, "I will not disappoint you."

Replacing his glasses, he opened the folder and shuffled through the papers. "I can never seem to find what I'm looking for." Shoving the folder aside, he looked up. "When are you finished with school?"

"This week. I have one exam to take on Tuesday."

"That's in your favor. Can you begin Wednesday?"

"This Wednesday?" Esther looked down at her lap. What if Cousin Gill hadn't hired anyone by then? How would her mother manage without her?

Mr. Bowden removed his glasses, his puckered lips creased into a smile. "You're worried about the pay, of course. I understand, you see. After all that is why we work, isn't it?"

She must get this job. Brent Insurance Agency had said they'd call her. She needed a job, not a promise.

"You'll be on two weeks' trial. Don't take that literally." Mr. Bowden chuckled. "After two weeks, I'll evaluate your work and determine whether you meet the criteria and the requirements necessary.

"Mmm..." He reached for her folder again. "There it is." He glanced up at her over the pages, his glasses resting on the curve of his nose, ready to fall. "You have filed a deposition on a Conrad Schmidt, kidnapping charges linked to possible espionage."

Esther sucked in her breath. "Yes, sir."

Mr. Bowden removed his spectacles and leaned back in his chair. The leather creaked with his weight. Only the tick, tick of the grandfather clock in the corner of the room disturbed the silence.

"Do you think there are more men like Conrad planning sabotage attacks on American manufacturing plants and citizens?"

Esther sat up straighter. "As long as there is a war in Europe and people who have divided loyalties and prejudices, yes, sir, I do."

"Do you think America will enter Europe's war?"

Esther did not flinch. "I think there is a strong possibility that we shall be forced to enter."

"Yes, well." He cleared his throat and leaned forward. He placed his spectacles back on his nose and wrote something in her file. "I'll start you at $0.40 an hour. You can figure on nine to five, eight hours a day, five days a week."

Esther gasped and did a quick calculation. Sixteen dollars a week!

Mr. Bowden frowned. "For a starting stenographer, without experience, that's not bad."

"I understand." Esther hoped her gasp had worked to her advantage. She and her mother were working for their cousin for thirty cents an hour. This job was more money than she had made in her life, but could she pay back her mother for the bank loan her college tuition had cost and rent an apartment?

"In two months, if your work proves favorable, I'll raise it by five cents an hour."

Esther was too stunned to say anything.

He plopped down his glasses, reached his left arm toward his intercom and pushed down the button. "Mrs. Ryan, come in, please."

The large oak door opened slowly. Esther wasn't sure what was expected of her.

As if reading her thoughts, Mr. Bowden smiled. "Mrs. Ryan, Miss Meir will be starting Wednesday. Make a note of that to payroll." He turned back to her. "Miss Meir, your first paycheck will not start until the week after next. You'll get paid for the three days. Then subsequently, you will receive your check every Friday for the previous week worked. Now, Mrs. Ryan, show Miss Meir her desk and, oh, get her acquainted with the staff and have her fill out the necessary paperwork."

He rushed them out with a wave of his hand. Then with a sudden clearing of his throat, he halted Mrs. Ryan's departure in mid-stride.

Esther made a mental note: Mr. Bowden clears his throat when he has more instructions.

"Make sure you keep abreast of current events, Miss Meir. I expect all my personnel to keep updated on the community." Mr. Bowden leaned back on his leather chair, his brows weaving into crescents above his dark eyes. "You have one day, Miss Meir, to get your affairs in order. Then, on Wednesday, you will begin your new life as my secretary. I expect the best, punctuality, loyalty, and above all, secrecy."

↶

"Mother, I got the job!" Esther danced around the laundry room as if on a stage in a gilded theater.

Her mother laid down the drapery, her face wet from the machine's steam, and applauding said, "That's wonderful."

Esther curtsied. "Thank you, thank you very much!"

"Okay," her mother sighed. "Now it's back to work. Here, hold these steamed pleats in place till they cool and I can tie them." Ruby peeked

104

around the corner of the open door, then wiped her hand across her brow. "Is the front door open?"

"Yes, Mother." Esther's eyes watered from the steam of the press.

"I hoped to let in a little fresh air."

"Here, let me do that." Esther set down the pleats that were pressed and hurried to help her mother carry another batch of heavy drapes to the presser.

"We've got to get these drapes pressed and pleated by the time Gill gets back from the bank. He was upset with me that they weren't ready for him to drop off before he left." Ruby put a finger to her thin lips. "Now let me see, yes, these are the last big ones." She patted her lips.

Esther scooped the yards of fabric into her arms.

"Stand back, Mother, I can lift them. You man the press." They worked in silence. Esther lifted the long heavy drapes onto the press, and her mother made quick and accurate folds in the pleats. As each panel was completed, she wrapped them with ribbons of paper to ensure their accuracy.

Beads of sweat washed over her mother's forehead. Her thin arms folding the yards of fabric on the presser.

"Mother, let me do that, you're not strong enough." The slope of her mother's thin shoulders displayed her exhaustion. The blue and aqua faded print dress she wore was as over-used and as worn-out as the woman it adorned.

"I don't think I'll ever be strong enough to move these heavy things."

"So why don't you tell Cousin Gill?" Esther was as guilty as Cousin Gill. She'd used Mother to climb the ladder of prosperity, to go to business school, hadn't she? Her mother's education hadn't gone past the eighth grade, yet she'd made sure both her children graduated from high school with honors, and when William won his scholarship, she moved them to Detroit to give her children a better life than she'd had.

"It was kind of your cousin to offer us a job and a place to stay until we could afford a place of our own. I don't know about his finances. Lots of people can't afford to get their cleaning done. I'm not sure he's making much profit."

"He's got us cooking and cleaning his big house for our bed and meals."

"Hush." Esther's mother looked around the room filled with racks and racks of clothes and drapes. Two men carrying out the bagged cleaning paused, looked at them, and then resumed their packing.

She walked over to her daughter and whispered, "Do you want someone to hear? We can't afford to lose the only job we could get, not with that bank debt to pay off."

The piles of drapes were chin level. Esther let out a huff of air. Why, God? He'd given her a chance to enjoy a better life than her mother would ever know. She didn't deserve this chance—Mother did. "The Depression's over for most, just not for us. It's not fair the way Cousin Gill is treating us."

"Fair?" Her mother's sharp eyes were unwavering. "The important thing is surviving. I'll never forget standing in line at the unemployment office. If it wasn't for our victory gardens, we might have starved." Mother wiped her pepper-colored ringlets off her brow. "I learned a valuable lesson during those hard times."

Esther looked at her. "What?"

"Never dwell on the have-nots; focus on the haves. 'Better is the poor that walketh in his integrity.' God will be there to lift you up. He can't do that if you don't take a tumble now and then."

"With my new job, I won't be able to help you much." Esther looked up from laying down another set of heavy drapes. "What are you going to do if Cousin Gill doesn't hire anyone? Who's going to help you?"

"I'll manage. I did when you and William went to that fancy dude ranch." Her mother coughed as the steam from the presser swirled around her head. "What company did you say it was downtown where you got the job?"

"A lawyer firm affiliated with the Special Services. They have an office over the recruiting department." Esther cringed at the sight of her mother's face, wet from the steam. "Mother, I can't stand seeing you work like this."

"Your cousin promised me that I'd just do seamstress work soon. He's just short-staffed. He told me the other day that he's placed an ad in the paper for more help." She nodded confidently. "Your cousin won't shirk his duties to his kin."

"I'll believe it when it happens. You're too dedicated, Mother, too hard-working. Why should Cousin Gill pay for another pair of hands when yours will work without complaint? Aunt Collina warned me, told me not to let you work too hard. But I might as well be talking in the wind, the good it does. You should've stayed in Kentucky. William and I can manage."

"You saw what your promises meant to that highfalutin bank person. He wasn't about to give you any credit." Mother lifted the lid, and steam floated up over their perspiring bodies. Her lips were drawn in a tight line. "We've got the devil by his tail, and you and your brother are going to be somebodies someday. Like your father wanted."

Steam spiraled its way upward, like wayward ghosts, into the high-arched ceiling. Secrets. Mother was a wealth of them, never revealing the darker side of life. "What happened to Buck Briggs, the man you were engaged to? Why didn't he come back?"

"Well, I guess you're old enough to know. Times were hard during those depression years. Buck got tangled up with those no-account political mafia men. When he got born-again, he was going back to disclose their rotten deeds. He wasn't going to run for governor, at least not on their coattails. They didn't like that much and—"

"Oh!" Esther covered her mouth. "He was such a good man."

Her mother grasped Esther's shoulders and gave her a shake. "Good doesn't protect us, nor get us through those pearly gates, only the blood of Jesus Christ can do that. Buck realized that truth and did the work of the Lord. Only God's armor can win this battle against the flesh, and I'm beholding to our good Lord for knowing Buck is in heaven awaiting—well, anyways, that was another lifetime. It was my decision to move up here. Remember that. You and your brother had nothin' to do with me leavin' Kentucky and coming to Detroit.

"Make me proud; that's your job, fulfill your destiny and do the best with the talents the good Lord gave you. That's all He asks of you, and that's all I'll ever ask." Mother placed a finger to her thin lips. "Now, let me see. I've finished the altering and this is the last of the big drapes."

Esther laughed. "You're telling me to shush feeling sorry for myself."

Her eyes hazed over, her lips crinkled into a large smile. "True. 'Cause no one can out give God. Doesn't that new job of yours prove it?"

The shop bell rang out its warning. "Ruby? Why is this door ajar? You got those drapes done yet?" Gill yelled.

∾

Esther's mother didn't look up from stirring the pot of beans. "Can you set the table, Esther? Your cousins should be coming through that door any time, and they'll want their supper."

"How many?" Esther dreaded seeing Gill after the way he yelled at Mother earlier that afternoon.

Mother paused, wiping her brow. "Just us and your cousin Gill and Elma this evening."

"Will William be here?"

"I hope so. Land sakes, I believe that boy runs on fumes. He ran out of here this morning, gulping down a cup of coffee and grabbing a biscuit on his way to an interview before his class. He's going to have a fit when he learns you got a job before him."

Esther got down the dinner plates and salad bowls and set out water glasses. Mother was making amends to Uncle Gill for being slow to finish the drapes by preparing a dinner fit for a king. "Mother, I'll make enough money for us to get our own apartment."

"Really?" Mother opened the oven door to check on the ham and sweet potatoes. "Good, they're done." Removing them, she put a pan of corn muffins in their place. "Who did you say hired you? Was it that insurance company or the law office?"

Esther took a deep breath. "Law. I'm in the Recruiting Building on the third floor of the Special Services law firm."

"Why did you pick that job? If we don't get in the war, they won't need you but a couple of months, and if there is a war, after the war they won't need you."

Esther turned. "We need the money, Mother. I'll do fine. Mr. Bowden assured me that they will be there indefinitely and that I'll get a raise in two weeks."

"That makes me feel better."

"What makes you feel better?" Cousin Gill's large bulk came through the door in a flurry of packages and bags.

"What have we missed?" Cousin Elma joined in. "I just knew I shouldn't have gone shopping. It was such a bore." Lifting her ample arms, Cousin Elma took off her hat adorned with a black peacock feather and small stuffed bird on its brim. "Here, Esther, take this and put it in that hatbox on the shelf in the hall closet."

Esther hurried from the dining room table where she'd laid the last plate and napkins. She wiped her hands on her apron and took Cousin Elma's hat. "Dinner will be soon. You might want to wash your hands."

"They do feel grimy from touching all those dress patterns." Cousin Elma patted her coiffure. "How you do like my hair? Just had it done."

Esther didn't know how to answer. Elma's round face resembled a tomato with a tuft of hair pinned at the crown of her head. After years of perms and colorings, she didn't have much hair left, just a small amount of yellow fuzz. "It's becoming, as usual," Esther said.

Cousin Elma turned. "Ruby, I couldn't find a dress that fit me right, so I picked up a pattern and cloth so you could make me one."

"I don't rightly know when I'll have time. But I'll look it over after I get the dinner dishes done."

"Thank you! Now, do tell me some good news. I'm bored silly with all this war talk."

Esther frowned. Lord forgive me, but oh, please, let me be perfect for this job so we can rent a flat. Mother's too loving; she's going to wear herself out trying to please everyone.

Moments later Cousin Gill took his seat at the head of the table, ready to eat. "I don't see that strapping boy of yours. Are we going to have to wait supper for him?" He reached for his newspaper.

Since when did Cousin Gill ever wait on them? "What can I do to help, Mother?"

Ruby set the bowl of steaming green beans on the table and surveyed the kitchen. "Can you get the pitcher of sweet tea from the ice box? And check the cornbread. It should be about done."

"Are these green beans from your garden, Ruby?" Cousin Elma lifted the bowl to her nose before taking a heaping spoon full.

"What?" Cousin Gill looked up from *The Detroit News*. "Wife, they came from our property, so that makes them mine."

Cousin Elma fussed with her hair, then frowned at her husband. "Your aunt Ruby hoed your dirt, sowed the seed, watered it, cooked it, and now we get to eat before she gets a mouthful. That makes it hers, and I think she deserves a special thank you. She didn't have to do all that." She forked a tomato onto her plate, and then slapped her red-tipped fingers down on the table. "But she did."

Cousin Gill straightened his paper with a loud noise and cleared his throat. "Thank you, Aunt Ruby, for harvesting such delicious produce for us to eat."

"My pleasure. It gives me satisfaction and a little piece of home when I find time to do my gardening."

Mother carried the ham garnished with pineapple and cherries to the table. Esther followed with the plate of cornbread. They sat down, just in time to fold their hands for Cousin Gill's prayer.

Her mother made sure Cousin Gill and Elma were served first.

"Mmmm, everything is delicious." Cousin Elma smacked her lips. "Now, I didn't forget." She giggled. "You know me better than to forget a tidbit of news. What were you two talking about in the kitchen when we walked in?"

Esther gulped. "I can't remember."

"News?" Cousin Gill looked up from his plate, chewing on a piece of ham. The juice seeped down his double chin. He wiped it away with his napkin that he'd tucked in his collar. "What news? Elma, you trying to drum up the latest gossip again? Woman, don't you realize we're on the pinnacle of a world war? If America doesn't enter it soon, Europe's going to fall to that barbarian. There's no telling what Hitler will do after he's got Europe by the juggler.

"And then there's Japan right on Hitler's heels ready to dominate the world with him. Their Japanese soldiers are systematically trained to commit brutal acts against men, women, and yes, even little children. They haven't got a conscience; that's been trained out of them.

"We didn't raise our boys for that. They're good Christian men. It's a shame. That's what it is." Before Cousin Elma could reply, he bent his head over his plate and crunched down on his ear of corn.

Cousin Gill's dentures bit off the kernels, crunch, crunch, crunch. No one spoke, just the crunch, crunch, crunching of his teeth on the corn.

He stopped, swallowed, and said, "It would be my guess that by this time next year, America will be waging a full-out war campaign against Nazi Germany, fascist Italy, and Japanese militarism—"

"We're sending England supplies." Esther couldn't hold her tongue in check any longer. "Roosevelt's cut off Japan's oil supply and some of our men have enlisted to fight overseas. The war could come to a screeching halt if Japan doesn't have fuel to run it."

Cousin Gill snorted, set his fork down, and drew his napkin from his collar to wipe his mouth before picking up the paper, reading where he'd left off. "This editorial right here says Europeans don't think our boys know one end of the gun from the other. That's why they're willing to *educate* them for us. Imagine that. *Educate* them to kill their fellow man." He slapped the paper with his hand, "It says here that 'while Germany and Japan were toughening up their youths to become a super race America is teaching their youths to be playboys whose only interest in bettering themselves is buying the latest zoot suits and purchasing the newest motor cars.'"

"Husband dear, what has that to do with anything? Our boys won't need to fight in that silly war—it's Europe's problem. We're hundreds of miles away and have the salty blue oceans keeping the world away from our peaceful shores."

"Wife dear, get with the times. Our world is shrinking. Maybe we have produced a playboy generation, but they're our playboys. They're good kids. And so what if we instilled good, solid Christian principles in them. How dare those people in Europe and Japan judge our boys for being young and impetuous?" Gill's eyes scanned the headlines. "See this right here? Looks like the draft board is getting ready for some serious work. I don't think they'd be doing that if the war department thought there was any hope that Roosevelt's oil embargo would work." Pointing to an ad in the paper. "Looks like they're hiring, too."

"We know. Esther got a job there. Well, close to there," Ruby said.

"What?" Cousin Gill peered around his paper.

"She's got a job in the Special Services Department."

"Hmm, I've heard about them. Why did they come to Detroit?"

The back door banged open, and William's long legs made quick strides toward the table. Plopping down at his seat, he reached for the ham and then the beans.

"Well, what have you got to say about your tardiness?" Cousin Gill's voice boomed across the dining room table.

William didn't stop. He nodded his hello, his cheeks bulging as he swallowed. He drew out a form, full of writing, set it down on the table, and then handed something to his mother.

"Twenty dollars? What's this for, Son?"

"It's my paycheck, Mother. I've been working for the Ford Motor Company for three weeks in the accounting department. I've got a one-year contract. Here." He tapped the papers on the table.

"But your classes at the University?"

"Yep, afternoons I've been at Ford Motor. Next semester, I've already enrolled in night school, and I'll be working for Ford forty hours a week." William gave Esther a wink. "Won't be long now, Sis."

"What won't be long?" Cousin Elma's hands clapped together in glee. "Oh my, more gossip, I can't wait."

"You might not like this gossip. It relates to yours truly, Cousin Elma, and will change your way of life." William bit into his corn with exuberance.

Chapter 11

The gold-colored name embossed in bold letters over the door of the little restaurant read, "Lafayette Coney Island." Two weekends of tedious apartment shopping had whisked by without a decision. Esther was determined this Sunday would not end until her mother and brother made their minds up. She glanced at her wristwatch: five o'clock.

William opened the door. Ruby stepped in first, and Esther followed. "This is the best little restaurant in Detroit to get a Coney Island."

"What's a Coney Island?" Her mother clutched her handbag to her black wool coat, as if afraid someone in the narrow room might snatch it.

"It's a fancy hot dog with chili, Mother. You'll love it," Esther said.

The jukebox in the back corner played Glenn Miller's "Tuxedo Junction." A food bar ran the length of the room. Esther waited to see where her mother and brother chose to sit before taking the aluminum barstool with the red plastic seat. The shiny tin ceiling, black and white linoleum floor, and tin wall paneling was different than any restaurant she'd been in.

"Mmm, must sell a lot of hot dogs here." Her mother's eyes were as big as a child's.

A waiter came forward. "What'll it be?"

"The house special, please, all around" William said. "Mother, you want that, right?"

Ruby looked down at the menu and nodded.

"Okay, a Coney with all the toppings and a Coca-Cola for each of us," William said. The waiter scratched the order onto a pad and left.

Esther withdrew some folded papers she had inside her purse. "So we decided. Saint Paul Manor or the Kingston Arms Apartments."

"What's wrong with the El Tova Apartments?" William nodded thank you to their waiter as he brought their drinks. "We can afford it."

"I thought we decided that apartment was out because of the high rent." Esther opened the paper. A picture of the large, four-and-a-half story orange brick building with limestone trim, orange terra cotta accents, and Spanish tile roof stared up at her. She pushed the paper toward her mother.

The name El Tova was carved on the scroll above the entrance, minaret-like towers projected from the gabled roof, and the entranceway was flanked with impressive lion figures.

"Too fancy for the likes of us," Mother said.

"We can afford it. Isn't that what we've been working for, to give us a little class?" William said. "I'm tired of feeling like a sub-servant."

"You children need to learn that no one can make you feel like that—but you. Quit worrying about pleasing others. Please God, and He'll take care of everything else. Now where's that paper showing the Kingston Arms?"

"Kingston Arms, that's the cheapest one of all. The only apartment they have left is on the third floor, and they don't have an elevator," William explained.

Ruby took a sip of her Coca-Cola. "You afraid of a little exercise?"

"Mother. You're talking about three stories. I hate to think about carrying up our furniture." William pushed the paper describing the Saint Paul Manor toward his mother. "What about this one? It's not as fancy as the El Tova, but not as plain as Kingston. At least it has an elevator."

Her mother looked at the picture of the red brick building designed for upper-middle-class families. It had plaster raised fronts with the scrolled embossed entranceway and gold-cased doors. "No, my mind's made up. You children need to save your money. Get a little recreation into your lives. Working all the time isn't good for the soul."

"How can it *not* be," William muttered. "It's all you've ever done."

"Here's your coneys." The waiter handed the bill to William. He reached into his pocket and produced the money.

Steam rose from the chili, sauerkraut, and onions covering the hot dog. Small, thin french fries and a side of coleslaw finished the meal.

Her mother was first to taste hers. Her pillbox hat bobbed back and forth on her head as each bite she took was bigger than the last.

"You like it, Mother?" Esther asked.

"I've had a hot dog with sauerkraut before but never with chili. It's real good. I might even make this for Gill and Elma."

Esther rolled her eyes at William.

William's brows arched like knife-sharp lightning bolts. "Your servant days are over, Mother."

Mother's gaze landed on her son like an eagle ready to battle. "Jesus said, whoever desires to become great among you, let him be your servant. Son, never begrudge the rich their wealth. Your cousin Gill isn't easy to work for, but he's fair. Besides, I've never worked for man. I've always worked for my Lord and Savior. Remember Proverbs 13:11? 'Wealth gotten by vanity shall be diminished: but he that gathereth by labour shall increase.' Learn to work hard for the Lord, always striving to learn more about God's wisdom."

William whirled around on his stool. The jukebox silent, the ball bearings on the stool rolled loudly. She couldn't see his face, but his shoulders were hunched as if he was weighed down. He spun back around, facing Mother. Silence. He looked like he was seeing his mother in a different light. He took a deep breath. "You're right. I've been absorbed in the foolish pursuit of people pleasing. My talent is a gift from God. I didn't do anything to attain my photographic memory, and it was because of your God-given wealth, Mother, and not my intelligence, we have come this far."

Truth germinated into reality for Esther that day as she sat on the wobbly red stool at Lafayette Coney Island. According to the world's standards, her mother was an illiterate woman, but she exceeded

William and her in common sense. When it came to knowledge or biblical wisdom, Esther would take wisdom over a doctorate degree from a prestigious university any time.

"I'll give Kingston Arms the deposit tomorrow," William said.

"Land sakes, I nearly forgot. Here, Esther." Mother pulled a letter out of her pocket book and handed it to her. "It's from your Aunt Collina."

"Why don't you read it out loud?" William said. "Unless it's personal."

Esther skimmed the contents and read. "Dear Esther,

"Your mother has written how proud she is of you and your brother. I pray you do not become unduly wrought with the high ideals your dear mother has laid upon such young shoulders.

"I am writing you to say, if you have a suitable place, I have transportation that can drive your horse to Michigan. Ruby thought it might help cheer you up and relieve some of the stress of the recent kidnapping you endured.

"Your loving Aunt Collina."

How had mother known that nighttimes were often filled with the nightmares of that kidnapping? Panting and running through the darkness...Oftentimes, waking up from night sweats, she would fall asleep by quoting Bible verses from memory. Every week the memories grew fainter, and now it was as if God had rewarded her for her faith in Him. Esther squealed. "My horse? Aunt Collina didn't sell her? Then the money for the bus ride and our stake came from Uncle Franklin?" She blinked back tears. "How did you find out about the kidnapping? William and I didn't tell you."

Mother patted her already-clean mouth with her checkered napkin. "I know, children. I understand your concern was to keep me from worrying. That's why I didn't say anything. I received this letter in the mail three weeks ago." She passed along a second letter, this one on linen stationery with an imposing seal at the top. "Go ahead and read it, Esther."

"Dear Mrs. Meir:

"It is with extreme honor I write this. Your daughter, Esther Meir, has proven to be a capable woman and a true American patriot in fighting off the attacks of Conrad Schmidt, a confessed espionage criminal for the Nazi government. With citizens like your daughter, this nation cannot go awry.

"John Nance Garner, Secretary of State to Franklin D. Roosevelt."

Ruby took the letter from Esther, folded it neatly, and put it away. "Now, William, you go find yourself a horse and put it at that stable you and Dottie have been riding at. I've already written Collina to send Esther's horse."

"But Mother, what if the war should begin?"

Mother waved her hand in front of her face like she was shooing a fly. "What if Jesus should return? We don't know if we'll be here tomorrow. We can't put our lives on hold just because we're afraid to live. No. You children need to pack up some good memories to get through the bad times.

"You've worked hard and you've done well for yourselves. Course I never thought you wouldn't. In the year we've been here, you've managed to achieve more than some people do in a lifetime."

Ruby raised her glass, toasting them. "Your Cousin Gill is sitting up and taking notice of me. Got me some help this week. I'm head seamstress." She set her glass down, shoved her spectacles up, and glanced at the papers describing the apartments. "I got my Christmas present coming early. I can't imagine what it will be like to sit in our own parlor and cook in our own kitchen, just the three of us."

∽

The workweek flew by for Esther. William had put down the security deposit on the apartment at the Kingston Arms. Then Mother, being her normal frugal self, got most of it back. She talked the Kingston Arms manager into allowing William and her to do the painting. The manager was so impressed by their work that he offered them a side job. William put a stop to that idea. He'd paint their unit and that was all.

Esther worked from dawn to late into the night to get the apartment ready and was happy to have an excuse for not seeing Eric or Dot. The memory of that Sunday after church sent a blush rising to her cheeks. Eric had not contacted her in the past three weeks.

Mother hoped to have their new apartment finished before Christmas, so they could invite Eric and Dot for Christmas cheer. Esther told her she would invite them, but for Mother not to get her hopes up. Eric had a large family, and she wasn't certain he could make it, and Dot was Jewish.

Esther didn't know how to tell Mother that Eric and she had broken up that Sunday they went to church together. She'd hope he'd call and apologize, tell her he understood. What she couldn't figure out is why God seemed to lay the guilt of this breakup on her. When she prayed for Eric, all she got in return was, "pride goeth before a fall" and Matthew 6:14 "if ye forgive men their trespasses, your heavenly Father will also forgive you." What did she do wrong but defend what Mother had said? "Wealth gotten by vanity shall be diminished: but he that gathereth by labour shall increase."

Well, good riddance, as Aunt Collina would say. She had more important things to think about, such as Saturday night and the Fenton auction. She was going there with William and Dot to find them a horse.

Chapter 12

Darkness had descended by the time William, Dot, and Esther reached the horse auction in Fenton. Cars and trailers overflowed the parking lot and onto the grass in front of a wooden two-story structure. The rusty-looking building had a large porch in the front with two tiny windows that resembled eyes. It was unpainted, like the mercantile store at Rock-a-Bye Dude Ranch. Esther stepped to the side as a rider galloped back and forth beneath a solitary spot light.

"Come on, let's get our numbers." William reached for Dot's hand, sidestepping a man mounting a horse. Inside the large barn were rows of wooden planked stalls. As many as four or five horses were tied up inside these pens, some with saddles and some without.

Esther started down an aisle where a pretty little palomino with a heart-shaped blaze on her forehead stood. Then she saw him. "Uh… What is Eric doing here?"

Eric stood not more than five feet ahead. He was bending over, picking up a big paint horse's hind leg.

She huddled behind some pens, then peeked out between the boards.

Eric's back was to her as he ran his hands over the black and white horse's neck. The matted mane and tail and muddy forelocks told of its owner's neglect for the big animal. A man dressed in Levis, cowboy boots, and a hat lounged just outside the stall doors.

"Say, do you know who owns this paint?" Eric said.

119

The man poured tobacco from his pouch onto a piece of paper and motioned with his head. "That gent over yonder brought a truckload in. Could be his."

A woman with long blonde hair and the longest legs Esther had ever seen stood next to—Oh, so that's it. Eric's dating someone else.

"Esther?" Dot frowned, her hands on her hips like a chorus girl.

"Shh." Esther put a finger to her mouth and motioned toward Eric.

Dot squatted down in the dirt and whispered, "William found a horse he wants you to see."

"Okay," Esther whispered back. "Lead the way."

Dot straightened.

Esther pulled her down. "Crawl. I don't want Eric to know we're here."

"You want me to do what?"

Esther peeked out from her hiding place. Eric was still busy examining the horse. Bending over, she scurried past the next few stalls, and then crept behind them, motioning for Dot to lead.

William stood in the back corner of the large barn, checking out a chestnut with a flaxen mane and tail, and a bay gelding with a white spot on its forehead. The horses lowered their heads, their ears pricked forward, and snorted at her crouching in the dirt.

"Esther, what's gotten into you?" William rested his hands on his hips like a gunnery sergeant and scowled.

Esther motioned with her index finger for William to bend down, then whispered, "Eric's over there. I don't want him to see me."

"Why not?"

"Well, we sort of broke up, and he's got some blonde bombshell with him. I'm not going to give him the satisfaction of thinking I'm following him."

"Following him? To Fenton? Hardly. Maybe he's been busy. Give the guy a chance." William grasped Dot by the arm. "Dot, you get up from there. Stand next to this chestnut.

"Just as I thought, you two complement each other." William smiled. "That horse has the same red highlights in its mane as you have in your hair. I could get the bay, and you could get the chestnut. Hmmm. No number. Stay here. I'll track down the owner and see if we can ride. Maybe I can make this deal before the auction begins."

William strode off, but quickly returned with the owner. The owner took one look at Esther squatting behind the pole and backed away. "What's wrong with her?"

"Man trouble."

"Oh." The owner belly laughed.

William bent over and whispered in Esther's ear. "We're going out behind the barns. You're welcome to join us; that is, if you can pry yourself away from that post you're cowering behind."

Esther followed, crouching behind Dot.

The owner saddled the chestnut and bay by his trailer. Both mares came from Battle Creek and were a cross between a quarter horse mare and an Arabian stallion. "I've come up with a breed that has impeccable stamina and safe enough for a child to ride." He took off his ten-gallon hat and wiped his forehead with his bandana. "I'd planned on doing more with the breed, but I've fallen on some hard times."

William and Esther put both horses through their paces. Esther dismounted and handed the reins to Dot. "You'll like her."

"What do you want for them?" William said.

"A hundred fifty each. They're worth every penny. These are good, well cared for horses."

"I'll give you two hundred cash for them both," William said.

The man rocked on his heels. "Well, I don't know."

"I do. There's a war coming. How do you care for a horse working for Uncle Sam?" William started to walk away. "What do I need with a hay burner I can't ride?"

The man's Adam's apple worked overtime. "Look here, it's a good thing I haven't registered them yet."

"Then I saved you the auction fee, right?"

"I need at least two hundred twenty-five for the both of them to haul them to your place. That is, if it's close."

"Okay. Do you know where Roxy's is in Warren?" William said.

The man nodded. "That's close enough." Opening up his papers, he wrote out a bill of sale.

William drew out his wallet and handed him the cash.

"Well, now, I'll get to watch the auction like a spectator." The man pocketed the money in his Levis. "You kids don't want to miss it."

$\backsim$

Esther's cowboy hat bumped on the crisscross beams overhead. She removed her hat, casting her eyes upwards at the rafters just an inch above her head. These were the only seats left. She had a bird's eye view of the horses running back and forth in an area no bigger than a ten-by-forty-foot room. People standing below, near the arena, elbowed for a better position to see the horses.

The auctioneer's words raced like a locomotive speeding down a rail. Figures ping-ponged back from auctioneer to buyers like lightning. Someone would raise their hand, and the bid escalated higher. She was afraid to scratch her nose for fear she'd buy a horse.

She spotted Eric near the pen. He stood a good head taller than any of the other men. She searched the crowd for the blonde. She didn't see her, but that didn't mean she wasn't there.

The horse Eric had inspected was led forward. A cowboy jumped into the saddle and galloped him back and forth a half-dozen times. He turned the big horse around and around on his haunches. The paint's hindquarters never left the inside of the circle. The cowboy galloped up and stopped within an inch of the wall—the paint slid across the dirt on its haunches. Clouds of dust floated upwards. Eric raised his arm and started the bid at forty-five dollars.

The auctioneer did his prattle, and then another arm went up for fifty, then sixty, all the way to a hundred. Esther held her breath.

"I'm bid a hundred, going, going—"

Eric raised his hand. "One twenty."

"One twenty going once, going twice, sold to the tall man in the black hat."

Esther spotted the blonde.

Like a hunting dog on a new scent, Dot pointed to the couple. "Who's that with Eric?"

The blonde's arms encircled Eric's neck. She bent her head forward and planted a long kiss on his puckered lips.

"I heard the smack from here." Dot slapped her knee in defiance. "How dare she do that to your guy."

"Not *my guy*. I never want to see him again." Esther climbed down from the bleachers. Eric looked up just then, smiled, and waved to her. She shoved her nose in the air and walked away, the thump of her boots resounding in her ears. She was done with Mr. Eric Smarty Breeches.

Chapter 13

The heavy rasp of the knocker jolted against the oak door and echoed into the living room. Ruby peeked around the corner of the dining room. "You want me to answer the door?"

"Who could that be?" Cousin Gill wadded up his paper, rising heavily from his chair. "I'll get it." His steps jarred themselves toward the front door.

With arms laden with the dirty dishes from their Thanksgiving Day meal, Ruby walked over and set the plates on the counter.

Esther, elbow-deep in soap suds, snatched another plate.

"I'm here to see Miss Esther Meir," the deep masculine voice said. "To take her to my parent's house for dessert."

"Eric?" Esther whispered.

Ruby peeked around the corner. Cousin Gill stood staring into Eric's stern face.

"She still has dishes to wash. Perhaps you can come back later."

"No, I can't."

Cousin Gill's face turned a burnt orange, which matched the pillows adorning his couch. In a shallow voice he cried, "Ruby? Aunt Ruby?"

Ruby wrapped her arms around Esther's waist and undid her apron. She whispered to Esther, "Go do your face and hair."

"No. I never what to see that grandstander again."

"Hush." Ruby touched a finger to her lips.

"Well, if it's all right with Aunt Ruby, it'll be all right with me." Cousin

125

Gill stomped back to his overstuffed chair, the springs complaining with his weight. He grabbed his paper and thrust the folds open.

Ruby stepped forward. The little boy who loved to chase the ice truck and sold newspapers during the Great Depression had grown up. She felt Eric's firm yet gentle hand clasp hers. "Shall we wait for my daughter on the front porch? There are things we need to talk over."

Eric's mouth twisted into a grin. "You don't need to worry about your daughter, Mrs. Meir. I've never met a woman with such strong convictions. I believe Esther and my mom will hit it off swell. That's where I'm taking her, to meet my family."

The dimples and inherent charm of this man who confidently smiled at her told her Eric was used to having his way with the ladies. As a little girl, Esther had never met Eric, to her recollection. William had once, during their Sunday dinner years ago. They were both so young neither remembered the incident.

Ruby wondered if Anna, Eric's mother, had met Esther. She didn't recollect. Would Anna remember the Meir name? Should she tell Eric she remembered him? "You remind me of my late husband, Eric."

"Do I? I remember Esther saying that he died."

"Yes. When Esther was just a baby."

"I'm sorry. That must have been hard for you. How old was William?"

"He was five. But tell me about yourself. What are your life goals?"

"I thought I knew; now, I think I need to check in with God first."

Ruby felt the overwhelming Spirit of the Lord telling her to pray. "Would you mind if we pray?"

"No, ma'am."

"Lord, we ask for Your favor on Eric, that You might show him Your wisdom. 'May the LORD bless thee and keep thee: The LORD make his face shine upon thee, and be gracious unto thee: The LORD lift up his countenance upon thee, and give thee peace.'"

She glanced up. Eric had his eyes closed. She resumed. "I claim Ephesians 6:11 to 17. 'Put on the whole armour of God, that ye may be able to stand against the wiles of the devil.' I also pray for clarity of purpose. I claim Proverbs 19:21, because many are the plans in a man's heart, but it is our good Lord's purpose that will prevail." She felt God's deep peace rest on her soul.

"You don't know it yet, but, son, God has a plan for you." She patted his hand before getting up off the wicker chair. "Get your Bible out and read it. Life's not going to wait around for you to figure out where your steps are leading. You don't want to go down a path you shouldn't be traveling. Our Good Lord will keep you headin' in the right direction with His Word."

"Yes, ma'am. Do I have your permission to court your daughter?"

⁊

Houses, maples, and elms dotted the canvas of scenery speeding past Esther's car window. "I don't know why I came with you. What happened to the blonde?"

Eric glanced from the road to her. Every once in a while, he pumped the gas pedal of his Ford Coupe to keep the car cruising without stalling.

"I'd think working at Wood Industries, you could afford a better car," Esther said.

"I'm putting myself through college, too. And the rest I'm saving for my own business."

"Where did you get this jalopy?"

"Not from a garbage heap, though I have to admit that most of the parts to repair it came from there. I built it during my senior year at high school. There was a hole right here." He pointed to where his foot rested, just below the accelerator pedal. "There wasn't any heat so I carried a blanket along. There wasn't any air conditioning, but for the hole in the floor." He turned. "Isn't it a beaut?"

Esther laughed in spite of her resolve not to. He drove up the drive to his parents' house.

There was something about him that remained a mystery to her. She glanced toward the white Cape Cod. Maybe the answer to the mystery was in that house.

"You want to know what your mother and I talked about?" His

eyes swept her face like a hawk's. "I asked her permission to court you. Guess I should have asked you first."

"I—"

"Wait!" He put a finger to her lips. "Give me a chance to redeem myself. I know you think I'm nothing but a flirt. I admit, I act that way." He looked away, then took her hand in his and squeezed it. "You want to know what you're getting yourself into in there?" He jerked his head toward the house.

"How many are in your family?"

"Eight, including me and my parents. Oh, and the Reverend Kelly might be here. We boys have the attic, and my two sisters the bedroom next to my parents."

He got out, slammed the door shut, and walked around to her side.

She still wasn't sure if the blonde was history; he'd avoided her question on that topic. Sneaking a look at her face and hair through the side mirror, she swung her legs out of the car, took Eric's arm, and climbed the steps to the large, covered porch. He'd invited her to meet his family. That had to be worth something.

"Esther Meir, this is Ann Marie, my oldest sister; Elizabeth, my youngest sister; and this is Anna, my mother; Pa's in the kitchen. The rest of the family you will meet later. They've left to visit their friends." Eric kissed his mother on the forehead.

Anna was a tall woman with bright blue eyes and a solid-looking face framed with a 1920's hairdo that resembled her Aunt Collina's.

"Meir...that name sounds familiar. But then Eric has told me so much about you I feel I know you, how you love dessert, so we waited for you to have ours." Her laugh was contagious.

Esther joined her. "Dessert is my favorite part of dinner."

Anna wrapped her ample arms around her aproned middle. "Sit down; make yourself at home."

Esther sat on the worn navy-blue velvet sofa next to Eric. His mother and sisters took the adjoining overstuffed matching chairs with floral pillows. An upright piano stood against one wall, and pictures of the family sat on the crocheted doily on the piano's top.

"You're different than what I expected a Southern girl to be." Ann Marie's no-nonsense gaze tallied her like a scoreboard.

Esther felt like she was being inspected for a contest she didn't care to enter.

Tan wallpaper with white seagulls in eternal flight covered the walls. The paper matched the oak woodwork, and the colors blended with Ann Marie's brown and orange plaid dress. "You don't have much of a Southern accent."

"I did when I first arrived. I've been practicing my diction."

"Ann Marie, her speech is softer than ours, and slower." Elizabeth smiled at Esther. "We run our words together."

Ann Marie nodded. "We come from a large family full of boys who like to run over your words before you've got the last one out."

Eric sniffed. "Smell that, Esther? Ma makes the best strudel in Detroit. Wait until you taste it. She got the recipe from her mother."

Anna's quick steps tapped across the wood floor. "I'll let the strudel cool a bit before I cut it." She crossed her arms and slapped her palms against her bare elbows, the sleeves of her knee-length dress rolled up. "Eric's grandfather worked on the railroads in Detroit, and his grandmother followed him and made money cooking for the railroad men." Anna pointed a thumb to her chest. "I was the oldest sibling."

Eric nodded. "Ma never slept beneath a roof until she married Pa."

"My Fred and the rest of my siblings built my parents the first home they ever owned," Anna explained.

"I see where Eric gets his height. I always wished I was tall."

"Me too," Ann Marie said. "I don't know how I got slighted. It's hard for me to see over the steering wheel at times. What about you, Esther?"

Esther shrugged. "I wish I knew. I don't own a car."

Anna brushed off the flour dusting her apron. "Would you like some coffee?" She walked past the adjoining dining room and into the kitchen. She came back with a coffee pot in one hand and a pint of milk in the other, and motioned for them to sit down at the dining room table.

"Ma likes coffee with her milk."

"When there's enough to go around, I do." Anne's apron pockets bulged with everything from napkins to silverware. She drew out a teaspoon from one pocket to stir her coffee, then took a sip.

A medium-built man with a thick mane of salt and pepper hair sauntered through the kitchen door. A taller man dressed in a long, flowing black vestment with a crucifix around his neck followed, smiling. His silver-white hair was cropped short and round as a bowl about his head, and in his right hand he carried a leather-bound Bible.

"Is John back?" said the medium-built man.

Anna smiled at Esther. "No, but Eric is here with his girl."

"How do, I'm Eric's pa. You can call me Fred."

He was dressed in a pinstriped vest and pants, set off with a heavily starched white shirt. He was two heads shorter than Eric, but stockier. His strong, square jaw and sharp hazel eyes didn't miss a thing. He reminded her of a picture she'd seen of a Nazi soldier.

Fred retrieved his pipe off the fireplace and took a small pouch of tobacco out of his vest pocket. "My John's got plans. Says if America declares war, he's planning to march right up to the recruiting office and join the Air Corps and learn how to fly a plane on government pay." Fred slapped his leg with his hand. "He's smart. Could be president someday, if he wanted."

"If I remember correctly, he received good grades all through school, even better than Eric's," the Reverend said.

Fred looked up at his son. "That right, Eric?"

Eric hesitated. "I was second-best in St. Thomas, five points lower than John."

Fred slapped his leg again. "That's my John, sure enough. I think he got my I.Q. A man, if he's going to amount to anything, has got to work hard to prove his worth in life."

"I'm at Lawrence now, Reverend Kelly. I'm planning to own my own engineering company someday."

"You are a very ambitious young man." Reverend Kelly slapped Eric on his shoulder. "You must be proud of your boys, Fred."

"Yep, can't wait for you to see how tall my John's grown. Why, he's a chip off the old block. Reminds me of me when I was his age."

Eric's face was flushed. Esther knew how that felt. She could never compete with William when it came to academics. What could she say to encourage Eric? Directing anything toward Eric's pa would be like tossing the comment to the wind. She glanced over at the Reverend. He's different. There's a bond between him and Eric.

"Eric rescued me from a runaway horse and saved me from a diving accident. He's got the grit and heart to accomplish anything he sets his mind to doing," Esther said.

Fred rocked back on his heels. "That's what I tell my boys, 'You can accomplish anything you set your mind to doing.'"

Reverend Kelly's smile showed a dimple to the right of his lip. "Young lady, you've summed up Eric and the Erhardt name nicely."

Anna carried in a tray full of hot strudel. "Here, Eric, cut some pieces for everyone. I'll get the ice cream."

An hour later, Fred leaned back on his chair and patted his middle. "Anna, that was delicious. I think you outdid yourself this time. Was it because of our little guest?"

"If she can keep Eric's roving feet in one place, then yes, I did."

"Now, Anna, he needs to be a roving playboy and have his fun. That's the only thing Eric's good at and excels over my John on."

Eric revered his pa. Even Reverend Kelly noticed.

"It had to be hard to feed so many mouths during the Depression," the reverend said. "I remember Eric helped out."

Fred puffed on his pipe, the smoke spiraling around his head. "All my boys helped. John had a job at the butcher's, made good money. Eric had a paper route and sold apples. Yep, I couldn't pay the all the bills if it wasn't for John."

Reverend Kelly frowned. "I remember Eric coming down the hallway at St. Thomas's, his face and hands red with cold from running through the streets delivering his papers before school. Sister Mary crossed his palms with her ruler if he didn't make it to her classroom on time."

Eric guffawed. "Dear Sister Mary, is she still teaching?"

"No, she retired, with regret, at seventy."

"Well, she deserves to rest. I'm sure her ruler must be worn out," Eric said.

Fred placed one thumb in his breast pocket, puffing on his pipe. "I don't believe in coddling my boys, makes them weak. They won't become the men God intended if they're coddled. A man's got to work harder than a woman to get into those pearly gates. God doesn't need nor want wimps in His kingdom. Eric here, being the third oldest, was the most stubborn of my four boys. But he never whimpered. Guess it didn't hurt him like it did the others."

"Yeah, between you and Sister Mary, I got my fair share of the belt." Esther gritted her teeth and looked away.

Eric walked over and opened the kitchen door. "Have you ever seen a basement that was dug after a house was built?"

"I didn't think such things existed," Esther said.

"Well, you've got to see it to believe it. See, that's where the truck dumps the coal down into the basement." A cold breeze swept through the back alleys. Esther hugged her arms close. Eric took off his suit coat and wrapped her shoulders.

"Thank you."

He smiled into her upturned face, his eyes soft, reading hers like a map. Then she heard the kitchen door reopen and out walked Eric's dad and the reverend. She could tell by the way Eric grew suddenly tense that he wished they hadn't followed them. "We'll be moving into the hard winter months soon." Fred gazed up at the sky.

The stars twinkled down at them like diamonds on black velvet.

Fred blew a puff of smoke into the air. "It'll soon be Christmas. I hope this war in Europe will be over then, so my boys won't need to fight."

"Germany, Italy, and Japan are a pin drop on the map compared to the rest of the world," Reverend Kelly said.

"That's the problem." Fred blew out smoke. The aroma of pipe tobacco mingled with the frosty air. "No one's taking Hitler seriously, but he's eating up countries like a pig gobbles up slop."

Fred rested his hand on Eric's shoulder. "You're tasting the good life now, the fun of kicking up your heels, having plenty to eat, nice clothes on your back, and a good job. Why you've got more education than Ma and I combined. I can't figure God out. Why would He allow you to fight in a war that's not your making?" He turned and puffed thoughtfully into the night wind. "I think by Christmas, we'll know for sure. My generation didn't finish the job." He patted Eric on the shoulder. "Son, annihilate these guys for good! You don't want to go back, or worse, your kids have to go over there! Least not for fighting. You got any words of wisdom for these young people, Reverend?"

"Remember, God only had one Son, and God loved us so much He allowed His only Son to suffer and die in our place. He gave us the Bible to follow and to learn by. Oh, Eric, here's the Bible you asked me for."

Chapter 14

*M*other, you were right," Esther said.

"Well, I try to be," Mother replied, wiping her hands on the dish towel.

"This move to Detroit supplied William and me with an education and good paying jobs."

Her mother pushed her toward the parlor where Dot, Eric, and William waited for them. "Go on now. I'll be there shortly."

Their apartment had become a snapshot of their lives. Esther smiled as she rearranged the picture of her then five-year-old brother sitting on a cow resting in the clover and other knickknacks Mother saved from her first home with Father in the cabin on the prairies of Colorado. Great-Grandmother's rocker brought over from Spirit Wind Manor sat next to their new blue couch. Eric joined her as she perused a picture of Aunt Collina and a thirteen-year-old Esther riding Magic. "I was so impetuous then."

Her fingers lingered on the picture of her and Eric taken at the dude ranch. Her thoughts whirled like a potential thunderstorm. Had God planned for Eric to be part of her destiny?

She gave him a glance out of the corner of her eye. The more she knew him, the more she saw his dependence on his father's approval.

Pleasant dinner music coming from the Zenith radio made for a pleasing backdrop to their conversations. "That was a good meal. I wish every day was Sunday." Eric wrapped his arms around her waist.

"First time I sat down at a Sunday dinner and did not have to hear Cousin Gill chomp on his corn." William dropped down on the sofa, and Dot followed.

Dot smiled into his eyes. "It's December 7, William. Remember you have seventeen shopping days left to find my—"

"We interrupt this program to bring you a special news bulletin. The Japanese have attacked Pearl Harbor, Hawaii, by air, President Roosevelt has just announced. The attack also was made on all naval and military installations on the principal island of Oahu.

"We take you now to Washington.

"The details are not available. They will be in a few minutes. The White House is now giving out a statement…"

Her mother's knees buckled. William guided her toward her rocker.

Dot covered her face. Her hands shook. "Are they going to bomb us next?"

"A Japanese attack on Pearl Harbor would mean war," the radio announcer continued. "Such an attack would naturally bring a counter attack….The President will ask Congress for a declaration of war."

"The horrors my relatives have endured," Dot said. "I still have nightmares and imagine Conrad's dirty arms on me. I don't know if I—"

"You will. We all will." William knelt in front of her and took her into his arms.

The commentator continued. "Two special Japanese envoys, Admiral Normura and special envoy Kurusu are at the State Department engaged in conference with Secretary of State Hull…this Sunday afternoon."

What? Esther couldn't believe her ears. What level of deception are the Japanese people capable of?

"And just now comes the word from the President's office about a second air attack on the Army and Navy bases in Malaya. Thus, we have official announcements from the White House that Hawaii and now bases in Malaya have been attacked. We return you now to New York, and will give you information as it comes in."

William turned off the radio. Silence followed, a quiet so deep and complete Esther's ears screamed for sound. She felt as if she'd gone deaf.

The squeaking of her mother's rocker broke the haunting stillness. Eyes closed, her rocker pillow cradled her head. "It's begun. Your Uncle Franklin said it wasn't over. That Germany and Japan would start another war."

She grasped a handkerchief from the pocket of her apron and dabbed her eyes. "It looks to me that our good Lord wants you to go to work cleaning out those evil dictators." She wiped her nose with her handkerchief. "Remember why your grandfather named his estate Shushan and how Aunt Collina fulfilled Esther 9:2. Yes, we've grown strong and united beneath one flag, as my father wanted. America is ready to fulfill his second prayer. I claim Esther 9:2, 'and no man could withstand them; for the fear of them fell upon all people.' Esther, hand me my Bible please."

Esther did as she was told, and Ruby quickly found the page she sought. "Lord, I claim Joshua 1:5 through 8, and I pray You will not allow any dictator to beat America or its allies. I pray Americans remain strong and courageous. Our children will continue to observe what they have been taught and do according to all the laws written in Your Holy Word, and this book of the law will not depart out of their mouths. We shall meditate therein day and night and do according to all that is written therein in Thy Holy Bible, amen."

Ruby looked up with tears sparkling in the depths of her eyes. "I expect you children might want to be alone. The upper patio deck is nice. You go right ahead. I'll be here when you get back and have your desserts ready."

༜

"You enlisting or waiting for the draft?" Eric said to William as they climbed the stairs to the roof. "I've got a year before I need to register."

"If I wait, they'll send me to the Army," William said.

The wind stroked Esther's hair, and feather-light flakes of snow caressed her cheeks. "Eric, are you thinking about enlisting in the Air Corps when you reach twenty-one?"

Eric hadn't thought that far ahead.

"It's so peaceful here." Dot sighed. "It's hard to imagine that for months in Europe planes have been bombing London and blowing up people's houses. How do those people survive?"

"They have shelters in the ground." Eric walked over to the metal railing. He looked out over the landscape and shoved his hands into his pockets. He wanted to sweep Esther into his arms and tell her not to worry. But how could he? He was scared, too.

Dot pressed close to William's side. "If Japan bombed Hawaii, what's going to stop them from bombing the mainland?"

William and Eric exchanged glances.

William wrapped his arms around Dot and kissed her forehead. "You ask too many questions."

She rested her head on his chest. "I know. One of the refugees from Germany that I helped said he can't understand how those Brits can stand the noise day and night, let alone the fires those bombs cause."

Esther joined Eric at the railing. The white flakes dotted the blackness and made a graceful decent earthward like little ballerinas. "You know God never makes a snowflake the same? Each one is different."

He drew her to him, enveloping her into his strong embrace, then bent and kissed her cheek. "Those snowflakes are characteristic of us. I know I could never find another woman like you, Esther." He blinked. That had come from him? Why couldn't he tell her how much he adored and admired her spirit, her forthrightness, her determination?

He'd been up half the night arguing with his father over Esther. Pa reminded him of their ages. Telling him that just because he'd turn twenty, that didn't give him the maturity or the resources to start a family. Pa encouraged him to enjoy the single life while he could. Esther would be around when the time came for him to settle down.

What if she found someone else? I've never met anyone like her. Was he what others said of him? Just a playboy? A wolf in a man's clothing who couldn't tell the woman he loved how much he adored her. Had he become what his pa desired?

The scent of her soap and the smell of her hair engulfed his senses.

She turned and drew his face closer and suddenly he felt her lips on his. Her soft, sweet lips. They were a part of her spirit, her heart of gold.

His senses spun out of control. His rising feelings for her replaced the stark and bleak reality, replaced the present with reveries of happier days. Her kisses halted his world from spinning away. Her touch communicated a world of security and peace instead of the unknown and the uncertain. He'd plan to tell her tonight how much he loved her. Now with the Pearl Harbor attack, the words got caught in his throat.

"Oh, Eric." Her tears made small pools in their liquid depth and spilled down her cheeks. "What will become of us?"

He drew her back into his arms and held her close. "The war can't last forever. Pa fought only eight months, and then World War I was finished." He nuzzled her hair. "I always wanted to learn how to fly. Maybe I'll try the Air Corps. Pa will think I'm trying to copy John. But after the war, I could take you up in my airplane, and you could count all the snowflakes in the sky. How about it? Would you like that?"

"Why couldn't Europe leave us out of their problems?"

Eric leaned his head on hers and stared into the darkness. "We have too much audacity. That's what Teddy Roosevelt said."

"You mentioned that very thing that first night at the Vanity." Esther said. "Your pa was right, Eric. He said he didn't think we'd see Christmas before we were in the war."

He bent down and kissed her. A whiff of her perfume tickled his nose when he trailed his lips toward hers.

"I pray God keeps you out of harm's way. Christmas won't be merry," Esther stuttered, "with our brothers and sweethearts preparing for war."

Eric closed his eyes, holding her close, enjoying the feel of her next to him. "I know, honey."

❧

Eric, his ma, pa, and siblings hunched in front of the radio. They were dressed in their robes. Ma handed him a piping hot cup of coffee and passed other cups around. Lamps and their warm stove kept the pitch blackness outside from entering in.

Eric worked the dial until the static subsided and he found a signal and the music of Glenn Miller filtered through the house. He cradled the coffee in his hand and waited. Suddenly, the music stopped.

Then Eric heard the well-known voice of President Franklin Delano Roosevelt whom he'd listened to as a boy, giving hope to the hopeless during the Depression years, now addressing Congress.

"Yesterday, December 7, 1941—a date which will live in infamy—the United States of America was suddenly and deliberately attacked by naval and air forces of the Empire of Japan. The United States was at peace with that Nation, and, at the solicitation of Japan, was still in conversation with its Government and its Emperor looking toward the maintenance of peace in the Pacific. Indeed, one hour after Japanese air squadrons had commenced bombing in the American Island of Oahu, the Japanese ambassador to the United States and his colleague delivered to the Secretary of State a formal reply to a recent American message. While this reply stated that it seemed useless to continue the existing diplomatic negotiations, it contained no threat or hint of war or of armed attack.

"It will be recorded that the distance of Hawaii from Japan makes it obvious that the attack was deliberately planned many days or even weeks ago. During the intervening time, the Japanese Government has deliberately sought to deceive the United States by false statements and expressions of hope for continued peace.

"The attack yesterday on the Hawaiian Islands has caused severe damage to American naval and military forces. I regret to tell you that very many American lives have been lost. In addition, American ships have been reported torpedoed on the high seas between San Francisco and Honolulu.

"Yesterday, the Japanese government also launched an attack against Malaya. Last night Japanese forces attacked Hong Kong. Last night Japanese forces attacked Guam. Last night Japanese forces attacked the Philippine Islands. Last night Japanese forces attacked Wake

Island. And this morning the Japanese attacked Midway Island....As commander in chief of the Army and Navy, I have directed that all measures be taken for our defense...No matter how long it may take us to overcome this premeditated invasion, the American people in their righteous might will win through to absolute victory."

Eric glanced around at each sibling listening intently as the members of Congress broke out in prolonged applause. A lump rose in his throat.

"I believe that I interpret the will of the Congress and of the people when I assert that we will not only defend ourselves to the uttermost, but will make it very certain that this form of treachery shall never again endanger us.

"Hostilities exist. There is no blinking at the fact that our people, our territory, and our interests are in grave danger.

"With confidence in our armed forces, with the unbounding determination of our people we will gain the inevitable triumph so help us God."

"I ask that the Congress declare that since the unprovoked and dastardly attack by Japan on Sunday, December 7, 1941, a state of war has existed between the United States and the Japanese Empire."

Chapter 15

"Close the door, Eric."

Eric did as he was told. Three weeks had come and gone since the attack on Pearl Harbor. He looked around. Nothing about the lavish office had changed in the intervening years since he began to work for Mr. Wattan. The wall of oak bookcases with ornate brass handles. The marble countertop and sink in the corner of the room with two shelves of brandy, scotch, and vodka. The impressive oak desk with its back toward the large-paned windows. Everything was the same.

He crossed the thick Indian rug of black, gold, and brown, and didn't bat an eye as Mr. Wattan stepped from behind his desk. That had changed. Mr. Wattan had not stood when Eric started here as a kid of seventeen. The summer he'd graduated from high school, he'd worked as a jumper for the *Detroit News*. The job consisted of hanging on the outside of a truck, standing on a running board and jumping off to drop papers off to various drug stores in Detroit. Happily, he replaced that job with becoming a junior draftsman. Three solid years of hard work had earned him his boss's respect.

Mr. Wattan moved one of the cherry-wood black leather chairs toward his desk, then extended his hand. Eric wrapped his work-hardened fingers around his boss's. Eric never realized how short his boss was. He was always sitting at his board when Mr. Wattan visited the design department. Standing before him now, the man barely came to his shoulder. He'd always envisioned his boss as bigger-than-life.

Mr. Wattan returned to his desk and sat down. "See these, Eric? I need every available draftsman to complete these contracts." He drummed his fingers on the executive desk and pointed at the new contracts covering one corner of the glossy finish.

Eric let loose a slow whistle. "That's a lot of contracts."

"I can't believe it myself."

"There's got to be thirty at least."

"Try fifty." His boss's glance swayed upwards. He grinned. "Sit down, Eric. I don't like anyone looking down at me. I believe you've grown. Or else, I've gotten shorter."

"Sir, my birthday being in a couple of months, I received my letter from the draft board telling me to register for the Selective Service."

Mr. Wattan rested back on his thickly padded leather chair, his gaze on Eric, and flipped his fountain pen through his thumb and fingers. "You don't know what your status is, right? So maybe I'm jumping to the worst conclusion. You might not be the first picked by Uncle Sam."

Eric frowned. Watching the juggling fountain pen, he marveled that Mr. Wattan would risk ink spatters on his neat white shirt. "I plan on enlisting in the Air Corps."

"What?" Mr. Wattan slapped the pen on the desk and leaned forward, his shoulders hunched as if to block a blow. Yet, by the looks of his flickering eyelids, Eric was pretty sure Mr. Wattan was glad the desk played referee. "Why would you do a fool thing like that?"

"I always wanted to learn how to fly. Besides, what better way to defend the country I love?"

Mr. Wattan stood. He walked toward one of the large windows that overlooked the parking lot, his arms behind his back. "How long have you been with us, Eric?"

"Three years. During that time, I've taken some engineering courses at Lawrence Tech."

"Have you got a girl?"

"Yeah."

He turned. "Bet she's a good looker. You wouldn't be satisfied not having the best. And you're willing to pass that all up to learn how to fly a plane and possibly get shot down over the Pacific and never be heard from again?"

"It's the lesser of two evils, as I see it. I'd rather fly than fight hand-to-hand combat across Europe and have some muddy bank for my mattress. If you really want to know, I don't care about fighting at all. I have my dreams the same as you. But I really don't have a choice, sir, do I? I didn't start this war, but it looks like guys like me are going to have to finish it."

"I understand. I have relatives who live in Hawaii and saw the Japanese bombing Pearl Harbor."

"Are they okay?"

"Yes, they are fine. My father maintains those ships. He talks about them as if they were his personal property." Mr. Wattan looked down at his fountain pen. "The United States government is asking my relatives to go to a special camp until the war is over."

"Do you think the Pearl Harbor bombing was an inside job?"

"They knew America's customs. They picked Sunday to bomb us. There's only a skeleton crew working on Sundays. And those Japanese planes knew the way through Kolekole Pass. That is the only place our radar wouldn't be able to detect them."

"How do you know this?"

"My uncle. He's a technician at Schofield Barracks. He was outraged that his mother country would do such a thing."

"If it will help you, I won't enlist. I guess when my number comes up, I've made up my mind. I'm going to jump into the Air Corps."

"Eric, you've got talent, a real gift for design. I don't want you to waste it toting a rifle in Europe. America can't afford to lose a generation of gifted men just because some madman wants to rule the world. I can authorize the right papers and get you a deferment." Mr. Wattan shifted through the contracts. "What is a war without the needed equipment? How can I get these done without men? You do what you think is best for your country. But consider our conversation."

Eric stood. "I will, Mr. Wattan. I don't want to let anyone down. Even if it means losing my life."

"I understand more than you realize. While my uncle was running with the pilots to get the planes in the air, he glanced up. There was one lone Japanese plane swooping down after them, flying so low Uncle could make out the style of the pilot's mustache. He looked at him and Uncle stared back, daring him to fire. The pilot banked his plane and flew away." Mr. Wattan wiped at his eyes and stood.

"My uncle came close to dying that day, but he said those were his planes and his ships, and this is his country, and he would have defended it to the last ounce of his blood."

Eric looked away. "I bet there were a lot of gallant actions that day. Good men dying like that."

"Some pilots did get off the runway, managed to fire some shots. The worst casualties were in the Navy. So many ships lost. They were so vulnerable, anchored in that bay with no means of escape. Father was beside himself—those were his ships. How dare they hurt his ships? Some of those sailors he'd known. Some he had dinner with. The sailors called him 'Grandpa.'"

"You're mighty proud of your family."

"I didn't tell you about my family for sympathy. Look, America can't afford to lose your generation. Who's going to be there to create the next aircraft, the next car, and a better communication system? When your number is picked, allow me to apply for one deferment. Think about that, will you?"

"If we don't stop this madman in his tracks, who's going to care what kind of car we drive if we lose our jobs, our homes, and, most importantly, our freedoms?" Eric extended his hand and they clasped hands. "Yeah, we've gotta face the truth like your father and uncle did. We aren't cut out to hide beneath a bush. It's not in our makeup. With God's help, we'll come out of this better Americans. You'll see, Mr. Wattan."

Chapter 16

The ticking of Esther's watch matched her heart beat for beat. Eight o'clock. She'd taken the earlier bus this morning. She couldn't afford to be late for work again today.

Six months had passed since Pearl Harbor. Every week brought more newsreels to the theaters, more war bond posters to the public, and more work for her and her boss. Last week she'd had to stay late four nights out of the five.

The Harper Street bus slowed to a stop to let passengers on, and then roared forward down Woodward. Several stomped last night's rain showers from their shoes. With no seats available, they clutched the rubber straps dangling from the bus's ceiling. Conversations mingled into a cacophony of jostling feet trying to remain upright through the forest of traffic lights and stop signs.

"Say, how far does that line go?" The passenger behind her pointed to the fifty or so men waiting outside a recruitment office.

Esther cupped her hands around the window. Did she know any of those men? Or boys, more likely, judging by their smooth faces and slight stature.

"From Jefferson Street to Woodward Avenue," replied a man dressed in a white shirt in the seat in front of her. "The numbers enlisting dwindled when the Allies lost in Java. The Navy win over those Japanese ships at Midway gave Americans a patriotic shot in the arm."

Esther straightened and reached for the handrail overhead when

147

the bus pulled away from the stop. "I didn't know there were that many men of recruitment age in Michigan, let alone Detroit."

"Sir." A young lady seated behind the driver tapped him on the shoulder. "Do you know if another bus has been dispatched?" One golden curl escaped from beneath her hat and fell prettily upon her shoulder as she continued in a coaxing voice, "My brother needs to get to the recruiting office today."

The driver shrugged. "The war'll be going on a few more months. What's his rush?"

"I don't want him to enlist, but he's dead set on it." She put a hand to her apple-red lips and looked around.

The bus driver guffawed. "Don't fret your pretty head. Saying dead doesn't put a jinx on anyone." He glanced back. "Sit back, I'm coming to a stop. Lafayette!"

With screeching brakes, the bus jolted to a stop. The door flapped open and the noise of the street outside filtered into the bus.

"Excuse me; thank you." Esther trotted down the steps to the whistles and catcalls of the men behind her. She smiled, thinking over what the bus driver said. Since the Pearl Harbor attack, every day the bus was packed with businessmen, workers, and boys barely out of high school. Uncle Sam's latest poster "We Want You" daily attracted youths from the farmlands to Detroit.

"Hey, are you going to be an Army WAC?" Two boys, who looked too young to shave, ran to catch up with her.

"Does it matter?" another man said. "You're part of the USO, right? You going to be at the Friday night dance?"

"Okay, sweetheart, I'm available for the first dance. Just take me away, doll face."

One cocky redhead who had joined the group took her elbow. "Don't listen to 'em. I'm the gent for you. Now what's your name, sweetheart?"

Esther laughed good-naturally. "I'm not part of the USO, and I'm not applying for a WAC position. I already have a job, which I will be late for if I don't hurry."

Fifteen minutes later, Esther removed her hat and coat and hung them in the closet. She hurried to her desk and collected the letters she'd transcribed, placing them in a folder marked Needing Bowden's Signature. Suddenly Mr. Bowden bolted through her door.

Startled, she said, "Mr. Bowden, your letters are here for your—"

"Good. Miss Meir, could you help in the Recruiting Office this week?"

"Why, of course. What do you want me to do?"

"I'm not certain. They're swamped. Intelligence is swamped, but our hands are tied. The Recruiting Office closes at five. Plan to work overtime up here until you finish your transcriptions." Mr. Bowden's hand shook as he reached for the folder.

"What's happened?"

Mr. Bowden dabbed the sweat off his forehead with his monogrammed handkerchief. "British intelligence deciphered the German U-Boat radio code and sent it to the U.S. Navy, giving the Navy ample warning of an impending mission directed at our American coast line." He dropped into a chair near her desk. "You'll never guess what our Navy did with the information. Nothing. Those German submarines are like a pack of wolves. In fact, American intelligence is calling them Wolf Packs.

"Right now, as I speak, German subs are making shrapnel out of our ships along the Eastern Seaboard. I just heard from North Carolina regarding last night's attacks." Mr. Bowden ran his fingers through his sparse hair. "Admiral King seems incapable of handling the situation. King's the only admiral left in the States. Our ships are virtually unprotected. All our admirals are fighting the Japanese in the Pacific, so now more American lives and ships are being lost every night."

Esther fell into her chair, the wind knocked out of her. "How many?"

Mr. Bowden swiped his brow. "About a hundred and fifty ships and a thousand lives. We look like idiots. Churchill sent a telegram to Roosevelt begging him to do something before all our ships end up on the floor of the Atlantic like the Pearl Harbor attack."

She was too stunned to say more.

"I just got a copy from Washington, D.C. Roosevelt is ready to call it criminal negligence. I have to start the paperwork. Admiral King failed to deploy destroyers and anti-sub vessels along our eastern coast. He also failed to impose a blackout, which allowed the Germans to follow our lights and beacons right to our shoreline. Roosevelt must replace Admiral King, but with whom? And do you know what they want us to do?"

Esther shook her head.

"This is top secret. Loose lips sink ships and all that stuff...turn off your light and keep it all hush hush. I have wired and called the governors and chief of police along the eastern seaboard to keep them updated."

Mr. Bowden rose. His tired eyes met hers. "Esther, pray. Pray like you never have before. Pray that Roosevelt finds someone that's not fighting in the Pacific to guard our shores here." Mr. Bowden lifted his eyes upwards. "I just don't know who's left."

The boys who had whistled at her just moments before danced before her mind's eye. Those young, innocent kids. Esther swallowed. "What should I take with me?"

Mr. Bowden sent her a blank look.

"To the recruitment office."

Mr. Bowden turned up his palms in helplessness. "I don't know. They didn't say." He shrugged. "Keep your ears open, Esther. And whatever you do, keep that innocent smile on your face." Mr. Bowden nodded. "Good. We've got to act like we've got everything under control. We don't need a panic. Keep the war in Europe...in Europe. At all costs." He took a deep breath through his mouth and breathed out slowly through his nose. "Take your steno pad and a sharp pencil." He started toward the door, hesitated, and looked back. "I can't say it enough. Keep your eyes and ears open for any strange occurrences and people. You know, like that Conrad guy. Anyone who doesn't act right, makes off-handed comments. You just never know."

She grabbed her pad and pencil and headed to the elevator. It was jammed, so she took the stairs. The stairs, too, were busy with young men and women standing, sitting, and talking. Saying their goodbyes.

A man with sandy hair that smelled like earth and sunlight all rolled into one opened the door to the large room now being used as the recruitment ward. He smiled at her. "Need anything, let me know."

Esther smiled back. "Are you the official door opener today?"

"I am until my number is called." He gave her a wink. "See ya later."

The information desk had five or so people around it. "Hello, I'm Esther Meir, Mr. Bowden's secretary."

"Yes, we've been expecting you. Can you register applicants?"

"Yes."

"Report to Betty, the nurse at Station 1. Through those white doors."

On the other side of the doors, rows of men stood in line with nothing on but their pants and shoes, a walking assembly line of bodies going through a gauntlet of tables with doctors checking their vitals and nurses administering shots.

A tow-headed boy who looked fresh off the farm rubbed his arm. "Ow. That hurt. What do I need a malaria shot for? I'm not going to the South Pacific."

A tall, stately woman about thirtyish mock-slapped his shoulder. "Soldier, you don't know where you'll land once you leave Detroit. Just leave your voyage to Uncle Sam."

Esther gathered her courage as the boy moved to the next station. "Are you Betty?"

The woman's dark hair was pinned up beneath her nurse's cap. She nodded her head toward the registration table. "I had to fire the last attendant. I couldn't read her handwriting. Do you have a sample of yours?"

Esther opened up her steno pad.

"I can't read that. What language is it?"

"Oh, shorthand. Here's a page of my handwriting."

"Mr. Bowden wants his coffee black tomorrow." Betty looked up. "Good. I take mine with cream and one cube of sugar."

Esther reeled back. Was she here to serve coffee? Esther glanced at the hundreds of men standing in line.

A doctor stepped forward. "Here's the stack of men who've passed the physical. Get them inoculated."

Esther peeked over the nurse's shoulder. "What are the requirements for enlistment?"

"As long as they're breathing and can stand on two feet, they'll pass."

Esther laughed.

"You think that's funny?" Betty chewed on her lip. "Men under twenty-one need a permission-to-enlist form from their parents. Everyone's placed in categories, and we expect them all to participate in the war in some capacity. Go through the lines and check off the shots each man receives. We don't want anybody missing one."

Three hours later, Esther placed a hand in the small of her back and rubbed, feeling a little woozy. She glanced at her wristwatch. Two p.m. "I need to take a little time to eat my sandwich. Where can I go for a cup of coffee?"

Betty glanced up after giving a man his shot. "You can't leave until you find someone who can fill in for you until you return."

Esther looked around. Everyone was busy.

Betty sighed. "All right, can you eat in fifteen minutes?"

Esther nodded.

"I guess I can spare you that long." She turned to the next man in line. "Stay put until I return. Do not leave this line, soldier." She turned to Esther. "Watch him."

The young man, who couldn't be any more than eighteen, rolled his eyes. "She's got to be kidding. I won't move a muscle for fear she'll wallop me with the next shot."

Betty walked toward a closed door, opened it, and yelled, "Carol, follow me, on the double."

Esther picked up her sack lunch and hurried toward the door left ajar. She spotted a pot brimming with fresh coffee, milk, and an assortment of donuts and packets of peanuts. She picked a chair with a high back and opened her lunch. One petite nurse, who had a large pink bow holding back her hair, puffed on a cigarette in the corner of the room, deep in conversation with another nurse.

A nurse poked her head through the doorway. "Mabel. Front and center. Betty's calling for you, and she better not find you hiding in here."

Mabel hurried out.

The girl with the pink bow walked over to Esther and sat down in a nearby chair. "So, how do you like our drill sergeant?"

Esther, caught with a mouth full of ham and swiss cheese, chewed and swallowed, washing the food down with a sip of milk. "Drill sergeant?"

"Betty. Everyone calls her the drill sergeant. Don't you think the name fits her?"

Esther took another bite of her sandwich and looked at her watch.

"Yeah, I can see she's got you jumping through her hoops. I'm Sally, by the way," she said, blowing smoke from her cigarette into the air. "If you let her, Betty will have you running all over the place."

Esther swallowed. "Betty is getting the boys through the line."

"Yes, all by her lonesome." Sally patted her blonde locks and leaned closer. Her blue eyes widened, like a cat ready to pounce on its prey. "The war won't be won by Betty alone."

The girl named Carol stuck her head in the door. "You Esther?"

Esther nodded.

"Betty wants you front and center. I can't seem to please her. And, oh, Sally-blue-eyes, Betty wants more needles washed and boiled to perfection. Pronto."

Sally doused her cigarette in a Coca-Cola bottle. "Remember what I said, Steno Girl."

Three nurses entered the room. Esther grimaced, recalling the men on the bus and those standing in long lines on the sidewalk. Soon they'd be in Europe. Then there were the German subs off their eastern coastline, and here Sally was hiding out in the lounge.

Esther hesitated before opening the door. "Sally, if you'd seen that long line of young men waiting on the pavement to do their patriotic duty this morning, I think your feelings might be different."

"Oh, you know all about what us nurses go through after spending one day with us?"

"Some of those boys probably are joining the military for the wrong reasons, maybe to get a chance to visit Europe. Just like some women join the USO to get a chance to be near lonely men. Or some nurses join to get close to some handsome GI."

Sally rose to her full height. "Now wait a minute, girlie, are you insinuating—"

"That shoe fits Sally-blue-eyes," one of the newcomers said.

Sally's face turned beet red, and she hurried toward the door.

Esther blocked her path. "I'm not name-calling. You have to remember why you're wearing that white uniform. The men need you, Sally, most of them aren't fooled by this patriotic flag waving. They know they're putting their lives on the line."

Eric's face shot through her mind. "They whistle and do catcalls to every pretty girl that passes by. That's to hide their inner feelings. Their determination is to protect us, no matter if it costs them their lives. That's the reason I allow Betty and people like her to boss me around."

Sally glanced over. The group of girls' mouths gaped open like hooked fish. "Well, you heard Steno Girl, let's get moving," Sally said. "We've got a war to win."

Chapter 17

From the balcony of Eastwood Gardens ballroom the band, busy tuning their instruments, sent melodies of distorted tunes to Esther's thoughts. William had brought her and Dot here for some relaxation after another grueling work week. But the stark reality of March 1943 slapped her in the face like an overzealous school matron. She closed her eyes and prayed. What's wrong, Eric? Why have you shut me out?

Eastwood Gardens. Simply saying the name soothed her distraught nerves. A solarium with its restful greenery was just a few steps away. February had left in a roaring snowstorm. March came in like a mild pussycat in comparison. In the glass-encased room, peace plants and hibiscus lined the inner walls of the glass dome-shaped area.

Only there was no time for relaxation because of what crossed her desk daily. Understaffed businesses worked around the clock in shifts to get the war equipment out in time to their GIs. Shortages of major wartime needs kept her Dictaphone humming as she typed out lists of military requests from D.C. to the Detroit newspapers. Through this network of communication, the population of the cities and towns across America replied. They scrambled into alleys and garbage heaps for scraps of aluminum, steel, and rubber, the response the same. "What more can we do for my husband, son, brother, and sweetheart across the seas?"

She looked down at her hands and grasped the railing. No, she wasn't here for relaxation. She was here to help Eric and William cope with their recent rejection.

The Air Corps didn't want Eric because he was color blind. Mr. Wattan told Eric he needed his skill as a draftsman to get the military equipment manufactured and reiterated his desire to file for deferment for Eric. Eric had refused any more deferments.

William felt the lash of refusal for the first time in his life. His photographic memory did him no good for this man's war. The deafness in his left ear kept him out of the Navy and Air Corps. There was only the Army left.

Notes from the clarinets, mingled with the sounds of the horns, weaved their magic tonic on her turbulent emotions. After the first grueling year of fighting, the only thing the Allies had accomplished was the loss of lives and the loss of British esteem for Judeo-Christian Americans.

European intelligence was full of jeers about American GIs who didn't know how or didn't want to gun down the enemy. Lord, help our soldiers, Esther prayed, recalling Cousin's Gill's words. Maybe we have produced a playboy generation, and so what if we instilled good, solid Christians principles in them. How dare those people in Europe judge our boys?

To boost morale, military intelligence sprang into action enlisting songwriters. Dinah Shore and others were soon singing God's praises to different lyrics with "Praise the Lord and Pass the Ammunition."

Emotionally wounded and physically maimed soldiers poured into the veterans hospitals in record numbers. Working with the FBI's Special Service Department, Esther was privy to information she often wished she didn't know.

The stage at Eastwood Gardens stood vacant. Teddy Powell, the band leader, had been arrested by the FBI on charges of bribing a draft official to evade service. He was to be arraigned soon before the United States Commissioner Stanley Hurd on charges of conspiracy to violate the selective service law. Some of Teddy's band members climbed the two steps, scraping their chairs along the wooden flooring.

Had Eastwood Gardens found a replacement for tonight? She looked around.

The irony of it all, Eric wasn't talking to her, which she suspected was due to his brother's heroic work in the Air Corps. William, too, was a blob of emotional pain.

Lord, where are You? We can't do this alone. We need You! More than ever now.

e⊃

Eric rested his foot on the copper footrest and hunched over the shiny mahogany bar. He glanced over at the ballroom floor.

"I bought some more war bonds on Friday," William said.

"Yeah, me, too. Ma's in a panic about her rationing cards. Said it's not enough to feed four, let alone eight. Make that seven, John's overseas flying bombers. Pa's got John's face plastered on our front window with a gold star next to it. Every battle the Air Corps enters is listed on the piano. Pa's proud of John."

William cleared his throat. "Read in the *Detroit News* that they're not rationing out any tires next week. Make sure you have a good set on your car. You won't be able to get any by April."

Eric nodded and turned toward the ballroom floor. He picked out the uniformed men and women. Blue, white and…were those others green or brown uniforms? He turned back to the bar, resting his elbows on its worn finish. "How's your sister doing? Dating anyone yet?"

"No one serious-like. She's around here someplace."

"She's a good girl. I wish her the best."

"Guess there's no way you'll let it slip why you two are not a couple?"

Eric grasped his drink, then turned back toward the dance floor and rested his elbows on the bar. "Esther deserves better. That's all I have to say on the matter."

"That's all applesauce and you know it." William faced Eric. "You want to be a part of this war as much as I. Really, I think Midway was the turning point."

"That's on the up and up. Our Navy's doing a bang-up job defeating the Japanese in the Pacific. You heard we defeated the Japanese in that Bismarck battle?"

William nodded. "They thought by sinking our ships at Pearl Harbor, we couldn't win. Well, they'll see what Americans are made of. You know, these dames are doing swell. Taking over the men's jobs in the factories."

Eric gulped down his drink. "The factories stopped making cars. The big three have voted to forgo the 1943 models so they can make planes, tanks, and jeeps. Packard, Nash, Studebaker, and Hudson have joined them. Detroit is an arsenal of democracy, just like the papers are saying. Did you happen to drive by Ypsilanti's Willow Run Plant? They're manufacturing B-24 planes in record numbers."

"Don't say?"

"You know how heavy a rivet gun can get holding it for nine hours a day? Well, these dames have to rivet these aluminum panels and do a perfect job on each plane. They have to, so these planes don't come apart up in the air." Eric scooped some peanuts from the bowl on the bar, then popped one in his mouth.

"I never thought I'd see the day a dame could work in a factory and perform a man's job," William said.

Eric wiped his mouth. "GM's Bill Knudsen has started the ball in motion for designing this new Sherman tank and Jeep. My company's got a piece of that contract."

"The Marines are doing some good things on land, too."

"Maybe I should have enlisted with them." Eric ran his fingers through his hair. "My courses at Lawrence Tech don't have enough people to warrant a professor."

"How long do you think before you'll be drafted into active duty?"

Eric turned back to the bar. Head down. "My boss makes me feel guilty because I want to fight, and Pa makes me feel guilty because I'm not."

"What you're doing is important to the war effort. I've seen that Jeep contract. The Army needs those vehicles." William leaned closer. "Now take my job, a lousy accountant. Any woman could fill my shoes."

The room grew silent as the master of ceremonies moved to center stage to the microphone. "Ladies and gentlemen, we are proud to tell you that our very own Glenn Miller is, 'putting a little more spring into the steps of our marching men' and has raised a million dollars in the war bond drive."

"Hooray!" a group of soldiers yelled over the crowd.

One soldier slapped Eric on the shoulder. "Remember me? I'm Bob Black, one of the Boy Scouts in your regiment. I heard Glenn Miller when I was stationed in London. He had a fifty-piece orchestra on Sloane Street. They were being barraged by German V-1 buzz bombs, but they played on. I tell ya, it was inspiring seeing that man's grit."

Eric nodded.

The soldier continued slapping Eric's shoulder. "I got an earful and so did my buddies, and did I tell ya the Army made Miller a captain?"

"No."

"Well, they did, captain of the Army Specialists Corps." The soldier shrugged. "Whatever that means. Well, I came over here to tell ya that your training helped me more in the field than boot camp did. You know, that survival stuff, especially that target practice, all of it, believe me, it helped."

"You're little Bobby?" Eric chuckled. "Bet you're hard-boiled now. If I recall, you were the one that cried himself asleep for two solid weeks wanting his mother."

"Yeah, you got the goods on me." Bob poked his chest with his thumb then leaned over. "Wish there were more guys in my division that had had you in their scout division."

"Eric?"

A petite blonde with an upturned nose and mascara-tipped lashes beneath large blue eyes smiled back at him.

Bob slapped Eric on the back. "Say, I'll see you around, just wanted to say hi."

The woman placed her fingers on the sleeve of Eric's coat, giving William a surveying nod. "You remember me? Nurse Sally. We didn't get our dinner yet."

"Sure, I remember."

e⌒⌒

"Say, girl, what are you doing over here all alone?" Dot wrapped her arm around Esther and gave her a hug. "What are you so deep in thought about?"

"I was thinking Eastwood Gardens is well suited for its name. Just look at those plants through that big picture window, the beautiful gardens a few steps away all lit up with lights. Those wrought iron love seats spaced within the alcoves of cherry and apple trees are so lovely."

Dot rested her arms on the cherrywood railing and watched the dancers. "William's made contact with a draft official to fill in the necessary papers so he can get on a battleship."

"No."

Dot nodded. "He told me during last Saturday's ride at Roxy Stables. You should have come. He was real talkative."

"I had to work." Esther sighed. "In a way, I can't blame him."

"Did you hear about McBrian getting killed?" Dot said. "Ann's taking it pretty hard. They got married before he shipped out. She looked so happy dressed in her office suit with a veil on their wedding day."

"She told me yesterday, if she'd known she was going to get married, she'd have stopped her mother from ripping her old wedding gown up for slips and undergarments. Now that he's dead, she wishes she had a better picture of him."

Esther looked at Dot. She'd worked with Ann at DuPont. Esther gentled her voice. "Who would have ever thought that it would be the little things of life that would mean so much?"

Dot's eyes hazed over. "Or that we never needed those little things in life to bring us happiness." Dot pointed to her legs, where she'd drawn a black line up the back of her calf.

Esther smiled. "That almost looks like you have on stockings. I admit, I'm getting used to not having them on."

"So the government confiscated all our natural fabrics. Guess what

DuPont is going to do now, and who's heading up the sales department."

"Who?" Esther laughed. "I declare, I sound like an old hoot owl."

Dot shined her already-sparkling red nails polished to perfection across the wide baby blue lapel of her suit.

"You? No kidding? Have they found a way to make nylons without silk?"

"Well, yes and no. I'm heading up the sales department, but we're starting into rayon production."

"You're no longer a secretary? How exciting."

"They had to promote me, seeing how their head guy was drafted."

"That's one way of getting ahead." Esther was happy for her friend.

"There aren't nylon stockings to be had anywhere. But at least, we'll have a few luxuries, if I have anything to say about it."

"What are luxuries when our men folk aren't there to see us in them?" Esther wove her hands into the folds of her altered business suit as she craned her neck for a glimpse of Eric's broad shoulders and handsome dark head.

"I like what your mother did to that suit." Dot tapped her sleeve. "Let me have a look at it."

"You're determined to get me into a better mood." Esther stood off, giving her a side view of her old, yet newly altered handiwork of her mother's gifted hands. "Well, maybe you're right. I've been enjoying my pity party much too long."

"It's a privilege we can't afford in hard times." Dot tilted her head. "Shorter skirts become you. They show off those shapely legs of yours. What did your mother do with the left-over material?"

"She donated it to the Red Cross for bandages."

"Good. If your mother has any more scraps, let me know. I've got a family in my flat that could use some rags. They're doing a business reprocessing the scraps into dishrags."

"Oh?"

"Her husband was killed during the Battle of Bismarck. Mary has never worked a day in her life, so I'm trying to get her started in her own business. She's good with the needle."

"Maybe Mother can see if she can get her a job at the dry cleaners."

"I'll tell her. Only, she has a little baby. I've been kind of helping her along with my food stamps. She'll be getting her own soon, but there's so much red tape, and the war department is frazzled just filling the servicemen's needs."

Esther looked over at Dot and put a hand to her lips. "Was her husband's name Robert Rizzo?"

"Yeah, they're neighbors of mine. I think I may have introduced them to you at the Vanity." Dot shrugged. "Don't know what good those food stamps will be. It's hard to get bacon and sugar as it is with my stamps." Dot leaned over the railing, moving her legs to the lively tune of "Pennsylvania 6-5000." "Look, isn't that Eric?"

"Sis." William spun her around. "Don't be a wet blanket. And stop looking at them."

"Eric's double-crossed you." Dot huffed. "Do something, Esther."

Esther turned her back on the ballroom floor, crossed her arms, and stamped her foot. "Who wants him? He's all wet, and I never what to see him again. Never."

"That's the spirit." Dot looked out at Eric and threw up her fist.

William pulled her hand down. "You're not helping the situation, Dot." William turned. "Sis, you may not think you look like a love-sick puppy, but you do. This dance won't last long. I suggest you find some other guy's arms to fall into and give Eric a wake-up call."

William was right. Esther glanced around. "There's a nice-looking man. I like the way his Air Corps uniform fits."

"He'll do." Dot gave her a shove.

Esther smiled when he looked toward her. As the last notes of the song came to a crescendo, the man in the snappy uniform stood by her side.

"May I have the next dance?"

"Yes, you certainly may."

He took her arm and smiled at her as they glided down the three steps to the dance floor.

Eric's familiar laugh filtered across the room with the notes of "I've got a Girl in Kalamazoo." Esther pretended she hadn't heard.

"Have you seen much action?" She smiled and batted her eyelashes.

The man's soft brown eyes met hers. "A little. Do you come to these dances often?"

"Not as much as I'd like. In fact, this is my first time to this ballroom."

"Mine too. I'm from Tennessee."

"Oh. Then we have something in common. I'm from Kentucky."

"Two Southerners here in our northern metropolis." Eric looked straight at her.

She ricocheted his glance and smiled back at her partner. "I'm sorry, what did you say your name is?"

"Thomas Cutter."

"How long have you been in Detroit, Thomas?"

"Two weeks. I've enjoyed seein' the sights immensely. A lady from the USO has been kind enough to give me a tour. This city is grander than a king's palace."

Sally sent her a catty look and smiled back into Eric's eyes. "You dance divinely."

Esther bit her lip.

"What did you say your name was?"

"Esther Meir."

Eric and Sally danced cheek to cheek. He maneuvered so he faced her. "Esther Meir, I thought that was you." Eric stepped closer. His looming height overshadowed Thomas and her.

Thomas frowned. "You know this fella?"

"I wish I—"

"Thomas?" Eric said. "Have you met Nurse Sally?"

Thomas looked from Eric to Sally. "No, should I?"

"Well, anyone who is anyone knows Sally, right?"

"Well, I do get around. Say, you're in the Air Corps?" Sally said.

Eric grinned. "You two need to get acquainted." With one sweep of his hand, Esther found herself locked in Eric's embrace.

Thomas was left empty-handed. "What—" He turned and politely smiled at Sally. She took his hand in hers and smiled.

"Poor guy. He doesn't have a clue what he's in for."

"Oh?" Esther kept her back ramrod straight, willing herself not to soften her demeanor or listen to his cheeky words and flirtatious charms. *All Eric cares about is the chase. He's just a big flirt and will never be anything else.*

He waltzed her around the room. She felt like a butterfly in its cocoon. No, it felt more like gliding.

There was never any thought about what to do when she was in Eric's arms. His guiding hand on the small of her back said everything. That gentle, yet positive pressure said he's sure, he'll take care of you, this way is the right way. His mouth came dangerously close. His warm breath tickled her hair. She attempted to step away, but his arm caught her.

His jesting eyes smiled into hers. His low voice, almost musical, whispered, "You're not taking my advances seriously, miss."

"Because you, sir, are nothing but a big flirt."

"Me?"

"You." She placed a finger on his chest. "To every poor girl in a skirt."

"Come, mademoiselle, to my inner chambers. Perhaps I can change that doubting heart of yours."

Esther couldn't stop the chuckle from escaping. Eric grinned. He secured her hand in his and walked her through the solarium's brick pathway. She laughed, and the notes of her merriment reverberated off the domed ceiling that twinkled with the patchwork of stars and full moon.

"Shush," Eric whispered. He led her deeper into the gardens.

A guy in a sailor's uniform and a woman in a long silk dress glanced up, finishing a lingering kiss.

"At last, a secluded spot." Eric drew her to him. The moon shone though the branches of a weeping cherry tree that had begun to bud, engulfing them in cross-like rays of moonlight.

"You have a moonbeam shinin' on your head, Eric." Esther smiled. He stared at her, as if memorizing her face. "What is it, Eric?"

"You remember I told you Pa said to go to aviator school?"

Esther nodded. Her eyes took in his square jaw, the proud lift of his shoulders. She watched his Adam's apple bob as he swallowed hard.

"I'm color blind. The grass looks brown to me. Nice, huh?"

Esther shrugged. "Things could be worse."

"I don't think it bothers me as much as it does Pa. He took it hard that the Air Corps wouldn't take me. I wish I hadn't told him."

"Is he color blind?"

"Yeah. He says it's his fault. I'm not looking forward to being in the Amy. But I know that's where I'm headed."

"The Army will be proud to have you."

Eric drew her close. His cheek caressed hers. He kissed her forehead and rested his head there. He sighed, as if a huge weight had lifted off his shoulders.

"Is that why you haven't called?" She loved being in his embrace.

"I don't want to hold you back, honey. This is good-bye."

"What? Are you saying that because the Air Corps didn't accept you, that's the reason you want to call it quits with us?"

"I don't have a choice. I hate failing Pa; I can't help that. I've conceded John is head and shoulders over me, figuratively speaking. Pa's stuck with me, but you're not."

"Why I never." She shoved him away.

"What?" He stared at her in amazement.

"Hey, keep it down over there."

Esther didn't give the disturbed lover a second glance but did keep her voice down to an enraged whisper. "I never want to hear such talk again. God gave both you and your brother special talents." She slammed an index finger on Eric's chest. "Stop looking to your pa for acceptance. Look to your heavenly Father. He formed you in your mother's womb. He loves you. He cares about you, and He has a plan for your life that no one," she poked his chest again to make a point of her last four words, "but you can accomplish."

"You're down right irresistible when you're angry."

His strong arms swept her into his embrace, blending her into his form. "Whatever happens to me…Well, let's just say, I thank God every day of my life I found you that night at the Vanity. Just keep on believing in me, Esther. I'll try not to let you or God down. I promise."

His lips demanded hers, hushing her rebuttal.

Chapter 18

With a screech of brakes, the bus lumbered to a stop. The door swung open, and Eric snatched a deep breath. A whiff of lilacs from a nearby bush intoxicated his nostrils as he stepped into a future he had no control over. Eric's draft notice said to report to Camp Custer on March 18, at seven a.m.

With suitcase in hand and dressed in his best suit, he'd given his younger brother his car keys with stern instructions to keep the car washed and polished. Then he hugged Ma and Pa and hitched a ride with a friend.

He hadn't wanted anyone with him at the bus station. He'd said his good-byes to Esther the night before. She'd taken his farewell like the good sport she was. She's a doll and too downright gorgeous for her own good. She won't last long out there with those Detroit wolves. The thought bothered him.

The bus door slapped closed behind him. There was no escape now. He looked around for a seat.

"Hey, anyone know where this Camp Custer is?" a tall, lanky guy with a face full of freckles asked.

"Near Kalamazoo." The stocky fellow in the back seat hunkered down and closed his eyes.

"I've got relatives in Niles. Is it near that?" the lanky guy replied.

"Close."

Eric sat alongside the man with the freckles. The bus rumbled down the road in a burst of speed. Freckle-Face continued to carry on a conversation with the guy in the seat ahead of him.

Eric needed a snooze. He'd gotten little sleep the night before. He'd kept his attitude upbeat. He was going to serve his country with everything he had. Yeah, his country needed him, and he didn't want his family to worry, especially not Esther. Getting hitched just because he didn't want someone else stealing his girl wouldn't be the right thing to do. Besides, he didn't know if he'd be back or if he'd end up with all his body parts. No, that wasn't what he wanted for her. No quick marriage before the justice of the peace for them. He wanted time. Time to be sure they each were ready for all the word *matrimony* meant. He rested his head on the back of the seat. The next minute someone was shaking him.

"Come on, soldier; it's time to earn your pay."

&

"Where's the rest of that bed?" Eric muttered. He walked past the rows of beds lining the whitewashed walls of the barracks, looking for one longer and wider. There was no way his frame would fit that. Not unless he slept like a pretzel. On each mattress sat a folded sheet and blanket, topped by a miniscule pillow and cover.

"Do they think we're dwarfs?" whispered a man standing at his elbow who was a head taller than him. "My feet are goin' to be hanging over the edge like a turkey dressed for Thanksgiving."

The door of the barracks opened, letting in the bright sunlight. The barracks sergeant, a short, squat man with permanent frown lines said, "Okay, men, listen up. Place your suitcases next to your beds and follow me. No talking in the ranks."

They marched single file into a large building. Eric was herded with the men who had the same height and build. There was a line for clothes, shoes, mess kits—you name it, there was a line for it.

"Hey, Mr. Sergeant, these don't fit." A small man, bone thin with eyes larger than his face, cowered before the hard stare of the sergeant.

He bunched the oversized waist with his small hand and lifted one foot showing five inches of dangling fabric.

The sergeant jutted out his pointed chin and glared. "You got in the wrong line." He pointed to another line. "Move!"

"What about mine?" Another man stepped forward and pulled at his too-large waist.

The burly sergeant scowled. "Where're you from, soldier?"

"New York."

"Well, this ain't no Park Avenue. Find a belt." The sergeant walked up and down the line. "My name is Sergeant Jones. Remember it. And remember you ain't at no boys camp. You're headin' to Fort McClellan in Alabama for boot camp soon. Believe me, you'll think of this place as a vacation spot. If your clothes don't fit, pin them. If they still don't fit, trade with someone. Now back to the barracks."

Eric was glad his fit. They marched back to the barracks in the same manner they had left.

Placing his things in the small locker, he got out his pencil and paper to write his first letter. Esther had been on his mind today. That flyboy, what was his name? Thomas Cutter. He and Esther had a lot in common, him from Tennessee. "Dear Esther," he began. The lights dimmed, then came back on.

One of the recruits called out, "Five minutes before lights out."

Eric tucked the paper away. The men around him hurried to brush their teeth. The lights flickered then went dark before they had time to get back to their bunks.

"Ouch."

"Say, that's my bunk."

"Then where's mine?"

"That ain't my problem."

Eric crossed his arms and placed them beneath his head, thinking of Esther. In fact, Esther was all he thought about, every chance he got.

Did she really think God had something special only he could do? The thought made him feel he was worth something, someone special. He always felt better about himself after he talked to Esther, like he could conquer the world. He closed his eyes, but that didn't stop his brain from working. He'd never met a girl like her. His eyes popped open as if he had springs in the lids. Esther didn't know how much he cared about her. Cared about her? A voice echoed in his head. Is that all?

He bolted upright in bed, bumping his head on the bunk above him. "Hey, watch it down there."

Eric rubbed his head. The thin light of a half-moon filtered through the barrack's window. At home, was she staring at the same moon, thinking about him? If so, what was she thinking? He had never felt like this for any woman. Never. Could this be what true love felt like?

In the days that followed, Eric performed the different athletic maneuvers that tested his dexterity to perfection.

Sergeant Jones handed him the piece of paper that proved he'd finished in the top ten of the two hundred or so men. He needed to finish at the top of his class, if he wanted to get Jones to grant him leave. Eric saluted sharply.

The only time he had to talk to the sergeant was the hour before dinner. That was their free time. Most of the men utilized it to soak their bunions and calluses from the grueling ropes and two-mile runs.

Eric stuck his chest out, anchored his shoulders in place, and opened the officers' door. Dressed in a clean uniform and polished boots, he waited in line for his turn.

"Yes."

Standing at attention, Eric saluted sharply. "Private Erhardt, sir."

"At ease, soldier." Sergeant Jones rested back on his swivel chair. "What is it, Private?"

"Sir, I would like permission to take a six-hour leave."

Sergeant Jones scowled.

His heart did a summersault. Jones' heavy dark brows hooded his eyes. He couldn't see the expression in them. So, did that look mean no? Eric cleared his throat. "I, I have some unfinished business to attend to before leaving for Fort McClellan." He had made up his mind to tell Esther how he felt about her. Of course, they couldn't plan to get married right away. Maybe they could get engaged.

170

"Woman business, no doubt," Sergeant Jones growled. "Half the men here have the same problem. Why should I allow you liberty?"

Eric didn't bat an eyelash. "Because I have some business—"

"If I grant you leave," Sergeant Jones bellowed, "what guarantee would I have that you'd return?"

"Sir, my word."

"Where's your sweetie?"

The quiet chortles of the men behind him emphasized his embarrassment. "Detroit, sir."

"We're shipping out in a day and a half. Permission denied."

"But sir, I've made arrangements to rent this car. I'd be back here tomorrow morning, before reveille, I promise."

"I can't risk it There's a war going on, in case you didn't know."

Eric closed his eyes. He couldn't tell Esther how he felt in a letter. The words wouldn't come. He opened his eyes to see the sergeant staring at him. He spun on his heels to leave. There stood Private Smith, that lanky, freckle-faced kid. What was he looking at?

∽

"Eric?"

Eric rubbed his eyes, focusing on the figure shadowed by the full moon shining through the barrack's window. "What?"

A tall figure bent over him like a sapling in a wind storm. "It's me, Smith. Look, my kid sister says she can get you down to Detroit and back before dawn. You want to chance it?"

Eric bolted out of his bunk, fishing for his pants. "Let's go."

He stuffed some clothes beneath the sheets, molding a silhouette of his form, then made his way outside. Smith's kid sister smiled at him as he slid into the passenger seat. Barely old enough to drive. "Thanks."

"No sweat." The gravel hit the bottom of the coupe as they sped away. They stopped for gas in Lansing. Eric ran toward a pay booth. "Hello, Esther. It's Eric."

"Eric? Is everything all right?" Esther's soft, musical voice sounded better to his ears than a Glenn Miller symphony.

"Fine. Only, I'm leaving Camp Custer soon, going to Fort McClellan in Alabama for basic training. After that, I don't know. I left a lot unsaid. Can you meet me at Central Park at the gazebo?"

"Okay, what time?"

Eric lifted his wrist, tilting his arm until the dials of his wristwatch were readable. Half past midnight already. How would they ever get back to Custer in time? "Around one forty-five a.m."

"I'll be there."

❧

The car's headlights loomed out in the hazy mist blowing clouds of moisture in the night wind. Esther clutched the gazebo railing, straining her eyes for a glimpse of Eric.

Eric took the three steps of the gazebo in a single leap, and she was in his arms. "Esther, I never want to let you go."

"I missed you something terrible."

He stroked her hair softly, and she felt his strength. His kisses wet her cheeks, her lips. "I could hold you like this for an eternity. My life is complete with you beside me. Hitched to the same star, you know what I mean?"

"Yes! Oh, I know all will work out for us. I keep reciting Romans 8:27–28 to myself, 'And he that searcheth the hearts knoweth what is the mind of the Spirit...And we know that all things work together for good to them that love God, to them who are the called according to his purpose.'"

"God made it possible for us to be together one last time before I shipped out."

He ran his fingers through her tresses as the prelude scents of spring wafted through the crisp night air.

"Hold me close. I can't bear this, this awful, awful war."

"Your hair, I forgot how sweet-smelling it is."

Suddenly she wanted to unburden her heart completely. Wanted to unload her worries onto his broad shoulders and let him pack them in his duffle bag and carry them to Europe where all this trouble began!

"Dot's trying to find work for Mary. She's having a terrible time working and caring for her little boy. She's tried the Willow Run plant, but the work was too much for her. She's very thin, and cries a lot."

"Mary…Oh, right, she was married to that Robert guy we met at the Vanity."

"Robert and Mary were so much in love, Eric. Now Robert's dead." She couldn't stop the sobs wetting Eric's starched uniform. She couldn't stop the misery from pouring onto him. Oh, she shouldn't have told him. She regretted she had.

Eric held her tightly. She could feel the warmth of his body taking the chill from hers. Felt the firm, unyielding chest muscles and the strong heart that beat within.

"I babysit little Bobby as much as I can for Mary. She volunteers at the USO in Detroit. But sometimes, when Mary doesn't know, I'm watching her, I see bitterness. When she comes back from that USO, I get the feeling she's thinking about her life and what it might have been without marrying Robert and getting pregnant with little Bobby." Esther glanced up. "Eric, was it God's purpose to have Robert die in this war?"

Eric kissed the tip of her nose. "That is not for us to know. What I do know is that this war cannot rob us of our memories."

She bit down on her lip to still her trembling, "I'll wait for you, Eric, until—" He laid a finger to her lips. "But I thought you came here because you—you know, hitch our lives to one star." She sent him a soft pleading look.

He kissed her wet cheeks, then his arm wrapped about her waist and his other around her neck as he bent her backward. His lips fused into hers, and she felt the tremor of his desire for her. Accelerated into a level of ecstasy she had never felt before. She moaned. This was real. Yes, he loved her, and she him. Song of Solomon 5:16 fell like honey from her lips.

"'This is my beloved, and this is my friend' and you are—"

"Hold up." A scowl swept his dark, swarthy face, masking his feelings like face paint covers a clown.

"What's wrong?" She was dumbfounded. Why the sudden change?

"Pa's right."

"About playing the field or working to prove your worth?"

He looked down at her from the tip of his nose. A stance she had seen him use whenever he desired to distance himself from his innermost feelings. "Your—sweetness engulfed my senses for a minute there. I need to be practical for the both of us."

Caught by the tide of circumstance, love had immersed them like a tsunami. They could drown in the waves of desire—or allow their love to grow stronger through their battles of separation. Evidently, Eric had chosen the latter. Esther sighed. Perhaps it was for the best, but for one concern he'd voiced from within the prison of his youth.

She locked her arms around his neck, caressing the back of his neck. She hoped to halt the tides of doubt locked in his thoughts from years of believing he must prove his worth. "Eric," she said, holding her eyes firmly on his. "What your father said is untrue. What your Father in heaven says is worth believing in. He tells us we are *already* worthy of His love! We don't have to work for it! It's ours to take. For by grace you are saved not by works. Not by our actions, by what Jesus did on the cross for us."

Eric reached up, took her arms in his, kissed them, and brought them to her sides. Looking at her, he groaned. "'Many waters cannot quench love, neither can the floods drown it…'"

Her sobs cut through the night like the dagger she felt lodged in her heart from Eric's rejection of God's simple plan of salvation. "Eric, what is it that holds your heart in chains?"

Bending low, he patted her on the cheek. She knew what that meant. He was donning his best cavalier mystique, along with a cocky smile. Has he fooled me again? Or is he pretending he doesn't—?

"Don't worry, sweetheart. I'll show those Germans what us fun-loving playboys are capable of. We'll keep that war where it belongs, in Europe. Then I'll be back and, well, we'll see about us then."

Esther placed her hand on her hip. "Oh, right."

A knowing look transformed his countenance, his eyes piercing her very marrow with their frankness. "Don't get yourself in a lather. I'll be back someday, Toots."

"Why, you, you Casanova!" How dare he use me this way, make me think he loved me. Well, I'll show him! "You mean you don't want to be tied down to a gal in the States until after you've checked out those Italian bombshells and those French mademoiselles. Then and only then will you come trotting back to me! Well, I just might not be available! Think about that when you're tramping through the mud and streams in Europe!"

       e⌒

A mountain of potatoes delivered by a dump truck that morning loomed before Eric. He didn't know there could be so many potatoes in the whole of Michigan.

"Start peeling. We'll be shipping out tomorrow morning."

"All these?"

"But, Sarge," Red said, "everyone else is gettin' three hours liberty. Don't we get at least an hour?"

Sergeant Jones stopped in mid stride and turned. Hands on his hips, his stern, scowling face surveyed first Eric, then Red.

Maybe it was Red's woebegone expression, maybe it was the relief Sergeant Jones felt knowing Red and Eric would be some other sergeant's responsibility, but big, threatening Sergeant Jones chuckled. Soon a full-blown laugh escaped his ruddy lips.

"Guess you'll think twice before you miss muster again." He pointed his thick finger at Eric. "What are you gawking at? Get peeling, Private," he barked. "If that pile isn't done before we ship out, there will be a bigger mountain of potatoes waiting for you to peel at Fort McClellan."

"I don't think I'll be able to look at a potato after this." Red watched the sergeant leave.

"Let alone eat one." Eric turned to the large, muscular man who had earned his nickname because of his bright red hair and freckles. "Why did you miss muster?"

Red winked. "What do you think? Had to see my little gal one last time and give her a little going away kiss, if you know what I mean."

Eric kept peeling. He'd worked the slicing into a rhythm and didn't want to stop. "How long have you two been married?"

"One week. It was a real short honeymoon. Made all the more rewarding, knowing I was shipping out. What about you?"

Eric kept his head bent over his potato. "I had some unfinished business." The swish, swish, swishing of Red's peeler grazing the smooth and pitted edges of the potato blended in with his.

"Oh, got scared, did ya? Well, don't worry. That just means the Lord intends for you to return, to finish up that unfinished business. My wife plans to live with her family until the war's over. They live on a winery near Lake Michigan. When the war's over, we'll move to my little ranch in Oklahoma. She hopes she's pregnant; she wants my baby bad."

Eric glanced up. Red winked.

"She'll live with her folks and raise our kid. That is, if worse comes to worst. How long have you known your gal?"

"Met her on a Friday night in August of '41 at the Vanity. Glenn Miller was playing that evening."

"A war sweetheart, huh? That explains it. I've known my Susie since we were little."

Red's words were a poultice to Eric's wounded heart. "You don't think it's a lack of love on—my part?" What if they got married and Esther became pregnant and he didn't make it back Stateside? Besides, his dad was right. What Esther said about grace had him puzzled. He'd always heard that works is what got you to heaven.

"Nope. Sometimes the careful ones end up being the lasting ones. You know what I mean?"

Eric laid down his peeler and massaged his palm. He doubted Esther would respond to his letters after what he said to her last evening.

"Hey," Red said. "We'll never finish if you stop."

"Sorry." He reached for another potato.

"This is my second KP, so I guess that makes me a veteran."

"So, you were saying?"

"My dad's first wife up and married him when he enlisted in the first war, then sent him a Dear John letter when he reached the trenches. About like to kill him, Dad said. Said he didn't have the heart to live. But about that time a little gal he'd grown up with started to write him, and what do you know, she waited for him right through rehab and all."

"Rehab?"

Red cleared his throat. "Dad got shell shocked something bad staying in the trenches for weeks at a time. The doctors didn't think he'd pull through it, but Dad's a survivor, and you know what they say."

"What?"

"Well, just that the fruit never falls too far from the tree." Red pointed his knife at him. "So don't lose heart; that little gal of yours sounds like the real McCoy to me."

Chapter 19

The *Empress of Scotland* rose like a cork in a bottle of cheap wine and slid down the choppy waves of the Atlantic like a sled skimming Mt. Everest. The motion left Eric's stomach on the upswing. The odor of cigar smoke, cooked cabbage, and unwashed bodies didn't ease his stomach's complaints in the ship's tight quarters, but he was determined to watch the poker game to the end.

Red crouched down on the ship's floor, his shoulders hunched forward, engrossed in categorizing his cards.

"Okay, I'll see you two and raise you three."

Red glanced up at the burly soldier, tossed down the money, and handed out the cards without a word.

Bubba scratched his ear. That was the signal for him to keep still. Eric knew when to get lost. Red, Bubba, and he had bet their pay, double or nothing, on this last hand, and Bubba didn't need Eric blowing it.

"I'm going for a little fresh air." Eric spoke in his most disheartened tone, hoping to sway the opposing team. But truth be known he preferred the autumn breezes of September to the stale stench of cigar smoke.

Eric glanced back before climbing the steps topside. Red didn't bat an eye. He threw down his full hand and laughed.

"Why, you bamboozled me. I should have known better than to play with loan sharks."

Red scooped the money with a sweep of his large hands, handed

Bubba his share, and hurried halfway up the steps to give Eric his. Eric's share tallied over a hundred dollars. He couldn't believe his eyes. "That's a lot of dough."

"Let's beat it. I could use a little fresh air."

Eric and Red climbed the metal steps topside. They leaned over the ship's railings bowed to one side as the wind whipped the seas, and the big ship slapped the waves of the Atlantic Ocean as if to say, "Look out, here we come." The spray felt good on Eric's face. He tasted salt and breathed deeply. "At least I washed away some of my grit."

"They're in a hurry to get us to Casablanca."

Eric gripped the railing and noted Red's white knuckles as an obstinate wave pounded the hull.

"Yeah. The Army wants to make sure all that training they gave us at McClellan is put to good use," Eric yelled over the roar of the waves. He squinted into the horizon as the cold seawater spray licked him again.

"Don't know why the brass had to ship us to Camp Shenango and train us some more before shipping us out to Europe. I feel like a beef cow getting ready for slaughter."

"What are you complaining about? We got paid. I think you're belly aching because you preferred the warmer climate of Alabama to the cooler one of Pennsylvania."

"No, I prefer getting it over with instead of playing this waiting game. Look, I've got to walk. This charley horse is giving me a work over. So, stop beating your gums and give me a hand."

Eric grunted. Red wasn't light. After weeks at boot camp, he had to be two hundred pounds of solid muscle. Eric took a firmer hold of his buddy when the boat began to rock. "They put us through some tough training so we'd be ready for anything. And they didn't spare any time getting us fit, feeding us like we weren't going to get another meal. I learned all sorts of ways to survive in the wilds."

"I talked to the captain. He hopes to arrive at Casablanca in another day." With each stride, Red took more of his weight off Eric as he worked out his charley horse.

"We've been on this ship for six days now. The *Empress* is making good speed." The ship lunged, and the spray off the bow blew salt water on them like a whale with a toothache. Eric grabbed the railing and supported both of them before they toppled on the slippery water-soaked deck.

"The front needs more men," Red panted. "The brass has pulled every soldier from inactive duty and put him in the front. This may not be any of my beeswax, but I think the big brass is planning a major battle."

"You on the up and up?"

"Yeah."

Eric cocked his head toward the bunks. The words "For it's hi! hi! hee! In the field artillery..." floated up from down below. The basses mingled with tenors as the men lifted their voices in song for the second stanza. "Well, will you listen to that? They started the singing without us."

"And they sound flat." Red shook his leg. "Come on, Eric, let's show them how to sing that song."

Eric followed his buddy down the thin steps. "What do you think Africa will be like?"

"Primitive. But I expect the city will be nice. Didn't you see *Casablanca* with Humphrey Bogart and Ingrid Bergman? I thought everyone saw that?"

"Well, you can't rely on a movie for the right information."

Red looked up and grimaced. "Right. We won't be in the ritzy neighborhood, that's for sure."

~

A brisk wind off the ocean swept toward the sea resort of Casablanca. Eric buttoned his Army-issued denim. He preferred the warm sleeping quarters of the ship to the shallow-walled rooms of the building the Army had turned into a barracks. They were moving out again, to where, Eric didn't know. He waited in line for further orders while Red powwowed with the locals.

Red and a native boy were in a serious debate over his mattress cover. The youth couldn't be older than twelve. He was clothed in some type of skivvy shorts, as were the group of boys huddled in a circle about ten feet away.

The Moroccan boy smiled. His irregular teeth gleamed white against his dark face. He extended his hand, displaying the glass beads strung on a thin rope, then added a moon-shaped knife.

"Now you're talkin'." Red took the items and handed him his mattress cover with the plastic overlay and the cotton crisscross underskirt.

The youth bowed, and bowed again, backing away. He drew a knife out that he'd tucked in his skivvies, made a slash down the middle of the cover, and placed his head through the opening and ran into the throng of the other natives. The boys touched it, cooed softly, and gave their friend admiring glances.

Red turned to Eric. "So much for the splendors of Casablanca."

Eric nodded and followed Red's gaze.

The city, with its paved sidewalks and roads and comfortable rooms, was for tourists. The only thing the resort supplied the native orphans were the scraps the undesirables collected from the kitchen's garbage.

"Get moving, soldiers, I haven't got all day." A sergeant with dirt-caked field boots and a coat to match pointed the way.

After a mile of walking, Eric climbed into a waiting boxcar. The odor of stale manure rose from the wooden floor's washed boards. He stared curiously into the boxcar's dark interior.

"Welcome to your new accommodations, men."

"This? But Sarge, where do we sleep?"

"On the floor."

"Where's the latrine?"

"Let's hope you took care of that before you climbed in." The sergeant counted the men. "Forty. Okay." He yelled down the line, "All full," then threw in his knapsack and climbed in. "Find a place and sit down."

"Get a whiff of that. It smells like livestock."

The sergeant snickered. "When there's a need, it'll accommodate eight horses comfortably or forty men."

"So that's why they call it forty and eight?"

"Right, Private." The sergeant sat. "It's better than walking. We'll be doing enough of that soon."

The door slid shut. The bolt sliding into place lent a finality to the discussion until someone from the back of the boxcar said, "Ain't we the lucky ones."

The boxcars growled and clanged against their yokes as the engine picked up speed. The noise of rails and the vibrating wheels beneath the wooden floor filled Eric's ears, and beams of light filtering through the wooden cracks of the boxcar accustomed him to his surroundings.

One man reached into a pocket and pulled out a pack of Camels. "You mind?" When the soldier offered him one, Eric shook his head.

The sergeant said, "Go ahead."

The match head glowed in the semi-darkness. He took a couple of drags on his cigarette. The smoke floated over Eric's head.

"You'll be replacements for the 34th Infantry Division, and you guys have been assigned to Company E, Rifle Company, 135th Infantry Regiment," the sergeant said.

"Where are we going?" Red asked.

"That's top secret. Presently, you're going to Oran to the Invasion Training Center for training in realistic street fighting, its obstacle courses, and live artillery barrages. The men you'll be joining will be there. They're battle weary." The sergeant shrugged. "Kind of beat up, but count yourselves lucky to be part of their regiment."

"Why, Sarge?"

The young private who sat across from Eric didn't look old enough to own a razor. He'd stretched his long, thin legs out in front of him, and his feet looked big enough to use as a pair of water skis.

The sergeant rubbed his forehead and stared at the wooden planks of the box car.

"Sarge. Why?" The young private wouldn't give up. Eric had to give the kid credit; he had gumption.

The sergeant squinted at the kid. "What's your name?

"Private Tommy Thompson, sir."

"Well, Private Thompson, you're joining an experienced company.

They'll be hard on ya.' You listen to them. They know the ropes. Yeah, you men are lucky. Pity the poor guy that gets a platoon still wet behind the ears, with a captain that don't know much."

"How long we going to be in here?" a young private asked. "I'm feeling claustrophobic."

The guy wasn't lying; the kid's face looked pale. The man with the Camel cigarette puffed away. The sergeant pointed to the queasy-looking private. "How old are you, kid?"

"Eighteen."

The sergeant cleared his throat. "The Germans are enlisting boys fifteen years old. Claustrophobic is just a word. You're a soldier now. You got to think like a soldier, and then your body will—"

"Really, Sarge? You get to feeling claustrophobic, too?"

The sergeant nodded. "In some fox holes. You ignore it. We're going part way across Africa. I sure wouldn't want to walk it, and I wouldn't be in such a hurry to get there, either, if you get my drift."

"Is it all right if I play my harmonica?" Tommy held up his instrument.

The sergeant shrugged.

"Mind if I join you?" Eric held up his harmonica.

The boxcar of soldiers sang their favorite Army song. "The coffee in the Army they say it's mighty fine, it's good for cuts and bruises, and tastes like iodine…" When one private started howling at the last rendition of "Gee, Mom, I want to go home," the sergeant sang along.

Tommy, in his too-large fatigues, tapped his big foot to the rhythm of his harmonica, and the other soldiers clapped to the tune of "Over There." The refrain stanza of George M. Cohan's masterpiece got every soldier in the singing mood. "The Yanks are coming, The drums rum-tumming everywhere. So prepare, say a prayer, Send the word to beware, We'll be over, we're coming over, And we won't come back till it's over over there."

Eric blinked in the bright sunlight, stretched his aching muscles, twisted from side to side, and bent over to touch his toes. After a day and night inside the boxcar, he had all he wanted of sitting.

"You men, front and center." A man with an unshaven face motioned with the butt of his gun.

"Gee, are we replacements or prisoners?" Red muttered.

"Replacements," one seasoned soldier replied, coming up behind them. "First Lieutenant Russell don't like to get close to the newbies. They don't last long."

Eric shouldered his knapsack and glanced at Sergeant Rusk.

The sergeant's boots were muddy and the shoelaces worn. His dungarees were caked with dirt, and the sleeves of his coat were as threadbare as his shoelaces. From the corner of his lips protruded a cigar, which he hadn't bothered to light, and which he didn't bother to remove when he talked. "Get moving."

"He takes after his lieutenant," Red whispered.

"Yeah, really makes you feel welcome."

"Atten-shun!"

Eric and Red fell into line.

"My name is Captain Kimble." The captain strolled back and forth, his arms behind his back, examining every soldier. His unsmiling face conveyed his no-nonsense attitude. A tall, lean man, Kimble had a way of moving like a big cat, reminding Eric of a backwoodsman he'd met once while camping in the Appalachian Mountains.

"How many here are replacements from another regiment?"

One man raised his hand.

Eric swallowed. Five soldiers stood behind Captain Kimble. Were these the only men left of his initial regiment?

Captain Kimble walked toward the man who'd raised his hand. "What regiment?"

"The 30th."

"They got beat up pretty bad."

"Yes, sir. I got wounded and went to the infirmary. No one knows for sure where my regiment is, so I got placed here."

The captain patted him on the back. "Glad to have you aboard. So, the rest of you soldiers are new to combat?"

The men chimed in unison. "Yes, sir."

A regiment marched by, Asian heritage, judging by the slant of their eyes, their dark hair, and butterscotch-colored skin.

"Sir, who are they?" Breaking ranks by talking was forbidden, but Eric had to know.

"The 100th Battalion and almost exclusively American Nisei, mainly from Hawaii. Now, men, here you see some good fighters. Examples of what you soldiers need to emulate. I just hope you guys prove half as good. Remember, you'll get out of training what you put into it."

From the corner of his eye, Eric followed the regiment until they were out of sight. He'd have to write Mr. Wattan about the Niseis.

The captain's steel-gray eyes stared into his. "Where were you stationed before, Private?"

"Had two deferments, sir, as a draftsman for an engineering firm."

"Did you ask to be transferred to active duty?"

Eric stood a little straighter. "Yes, sir, when the need arose. I guess the need arose."

"Indeed it has." Captain Kimble stepped back. "Well, recruits, my soldiers and I will give you some training you did not receive at basic. This training will help you perform your duties and get you back safely to the States. So listen, learn, and acquire the skills my men and I have learned the hard way."

Eric accepted a patch from Sergeant Rusk that he was to sew on his jacket like he did his 34th Red Bull patch. This new patch had a design of a shield with a three-leaf clover in the center. Blue letters etched around the shield read, "To the Last Man." The patch awakened the words of Ephesians 6:11, put on the whole armor of God...and Ephesians 6:16, above all taking the shield of faith...to his thoughts. Is God preparing me for what lies ahead?

"Captain," Red said, looking down at his patch. "I mean, sir, just where are we going after this training?"

"To hell and back, soldier."

Chapter 20

September 9, 1943, Allied Invasion at Salerno

"What's wrong with this bread?" Red pointed to the small colored spots he'd noticed. "Mold?"

Eric crouched to a kneeling position and held the bread up to the light streaming in from a port hole. "Mold doesn't move; they're bugs." Eric smirked, resting back down on the ship's nail-hard floor, and bumped two soldiers. He doubled up his long legs and attempted to find a spot on his bottom that wasn't numb. Two days had passed since reaching Salerno, Italy. "Looks like we've overstayed our welcome."

Dick, a big burly man with a mass of muscles like a wrestler, leaned over and said, "Welcome to the Army, soldier." He flicked the bugs off and bit into his bread. "Eat up. You never know when your next meal will come, and scuttlebutt is we're leaving our lovely Hilton accommodations at zero hundred hours."

As midnight arrived, the moon cast a yellow glow over the white-capped waves, and the dark mass of men comprising the 135th Infantry plopped into the water. The waist-high tide pulled on Eric's legs. He struggled to keep his rifle high over his head as he bent over, working to keep the clothes and food in his backpack dry. He spit out some seawater from a cresting wave and walked forward.

The sea's rumbling against the boulders filled Eric's ears. Usually, he loved to hear that noise at night, sitting with a girl on a sandy beach.

But now, it sounded more like a prelude to a horror flick. Reaching the foamy beachhead, the current sucked at his boots as if unwilling to relinquish its prey. He jumped out of the seaweed that could be hiding jellyfish ready to send its stingers deep into his legs.

They rushed out of the shoreline toward the rocky expanse. The forest extended long branches and sucked them into its depths. The men blended in with the forest like nomads.

Sergeant Rusk's cheeky face was contorted in corkscrew creases, much like a bulldog's. He removed his unlit stogie from between his teeth and motioned for them to draw near. "The third division of the 36th came ahead of us. They took a heavy beating from the Nazis."

"We lucked out," Dick said. "Getting dropped more north. Hope our luck holds."

They kept to the forest, stepping carefully through the maze of trees as they traveled toward Naples to regroup with the rest of the 34th Division. Eric blinked the sweat out of his eyes. After ten miles of jogging and walking, his adrenalin was wearing down. He took deep, labored breaths, fatigue setting in. Up ahead, Dick handled the rocky upward terrain tirelessly. The sun crested the hill as they reached Naples. Eric and Red collapsed on the ground. Here the unit stopped to regroup.

"Take out your C-rations; pass the word on. Take a nap," Dick said.

Eric thought a meal never tasted better. Just a moment to rest, and a hand jostled him awake.

"Okay, soldiers, time to unload."

The private next to Eric snapped a picture of Sarge. He frowned.

"Unload what, Sarge? All we brought was our knapsack."

"All you need is your tent, raincoat, C-rations, and canteen in your backpack, and your rifle. That's it!"

The private held up his camera. "But I promised to send my family pictures with my letters."

"This is no vacation, soldier. Bury it. That knapsack's going to feel real heavy marching twenty miles a day."

Eric emptied the contents of his sack. He'd collected a lot.

Soldiers discarded cameras, extra clothes, and souvenirs. One guy looked down at a small Bible they got the day they boarded the *Empress of Scotland.* Eric looked down at his own New Testament that was no bigger than the palm of his hand. Sarge had said to write only their name in the cover, nothing else. If the enemy should confiscate their belongings, anything else could provide valuable information to German intelligence. He flipped to the first page, "As Commander-in-Chief I take pleasure in commending the reading of the Bible to all who serve in the armed forces of the United States… It is the foundation of strength." His eyes landed on Franklin Roosevelt's signature. Eric placed the book in his chest pocket. He had a piece of the good old USA and the God who could get him out of this place still breathing, and he wasn't letting either go.

He kept his extra pairs of socks. He knew from his Boy Scout training the value of keeping his feet dry. He shoved his castoffs into a hole some soldiers had dug. Someone had tossed a Bible on top of the pile, but before the first shovelful of dirt fell, Eric made a grab for the Scriptures. Soldier boy's going to thank me.

The 34th Infantry Division split up. The rifle division moved ahead. Eric glanced back and swallowed. It's just us and the Germans now. Captain Kimble motioned for the tall, lanky youth Eric had noticed earlier. He had told the captain where the rest of the Infantry was. Captain pointed for the man to go on ahead.

Sarge stuck up his thumb, the motion to follow close.

"Where's that kid going?" Eric muttered to Dick.

"He's our runner. He goes up ahead to sniff out any Germans."

"That sounds kind of dangerous."

Dick snickered. "Yeah."

They walked single file through dense woods, dark now that the sun had set. The sounds of a rushing river filled his ears. Red held his rifle above his head.

As they came into a clearing, the noise of a rapidly flowing river up ahead swelled around him. The river ran a half-mile wide, and the rays of the moon gleamed on the foaming white caps as the water splashed over rocks and boulders. Along the eroded shoreline, the turbulent waters, brown from the previous storm, exposed tree roots and debris.

Two men took off their boots and waded into the foaming river with a heavy rope.

Twice the current of the Volturno River tossed the two soldiers like paper boats downstream. They came back up on the bank, panting for air. Then moving upstream a ways, they waded in, swimming in spots until they crossed to the opposite shore, where they tied the end of the rope to a sturdy oak.

Dick and a couple of other soldiers tightened their side of the rope and motioned for them to move in single file. Captain Kimble went first, followed by First Lieutenant Russell, then Sergeant Rusk. Dick raised his rifle over his shoulder and with his other hand seized the rope. The river quickly wrapped around his ankles, knees, and waist, then rose chest high. The current swirled like a rattlesnake around him.

Eric tucked a pair of dry socks under his helmet, placed his rifle in one hand and the rope in the other, and then waded in. The cold water swirled around his pant legs. He fought to stay upright. This river was worse than the Atlantic, and a lot colder. He forced his legs to move against the rapid current sweeping down the river. Every step had to count. His boots slid over the rough rocks. What he didn't need was to sprain his ankle. His legs grew numb.

Red struggled to stay upright. The two men in front of Red tried to balance themselves across a boulder that broke the waters and swirled every which way but to the shoreline.

Sergeant Rusk, now on shore, motioned for them to hurry. Reaching the shore, Eric looked back. The little guy who'd muttered the water was cold was at a disadvantage. The water swelled to his chin. Eric leaned forward offering his hand.

As if he'd tripped a guide wire, intense mortar, artillery, and machine gun fire exploded before Eric's eyes. One soldier spiraled into the air and landed back in the river. A mine went off, and then the machine guns started their rat-a-tat across the bank. Eric flopped down like a hooked fish and wiggled his body up the bank. A man who had been near where the mine exploded clambered out of the water alongside of him. He was bloody. Eric recognized him as one of the lieutenants. He reached out to help him.

First Lieutenant Russell grunted. "I'll be all right; go on ahead."

Captain Kimble's filtered drawl oozed through the smoke. "Come on, men. We can take them." He waved the men forward.

Russell, blood oozing down his pants leg, followed Kimble.

Machine gun fire sprayed the dirt in front of Eric. He fired and fired again. The woods were alive with SS Troops. A German wrestled him to the ground. The German had his knife out before Eric could think. Eric flipped him onto his back like a turtle on its shell.

"Finish him off, soldier."

"Kill him."

Eric looked up.

The German tossed Eric off like a rubber ball, his knife gleaming in the blast of another shell. Dick's bayonet went deep into the German's back.

"What's the matter with you?" Dick scowled. He shoved Eric aside as another shell went singing past their ears. "Leave that thou-shalt-not-kill stuff in church, 'cause if you don't, the only way you get back to the States is in a body bag. It's every man for himself out here."

The gleam of a rifle two yards away was pointed at Dick's skull. Eric fired. Mortar pulverized the ground four feet before him. He covered his face with his arm to deflect the debris. The rat-a-tat of a machine gun in the distance added to the ear-splitting humbug. He crouched and ran forward. The path changed into a well-worn trail.

Eric slipped around a tree, saw the helmet of an SS trooper, and fired. The man fell.

Dick ran up, fired at another German, and looked down at them both. He kicked them in the gut. "Only way you can make sure these Jerries aren't playing possum on ya." He motioned with his hand for Eric to follow.

"Spread out; pass it on."

Red joined him, and they nodded their hellos. Eric kept his gun finger cocked, ready to fire. He looked around a tree, then moved forward, keeping the soldier in front in his eyesight. Hope the guy knows where he's going.

He thanked God he'd kept his ammo dry. He could be the one lying face down in the leaves. A noise in the thicket—he turned. Was that one of their guys—or a German? The haziness of mortar and artillery fire filtered through the trees. The smoke blurred his vision.

"Germans, three o'clock." Red squatted down.

Eric's heart beat like a drum. He had to make each shot count. Someone cried. He looked around. Another German? The woods crawled like fire ants with them. Eric bit down on his bottom lip. Sarge said that was one of the German's tactics—to pretend to be a hurt GI, leading the unsuspecting soldier into a ring of Germans. The bullets of a machine gun churned up the dirt ahead of them. Eric jumped into some leaves, dirt and leaves flying everywhere. Eric and Red crawled their way forward.

Dick nodded his head toward the German outpost. "Stay here." Dick crawled forward, slinking like a caterpillar along the dirt beneath the heavy fire discharged from the machine guns housed in a well-encased dugout. He made his way to the outpost, pulled the pin of his grenade, and tossed it in. The explosion was deafening. Smoke and debris flew everywhere. Eric stuck his head in the dirt as particles hit his helmet.

"Okay, men." Captain Kimble jumped to his feet and ran toward the outpost. With his rifle cocked and ready, the captain waited, motioned the others to follow. Entering the building, they found one German who had survived the attack.

Captain Kimble surveyed the mute prisoner as Lieutenant Russell patted the man down, the prisoner's eyes expressionless.

"Sir?" Russell handed Kimble the confiscated documents.

Kimble leafed through them. "Take him back to headquarters for questioning."

"Sergeant Rusk, pick some private to take these documents and the prisoner back to HQ."

"Yes, sir."

Rusk turned, surveying the GIs. "You, big guy, front and center."

Eric didn't flinch a face muscle as he stepped forward.

"You think you can find your way to battalion headquarters and back tonight?" Rusk said.

"Yes, sir."

"Okay, here are the papers I want you to take. If he tries to escape, shoot him. Shoot to kill." Sergeant Rusk removed his stogie, wet from the river crossing, from between his yellowed teeth, and butted the prisoner's chest. "You savvy?"

The German, his hands tied in front, eyed the sergeant, then Eric.

Eric narrowed his eyes and returned his gaze. The German sported a medium-sized build but couldn't be more than five foot, eleven inches high. Sandy-blond hair showed beneath his Heer helmet, and his cold blue eyes looked into Eric's without blinking.

"Get going." Eric prodded the man with the butt of his rifle. As Eric passed with his prisoner, the trailing GIs tossed a half salute to Eric and wished him well on his assignment.

Eric poked the German with his bayonet. He could smell what the German had for lunch. "Don't get any ideas, I'm tired and I'm hungry and I'm not in the mood for trouble."

Sudden movements at ten o'clock made him hoist his rifle. Nothing. Must have been a possum or some other night critter. At the river, crickets and bullfrogs were busy harmonizing with one another.

That's a good sign, didn't hear a peep out of them before the attack. Must mean the coast is clear. He pushed his prisoner forward. The crack of a rifle shot split through the crickets and bullfrogs' duet. Great, a guy can't even trust a bullfrog. Eric ducked, pushing the German to the ground. Using him as a buffer, he fired back. He could just make out the distant shine of a rifle stock. He fired. A groan, then…the German landed hard. Eric pushed his prisoner to his feet. The SS trooper stared blankly up at him.

"Come on." Eric blinked, trying to get the dead man's face out of his head.

Reaching the river's edge, he motioned for the German to grab the rope. The man hesitated. Eric scowled and shoved him toward the river.

The river was about ten degrees colder than earlier. His damp clothes felt like a wet sheet in February as the frigid air and freezing river water enveloped him. The German's breath came out in gasps. Eric pushed his prisoner onto dry ground on the opposite shore, feeling like a glacier had formed around each leg.

"Keep moving." He had no intention of catching pneumonia. Eric cupped his hands and blew on his fingers, then rubbed them together. The slosh, slosh of river water in his boots made walking uncomfortable, and his clothes weighed a ton.

❧

Eric pushed the German through the open tent flap, blinking at the bright light coming from the lantern. The smell of fresh coffee, a pot of beans heating in the skillet, and some kind of soup—maybe stew— met him as he entered. His stomach growled, reminding him he hadn't eaten since noon. He surveyed the room, spotting both Colonel Ward and his aide. "Sir," he addressed the aide, "I have a prisoner for you and some papers."

"Attaboy, soldier, where did you capture him?"

"German outpost, north of the Volturno River crossing."

"Bring him here," Colonel Ward said.

"Yes, sir."

"You hit a lot of resistance?" the Colonel asked him.

Eric saluted. "Yes, sir." He handed Colonel Ward the folded papers he'd placed inside his coat. "These papers were confiscated from the prisoner by Captain Kimble."

Colonel Ward glanced through the papers. "You give Captain Kimble an objective, and he doesn't quit until it's done. He's got the grit I wish I had in every one of my captains. Did I say he's from Kentucky?"

The aide, with a cup of joe in his hand, walked back with Colonel Ward to his table.

"No, sir."

Colonel Ward became engrossed in what Eric had given him.

"You look chilled. Coffee?" the aide asked the prisoner.

The German nodded and rubbed his fingers.

Eric scowled, seeing the man untied and handed a steaming cup of joe, then given a blanket to wrap around his shoulders to ward off the chill.

Eric licked his lips, almost tasting the hot coffee. Yeah, that's stew. He sure could use something hot inside him right now. And some dry clothes and boots, too.

The officer approached Eric, eyeing him.

Eric rubbed his muddy hands across his dungarees.

"Get back to your platoon, Private." The officer saluted in dismissal.

"Yes, sir." Eric saluted sharply.

"Oh, and close that tent flap. It's getting chillier. We just got this place warm."

Eric glanced back at the prisoner just before loosening the flap. The German held a plate of beans on his blanketed lap and a cup of joe in one hand. The man emptied his mug, set it down, and reached for a bowl full of steaming-hot stew.

Eric drew his wet coat closer around him. Blowing on his hands, he shouldered his rifle and walked back to the river. He reached for the rope and plunged his body into the swift current. He'd thought the water was cold, until he experienced the lack of welcome in the HQ tent.

What next?

Chapter 21

*I*taly's roads had turned into mud bogs with the autumn rains pouring their dampness into November without a letup. Eric and six other men put their shoulders to the back of the major's jeep. The Willys MB canopy top afforded the major protection from the rain but not for the foot soldier.

Black mud and brown water splattered the soldiers clothes and faces. Eric's boots, caked with two inches of mud, felt glued to the ground. "One, two, three, push." The jeep sank deeper into the oozy mire.

First Lieutenant Russell wiped the mud off his face and onto the sleeve of his coat. The slop, slop sound of his boots made a suction noise. Walking to the passenger side of the jeep, he saluted. "Sir, you'll have to wait for the winch."

"Italy's nothin' but a mud hole." Mud caked Red's face. He rubbed his eyes and blinked, looking like a raccoon. Except Sarge's face was funnier. Mud filled every crease of his large bulldog face. Eric laughed.

"What the blazes is there to laugh about?" Sarge wiped mud off the spattered back window of the jeep and snatched a look at his face. "Humpf. I look like Winston's bulldog smoking a stogie." He turned. "You sorry guys don't look any better. You're all a bunch of dog faces."

Eric wiped the grit from his teeth with his index finger, then spit.

Russell laughed and motioned them forward.

"Yep, we're the Dogfaces and, you know, I can't remember a day it hasn't rained in October."

"Well, it's the middle of November and still raining." Red stamped his boots to clear some of the mud off.

"I've gotten used to having my clothes wet and damp." Eric tapped his helmet. "At least I'll have a dry pair of socks to change into tonight."

"Gotten used to changing into dirty socks, have ya? That malaria you got after Naples still got a hold on ya?" Red said.

"I feel okay." He picked up one foot thick with the quagmire of mud. "This rain has got to stop soon." Eric looked up.

The clouds hung like grey rags before the sun, making telling the exact time of day difficult. His eyes scanned the distant woods. He'd gotten used to looking around, pinpointing any shadows that didn't belong to the trees. Being a runner a couple of times before he got sick had taught him to depend on himself.

"I don't think I can remember a day since our landing when I had an outfit of dry clothes," Red said.

As if in answer, the sky opened up, and lightning flickered through the clouds followed by a clap of thunder. Eric pulled his coat collar up, then noticed it. That shadow had moved. "Something moving at two o'clock in that band of trees."

The GIs crouched beside a bank and waited. The rumblings of German tanks on the wooded hillside blended with the rumble of thunder. The tanks soon filled the woods with a noise like a swarm of hornets.

"How are their tanks moving, when ours are stuck in the mud behind us?" Tommy said.

Captain Kimble told the radio dispatcher to alert the caissons, then motioned for the men to circle the tanks.

"He doesn't want them practicing their target shooting on us," Eric whispered to Red.

Using the trees as shields, the Dogfaces dug in and waited. They didn't have to wait long. Germans ahead of the tanks snatched pine needles, branches, whatever to keep the tanks from getting stuck in the rain-drenched ground.

"They don't know we're here," Sarge whispered. "There's probably a German division following."

Eric squinted in the dusk. Shadows lurked from every tree, and he struggled to tell GIs from the Germans.

Captain Kimble motioned for his men to take the little hut two yards from their path. The men rushed toward the structure made of straw and wood.

The hut's dirt floor was the first dry place they'd been in for three weeks. The back of the hut opened to a grape arbor. Stationing along the walls, they waited.

Three tanks rolled into view. The foot soldiers couldn't be too far behind. Eric looked around, wondering if this might be a bad idea. Straw would make great fodder for hand grenades, let alone tanks. The men with bazookas moved into action. Irishman O'Brien ran out of the hut followed by Bob with the shells for the bazooka. They made their way toward the tanks.

Vulnerable, looking for something to hide behind, the tough little Irishman from the Bronx crawled behind a tree and knelt. Then Eric saw the German, his gun pointed at O'Brien's back. Eric squinted into the scope and—bam. The noise echoed in his ears, stillness.

A flash of light...boom. O'Brien's bazooka met its mark. Fire bellowed out of the side of the tank. Like popcorn on a hot skillet, Germans jumped out of the sweltering-red vehicle. Another tank exploded. Suddenly, the forest was alive with crawling or running Germans.

Where was that Irishman now? Red flames lapped the sky. Another tank met its doom. No doubt he's alive. Eric knocked off a couple more soldiers. He bent down, loaded his rifle, cocked, and fired. This skirmish felt like a turkey shoot, only, it wasn't turkeys he was shooting. Sweat drizzled into his eyes. He blinked. His fingers wrapped around his lifeblood, his ammo. He reloaded and fired into the thickening soup. Thunder cracked like a quake overhead, and a flash of lightning lit the sky. Another tank sent sparks into the gathering darkness resembling Fourth of July fireworks. His buddies kept up the volley of shots.

"Hold it, men," Captain Kimble called.

Eric paused. The last tank in the line turned and disappeared into the night. Quiet as thick as the previous thunder and noise of the guns fell upon his ears. Then he heard a groan coming from a nearby tree. The dense fog and gun smoke made identification difficult.

"Could it be O'Brien?" Red poked his gun out of the window and looked through his scope, moving the muzzle slowly around the perimeter. "It could be a Kraut pretending he's our GI."

The smell of wet clothing and the sizzling odors of gunfire filled the close quarters. Eric knew there would soon be another odor to mingle with the night wind.

"Where's O'Brien?" Captain Kimble said. Bob shrugged.

The soldiers stared out the hut windows. The groans started again.

O'Brien had saved their hides. Greater love has no man than this. "I'm going out there and find out who's doing that groaning and where the Irishman is," Eric said.

Red put a hand to his chest to stop him. "Don't be stupid," he hissed.

Eric shook off Red's hand and gave a smart salute. "Captain, permission to find O'Brien."

Captain Kimble glanced through the hut's window, then turned. Deep shadows circled his eyes. Fatigue jagged across his face like a map. "Permission granted. Take someone with you."

Dick clutched his rifle. "I'm volunteering."

A crack of lightning followed by thunder and a volley of rain washed over the rear of the hut as Eric and Dick made their way to a clearing. Eric blinked through the small waterfall spewing over the brim of his helmet. They ran a crooked line toward the trees, their boots splashing through ankle deep water. A flashlight would come in handy right about now. Yeah right, if he wanted every Jerry within a mile to know where he was.

"Nothin." Dick pointed to a clump of bushes.

Eric looked down. Five Germans lay stretched out behind the waist-high blackberry bushes. One was still warm.

"Get going," Dick hissed, looking around.

Eric followed. Something didn't feel right.

Dick stopped. He pushed Eric behind a large oak and put his finger to his lips. Dick bent down and then got up off the wet ground and moved forward. Eric got through the forest without cracking a twig, then saw the three Germans. Raindrops splattered the leaves, making enough noise to drown out the Germans' conversation. They moved closer. Eric heard an unmistakable groan coming from the gully. Two feet below the enemy, O'Brien's head and shoulders rocked back and forth.

Eric shouldered his rifle, looking down the scope. One German put a hand on his companion's gun and motioned to the other to leave.

Eric and Dick lowered their rifles and waited.

"An eye for an eye. They spared the Irishman; we'll spare them," Dick muttered.

∽

"Men, we're blessed tonight." Captain Kimble lifted his canteen. "We've got a roof over our heads, and O'Brien's going to be fine."

O'Brien nodded his curly head, then bent over to look at the cauterized bullet wound in his leg. "You did a nice job." He buttoned his shirt across his hairy chest.

"You must stay pretty warm with that inner layer of hair. It's got to be better than long johns," Dick said. He stirred the embers of the small fire they used on O'Brien's wound and now brewed hot joe to warm the men. "Yeah, I bet when you go bear hunting, you meet a lot of your kin."

"You can laugh if you want. My daddy said it was a present from my great-great-grandfather who came to this country during the potato famine, so I wear it proudly, I do."

"Well, O'Brien, I'm glad your great-great-grandfather made the voyage." Dick held up his tin cup. "You've proven a capable bazooka man. With me, the contraption is as unreliable as a woman."

"Depends on how the bazooka is cared for." O'Brien cradled half the weapon onto his lap, took out a cloth, and cleaned the barrel. "And, I might add, if you handle a woman gentle-like, I be thinking, will do just as admirable."

"Captain, can we start a bigger fire and get our shoes and clothes dry a bit?"

The captain shook his head. "Could be Jerries in the nearby woods. Count your blessings there's enough fog out tonight to hide what little smoke and, hopefully, smell this fire makes."

Eric checked a second pair of socks. Still damp. He unlaced his boots and removed the wet ones, then let his feet air.

A large clap of thunder sounded followed by the wailing and cracking of a tree not two feet away. Rain peppered down like an out-of-control machine gun. Drops of rain penetrated the roof.

"If you thought it was muddy out there before, you should see it now." Eric stepped back from the window and rubbed his face clean from the rain.

"Yeah, you can't see the mud with all the mini-streams flowing around the hut." Tommy walked back from the door, his long, thin legs sticking out like scarecrow limbs from on top of his massive black boots.

Eric remembered thinking, back on the train, how Tommy's feet resembled water skis.

Tommy plopped down next to his knapsack and began rummaging through its contents. "Gee, Captain, I wish you'd let me play my harmonica. I'm going to forget how."

"We need to find Tommy some boots that aren't so big for him." Sergeant Rusk plopped down and sat cross-legged. He opened his knapsack, drew out his cigar, and placed it in his mouth. "Well, do you gents want an invitation? Sit down, make yourself comfortable."

Tommy shrugged. "My shoes fit fine. Pa's bone-thin, too. He could eat a side of beef at one sitting and not gain an ounce. Guess I took after him."

"No need to worry, staying at the Ritz." Dick unloaded his mess kit. "I had a cousin like that."

The sergeant took a swallow from his canteen, then opened up his C-rations, all the time keeping the cigar in the corner of his mouth.

"Sarge, are you ever going to smoke that cigar?" Tommy asked.

"What, this?" Sarge said.

"Last time I was home, that's what that thing dangling out of your mouth is called," Dick said.

Sarge flicked imaginary ashes. "Son, I don't smoke. It's a nasty habit."

Captain Kimble looked up from his mess kit. "Sergeant, Tommy asked you an honest question. He deserves an honest reply."

"Well, once, I did." Sergeant Rusk sighed. "But now my only connection to tobacco is holding this in my mouth. It's become my pacifier. After nurse-maidin' you sorry GIs, it gives me pleasure. I never needed it until I took this here prestigious position."

The walls creaked and moaned as the wind and rain battered the sides and roof of the hut. A raindrop plopped on Eric's forehead, spattering him in the eye. He got up and chose a spot toward the grape arbor. He opened his mess kit, rubbed his thumb across the profile picture of Esther's face he'd scratched with his pocket knife onto the inside lid. Tearing open the packet of dried beans and meat, he took a bite, swallowing the food down with a drink from his canteen.

"Anyone want my beans for their jerky?" Red asked.

"Here, I'll swap."

Eric reached into his pocket and took out his mother's cookies. This was the last of them. He opened the brown paper carefully. The cookies were crumbs. They tasted stale. But that didn't stop him from pouring them into his mouth. He licked the paper clean.

"Hmm." Red sat down next to him, still chewing. "I just can't figure why, but my wife's cookies taste better than anything else in this mess kit, even though they're soggy."

Eric nodded. He drew out his unfinished letter to Esther.

"That a picture of your girl?"

"Yeah."

"She's pretty. Is her hair really that long? I mean, it flows down her back like that, all fluffy and wavy like? Gee, she's beautiful. No wonder you're not giving up on her. A man would be a fool."

"Get some sleep," Sergeant Rusk said. "I'll take guard duty first."

Eric folded his unfinished letter into his pocket. Taking a last look at Esther, he closed his mess kit before pulling out Esther's last letter.

Eric, my darling, I'm claiming Psalm 91:7, 11, and 12 for November: A thousand shall fall at thy side, and ten thousand at thy right hand; but it shall not come nigh thee...he shall give his angels charge over thee...They shall bear thee up in their hands, lest thou dash thy foot against a stone. I miss you terribly, and just in case my cookies and letter don't reach you in time for Thanksgiving, have a blessed one and know I am praying for your safe return.

Eric pulled on his socks and boots, unrolled his blanket, and stretched out beneath the grape arbor to sleep. He smiled. Drops of rain spattered his forehead as the storm raged on outside. Memories of that Labor Day week when he and Esther had met and he saved her from that swimmer pelted his dreams. How he dived into the pool after her and felt her body next to his as the water washed over him. Water flowed over their warm bodies—

"Hey, Eric, get up." Red's grin looked as wide as that Volturno River. "You're just about to wash out of this here hut."

Eric dropped his arm into six inches of rainwater. "No wonder I was dreaming about swimming."

Red tried to wring some of the rain from his soggy coat. "Glad you had a good night's sleep. I didn't." He started to shiver. "I'm wet through to my marrow."

"Here, take my coat; I'm not cold."

"You will be if you take off that coat. Keep it on. I'll get warm when I start walking."

The strap of Eric's rifle fit the groove in his shoulder. "I can't figure out what keeps us from getting pneumonia."

"Should get our winter gear soon. But if we could have had a fire big enough to dry our clothes—"

"A fire could be seen for miles." Eric stepped out of the hut into an ankle deep puddle. "I'd rather chance pneumonia than risk getting caught by the Jerries and end up in one of their POW camps."

Red shivered.

Chapter 22

Esther's coffee steamed the office window as she gazed out at Woodward Avenue, watching the Christmas shoppers bustle down the sidewalks. Thanksgiving and Christmas of 1943 had long ago come and gone. Now the calendar read December 1944. Esther and Eric's mother, Anna, had grown close. They had received an occasional letter from Eric telling them not to eat too much turkey on Thanksgiving, or not to worry about him if they didn't receive much mail. His regiment was always on the go. He had to wait to get into his bedroll to write, and it was often hard for him to find paper and pen.

He remained upbeat and asked her to send him a picture of herself. In his December letter, he wrote from his hospital bed. "I have jaundice. I'm feeling okay." He assured them it was nothing to worry about, adding that his cute nurse was very attentive to him. "Whoopie!"

Did he really think she'd fall for that? One thing was definite. Eric was keeping her at arm's length. Why? Is it that bad in Italy that he didn't want her hurt if he didn't make it back?

Staring out the window, Esther sipped her coffee. She had sent him a picture of her and Dot standing by the Christmas tree at the apartment. A car honked below her. With the speed limit thirty-five miles per hour, and their ration books running out of stamps before the end of the month arrived, the norm had become to walk whenever possible.

She watched as a Ford waddled down Woodward with a steel rim in the rear of the car attributing to the imbalance. Tires were allotments.

Most Detroiters did without instead of having their GIs go in want.

Flakes of snow from the night before festively cloaked the maples and oaks dotting the street. Streetlights garnished with evergreen sprays and holly added a feeling of goodwill toward passersby. After she finished her regular job, she worked in the hospital on Mondays and the USO Building on Saturdays. She'd met Thomas Cutter in both. He'd gotten some shrapnel in his leg when his plane went down in the Atlantic. She'd invited him over to share Christmas day with her mom, William, and her.

Esther smiled, remembering the fun Eric and she, and William and Dot had riding their horses in the snow at Roxy Stables. Those happy days now felt like a dream.

William had been drafted into the Army six weeks ago and was currently at Camp Shenango in Pennsylvania. Mother hoped he would get a furlough soon. Dot said they were unlikely to see him, after receiving coded letters from her relatives who wrote how life-threatening the war in Europe had become.

She sipped her coffee, devoid of milk and sugar, as she prayed over the heartbreaking news of lost soldiers. Every house window had gold or silver stars shining on their pane. The casualties list was the first page people read.

A knock on her door sent her to her desk. "Yes, come in."

"Mr. Bowden is asking for you."

She reached for her steno pad, then headed to his office, her heels echoing in her ears. With all the problems overseas filtering into many of the big cities, the FBI had been busier than ever. Esther never knew what to expect from her boss. Snatching in a deep breath, she knocked.

"Come in."

Two men stood when she entered the room. She looked from one to the other. They looked familiar. A medium-built man with wavy brown hair and long, sloping sideburns smiled down at her. "Miss Meir, allow me to introduce myself, Mr. Smith."

Esther knew that many of the agents used common names and never revealed their true identity. "How do you do, Mr. Smith?"

"Miss Meir?"

Esther's attention switched to the second man. Shorter than Mr. Smith, heavy-set and balding.

"Miss Meir, I'm Mr. Jones. It's a pleasure to meet you."

Mr. Bowden cleared his throat. She turned attention from Mr. Jones to her boss. "Yes, Mr. Bowden?"

"Miss Meir, take a look at these pictures. They're very graphic. The Pentagon wants to release some information to the public, but they need to know if it will help or hurt American morale. I have explained to these men about your Jewish girlfriend and your abduction by a Nazi informer."

Esther snapped her fingers. "That's it. You're the men Dot and I first told about our escape. How could I have forgotten? I do apologize."

"Apology accepted. Can you help us determine which photos to use and how much information to release to the papers?"

Mr. Bowden handed her the photos. "You might want to sit."

She set her steno pad on her boss's end table and moved toward one of the comfortably padded leather chairs.

Mr. Smith sat in the adjoining leather chair. "These first ten are of a Nazi concentration camp. The camp is designated for the systematic extermination of undesirables, which include Jews, Gypsies, homosexuals, the mentally retarded, and others. At a glance, it looks like a work camp. Barbed wire fences, barracks, concrete floors, bathhouse. Now, look closely at this bathhouse, see anything strange?"

Esther stared at the black-and-white photo that had been smuggled through by one of their European patriots. Cement blocks went from ground to ceiling, making seeing anything else difficult because of the interior darkness. "Is that a spy hole?"

"Miss Meir, this is not a normal shower," Mr. Smith said. "See that spigot. It's too small. It looks like they pump hot air into those five-yard square rooms and then—"

"Gas?" Esther clutched her throat. "How many people do you think have gone into these gas chambers?"

"Nearly two thousand people could be disposed of simultaneously."

Esther closed her eyes. She braced for the next photo. Dead GIs lay in a narrow grave. A Japanese soldier astride a horse was laughing as his samurai sword beheaded a GI. Another bayoneted a soldier. Esther looked up. "Is this Bataan? That march where the *Manila Times* claimed our prisoners were treated humanely?"

"We have prisoners who escaped from what the Pentagon is calling the Bataan Death March. Our government has documented evidence that it was brutal savagery the Japanese inflicted on our American soldiers."

Esther turned to another photograph. A group of GIs sat on the side of a mountain, hunched inside a half-pup tent. They were unshaven. Some smiled a toothless grin at the photographer. Their gaunt, bearded faces and thin coats looked ghastly, unsuitable for the cold, snowy landscape. The caption read, "9,000 men in battle losses before penetrating the Gustav Line. Pneumonia, trench foot, and sickness due to exposure, cause loss of 50,000 Allied forces."

Esther glanced up. "Where was this taken?"

"Near the Volturno River. Some place near Monte Pantano and Monte Marrone."

She looked closer at the snapshot. Could one of these men be Eric? She couldn't detect a set of irresistible dimples beneath that beard, but one man's eyes stared back at her. She jumped up, spilling the rest of the photos off her lap, and paced back and forth. Eric's last letter mentioned the Volturno River and Monte Pantano.

"I feel bad for those guys. Intelligence intercepted a message from the Gestapo. Hitler stating, 'Lance the abscess south of Rome.' Hitler is obsessed with showing the world what he can do with his three-hundred well-fortified machine guns. According to our intelligence sources, he's sending over twenty thousand more troops into the area. We've sent a message to Washington."

"They'll be outnumbered three to one. The Allied forces are strained like a rubber band, needing more troops in the Pacific," Mr. Jones said.

Esther scooped the photos from the floor and handed them to Mr. Smith. "Never underestimate the strength of our prayers, gentlemen. American Christians need to know the complete truth, because when

Christians pray, God listens."

Mr. Smith shuffled through the photographs. "We can't release this type of news now. It'll ruin everyone's Christmas."

So? Their GIs needed their prayers! Esther's fingernails dug into her fisted palm. "These men need winter gear and our prayers."

"The 133rd and 135th rifle divisions are always on the move. We can't get winter clothing to them because they're gone before the trucks get there. We'll release the news to the newspapers about the gas chambers after Christmas, first week of January. We were going to wait until February. But because of your concerns, we will up it a month sooner," said Mr. Jones.

"Regarding those rifle divisions," Mr. Smith grunted. "Colonel Ward has found out about the winter coats."

⁂

Inside the foyer of the Kingston Arms, Esther opened their mailbox and thumbed through the letters, looking for Eric's strong penmanship. She took his letter out of the stack and clutched it to her bosom. Her high-heel shoes tapped out a peppy note on the apartment steps as she danced up the stairway decorated in pine garlands.

"Mother, we've got two letters, one from Eric and one from William."

Her mother hurried into the parlor, wiping wet hands on her apron. "Oh my, do you think they got your letter about President Roosevelt winning the election?"

"Oh, Mother, I just saw a recent picture of him at work. He looks so tired."

"I wonder if they heard the news about Glenn Miller."

"I wrote Eric about his plane being missing, perhaps shot down. It's a shame. We're going to miss him."

Esther smiled as her mother tore open the letter from William. "I don't know why I'm bothering to open this. William has already written Dot everything."

"I hope he doesn't write her his proposal."

"William has much too much romanticism in his bones to do a thing like that. He's like your father in that respect."

Esther clasped her unopened letter to her bosom.

Mother took a seat in her rocker. "I wish William and Eric could be here for Christmas. It doesn't feel like Christmas, with so much sadness."

Esther walked to the little tree she'd placed by the window, hoping the passersby could see the Christmas lights. "Cheer is hard to come by, but we have to keep our morale up."

"William writes he bruised his leg something awful during boot camp." She clicked her tongue against the roof of her mouth. "It's a wonder they took him. His hearing loss hasn't changed."

"They're taking everyone that's not married." Esther covered her mouth. "Oh, I didn't mean that to come out the way it did."

"I know what you mean. William's still proud to be away from that desk and going overseas to fight."

"Here's what Eric writes, Mother." Esther's vision blurred reading:

"My little Bible is getting a workout every chance I get. Sometimes I see the eyes of the man I killed that day, staring back at me, and I open my Bible and read some passages and close with

'Now the day is over.

Through the long night-watches

May Thine angels spread

Their white wings above me,

Watching round my bed.

When the morning wakens,

Then may I arise

Pure and fresh and sinless

In Thy holy eyes.'"

Dear Jesus, bring Eric home safely. Esther looked up. Mother was just as teary-eyed.

"'I fear no foe, with Thee at hand to bless.' Lord, forgive Eric and all your boys who are doing their duty to You and country…Brother sends you his love. Is there something wrong, Esther?"

Esther clasped her hands together. "Oh, Mother." She ran to kneel beside her mother's rocking chair. She laid her head in her aproned lap and sobbed. "I love Eric. I'll always love him. I'll never love anyone like I love Eric."

Mother patted her head. "That's the way it was with your father. When he was sick and dying, I didn't know how I was going to manage. He said his only regret in leaving was me. He hated to leave me with two little ones to rear alone and wished he'd never married me." Mother sighed, closing her eyes. "I told him that marrying him had made me complete. That I could wish for no more in life. I had known the love of a good man. Many women go through life, never having known love like I had. Did I ever tell you that it was your father who first put me and Buck Briggs together?"

"No."

Ruby smiled. "Your father wanted me to marry Buck. That way I could stay in Colorado and keep our homestead. Well, the good Lord had something else planned unbeknownst to your father and me. Buck Briggs found his Savior in Detroit at your Uncle Franklin's home. That made him a new man, ready to do battle with those gangsters."

Esther wiped her eyes. "And that's how he died?"

Mother nodded. "Buck had to expose those corrupt politicians like our boys have to stomp out Hitler in Europe." Clutching William's letter, she took Esther's hand, leading her to the window. The noise from the street echoed up. The street lamps twinkled, and gentle flakes of snow gracefully floated to the ground.

"Buck died for his convictions." Would that be Eric's fate?

"Being a war bride brings more trials than most marriages. It's a lot like being a widow battling the parched prairies of life. You see, after romance, comes commitment, that part of a woman's love that goes beyond self, to that selfless love that took our Lord Jesus to the cross. A woman needs to remember that. She's the anchor for her husband and her children. Her light of faith must never dim."

"I don't see how Eric is going to survive. Mother, the Germans outnumber the Allies three to one in Italy."

William's letter floated to the floor. "William won't be here for

Christmas. He'll be spending his Christmas somewhere else—I pray it's not in Italy," Mother said.

Chapter 23

Tommy's head poked in between Eric and Dick. "Hey, is Rapido the name for every river in Italy?"

Eric looked up from his letter. "Nah, it's one river."

"I'm growing fins on my feet with all these Rapido crossings."

Eric finished writing "January 10, 1944" on his letter, pocketed the page, and moved over for Tommy to join them inside their pup tent, which offered minimal shelter from the nail-biting wind. The kid had grit. What hand-to-hand combats, barbed wire, and mines couldn't do, the weather did. GIs filled the medical beds with trench foot and pneumonia.

Dick glanced over. "You like your new winter coat?"

Eric scrunched beneath the wool lining. "Wish I had it about two months before."

"The scuttlebutt is Colonel Ward found out that there wasn't enough winter gear to go around for his troops." Dick leaned closer, lowering his voice. "Colonel Ward threatened to take the coats off personnel's backs if they didn't find everyone the proper winter attire."

"He did? Well, my coat came in handy during that snowstorm and blinding gale we went through to relieve the 36th." The ashen faces of the soldiers sent a shiver down Eric's backbone. Don't give up hope. Esther's letters were his lifeline. He'd sometimes get six letters from her when the mail caught up with his division.

Her perfumed stationery got him kidded, but he could tell by his

213

buddies' itchy ears and the way they pored over their little Bible that their faith was renewed when he read out the verses Esther claimed that week for their safety. Ephesians 6:10–18 had become one of their favorites. He especially liked "Put on the whole armour of God… Above all, taking the shield of faith." Esther wrote how the churches throughout Detroit were filled to standing room only with families praying, beseeching God to bring their loved ones home.

That had been the general theme for Christmas Day. Though the trimmings were primitive, the turkey and dressing were plentiful. The chaplain wasn't sparse on the Word. When the chaplain had spoken about God sending the angels on that first Christmas to the shepherds sleeping on the cold, hard ground guarding the sheep, the GIs could relate. Especially knowing his regiment had to move to the line the next day.

"The Lord God sent His son as a symbol of His love. Jesus died on the cross for our sins, and each Christmas we celebrate that priceless gift. You men understand the loss of being separated from loved ones, war in all its hellish forms—but I feel that some here might feel something more is missing in your life.

"My Christmas message will answer all your questions and will bring you lasting peace.

"The only the atonement from sin is the blood of Christ. The cross and His resurrection are man's only hope. God says, 'I love you and I can forgive you.' Humble yourselves and admit your sin. Turn by faith to Jesus Christ. 'For by grace are ye saved through faith; and that not of yourselves: it is the gift of God: Not of works, lest any man should boast.'"

He was beginning to see Esther knew a heap more of the Bible than he. Was she right that he didn't need to prove himself to her or God?

Lord, I'm a sinner, and I ask you to forgive me of all my sins. Especially the fifth commandment, "Thou shalt not kill." I come before you in faith, believing. Amen.

This war had to end soon. The sleet changed to big white flakes that floated down upon the soldiers. Eric remembered a December night with Esther. The Pearl Harbor attack had changed the lives of every American. They had stood on the roof of the hotel that evening feeling the snowflakes falling on their faces. No two are alike. Yeah, the war can't last forever, but it sure could make a man miserable before it was over.

Red spat in the snow. "That Rapido River don't look inviting."

The sweeping current of the river tossed five-foot logs and branches like a circus juggler. On the opposite bank, a mountain of mammoth proportions peaked toward an ash-colored sky. On the mountain's crown, a building rose from the boulders as if a part of the rocky formation, an impregnable rock.

"Captain, what's that building called?" Tommy asked.

Eric, Red, and Dick stood and offered the captain a snappy salute.

"At ease, men." Captain Kimble smiled. "It's the Monte Cassino Abbey, Tommy."

"Gee, that sounds kind of religious."

"It's full of holy artifacts, and was founded in A.D. 529 by the Benedictine order."

"Catholic monks?" Tommy said.

"German SS Troops confiscated it from the monks." Kimble's steel-gray eyes softened. "It's up to us to save it before the British turn it into a stone quarry with their bombers. You can tell your children someday how you saved the Abbey."

Eric got out his binoculars. Rows of barbed wire five feet high stretched out thirty feet from the river bank and extended around the perimeter of the mountain like a giant worm of metal. The fence reminded Eric of the rolled bales of hay at Rock-a-Bye Ranch.

Red whistled. "Must be enough wire there to fence in all of Oklahoma."

"Some of the 34th tried to get up the bank of the mountain's backside. The terrain proved too steep. It's the only way, soldiers. Cross the river and go through that barbed wire and mine fields. We've got to capture the Abbey."

❧

Eric rolled the dead soldier aside. He clasped the wire cutters and attacked the barbed wire. They were like pheasants at a gun range. Sitting, or should he say, lying targets. He'd seen what the sharp metal of barbed wire could do to a horse. A mare had galloped right into the fence and torn a two-inch hole in her chest. Flesh and hair were ripped away, and the hole stopped within a half-inch of the horse' windpipe. If that could happen to a thousand-pound animal, he could visualize what it could do to a two-hundred-pound man.

A twang interrupted his thoughts. He ducked in time to miss a sniper's bullet.

"Let me at that thing." Dick snatched the wire cutters from him and began cutting. "Got it!"

They inched their way through the opening in single file. A bullet whizzed past his head. Eric got a bead and fired on the sniper. Now he knew what a turkey felt like, pinned in on every angle.

Shivering from the river, cut and bleeding from the barbed wire, their rifle division was crawling their way through the middle of a minefield, trapped like a rabbit in a snare, and they hadn't gotten a toe-hold on this mountain.

Sarge inched his way along. Eric felt Dick's hand on his shoulder. He got up from his belly and sprinted across the minefield. Eric took a solid breath, rose to his feet, and followed. Red was close behind. A machine gun ripped the ground two feet in front of him. Eric squatted down and ducked. Dirt and debris flew up. Dick had reached a clump of trees. Eric's heart felt lodged in his throat. He jumped up and ran a diagonal toward a dugout where Dick was doing a good job of cleaning out the Germans. The machine gun's rat-a-tat-tat trailed his steps like a rattlesnake. He dropped to the ground.

He inched his way forward on his belly, squirming like a worm. Dick helped him into a good-sized dugout the Germans didn't need anymore. God, please be with Red and the others; help them get through. Blood oozed from Eric's hand. He ducked. The machine gun blasts zinged into the boulder just a yard from him. Dick inched forward, his toes feeling for the next toehold.

"Kraut pillbox, two o'clock." Dick reached into his pocket, removed the pin from a grenade, and pitched it. The grenade fell short of the pillbox and jack-hammered onto the rocks.

"You've a lousy pitching arm." Eric's fingers closed around a grenade. He looked at his bloodied palm, flexed his fingers, measured the distance, and pulled the pin. "One, two..." He flung the grenade right into the pillbox. The explosion was deafening. "Sort of like the Fourth of July fireworks."

"Luck," Dick muttered. He inched his way up the hill.

Artillery covered the mountains with a heavy residue of gunpowder fog and the stifling smell of sulfur and human flesh followed. Eric looked for a trench, maybe another dugout to burrow into. Dick spied the hole first and threw himself in. Eric followed. A red-bearded man snaked his way through the debris, dragging his tommy gun and rifle. His bayonet was fastened on the stock, sort a like a dagger.

"Attaboy."

"Yeah, you left me a pretty good trail of blood. What'd you do, try to peel that wire away with your bare hands?"

Eric stared through the foggy mist, attempting to penetrate the gathering smoke. "Where's the rest of the guys?"

Dirt mingled with sweat and snow covered Red's face. "God knows."

Eric's trigger finger itched to make amends for his buddies. A bullet whizzed past his ear. A machine gun fired in the distance.

"Those sorry Krauts," Dick muttered.

"This place ain't a spot I care to die in. Maybe we should get out of here," Red said.

"Might be better to stay put tonight." Dick leaned against a boulder. "We'll be easy targets out there."

A noise from above. Eric craned his neck and peeked over the edge. Five SS troopers were making their way down the hill toward them.

They'd been fighting mostly with grenades because they couldn't see over the steep hills and rocks to use their rifles. Eric was glad to feel the familiar barrel in his hands. He lifted his rifle and picked them off. Some didn't take well to being shot. Their screams echoed over the mountain as they fell with loud thumps. The smoke from the battlefield floated about them like ghosts during a Halloween prank.

Time seemed to stand still as they scrunched down in their dugout waiting for the next onslaught of SS Troops.

"I've got one shot left." Red felt in his pockets for more ammo.

Dick reached into his pocket, produced two more rounds, and handed Red one.

Eric checked his supply. He had one round left. The iron grip of fear took hold of his chest. The hours ticked by, drawing the darkness like a shroud about them.

Like a rabbit in its burrow, Dick slouched deeper into his coat. "It's going to be a long night. Too bad those SS troopers didn't land a few feet in front of our hole and not plummet over that mountainside."

Red reached for his canteen, shook it. "Got one drop left. Yeah, we could have used their rations, too."

Eric reached for his. "I haven't got much, but you're welcome to it."

"I can't believe it." Red lowered his head to his sleeve and sneezed. "After months of rain and walking through that river for weeks, I'm out of water. Can a man be so unlucky?"

"What's that?" Eric heard the soft braying of a mule. He strained to see through the pitch-black.

The moon, now free of an obstinate cloud, bathed them with light. Eric glanced up. The moon was directly overhead. Midnight. The clouds gave way and the sky was clear. A moment later, the animal emerged from the smoke, its head hanging low to the ground.

"Look. Bet those cans have water in them."

Eric squinted. "Bet those saddlebags have ammo. Cover me."

"No." Red pulled him back. "I want the drink."

"Yeah, but you're slower than molasses in January," Eric retorted. He slid out of the foxhole and talked in soothing tones to the mule, trying to coax him closer. "Good boy, come here." The mule hesitated, then started to walk away.

"Mule, here boy."

A bomb lit the sky. The mule brayed and started to climb the mountainside. Eric leaped and caught the harness, stroked its head, and led the animal toward their foxhole. "You're Uncle Sam's mule. That's our water and our ammo, not the Jerries'. Where's your patriotism?"

Grabbing a can, he flung it to his buddies. The strings of ammo came next. A bullet whizzed past his ear, and Dick's answer was to send the SS soldier tumbling down the mountain. Eric crouched behind the braying mule just as a missile zinged over his helmet. The mule backed away. Eric snatched the saddlebags then slapped the animal on the rump, heading him downhill. The mule broke into a loping gallop. Eric dove for the hole before that sniper's bullets could find him. Dick sprang up and fired on the sniper.

Red gulped down the water, his Adam's apple working overtime trying to swallow fast enough.

"Thought you were a goner." Dick wiped the sweat off his brow.

Eric inhaled, gulping down air like a drowning sailor. "I could feel the wind from the bullet near my cheek, and that's as close as I care to be to a slug."

"There's some of our men." Dick waved.

Three joined them.

Jimmy's young face lit up. "Eric, Dick, Red, gee whiz, am I glad to see you guys."

Eric patted Jimmy on the back. "That mule's probably halfway down the hill by now."

One man waved the point of his rifle in the mule's direction. "Nope, don't think that mule will be going anywhere."

Eric looked out.

"He got a shell in its side."

He sank back into the dugout. "That mule didn't ask to be a part of this war."

Dick slapped Eric's coat. "Did you? Did any of us? No. That mule didn't suffer half as much as we might before we get out of here."

He peered into the night. Only the cries of the wounded met his ears.

"That guy sounds close," Red said. "Sometimes I think hearing them is the worst."

The wounded soldier's voice echoed in the stillness.

Eric spat. Dear God, what do you want me to do? A breeze blew across his face. He shouldered his rifle and muttered, "Cover me with

Your armor, Lord." He sprang out of the hole and ran toward the sound.

Out of breath, Eric whispered, "Soldier?" The light ash-blond head of the guy looked up.

"William? What the devil are you doing here?"

William doubled over, panting, "Uncle Sam…needed more men."

"Where are you shot?"

"My…side."

"Grab my neck." Eric hoisted him up on his shoulders and ran across the yards of rocks and debris. The ring of a bullet ricocheted off a rock nearby. He flattened himself and laid William out, pretending to be dead. Two Germans ran toward him. He would have one chance to land them both. His bullet echoed down the hilltop. One German fell to the ground; the other flung himself forward spread-eagle with a grenade in his hand. Eric thrust his bayonet into his middle and flung the grenade into a clump of trees. The light from the explosion revealed his cover. He grimaced. The first man's eyes stared blankly up at him. William had passed out. Eric picked him up buddy-style and ran to their foxhole.

Dick clasped William by the shoulders, then motioned toward Red. "He's been asking for ya. I'll take care of your buddy."

Red crouched in a corner, shivering. He looked up and grinned. "I, I think I drank that water too fast."

Eric felt his head. He was burning with fever. Eric laid his jacket over Red, tucking the damp wool around his shoulders.

Red closed his eyes. "That feels good. I'll be all right in the morning."

"Sure, Red."

Dick applied sulfa to William's wound, then bandaged it. "He's lost a lot of blood. Get some sleep, Eric. I'll take the first watch."

"Will William make it?"

"Good as new in a couple of days, only…" Dick eyed him.

"I said not to worry." William tried to rise, then fell back, mumbling. "I'm not about to let…a flesh wound stop me."

"I should have known he's a friend of yours." Dick pushed William down. "Okay, Private, plan on lying low for a couple of days, if you can." Dick rocked back on his heels and sighed.

"I knew I'd be fine. Did you feel that wind?" Eric asked.

"Feel what?"

"You know, that wind just before I jumped out of the foxhole."

"What about it?"

"There's a passage my gal told me about in the Bible. John 3:8. Whenever the wind blows and I find myself doubting, I remember. It's up to God. 'You canst not tell whence it cometh, and whither it goeth…'" Eric drew out his Bible and brought out "A Soldier's Prayer." Dick recited it along with him. "O Christ my King, on bended knee, My Leader I salute; Help me to serve Thee faithfully; Sin's error to refute. I beg for grace to do my part Throughout this mortal war; For courage and a soldier's heart Through cannons blast and roar. Protect me when Death's flags are high, But if it be Thy Will That I should die, then let me die Thy friend, thy soldier still." They glanced toward Red and William.

"You got that right. God tells you when your number's up." Dick leaned his back on a boulder, stretched one leg, then the other. "My little Bible is vital for survival. It's the only thing you can count on out here." Dick patted his inside chest pocket where his Bible lay. "You'll never meet an atheist in a foxhole."

Chapter 24

The dark sky weighed as heavily as Eric's mood. The foxhole gave him and his buddies little shelter. He brushed away the snow and ice, his Army coat cracking like popcorn. William, the master accounting bookworm, had proven his gutsiness battle after battle, never complaining about his rib or his gashed leg. They'd manage to cover ground to the Abbey and captured six prisoners. Then the Germans reinforced their troops. Now, they were stuck in this trench.

The early morning mists floated on the hill below them. Or was that smoke from last-night's bloody skirmish? "How do you think the 168th is doing?" He met William's penetrating gaze.

"They looked spent when we passed them near Highway 6. You think they made it up here to Hill 593? We could use the back up."

Eric peered down the mountain.

"If those Nebelwerfers would let up, we could take the Cassino with no problem, even with no back up," Dick said.

"Is that the bomb's real name? I thought it was called Screaming Meemies?" Tommy said.

"Yeah. That's the bomb's real name," Dick said.

Tommy, his helmet cradled in his hands, crouched next to Eric. Eric pretended to pull an imaginary whisker from Tommy's face.

"Leave that alone." Tommy felt the side of his jaw, his eyes as wide as a child's on Christmas Day. "Did I have a whisker, really?"

Eric chortled. "Don't worry. Facial hair comes when you least expect it.

You'll remember the days fondly when you didn't have to shave."

"I know what that bald-headed rooster back on Pop's farm felt like, strutting alongside those feathered birds...paltry."

Eric tasted the bitter gall of his flirtatious actions with the gals and looked away. "Manhood's not measured by whiskers, Tommy. Being born a male isn't our choice." Eric fingered his rifle. "Being a man is."

Tommy rubbed his smooth chin. "I never thought of it that way. Just before I shipped out, Pop said, 'Do what you must to honor God, protect your country, and when you get married provide for your family.' I want to be just like Pop. He's a great dad and good to my mom. I hope to make him proud of me some day." Tommy smiled. "So, what are we looking for?"

He and Tommy had something in common. Eric rested his rifle on a boulder. "That was my last food ration, and I'm running low on ammo. I'm looking for a supply mule."

Tommy pointed to two mule carcasses. "The Germans killed them."

Eric rubbed his nose. The stench had haunted his dreams. Or did he smell the bodies of fallen soldiers? Overturned vehicles, abandoned shell-casings, and disabled tanks littered the hill. His throat felt like sandpaper. Along with no food or ammo, they'd run out of water. He bit into a handful of snow and rolled the frozen water around in his mouth. For four days, the rear unit volunteers had not ventured up the treacherous mountain and shelled terrain to evacuate casualties.

What was that? A shiny object further up the hill captured his attention. Must be a steel pillbox half-buried in the side of the mountain. He pressed on Tommy's shoulder. "Get down."

"Now I know what a duck feels like on opening day."

"Why'd you enlist instead of waiting to be drafted, Tommy?"

"Because the war might have been over before I reached twenty."

William sat up. His expression held a calculating edge, and his smile did not quite reach his eyes. "That's what's wrong with youth. They're always in a hurry to go nowhere."

Needle-cold pricks of sleet pelted Eric's face. He spotted a familiar figure. Eric smiled over at Tommy. "Looks like we're moving out."

Captain Kimble jumped into their foxhole. "I figured you men needed a little exercise after sleeping in." He pointed toward the steep incline. "Let's see what's going on in the Cassino."

The rifle company inched their way forward in a football game of chance, tossing hand grenades in the air and running forward before another blast from the machine guns intercepted their maneuvers. But their plays, if not completed, had life and death consequences. No telling how many of his rifle company was left. Eric looked around. He bolted from boulder to boulder as they struggled north toward their objective, Highway 6, and their goal of isolating the Abbey. They hadn't gone thirty feet when the Screaming Meemies began, then the rat-a-tat-tat of the machine gun.

"Ow unh!" Tommy slumped toward him.

"Tommy!"

Tommy's arm remained outstretched as his body bounced backwards. "Help...me."

Eric bent down, his arm outstretched as Tommy's body rolled and bounced, hitting boulder after boulder down the steep mountainside. Eric searched for a place to climb down. Dick and Red pulled him back.

Dick shook him by the shoulder. "Let him go."

Eric shook them off. Tears oozed wet streaks down his chapped cheeks. Why, God? Why Tommy? Dick seized him around the neck, shoved him to the ground, and hissed in his ear. "Soldier, Tommy's number was up. He's with Jesus. Come on."

Eric wasn't leaving this hill until he killed every German there. The Germans counter-attacked. Each attack melted the Allies' numbers. Eric threw hand grenades until he thought he'd dislocated his shoulder.

He ran forward and sank his bayonet deep into a German. Their faces were so close he smelled sausage and wine on their breath. Blood splattered his face. He didn't know whether the fluid was his or the German's. Red spots stained the white snow. Helmets with the swastika lay strewn about the ground, mingling with helmets bearing the Stars and Stripes. Eric planted his boot in the back of a dead German and panted, bending his head down to his knees, gasping for air.

Kimble's eyes stormed out his anger. "Come on, men. Let's get out of here. We're sitting ducks. We gotta find someplace to dig in for the night."

Long hours later, Eric calculated the time to be just after four a.m. The smoke in the foxhole was so thick he needed his Bowie knife to cut through the haze to see the man not three feet from him. The wind carried the residue of gunpowder and flint to his nostrils. He coughed and reached for his canteen, taking a swig. He grimaced at the taste of the water and screwed the cap on.

"I'm out of ammo and on my last grenade," Red said. "You got any?"

Eric shook his head and wiped his mouth with the back of his hand. He'd counted five counterattacks, including the two outside the Abbey.

"We've got to hold them off for another hour." Dick removed his helmet and rubbed his forehead with the sleeve of his jacket. His eyes were like deep sockets in a mass of dirt and sooty snow.

Red's eyes fluttered as much as his hands. He reached for his canteen but couldn't seem to find his mouth. Eric looked away.

Tommy's face, his body somersaulting down the mountain, haunted Eric. Every time he closed his eyes, he pictured his young friend out there, at the bottom of the mountain waiting for a litter to take him and pile him with the rest of the dead soldiers. Eric aimed his rifle and waited.

Dick opened a can of stew and stared back. His voice grated Eric's already heightened senses like coarse sand on skin. "Look, I know about those ghosts that plague a man's thoughts." He pointed his fork at him. "The way I see it, Tommy's in heaven because God didn't think he needed to suffer any longer, 'cause of his innocence. But being the sorry GIs we are, we have a lot of penance to do." Dick took a mouthful, chewing thoughtfully. "God's picked us to finish this here mission, so Tommy and the others didn't die in vain."

Eric set his rifle down and glanced away. Penance? He'd prefer a couple of Our Fathers and Hail Marys to this.

"You can look at it as a kind of honor. Come on, get your chin up off the ground. What's the matter with you sorry GIs? Christ wouldn't put us here if He didn't think we could do some good, like take this hill."

"Suppose we take the Abbey. And after that, then what?" Red's bottom lip quivered. "Another hill and then another and then—When's it going to end, Dick? When we're dead at the bottom of some rock quarry?"

"When?" Dick's arm shook, trying to unscrew the top of his canteen. "When we kill these Krauts and mail them in body bags to Hitler. We didn't start this war, but I'm sure plannin' on finishin' it. With God's help, I am."

"What's that?" Eric aimed his rifle.

"Holster your guns, you sorry GIs." Sarge jumped into their hole. "Orders from the brass, we're to pull out ASAP."

"What?" Dick groaned. "Can't Clark make his mind up? Just give us some men. We got more holes in our flanks than Swiss cheese. Come on, Sarge. We got to finish it up and take the Abbey."

"The British want a try at it." Sergeant Rusk shrugged and rested his large hand on Dick's shoulder. "Kimble says he's got enough dead heroes; he's met his quota. He needs to keep the rest of you alive."

Eric slammed his helmet on the ground and bit his bottom lip so hard he drew blood.

Sarge nodded. "You think I don't know how you feel? Look at it like this. Here's your chance to get off Cassino. Don't you want that? You all need a rest. Why, Red here can't even find his mouth."

"You don't see me belly-aching." Red buried his hands in his armpits. "My hand's tired from throwing those grenades, that's all."

"Not my call. Brass has ordered a cease-fire. We're moving out; pass it on." Sarge disappeared into the next foxhole.

"We could've taken that Abbey if we had more manpower." Dick said.

"What's it all been for?" Red lowered his head between his knees.

"I'm not going!" Dick threw his empty can out of the hole.

Captain Kimble jumped out of his foxhole and into theirs. His steel-gray eyes burned into Dick's and then Eric's. "I'm not in the mood for backtalk. The British are sending in their Indian Gurkhas. I lost all the GIs I can handle."

"Now that we got Jerry pinned in, those Gurkhas think they can finish it, huh?" Dick said. "They're going to take us off our mountain after we made it into Cassino? And we're to let some Indian Gurkhas get the credit?"

The stern lines of Kimble's face softened, yet his smile did not quite reach his eyes. He slapped Dick on the shoulder. "Every time the Krauts moved, you clobbered them back." The southern twang of the Kentucky hills covered their foxhole like a familiar sonnet. "Every one of you soldiers deserves a medal."

"Captain?"

"Yes, Dick."

"What's the date?"

"February 14. "

"We're leaving on Valentine's Day?" Red's mouth drew into a big oval.

Kimble shrugged. "Guess it's Clark's way of remembering the date."

The soldiers stepped out of their foxholes.

Eric counted the survivors, "One, two…"

Three dozen Army medics with stretchers made their way up the hill. One called out to him. "Private, lend a hand."

Eric followed and helped First Lieutenant Russell from his foxhole. Dick caught Red before he fell.

"Let go; I can walk. Ow."

"Come on, you stubborn Irishman." Dick wrapped Red's arm around his neck.

Eric looked at the captain and Sarge, then William. "Including us, makes six."

Dick dragged in a ragged breath, his brows drawn close. "Six men made it out of our rifle company?"

"Yeah, six of us who are able to walk off this mountain."

Red grimaced. "Well, we sure did make a ruckus."

Coming down the mountain, Eric glanced at the thousand or so logs piled at the base in a jumble like pick-up sticks. "I wonder what they plan to burn?" He gasped. "That's not logs. That's dead men, piled up like logs." The horror stretched before his eyes in the golden hues of dawn as far as he could see.

The British Indian Gurkhas stared as he neared them.

William's hoarse voice broke the silence. His words weighed like ten pounds of lead on Eric's ears. "We must smell pretty good, the way these British part like the Red Sea when we get near."

"Yeah, we look like we should be stacked alongside our buddies," Dick muttered to Sarge and Captain Kimble.

Red glanced over at the corpses, and Eric choked back a bitter sigh. One of those bodies was Tommy's.

"Stand tall," Captain Kimble ordered.

Eric squared his shoulders. Six abreast they met the stares of the British soldiers and Indian Gurkhas.

One Gurkha, his head wrapped in a white turban, came forward, his high-pitched voice anxious and confident. "We take hill."

One Indian fell in step alongside Eric. His lips displayed irregular teeth in a mammoth smile.

Hands fisted at his side, Eric watched the Gurkha run in front, causing Eric and the others to stop. From the folds of his tunic-type pants, he produced a long, slightly arched knife. "We go up, slash, slash the Germans. We attack, attack, to the last man. You see."

"To the last man?" Where did this Gurkha hear that? It was his company's motto, and he didn't care to hear it on that Indian's lips.

The Indian pointed to Eric's insignia and said, "To the Last Man."

His infantry regiment patch. So, the man could read English. Eric had done some research about his patch. It originated from the 1st Minnesota's stand at Gettysburg. Well, they certainly lived up to that patch this day.

Eric watched as the stretchers with soldiers were carried past them. Captain patted Eric's shoulder. "Well, men, it's off to the King's Palace."

"Really, Captain?"

"Yeah, son, soon as you all check into sick bay and pass inspection."

Chapter 25

The building's whitewashed walls gleamed in the bright morning sunlight. Delicate ivory plants spiraled downward from its gothic roof and walls. All that was missing was the gondola music to complete the picturesque scene.

Eric whistled. "When we captured Sant'Angelo d'Alife from the Jerries that first week of February, I didn't notice this place."

"Me neither. Course I was trying to keep breath in my lungs, running up and down these hills, fighting." Red kept looking up and walked right into one of the potted plants decorating the outside veranda. "Nice piece of real estate."

"We lost fifty good men in this place." Dick glanced over his shoulder. "Hey, Sarge, is this really the building people call the King's Palace of Italy?"

Eric cocked his head, straining his ears over the ping-pong conversation of the servicemen's voices swelling around the mansion like buzzing hornets.

"Yeah."

He glanced at the men beside and behind him. The dirt-stained pants and worn elbows of Dick's and Sarge's jackets were a carbon copy of his own.

"How long are we here for?" Dick asked.

"Where is here?" Red asked.

Sarge removed his sodden stogie like it was a lollipop. He pointed to the majestic double doors. "We're thirty-two kilometers from Naples. This is where the rear echelon lived. Make sure you stick your little pinky out when you eat in the king's dining room."

"Yeah, well." Dick glanced toward the building. "How long do we have to break this place in, Sarge?"

Sergeant Rusk's gaze lingered. "Long enough for us to get replacements and you boys some clean duds."

Eric elbowed William and Red. "You know what that means?"

"Yeah," Red said. "Means we've moved up in the ranks to *seasoned*."

e∽

The late afternoon sun filtered into the dimly lit room Eric occupied with Red and William. They'd groomed themselves as best they could, then napped. Eric ran a comb through his thick wavy black hair. His washed and shaven face felt bare. He didn't have any other clothes to put on but his dirty ones.

"Come on, pretty boy." Red shoved him toward the door.

William, Red, and he strolled into the eloquent mansion's ballroom that had been turned into a makeshift bar complete with scrolled ornate tables and cushioned chairs borrowed from the various rooms of the estate.

Eric squinted against the bright light and reflecting surfaces. William glanced at him, then back to Captain Kimble, who was slumped over a table. Dark circles surrounded his eyes as he stared at them over a glass of wine. Eric grimaced. *He's seeing the faces of his absent GIs.*

Two British soldiers walked in, looked at Eric, then their captain. Eric balled his fists.

"Sorry, chaps, about your misfortune." The Brits diverted their eyes, walking toward the bar. Eric inhaled deeply. *Had they been making fun of the Americans? Or was he reading into their look because he felt like a pitiful loser?*

The stale reminder that Europeans had thought of Americans as playboys rubbed salt into his open wound when they had to give Hill

593 to the Gurkhas. Tommy's youthful smile interfered with his sleep. Why did those men have to die?

Dick's comment made sense. Tommy had fulfilled his calling and had gone home. He was too young to face the evils of this life. What would Pa recite from Shakespeare? The coward dies many deaths, the brave only one. Lord, will I die bravely when I know a bullet's meant for me?

Dick put an arm around Eric and Red. "Captain, can you believe these kids made it? Must have been my nurturing ways."

Kimble blinked. He lifted his hands from the polished table, his laugh like furniture scraping over a tiled floor. Sarge, Dick, Red, William, Eric, Lieutenant Russell, and O'Brien just out of sick bay, circled their captain and patted his shoulder.

Sergeant Rusk clicked his tongue like a cackling hen brooding over her chicks. "You look like a bunch of starved scarecrows that couldn't chase a crow away if your life depended on it."

Dick had a stogie cradled between his two fingers and did an imitation of Sarge. He bit off the end, placed the cigar in his mouth, lit a match, and puffed until smoke circled his head like a wreath.

Red slapped him on the back. "What are you going to do, Sarge?"

"Do? Well, I just might join him."

Dick removed his stogie.

"Come on, let's fill our stomachs with some good wine. That's the only thing these Italians have a large supply of."

"You plan on leading this young man down the alley of your bad habits, Dick?" Sarge guffawed. "I taught you better than that after two long years together. And didn't I say smoking was bad for your health?"

"Sarge, you surely did." Dick bowed his head. "But those Nazis just up and shot all my good manners right out of me, and that only leaves the bad ones. Come on. You deserve a reprieve, too."

The sergeant laughed. "Don't mind if I do. Some WACs should be here soon. They plan to give you a good time this evening, dancing the night away. That is, if you sorry GIs know how to dance."

"You kidding, Sarge? Music, too?" Eric looked around, spotted a couple of local Italian girls, and smiled. He and William found a table close to the bar and the dance floor. A few WACs and a couple of Italian girls stood behind the bar.

Dick pulled over a couple more chairs to join Eric. "Come on, honey. We're friendly. Come sit with us." He and Eric stood, motioning to the chairs.

A cute Italian girl with large brown eyes circled Eric's arm with her petite hands. Eric leaned close to her ear. "You're cute. Do you speak English?"

She nodded. Her long dark hair bounced around her shapely bare shoulders. Silky lashes framed her large, expressive eyes. All this encased in a heart-shaped face. Wow, he felt lucky tonight.

Eric guided her toward a chair next to his. "Well, then, why don't we get to know each other better. Maestro, where's the music?"

The scraping of chairs on the wooden floor and the soft mumbling of the men walking into the saloon erupted into vociferous catcalls, and someone yelled, "Russell, when are the WACs getting here?"

First Lieutenant Russell looked up from his place at a table with Captain Kimble.

"What's the matter?" Dick muttered. "Don't tell me, I've heard it before. The WACs aren't coming 'cause we're smelly and there's some fly boys here that smell better and aren't as battle-scarred as us, right?"

"They were supposed to be here," said First Lieutenant Russell.

The WAC behind the bar, a girl in her early twenties, said, "Sorry, the WACs are at the movie theatre with the Air Corps."

"But I wired ahead that we were coming in." First Lieutenant Russell walked to the bar. "These men have been battling up the Boot for over five months. The least they could do is give them a decent time." He leaned closer to the WAC and whispered. "Dance with them, give them a reason to—"

"That isn't my fault."

Lieutenant Russell spun on his heels and banged through the door, letting it flounder on its hinges.

"Stay here, sweetheart. I'll be right back." Eric pivoted William off his chair and out the door.

"William, duck." They peeked out from behind the building. Eric whispered into William's good ear, "I never saw Russell so hot under the collar before."

Russell turned down a crossroad.

"How can he walk so fast with those busted ribs? He couldn't put one foot before another and had to be littered off. He's got to be running on pure adrenalin, or he's doped up on pain meds," William muttered.

Russell plowed into the movie theatre, where he climbed the stairs two at a time. Straight to the head projector. Eric and William waited at the bottom of the stairs. Russell's voice penetrated the walls, sharp as a bell. "You shut that projector off or else I will."

"Yes, sir."

Eric and William blended into the shadows of the back room when Russell thundered down the stairs. His combat boots echoed like Indian war drums in the quiet room as he stepped onto the stage. "Excuse me, ladies, but I've got the 135th out there waiting for you. They've been fighting a gruesome hand-to-hand combat battle against overwhelming odds at Cassino, and against Germany's well-fortified and horrendous weaponry. Every time they were asked to attack, they did. They lived up to their platoon motto and did it with determination and ferocity.

"I'm asking if you might find time out of your, um, schedule to give these well-deserving men a few hours of your feminine charms and a reprieve from their memories?

"Yeah, they're rough around the edges. They have to be to endure what they did. They don't smell real good. Their clothes are as dirty and worn out as they are. Their boots aren't so shiny, 'cause they've been walking twenty miles a day, fording rivers. They've been doing a job not many men are capable of, fighting unselfishly with all they got, and I want you to give these heroes a little of your charms—tonight." Silence. His eyes swept the room.

One woman, then another stood. Soon every WAC was walking toward the door, following Russell back to the dance hall.

"You haven't said a word since we left the movie theatre. What's up?" William said.

"I always thought Russell was a prima donna. But he sure did eat the same dirt we did." Eric stopped. "Who else have I been wrong about?"

William didn't hesitate. "Esther. You've been wrong about my sis. If you ever win her heart, she'll love you back with the kind of love that won't quit."

⁊

The next morning, Eric bounced back and forth in the truck full of GIs, but he didn't care, just as long as he kept his head level. He smiled. He'd known that about Esther, but to hear William say the words was like music to his ears. Was he close to winning her heart? Sounded to him like William thought that was a definite possibility.

"You reliving last night?" Dick asked.

What did Dick know? Or what did he think he knew?

"That little Italian gal really got the hots for ya. Sending for her mama like that. Was her mama's spaghetti as good as she said it was? Bet they poured more wine in ya, too. That's how these Italian moms get their daughters wed to American GIs."

Come to think of it, what had happened? Eric bowed his head. "Ow." He had a major hangover. Had William heard what Dick said? Eric glanced over at William, who responded to Eric's unvoiced question by crossing his arms.

Eric buried his head in his hands. What happened? Half the time his thoughts were on Esther, and the other times he...He wasn't dreaming. He'd awoken in that little Italian gal's bed. He remembered now. He'd crept out of the house before dawn.

Dick's grin reminded him of a hyena with a toothache. William had turned his back. Gee, my luck to have Esther's brother in my rifle company. "Did you find a gal that liked your taste in stogies?"

"Yeah."

"Did Sarge say where we're going?" Red said.

Dick shrugged. "We'll know when we get there."

The truck came to a screeching halt. Rows of white tents gleamed in the early morning sunlight.

Dick whistled. "Where do you s'pose they found all those tents?"

"Okay, everyone, line up," someone ordered.

They piled out of the truck.

"You'll be assigned eight men per tent. First, step this way."

Eric walked with the soldiers to a trailer.

Dick frowned. "It's a delousing trailer."

"What's this white powder?" Red backed away, coughing.

William's face turned pale.

"You haven't lived till you've breathed that powder." Dick muttered. "Move, soldier."

Eric grimaced. "I'm beginning to understand what cattle feel like."

"Back on the ranch when we put the cattle through, we used an electric prod to move the slow ones." Red guffawed. "Good thing they're not from Oklahoma."

Dick removed his stogie and looked at the steaming showers. "What am I going to do with this?"

The man directing the soldiers to the next station grabbed the cigar and scrunched it beneath his boot.

"Hey, you know how long I had to wait to smoke that?"

"You want me to get my prod out?"

William held up a pair of pants. "Whose clothes are these?"

"What do you care? They're clean and mended."

Eric smiled, stepping into his clean clothes. For the first time in months, he didn't feel something crawling on him. His new outfit fit him better than the first set had. Now for the final test, the boots. Every infantryman depended on two things: his rifle and his boots. If they weren't the proper fit, well, you limped along in discomfort for miles. He looked at his old ones. The sole was worn through, the laces nearly gone. There was no way of salvaging them if these new ones gave him problems. He stood, walking back and forth. "Not bad. How do yours feel, Red?"

Red walked the length of the building. "Pretty good."

Eric's division gathered outside the tents. The rumble of bombers overhead had him and everyone else within hearing distance watching the huge planes lumber toward Cassino and the Abbey.

Captain Kimble walked forward. "The Allies and British Indians have left the mountain in defeat. The British Indians lost the ground we took. Here's what's going in the record book."

He unfolded a sheet of paper. "Though the Battle of Cassino proved a failure because the Division failed to take its objectives, yet for those who were there and who knew the difficulties—to those men, Cassino was the outstanding achievement in the Division's history."

The captain coughed. "In spite of the most rigorous air support, the British lost ground, which our troops gave to them. It is now a matter of record that successive attacks by troops several times as numerous as we also failed to capture the fortress. The Allied attack finally achieved its goal. No less than five divisions were required to finish the task that the 34th so gallantly began and so nearly completed." He looked up and saluted. "Good work, men. I can't tell ya how proud of you I am."

Chapter 26

*I*n the entranceway of her apartment building, Esther opened the door for Dot, then shook off the snow and retrieved the mail. She hugged the four letters to her tailored wool coat. "Dot, I got two letters from Eric and two from William." She turned to Dot and smiled. "See? They're all right."

Dot's hair fell to her shoulders in an assortment of tossed curls, framing her makeup-free face. Usually, Dot was a picture-perfect copy of the latest up-do and clothing fashions. Esther always kidded her that *Life* magazine could photograph her anytime and she'd look gorgeous and glamorous. Today, however, Dot looked like she'd just gotten up, her usual confident demeanor swept away like last spring's tulips.

Dot held up her letters. "I got three from William. I haven't heard from him in months. Do you suppose he is having second thoughts? I'm afraid to open them alone."

Esther hugged Dot. "Come on. Mother's back from the cleaners. We'll open them together."

Dot bolted up the stairs and into the apartment. They tossed their coats on the closest chair. Esther snapped on a lamp as she whispered a hurried prayer. "Mother, I'm back from work, and Dot's here."

"Dot, can you stay for supper?"

"I guess. Thank you, Mrs. Meir."

Esther looked down at the letters. Today, her boss had buzzed with the news about the fighting going on in Italy. Warning leaflets of the brutal battle had been dropped by shell on Sunday, February 13, to the local Italians from the Fifth Army, telling every Italian civilian to evacuate. That's part of Eric's and William's 34th Infantry Division. Valentine's Day had been worse. No news came through the wires.

A rapid knock on the door caused them to jump.

"Get the door, Esther," Ruby called from the kitchen. The noise of dishes clacking followed.

Esther opened the door to let in a tall woman dressed in overalls and wearing a bandana tied around her curly blonde hair. A little girl with Shirley Temple type blonde curls clutched the woman's hand.

"Rosie, so nice to see you."

Esther's mother entered the living room, wiping her hands on her apron. She hugged Rose and bent to speak to Betsy. "And what is your little dolly's name?"

Little Betsy's face lit up as she held out her hands, displaying her dolly, the mirror image of her.

"Mrs. Meir, sorry to bother you, but do you happen to have those alterations done to my dress?"

"Why, yes, I do. Would you like some coffee? I've just made a fresh pot. Dot, how about you?" Esther's mother walked toward the bedroom.

"Yes, just what I need. A good cup of joe."

"Well, help yourself to the coffee cake, too. I made it from a new recipe. It's probably better for us, with little sugar and less flour."

Dot's heels stamped a resounding pattern against the kitchen linoleum floor.

Esther bounced Betsy on her knee. "How about you, Rose?"

"No thank you, I need to get home. Betsy hasn't had her dinner."

Ruby returned, holding a black silk dress neatly ironed and hanging on a hanger wrapped in plastic. "Here it is."

"How much do I owe you?"

"Pay me when I get the rest of your dresses done."

"Daddy will be home tomorrow." Betsy hugged her dolly close.

Rose glanced at Esther. "He wrote he was injured somewhere near

France, when his plane got hit. I don't want him to see me in these. I'll sure be glad to put on a skirt again. But what else can a woman wear in the factory?"

"What do you do?"

"I do the riveting on the B-24s at the Willow Run plant." Rose nodded. "Yep, we turn them out one plane an hour. My sister on the West Coast says they're doing the same, only with their Liberty Boats. At least that's what they call them. She works for Kaiser Manufacturing. Sis says they don't look so pretty, nor ride so well, but they're getting the job done."

"Oh," Esther looked more closely at their visitor. "Have you seen that poster? Rosie the Riveter. Is that you?"

"Oh, that thing. No, that's not me."

"Just the same, I envy you. You're doing something for the war effort, for our men." Esther hugged her.

Rosie's sobs said what words could not. Her shoulders heaved with her silent tears. "If it'll mean my Roy…will get back to us…it's all worth it." She patted her eyes with her handkerchief. "Just pray. All us gals pray every morning that each plane built carries our flyboys safely home."

Esther choked back her tears as Betsy held up her dolly. "Her name is Betsy Lou."

Esther bent down. "What a pretty name. How old are you?"

"Five." She swayed back and forth. "Daddy sent me Betsy Lou. He made it to look like me from a photo mama sent him."

Esther cleared her throat. "Where is he stationed?"

"Someplace in England," Rosie said. "This will be the first leave he's had since he joined in '41. Oh, I pray it's not cancelled like the others."

Esther let Rosie and Betsy out and closed the door. "Mother, we've received four letters, two from Eric and two from William. Dot's got three. Let's pray first."

∽

U-boats. For as far as Eric could see from his position on the ship.

"March 23, 1944," Red muttered as he jotted the date down.

"Why are you writing that down, Red?" Dick asked.

"'Cause I'll forget if I don't. How do you spell, you know, that beachhead?"

"A-n-z-i-o. It's not that hard to spell." Dick fumbled with his knapsack. Eric frowned. That wasn't like Dick to get distraught over a little thing like spelling Anzio. Red wrote the word down on a piece of paper, then folded it eight ways, and tucked it in his chest pocket.

"It's a letter to my wife. I wrote her about that parade they had for General Clark that we participated in. She wants to know everything I do, so, well, just in case I don't get back, she can tell my son. My wife says she's not worried about me making it." Red looked down at his hands. "I haven't seen my son, and I can't help wondering what will happen to my wife and kid if I don't make it."

Eric patted him on the shoulder. "Your wife and son have a permanent place to live with her parents." Just the same, he was glad Esther didn't know how much he burned inside with love for her.

White caps skimmed across the green-blue turbulent sea. Eric didn't deserve Esther. That Italian girl's mama almost snared him into marrying her daughter. If Dick hadn't stepped in, she'd have gotten her way.

Dick wasn't just a veteran to the Army, he was a veteran to the wiles of desperate women. He'd taken Mama by the elbow and walked her up the cathedral steps and to the priest. She'd confessed the truth. Yes, a tearful mama had lied. Eric had done nothing to her daughter but give her a sweet kiss on the lips before falling asleep in an exhausted stupor.

Dick's hand shook violently. Though the wind coming off the ocean was cold, beads of perspiration dotted his forehead like water on a duck's back.

William noticed it too. The telltale sign of war fatigue. How had the medics missed the symptoms? Must have looked the other way.

Dick swabbed his hand across his brow. He looked out over the waters, his jaw clenching and unclenching as he gritted his teeth. "Me, Sarge, and Captain are the only ones I started with in '41. My luck has got to be playing out soon. I'm living a stacked deck."

Eric felt inside his pocket where he'd hidden his Bible and Esther's letters. He'd gotten mail from Ma, his sisters, and Esther. Ma had been ailing with a cold. He wished there was something he could do to help her. He'd received some prayer pamphlets from Ma, too.

Esther filled her letters with encouragement and hope. That gal has a way of making me grateful just to see the sky. He hadn't written anything that would tell her how much he loved her and didn't intend to anytime soon. Like Dick, he felt Esther was better off not knowing until when—and if—he returned home. Even Red, a family man to the core, wasn't sure what God had in store for him. William, on the other hand, was the type of guy God would keep safe.

The Cassino battle had made him face the sharp reality about the brevity of life in the infantry. The Bible says, I am but a mist that appears for a little while and then vanishes. If the Lord willed, he'd get home. He didn't want Esther to love him. Not until he returned.

He narrowed his eyes against the spray coming off the waves. He had regularly visited the Santa Maria della Valle and the other churches in the area with some of the guys. There were plenty to choose from, and the Archangel Michael was the village's patron saint. He figured that had to be worth something to keeping a guy alive. A snapshot of dismembered bodies littering the minefield flashed before him. He reached for his Bible. It was the only way to quench the horror. Sprays of salt water slapped his face. From memory he quoted John 5:24, "'He that heareth my word, and believeth on him that sent me, hath everlasting life…and has passed from death unto life.' Think of that, you sorry GI. Tommy made it first, but we're destined to be together."

"Okay, and that's supposed to make me feel better?" Dick said.

⁀⊘

Esther clutched Eric's letters and ran toward the kitchen. Dot hunched over the table, her head in her arms. Sobs shook her shoulders.

"What's wrong?" Esther asked, viewing the scene.

"There, there, dear," Ruby consoled. "William loves you. Don't fret your pretty little head about it."

"No. No. He doesn't love me, Mrs. Meir. William couldn't have written those things if he did."

Esther picked up the opened envelope. Then she looked at her envelope. "You read the last one William wrote first." Esther thumbed through Dot's letters. "Read this one. Mother, read yours."

Dot dried her eyes and read, smiling as she went. She looked up at Esther's mother.

"William is his usual kidder." Ruby smiled and continued to read.

Esther took a deep breath and opened Eric's more recent letter. She seesawed her teeth across her bottom lip as if trying to cut a groove. "Oh dear." Well, she'd expected as much. The grief Eric had held in for so many months spilled across the pages to her, communicated not so much in what he said as the words he used.

She struggled to make sense of his letter through the blacked-out portions and the innuendoes and unfinished sentences. Fear that the enemy might intercept the mail had resulted in censorship and a warning for servicemen to limit details of the battles. "Loose lips sink ships" was a phrase everyone knew by heart.

Eric's thirst for spiritual water was clear to Esther, and he needed nourishment to understand why so many good men had died and he'd been spared. For how long, he wasn't sure. He wrote:

I've been memorizing those Bible scriptures you write in your letters and have been reading my Bible every chance I get. But I still see my buddies' faces every time I fall asleep. Esther, I'll never take my freedoms for granted again. There has to be a reason why I was spared and men like Tommy died. Right now, the verse that keeps coming to my mind is the last one you wrote me. 'Greater love hath no man than this, that a man lay down his life for his friends.'

Dot dabbed at her eyes with her handkerchief. "I'm beginning to see what's wrong. William's afraid he's not going to make it. He's trying to…Well, it won't work, mister; you'll not get rid of me that easy."

Esther patted Dot's arm. William was as solid as the US Treasury.

When he told a woman he loved her, he did. "I know, Dot. At least he has confessed he loved you." The one thing missing in Eric's letter was the I-love-you part. The thing he desired from her right now was her prayers and Scriptures. "I'm not sure if Eric will ever tell me that he loves me."

"William has his misgivings about that, too." Mother handed William's letter to Esther.

Eric cut a memorable rug with a cute little Italian girl. She took him to meet her mama. Ha, ha, Eric's still the suave, debonair playboy who every woman loves to be with. Trouble here is that these Italian mamas are determined to get their daughters wed to some GI by any means they can, just to get them out of this hell hole Hitler has created. You can hardly blame them. But their tactics include getting the GI drunk with wine and not knowing what happened the night before.

She looked up. "I hope Eric has sense enough not to fall into that trap again."

"Again?" Dot looked up from the letter she was reading. "Let's hope that never happens to Eric again."

A knock at the door startled them.

"I'll get it." Ruby said, making her way to the door. Her mother's words filtered into the kitchen. "Why, Thomas Cutter, looks like you've got yourself some new stripes on those handsome shoulders of yours. Did you come here to brag?"

"No, ma'am. I came to see Esther. Think you could put in a good word for me? I'd like to take her to see a movie and grab a bite to eat before I ship out."

Esther had words of refusal on the tip of her tongue, but her mother spoke for her.

"I think I can arrange that."

Chapter 27

Eric walked through the debris washing up on Anzio's beach. He swatted at the flies buzzing in his face.

"This was a beautiful resort once." Sergeant Rusk's stogie poked a hole in his frowning mouth.

Eric walked farther up the beach where remnants of nightclub signs dangled from their hinges. Some of the buildings had gaping holes in their roofs.

"Look," William said. "Here come some Jerry fighter-bombers."

"Must be the welcoming party," Dick replied.

The planes wove through the clouds like a party of vultures looking for dessert. Three British attack planes rose to the challenge and put on a demonstration of a cockfight of skill and dexterity. The winner got to live. The planes shone like ebony against the crystal clearness of blue sky. However, that was not to last.

Gray-black smoke marked the sky like a newly dug grave as the German bomber plummeted out of control, screeching and bellowing smoke. The plane spun around and around like a tornado had a hold of its tail, then the plane was gone, swallowed into the dark sea.

A German bomber zigzagged through the smoke of the downed plane, gliding over the waters, its tail on fire, aiming for the beach and the GIs. An American gunner got a fix on him just as he reached the beach. The plane's bombs exploded into a colossal ball of fire, and billowing black smoke erupted. Eric and his buddies ran toward the

247

scene not more than twenty yards away. All that remained was a swatch of clothing and the plane's tail section.

Sarge removed his stogie and smacked his lips. "So much for our welcoming party. We'll wait here for dark before we hunker down in our foxhole. Make yourself comfortable in your new home, guys. We'll be here a while."

As midnight drew near, Eric ducked his head as the eerie Screaming Meemies sought another victim. Soldiers, bending low to the ground, gathered supplies and food, or relieved themselves. The terrain was the opposite of Cassino. Flat, like a farmer's field, the land stretched out ten miles at its widest point and no more than eight miles deep, crisscrossed with canals and drainage ditches.

Sarge pointed to the distant hills. They loomed over them like a prehistoric animal. "Any movement during the daytime will draw their fire. Find somewhere to hunker down, a canal, a ditch, or an abandoned foxhole."

Dick pointed to a ditch a few yards away. "Guys. Over here." The floor was muddy and sodden with roots and debris. Their foxhole backed up to another trench. "This'll work."

"Yeah? Well, everyone in that hole got hit by them bombs." The soldier from the next foxhole poked his rifle toward the hole. His face was so black with grit and dust from the bombs the only thing visible on him were his eyes and pink mouth.

"We'll chance it."

O'Brien, Eric, and William jumped in.

"But, Dick." Red's whiny voice carried across the quiet battlefield.

His face two inches from Red's, Dick retorted, "Don't feel I'll be offended if you don't like my accommodations."

The light from the rockets cast an eerie amber glow like a halo around Red's beard and hair.

"Lightning never strikes the same place twice. Relax."

Shells, one after another, lit the night sky. The rear Allied artillery fired back.

Red ducked and jumped in as dirt and debris from the bomb

sprayed him. "A guy could get killed in the crossfire."

Eric spotted movement across the sand straight ahead. "Twelve o'clock, can you see who it is?"

Another shell sang over their heads and landed fifty feet back.

"It's a Kraut," William said.

Eric took careful aim and fired. The man collapsed.

"The ground's crawling with them." William took aim and pulled the trigger.

Midnight rolled into three a.m.

"When does a man get to sleep around here?" Eric muttered.

"We don't," a disembodied voice whispered from a nearby foxhole. "We keep firing, covering our heads, and pray."

"You think it's bad here. Try the hospital to the rear," a man in a foxhole to the left of them whispered. "That place's a morgue. I know, I was there. See the way those shells are going over our heads? Well, they often hit dead center back yonder trying to blow up our supply depot."

A rebuttal shot came from their rear. A blast that had proven too short sent mud spilling over Eric. He ducked, then looked up to see who got hit. "That's from our side."

The torturous, agonizing hours wore on. The rocket artillery lit the night with an eerie light. It was kill before being killed here.

"When does a soldier get to relieve himself?" Red whispered.

"Over to the east in that clump of trees, only, don't do it too often," a GI said. "Your chance of getting killed with your pants down is greater."

Another GI popped up from his hole like a groundhog. "Or," cupping his hands around his mouth he whispered loud enough to hear, "if you're too much of a scaredy-cat, you live with the stench." He pointed to a couple of lieutenants who had never been seen venturing from their foxholes.

Eric started to climb out, but William pulled him back.

"Be smart. They still outrank us, even if they're not as gutsy as us."

"Gee, William, I just wanted to make sure I could recognize them."

"You will, by their smell."

Days and nights melted into a month. During the day, flies buzzed in swarms around the corpses, their incessant wings landing on the dead and the living. Eric slapped a blue jacket buzzing at his face. Soon, three more joined the first, landing on his legs, shoulders, and hand. Eric whipped the air with his arms furiously, then crumbled in a heap in his hole, exhausted. He couldn't fight the pests any longer.

Bombs and artillery kept them up at night, and the flies pestered them during the day. The weeks were taking their toll on him. His nerves felt like bits of raw meat. The sunlight boiled his skin, and the moon chilled him to the bone at night. And then there was the rain.

He couldn't sleep, and when he did, he'd wake shivering from his nightmares. William and he were guarded with the letters they wrote and the ones they received. Eric glanced over at him now.

William's face was back to being that pasty white color, his eyes sunken, and his friend stared blankly back at him before returning to his scrap of paper. *Was he saying something about me?* Eric looked away. *What did it matter? What could he write Esther? Not about Anzio. He didn't know if he'd survive another hour. It'd be easier just to…quit. If Esther knew what he'd done, the men he'd killed. What kind of love could he give her? What kind of man would he be after the war? Pa's right, he'd never amount to much. Yeah, his brother John was the winner. He made it as a flyboy. All Eric was good at was dancing and flirting. He's a playboy trying to pretend he's someone—*

"Hey, sir?"

Eric looked up at a soldier, no older than his kid brother and nodded.

"Is the 168th up ahead?"

"Yeah, but climb in here. You won't make it. The Jerries will gun you down. Come on, we've got some room to spare."

"No, sir. My orders are to report today."

"Well, it'll be dark by nine. That'll make it still today. Get yourself in here."

"No, sir, I've got to obey my orders." He walked forward.

"Private," William yelled, "get back here."

The kid turned. A cocky grin sweeping his smooth face.

"That gutsy kid will make it. Good for you, kid. Is there anything impossible for youth?" William slumped down in his hole. "I felt like that once."

The rat-a-tat sound of a machine gun went off. William jumped up. Eric grimaced as the young private fell forward, his body jumping from the bullets hitting him.

"Those sorry Krauts and their machine guns. Don't they ever stop watching us? We're pinned in here like rats," William said. A Screaming Meemie shot over their heads. "There they go again, those rockets. They're—" William covered his ears. "Like, like, banshees, demonic."

Eric glanced to a foxhole where some long-time veterans sat slouched down like beaten, whimpering mutts. Even seasoned soldiers were having a tough time. The constant bombardment, the noise, and blaring light of the explosions made sleep impossible. Succumbing to exhaustion was the only way a soldier found rest. GIs that didn't get hit got the aftermath of flying dirt, shrapnel and worse—airborne helmets, boots, pieces of clothing. And body parts. Dick's teeth started to chatter.

Dick's shaking had grown worse. He refused to go to the hospital. He had trouble drinking from his canteen—even holding a spoon. Eric and William took turns holding his canteen and lifting his spoon to his lips.

Somewhere between the kid dying and dusk, Eric slept. The noise from the rocket artillery woke him. Some men in a nearby foxhole spoke in hushed whispers. Their conversation rose to hallucinating screams, jabbing his heart like an ice pick. The low-lying heavy clouds hid the moon and stars from view. The night sky was as dark as pitch.

"Stop." Someone yelled. "Make them stop. I can't stand it any longer. I tell you I can't."

William woke with a start. He'd appointed himself the designated comedian, their GI psychologist who channeled the men's thoughts into acceptable avenues of distraction. "Look, dinner time," William yelled. "What do you think's in the pot today, possum or muskrat?"

Another soldier picked up where William left off. "I saw a skunk a while back." A group of GIs laughed. The two men stopped their screaming. "Here come the mules." The daily provisions of food, ammo, and letters had arrived. That is, if you could catch the four-footed delivery animals. Eric stretched out his hands for their canteens, while watching the progress of their four-legged waiter in the distance. He grinned back into the sweating faces of the men in his trench, then turned and clucked at the mule. "Here boy, no, not that way. That mule must be part jackass."

The men laughed.

"Where'd he go?" A rocket flew overhead. With one lunge, Eric jumped into a neighboring foxhole, then jumped back out and ran toward the mule who'd taken an alternate route. He hadn't eaten anything all day. He wasn't about to let that mule get away. "Easy, good boy."

Halting the mule, he looked down into the scared eyes of the crouching quartermaster. "I thought the mule was on its own tonight."

"Here," the quartermaster said, reaching for his mail pouch. "See if you can find the men these letters belong to."

Eric busied himself with pouring soup into their canteens, and then reached for a pack of bread and ammo. He layered his shoulders with the supplies, then flattened himself as another rocket screamed overhead. "So now I'm the mailman?"

The quartermaster shuddered. "Everyone I found was dead. You're the only one I've seen crawling out your hole this week. Good luck."

Explosions lit the sky one after another, forcing Eric to belly back to his hole, feeling more like a mole than a man.

After eating his lukewarm soup, Eric passed the letters around the best he could, tossing them into the various foxholes. Some of the men were dead. Those letters came back to him, and he carefully pocketed them to return to headquarters. He sat down to read his. At least the bombs gave him enough light to read. He tore open the letter from Esther first.

"Eric, I want you to know that I love you with the love of our Savior, Jesus Christ. I always shall. This Bible passage came to me while I was praying for you and your regiment this morning. I felt that God wanted for you to—"

"Duck, you sorry GI that one is heading—"

The quing quang noise of the shell split through the soldier's words. This is mine. It's got my number on it. Eric fell face down, covered his head, and waited for death to come. He peeked out. The bomb had missed the men in the foxhole behind him, too. It had spiraled into a dirt mound. One of the guys wiped his forehead, then held up his hands clasped together, the code between the Red Bulls of being too close for comfort and victory.

Huh! Guess God's not done with me. Eric sat back up and read. "'For I am persuaded, that neither death, nor life, nor angels, nor principalities, nor powers, nor things present, nor things to come…shall be able to separate us from the love of God, which is in Christ Jesus our Lord.' Not even the valley of death can harm you, a child of God. Death is only a shadow for a Christian. A shadow can't harm you. If you should leave me, Eric, we'll meet again in a better world than this one."

William crawled over. "What happened? Bad news from home?"

Eric handed him the letter.

William read the words and sat back, resting his head and shoulders on their dirt walls. His Adam's apple jerked up and down his throat. They both laughed. William slapped Eric's back, then wiped at his eyes, "You got yourself a winner and good luck in winning any battles with her in the future. How did she know?"

Eric shook his head. "I never wrote her how bad it is." He sniffed. "I can't believe I read that last line after I thought that shell had my name on it."

William nodded. They didn't speak. Both knew the words of Romans 8:38 and 39 had brought them back from the precipice of self-destruction.

Sarge jumped into their foxhole. "The shells have relocated. Our lines are down. We need to tell headquarters they've shifted their points of delivery. Eric, you're the best runner I have. I've got a list of casualty figures and points of artillery fire."

"Back to headquarters?"

"Yep." Sarge looked around, then down.

Something was eating him.

"Look, you need to take someone with you. If you don't make it, well, it's imperative this paper gets to the major general. A lot more lives than yours—"

"I'll volunteer, Sarge," William said.

"No," Eric hissed. "You want to get killed?"

"No more than you do," William whispered. He reached for the men's empty canteens. "I'll fill them up. What are you gentlemen's requests? Milk, more soup, what?"

"How about a fifth of Scotch or red berry wine?" Red said.

"Forget it. The brass confiscated it all for themselves." Sarge wrote down a few more changes he'd calculated and handed the paper to Eric. "Godspeed to you both," Sarge said and scurried back to his hole.

"Watch out for the foxholes." Eric said. "We don't need to break a leg." The plan was to wait for a shell to explode, then bolt like a scared deer before the next bomb came. They waited. The skies lit up like the Fourth of July, enabling Eric and William to map out the best course to the rear line.

"Eric, William, be careful," Dick said.

Eric nodded, jumped out of the hole, and sped away like he was running a touchdown for his high school football team. He dodged the holes with William as his linebacker. With heads down, they ran as if their lives depended on this mission.

Men in the foxholes cheered them on. Eric knew he'd never forget the moment. What a way to go. They reached the end with seconds to spare. A shell rippled through the night sky, its devilish scream silencing the cheers of the men.

Eric and William knelt down, arms resting on their shaking legs, and sucked in air like half-drowned swimmers. Then they prayed, giving over their heartfelt thanks to an ever-watchful God. Walking down the line of tents, they found the general's and then waited for their turn.

"What have you got here?" the major general asked.

Eric saluted and handed the general the paper Sergeant Rusk had given him.

"Good. We'll take care of it from this end."

The dirt roads were crammed with supply trucks attempting to get out beneath the cover of night. German artillery lit the sky. They ran behind a tree for cover.

William motioned for Eric to follow him to the mess tent. "Come on, they've got to have more food than our little mule can carry, and let's pick up some carrots."

Eric looked at him like he'd lost his mind. "You didn't chase that mule half a football field like I did. What do you think this is, a delicatessen?"

"Well, we need to put in our requests for Easter dinner. I prefer ham. What about you?"

"Anything but liver."

Chapter 28

April 10, 1944

The Detroit USO was busting its seams with men in starch white, forest green, and royal blue uniforms with shiny brass buttons. Just about every branch of service was parading around the dance floor. Men on crutches, some with bandages on their arms, and even a few with bandages swathing their handsome heads like Thomas Cutter.

Esther had to hand it to Thomas; he was quick on his feet and could dance the fox trot, polka, and the waltz divinely. She enjoyed his soft drawl of her beloved South, but try as she might, she could not feel the slightest affection for him. Whenever she saw a man with a mustache dressed in his Army dress uniform she immediately thought of Eric. Oh, Eric wrote her, and he always started his letters with "Hello Honey." He even sent her some Stars & Stripes stationary from Italy as a souvenir. He was pleased to learn she went to church for Easter with his mom. He'd written back to her saying, "Hope you liked it...keep praying...if you talk to Mom don't tell her anything that might make her worry..."

Is he writing that Italian girl he met? That thought had entered her mind once too often.

In one letter Eric wrote: "I try to picture the way it might be when I come home. I do a lot of dreaming about you, no lie." Was he remembering that night so long ago when he'd gone AWOL to meet her at the gazebo before shipping out?

He always asked her about her health, how she felt, and how her mother was doing. Very little about his present circumstances. He talked most about the weather. She felt like writing back, "We have weather here; what about us? Whether we will be together, or whether we should move on after the war?"

Eric had written in his last letter, "I keep praying and hoping it'll turn out right, honey—it's our whole life and there can't be any mistakes…" He'd ended his letter with, "Love & Kisses…" That's a common valediction for—

"Esther, you are absolutely the loveliest girl here." Thomas Cutter's eyes sparkled into her's. His arm pulled her closer as he lowered his head toward her. She turned. His kiss landed on her cheek.

The waltz faded to a close. He continued to hold her tight, as if she belonged to him, like the star-struck lovers smooching along the wall there.

They were practically the last couple to leave the dance floor. Except for that couple kissing each other a few feet away. Thomas glanced over at them and bent his head closer. "Why," he said in his infectious southern drawl, "I believe you're prettier than the girls I knew in Tennessee. You want to come away with me—"

"Why, sir. Little o' me? What are your intentions?" she said in her best drawl.

But he wasn't joking this time. He's been polite, genteel, and had gone out of his way to make last Christmas special for her and Mother.

Mother liked him. She thought him a favorable and suitable partner for her. Mother told her to weigh her decision. After all, Thomas was handsome, and he definitely liked her and didn't hide his feelings about that. Most of all, Mother said, he was the dependable type.

"I've rented a car. I could take you for a drive along the Detroit River? The lights are beautiful on the water this time of night. And, to our advantage, there's a full moon out tonight." He pulled her closer. His hot breath tickled her cheek.

She smiled and gently pushed against his chest. Dependable, yeap. He expects it's payday time for all his presents and gentlemanly manners. "I need to freshen up a bit before we leave." She started to walk away, turned and clicked her fingers. "Oh, foolish of me. I forgot to ask you." She played her fingernails on her lips. "Is it okay if I ask Dot? I'm sure she'd love to see the river in the moonlight, too."

"What? I was thinking of something more intimate."

The other soldiers saw the makings of a good jab. "Hey, soldier, you in need of a cold shower?"

"Maybe that bang on the head knocked something loose inside."

"I don't think he's thinking much about his head right about now."

More heehaws, and a red-faced Thomas stomped off the dance floor to their table.

Her heels clicked against the linoleum floor. Memories haunted her with every step. Why were Eric's flirtatious innuendos always humorous and tantalizingly enjoyable? He would have handled that kidding graciously and managed to kid them back with equal banter.

Why hadn't their relationship blossomed into more than a friendship? She hadn't wanted to like Eric further than friend-brother relationship, yet, hard as she could, hard as she tried not to—she'd fallen in love with him. Why?

Amidst his letters telling her about his hospital stays for jaundice, pneumonia, and deprivation, he acted like it was a great time seeing all the pretty nurses! The lack of water during the summer months, the lack of warm clothing during the winter months, all he'd write was "I could use a good hot shower to take the chill off." Eric sent humor and a good-natured assessment of the plight of him and his buddies. Only when a close buddy died would he allow her into his nightmarish world and hint of his grief. Oh, she'd almost forgotten that Italian girl.

But Thomas had had his own narrow escapes. His plane had been shot down twice, and luckily, he was rescued before a Japanese submarine captured them up in their little life raft. Thomas was recuperating from a bad slash on the head from his last narrow escape. He should be reporting back to duty soon.

He had had a hard time of it. He'd get the shakes whenever he overheard one of the soldiers talking about getting wounded, or their plane getting hit. He'd gone through some agonizing days before he was rescued in the Pacific by the Navy. She shivered recalling his narration of all the terrible details of the battle and later the ordeal of bobbing in that little raft assaulted by the sharks. He was the complete opposite of Eric. Thomas never spared her the morbid details of war. He'd confided in her that he didn't have any desire to rejoin his regiment.

The upside was, he'd made the Air Corps when Eric couldn't, and Thomas never spared words telling her how much he adored her.

Those same adoring words seemed to get stuck in Eric's jugular. Esther opened the powder room door. Yes, she would try harder to fall in love with Thomas.

"Oh, here's the girl of the century. You dumpin' Eric for Thomas?" Sally said. "Or stringing both along 'til you decide which will make the most money—or have all his body parts after the war?"

"Red doesn't suit you, Sally girl. It just makes you look real desperate." Dot said, looking up from applying her fuchsia-luscious lipstick. "Keep those jealous fangs hidden, sweetheart, before word gets out. There are plenty of men out there for the picking. No GI wants to get close to a sour grape!"

Esther didn't care what Sally thought of her. She grasped Dot by the arm and pulled her toward the entranceway, the only place quiet enough where they could talk and hear each other. "Dot, you want to go for a ride with Thomas and me to see the Detroit River?"

"Hmm, when are you going to spring it on him that your heart belongs to a man who loves making mud pies?"

"Eric? He's a flirt, stubborn as a mule, obstinate as a billy goat! Why would I pine over someone like him when I have a handsome pilot that adores me and gives me nice presents and takes me places?"

"You trying to tell me you don't love Eric? Well, I'm not convinced."

Esther took a deep breath. "The last thing a woman needs to do is to make a decision with her heart."

"Really? I'm all ears."

"Well, it's like this. I like the southern climate, I have relatives in Kentucky, and doesn't it seem more practical to think of liking a guy from the vicinity more to my liking?" It sounded so practical. Then why, God, am I having such a hard time with this?

"I have one question, and then I'll back off with the advice." Dot walked forward. Her heels echoed in the foyer, and a chilling draft wafted through a small crack in the door frame. "Why, when I talk to so many soldiers with missing body parts and wrapped up limbs who are chomping on the bit to get back into the fighting to help their buddies out, is Thomas Cutter willing to wait on the sidelines. He's not in a hurry, Esther, to get back in the fight. You really want a guy who hightails it for green pastures?"

Esther bit down on her lip. "Well, wouldn't you? Maybe he's the only sensible one here." Still, that was something she wondered about too. Maybe it was just his love for her that kept him not wanting to rejoin his unit. Or was she the excuse he was using to deceive himself?

Chapter 29

Easter came and went. Eric checked off the days from the calendar he had made.

"Come on, you sorry GIs." A smile plastered across Sarge's stubby chin. "Brass is tired of sitting. Says it's time to kick some you-know-what. We've been attached to the 1st Armored Division. We plan to mow those Krauts over and then move onto Rome."

"Well, you'd think after two months of fighting in those foxholes, we could get a little R and R." Red kicked the dirt on the road.

"After two months of flying shells and bullets, I'd think you'd be glad to feel your feet beneath you again. I'm glad it stopped raining." William matched Eric stride for stride. "The countryside is pretty, what with that green grass and the smell of spring."

"Yeah, well, this ain't no May-day hike through the woods. Keep your eyes open and look for snipers," Sarge grumbled.

"What's that rumbling I hear, Sarge?" Dick perked up. "It can't be a train. I know the feeling all too well. I was a conductor before the war."

"Eric, do you hear a rumbling noise?" William asked.

Eric nodded.

William looked down.

"It don't feel right." Dick's left shoulder twitched.

"Well, maybe Jerry's brought a herd of elephants in to help beat us." William placed his hand on Dick's shoulders and rubbed.

Sarge shook his head. "Don't you GIs remember your training? We

263

talked about Slim Bertha, the Germans' 28 cm Railway Gun."

"The one with the barrel seventy feet long? I thought you were kidding." Red's mouth dropped open. "There ain't no way."

"Hear that?" Eric shouldered his gun. Budding trees and flowering bushes chocked with underbrush not more than ten yards from the road made a great camouflage for bushwhackers.

Sarge stepped up his pace, and Eric jogged up next to him.

"Now, let's see, the maximum range is 68,240 yards."

Eric bent over, winded from his jog. "Or thirty-eight miles."

Red turned around. "Hey, how did ya figure that so fast?"

"I'm an engineer. It's my business to know."

The sergeant shook his head. "I'm surprised you're not in the Engineering Corps. How did you get to be a doughboy, Eric?"

"They needed reinforcements. You want credentials? William has a bachelor's in finance."

The ground rumbled beneath Eric's feet.

"Snipers, three o'clock."

Eric, Red, and William dove behind a tree to the right, Sarge and Dick ran on ahead, taking cover in a stand of young evergreens. The tops of their helmets stuck just above the crowns of the trees. Trees better suited for adornment with candles and popcorn garlands than with helmets.

The dirt road that seconds ago had over two hundred foot soldiers tramping its ruts flat was empty. Eric held his breath. For a minute, he thought an earthquake had caused the tremble he'd felt from his toes to the top of his head. Peering through the hazy half-light of the setting sun, he saw the reason.

Red whistled. "I see it, but I don't believe it."

Eric rubbed his eyes. That's a gun? A troop of German soldiers walked before the biggest gun he'd ever seen, laying down the track as other soldiers walked alongside.

William blinked. "Gee whiz, it's big enough to straddle like a horse."

A monster of a 28 cm Railway Gun lumbered down the track like some circus elephant, mulching to pieces anything stupid enough to get in its way. German SS troops looked into the woods, firing at anything that moved.

"Just how are we going to get out of this one?" Red muttered.

"With dexterity." Eric took careful aim with his rifle, then fired three shots, knocking off a German with each. He then inched his way toward the rear of the big gun. Even a monster this size had to have an end. He watched as the metal terror, better known as "Anzio Annie" took her slow time down the rails, seemingly in no hurry to vacate the area.

Red and Dick followed, knocking off two more Germans, retreating behind their cover of trees and brush.

More SS troops appeared farther down the trail, their rifle shots exploding around them. Eric and William ducked into cover behind a clump of trees. A groan came from Eric's right.

Eric turned. "Dick?" Dick rolled on the ground, holding his left leg.

Eric looked around. "Anyone see the medic?" Bullets whizzed about them. The big boom of Anzio Annie shook the ground like an earthquake. He clasped a sulfa packet and sprinkled the powder on the gaping hole in Dick's leg. Unbuckling his belt, he ripped the canvas strap from around his waist and tied a tourniquet above the wound. The crusty Irishman knelt beside him.

"O'Brien, I'm going to take Dick to a medic."

O'Brien nodded and picked his way to the front with his bazooka and Bob carrying his shells.

Red joined Eric. "You can't go back—it's worse there. And they might have bombed the hospital." Red looked down at Dick. "Is he unconscious or—" He shook his head and bent lower, listening for a heartbeat. "He's alive."

Eric got up from his knees and crouched over his wounded friend.

"Don't be a fool! Dick wouldn't want you to try it. You know what the odds are of you getting back alive?"

"Pretty good." Eric grinned. "It's dark enough, and I'm fast enough on my feet to give these Jerries a good run." He patted Red's shoulder. "I'll try and take a couple down with me."

"You got a date with death?"

"Watch Dick a minute." Eric checked out the terrain, spotted a sniper and shot off two more bullets, and hurried toward his friends.

He poked Dick awake. "Can you walk, Dick?"

Dick started to tremble. Convulsions shook his body.

Red helped Dick up and heaved him across Eric's shoulders. "I'll cover you."

Walking farther into the woods, Eric made a diagonal turn and a beeline toward the medic's tent. At least, where he thought the tent would be. He almost tripped over a tree root and had to stop several times to catch his breath. He murmured encouragement to Dick, who lay across his back like a sack of potatoes. Only heavier and more valuable.

∾

"Lay him down here, soldier." The doctor cut Dick's trouser leg.

Dick mumbled. "What do you think you're doin'?" Then he fainted.

"He's lost a lot of blood." The junior medic, a youngster not as old as Eric, peered over his shoulder. Heavy dark rings circled the young man's eyes. His ashen complexion and gaunt cheeks told the infantry story—too much work, too much fear, and not enough food or sleep.

The doctor examined Dick's grazed forehead and the wound on his left arm. Then turned his attention back to the bullet wound that still seeped blood.

"He's going to make it, right, Doc?" The big guy looked so helpless. Eric swallowed hard. Flashbacks of that river crossing, the hut. He looked away.

"He'll make it."

"His leg?"

"He'll keep it."

"I'd better get back."

"Wait."

Eric paused in the door of the tent and looked back at Dick fighting between unconsciousness and life.

"Look." The doctor sent him a kind glance. "Grab a cup of joe."

He might as well ask him to commit hari-kari. "Doc, my buddies are dying out there. They need every man that can carry a rifle."

"What can one GI do? Or do you have a plan the brass overlooked?"

"A plan? Yeah." Eric greeted the doc's penetrating gaze with one of his own. "We'll derail the beast one track at a time. And send Jerry running back to Germany with that contraption up—"

"I've got the picture, soldier." The doctor smiled. "I wouldn't want to move these sick men again."

A nurse walked over to sponge the blood from Dick's arm and leg. The rumble of a half dozen tanks filtered through the tent flap. Eric stepped out. The half-track vehicles with their 105-millimeter howitzers rolled up.

A first lieutenant ran up to Eric. "You know how to get up that hill and through that brush to Anzio Annie?"

Eric saluted. "Yes, sir, I do."

"Okay, soldier, wait here."

Eric turned to the doctor. "Doc, you won't have to move anyone, because we're going to stop Anzio Annie dead in her tracks."

The doctor returned to the operating table, glanced at the nurse and smiled. "And Japan didn't think our fun-loving boys could fight, huh?"

"Playboys," Dick muttered.

The dark-haired nurse with the pretty smile patted Dick on his good shoulder. "Yes, soldier, now you rest."

"Yeah, Toots, a bunch of playboys out to lick the Krauts."

The doctor joined Eric outside and lit a cigarette. "Waiting for the anesthetic to take over before I operate."

The gathering tanks bunched together like cattle waiting for their trail boss. Doc whistled low. "Dear God, help our boys save the world from a mad man."

Eric saluted sharply. "Yes, sir. He is." Eric jogged alongside the tanks, waved his rifle in the air, and led them up the trail he'd run through not an hour before.

Chapter 30

The dust the caissons stirred up made it hard to see. Coughing because of the fumes and dust, Eric ran to catch up to Red and Captain Kimble. The roar of engines from the artillery trucks echoed like a ragged drumbeat in his ears.

Red's facial hair, a cobweb of dust and debris, demonstrated his exhaustion and complete abandonment of the rules. His frustration showed in the irate tone of his voice, which carried over the rumble of moving machinery. "Hey, Captain Kimble, why are they gettin' to Rome before us?"

"Orders. We're gonna swing around this perimeter and take out German snipers."

"We already did the hard job of disarming Anzio Annie and got those Krauts running scared. Where's our rights?" Eric said.

"Yeah." O'Brien took a drink out of his canteen, poured water in the palm of his hand, and wiped his eyes. "They'll get all the lassies before we get there."

Kimble guffawed. "Lassies is it now? You all better get your attention on those woods over yonder."

Like a pit bull with a bone, Red countered. "But, Captain, we fought the battle and those guys are gettin' the glory."

A GI popped his head up from the top of his tank and laughed. "See ya in Rome."

Kimble frowned.

The man paled, saluted, and like a rabbit in its hole popped back into his tank.

Kimble's broad shoulders swept a circle as he pointed to the trees, shrubs, and underbrush lining the road. "Spread out, men, and stay alert. There's probably a dozen snipers waiting to nail us. The war's not over yet."

Eric stepped up his walk, hurrying past Red. "Captain, sir. You were saying something about it being almost over. Do you mean Rome or the war?"

"What day is it?"

"June 6."

"Remember it. It'll be something that goes down in the history books for your future children to read about."

Eric walked stride for stride with the captain. "Because of Rome?"

"That's part of it. A big D-Day invasion of Normandy is happening this minute. The Allies are going to hit the enemy by surprise. They couldn't have done it without our help. We kept half the Jerries busy defending Italy. France is ready for the taking. Remember that. My hat's off to you boys for not giving up." He patted Eric's shoulder. "I've been blessed having a good shooter like you in my outfit."

Captain Kimble smiled. He looked up the road and back to a grassy knoll where a tree with a wooden seat constructed around the trunk gave an inviting recline. "Say, you GIs hungry? I'm gettin' real tired of eatin' their dust. We'll stop here and let it settle."

"Well, my stomach thinks a Nazi's slit my throat." Red plopped down on the grass and searched his pack, pulling out a C-ration.

"Captain sat on the wooden bench, took his helmet off, and wiped his face. "Tomorrow I'm plannin' to sleep in a real bed with clean, sweet-smelling sheets."

"You mean you don't want to bed down on Mother Earth?" muttered First Lieutenant Russell, who sat to the Captain's right. "I think these Italian ants and spiders are going to miss us. But they've left enough marks on my skin to last me for months."

Eric plopped down on the sweet-smelling clover, resting his back on an apple tree, one of many dotting the orchard behind. The tree had a few blossoms left and the scent of the fragrant flowers lingered. A peace he'd not known for a time enveloped him as he thought about the war's end. It was hard to believe—

Bam! The twang of a sniper's bullet split into his reverie. Eric slammed his face into the grass as he hit the ground, tasting stale dirt and spit. His lunch flew across the lane and landed in a puff in front of him.

Captain Kimble tumbled forward, his head—

"No!" Eric reached his beloved captain first and reverently laid him down in the dusty road. A bullet whizzed past him. Eric dove, flattening out like a pancake on a griddle. Using his elbows, he dragged his body behind a tree. Dust clogged his throat, but he managed to choke out the words, "He's mine."

Bending low, he ran toward the gnarled apple trees. A shot zinged past his shoulder. He huddled closer to the wrinkled trunk, his eyes squinting into the half-darkness of the forest. The taller forms of pines and elms stood like silent sentries against a cloud-tossed sky. Aged trees cast ominous shadows where night reigned. Were there ten or just a handful of Germans waiting for him in there? He slithered across the uneven ground, his nostrils absorbing the aroma of last autumn's leaves and this year's foliage. A mist of gun smoke floated in the air.

A glint of steel touched by a ray of sunlight glistened between the brown tree trunks to his left. He took careful aim. His shot echoed amongst the trees.

"Ahhh…" A German thumped to the ground. Eric stood. A noise near his elbow. He turned. His ears rang from his first shot. God, help me. Was that noise a German or one of my buddies? His trigger finger shook.

"Hello," a heavy-accented voice said.

"Name your division," Eric panted. "Answer me." Shaking as if he'd stepped out of the Atlantic in February, he yelled. "Answer me. Or I'll shoot your sorry head off the way you did my captain's."

A noise rustled the dried leaves. He turned and fired. An SS trooper dropped from behind a tree. He squinted as shadows from tree branches floated in the summer breeze. What's that? A shot zinged past his left ear. Another followed.

He fired. A groan, then silence. Eric blinked away the sweat rolling down his forehead. His heart raced like a freight train out of control. Someone grabbed his shoulder. He spun. The butt of his rifle aimed, ready to slam into a German's face.

"Hold up; it's me, William."

"William." Eric dropped to his knees. "I think—I think I nailed three."

"I got the one that said 'Hello.' Come on, let's get out of here."

Eric nodded, stumbling over his feet as much as the roots and debris littering the ground. "The captain? You saw?"

William nodded. "I was across the street from him."

"Let's get out of here."

"Yeah, it's time."

❦

The week that followed blurred before Eric's mind. He knew it did with the other soldiers in his division. He munched on his rations haphazardly. Lieutenant Russell walked up. "Follow me." They made their way to a tent that some of the brass occupied.

Eric saluted sharply.

"Corporal Erhardt, you have two decisions to make," Russell said. "You've got a chance to leave the 5th and go to the new Engineering Corps."

Taken by surprise, Eric blurted, "But I'd be letting my buddies down. We're a team."

The Lieutenant's voice gentled and his steel-hard gaze softened. "You have a chance to serve your country in a larger capacity. Brass needs a knowledgeable engineer to study aerial photos and mark the mines on a map so we won't send our troops blindly into a minefield. A lot of work has gone into this. You'll be a part in that, Eric. You could save thousands of soldiers from being dismembered—or killed— accepting this promotion. I told them if anyone knew what was at stake, you did.

"This leads me to your second choice." Russell patted him on the shoulder. "I decided, and it has been unanimously accepted by the men of our division that they want you as their next captain."

"You mean, take Captain Kimble's spot?"

Russell nodded.

"Sir, I could never fill Captain's Kimble's shoes." Eric looked away. "If it is all the same to you, I'll take the Engineering position. But what about William? Sir, he has a degree in accounting. Is he coming?"

Russell's brows puckered. He ran a thumb and forefinger across his whiskered chin. "William—is his last name Meir? He's been assigned to another department, too."

Chapter 31

Esther strolled down the sidewalk near the Detroit River, Dot at her side. The humbugs and snide comments about the latest accomplishments of the Allied Forces overseas cascaded into car horns and human exclamations with a rumble that resembled thunder.

She absorbed the scene of shop owners running into the streets and slapping passersby on the back. Even Dot, who had been quiet for weeks, was in high spirits.

Her friend's powder-blue perfectly tailored suit fit her tiny waist like a lady's opera glove. Pinned-up auburn tresses on either side of her oval face and a layer of rouge with matching red fingernail polish decorated her attributes fashionably. But now there was a glow to her countenance that wasn't present a year ago.

Esther couldn't understand why she wasn't glowing. Her nerves resembled butterflies banging in her stomach. Eric, do you truly love me? Don't string me along like a puppy on your leash.

Dot's mouth tipped in a Mona Lisa smile. "Isn't it exciting?" She slapped the front page of the newspaper. "I still can't believe it. 'Normandy's D-Day Invasion tremendous success.' The war should soon be over." Dot touched Esther's arm. "What's up with you today?"

"Nothing. I was more interested in the exploits of Eric's and William's infantry unit."

"Oh, me too. I wish General Clark could have had more coverage, not just that little picture of him beneath that big picture of the Normandy Invasion."

"That reporter didn't do General Clark justice, placing the General's entrance riding into Rome in a jeep in the lower corner of the page. How did he title it? Something about being victorious, like a modern-day Caesar? And those soldiers looked...Why weren't they cheering like the soldiers in France?"

Dot wrapped Esther's arm within hers. "Oh, you worry too much. You always read trouble into everything. Relax and enjoy the moment. Just think, William and Eric will be home soon." Dot stopped and placed her free hand to her heart, her voice anxious. "Now that those prisoners of Germany's concentration camps are liberated, I can witness to my Jewish friends about the saving grace of Jesus."

Esther patted her hand. "God will use you to reach your Jewish friends. Without Christ's love, how can anybody face the atrocities this war caused?"

"Our infantrymen who liberated the camps couldn't believe their eyes. GIs are used to seeing maimed bodies, but our soldiers vomited when they saw the gashed eyes, the disjointed limbs, and skeleton-like bodies of those half-dead Jewish people. Some of the prisoners they couldn't save; they died in their arms."

What had Eric seen? Been through? Esther's thoughts weighed her heart. "I read our soldiers made the villagers dig the graves."

Dot's brows drew close. Her happy outlook turned topsy-turvy. "Did the German people know how bad it was and do nothing?"

Esther wished the words weren't true, but intelligence said that facts were facts. She dragged in a ragged breath. "Some civilians were brainwashed into believing the undesirables of society needed to be punished. But other German and French civilians did brave exploits and fought against the Gestapo evils, oftentimes landing in the concentration camp themselves. And I think some Germans were too afraid of the Gestapo to try and stop Hitler's atrocities."

"You think William and Eric will be different?" Dot removed her arm from Esther's and wrung her hands. "I mean, you hear so many horror stories about shell-shock and how some men change emotionally. After all, they took human lives."

Her words sent a pang to Esther's heart. She had the same concerns, and now to hear Dot speak them aloud made them seem true. In Eric's last letter to her he'd written:

The war might be over for some in the States but it's all over but the fighting here, honey...I don't want to go home and have to come back...

What had he meant? Her gaze flitted from her friend to the river. "You know, they wanted to make Eric captain after—

"I know, William wrote me."

"Now that Eric's an engineer at Lake Como, his letters should become brighter." "

God cares. He cares so much about us to send His Son to save us from Satan. For Eric to find William at the battle of Cassino, William said that the Holy Spirit had to have guided Eric. God is capable of carrying them through their bad war memories, too."

I wish that was all that was bothering me. Esther turned, surveying her friend. "William's the rock of Gibraltar. When he said he loves you, you can take his word." Eric refuses to commit. She took the crumbs left from her bagged lunch and cast pieces of her sandwich over the river. Seagulls swooped from a sun-drenched sky, catching them before the bread could land on the white-capped waves.

Dot tucked a tendril of hair behind her ear. "Being kidnapped by Conrad, I was forced to see the truth about my shallow life. This war experience might change a lot of soldiers' outlook on life. Oh, did I tell you, two of my aunts who got taken by the Germans were freed from Ravensbrück. Soon as they are better, they'll be coming to America. Both of my uncles were killed. Pray, Esther, that I can show our Savior's love to my aunts."

Esther studied her friend's face. "Speaking about love, what about you and William?" Her question sparked a reaction like a jewel uncovered in a mine. "Dot, you're blushing. That's got to count for something. So, my lop-eared brother did propose. Mother thought he had."

"Well." Dot waltzed around the carpet of grass, her arms outstretched. Was she hugging an imaginary William? "Is it that obvious? Oh, I want to scream for joy. I never dreamt that time at the Vanity could be the beginning of love." Dot faced her. "What about you and Eric? At the Vanity, he had eyes for only you. Aren't you secretly engaged, too?"

She slumped down on the park bench, buried her head in her hands, and sobbed. "I, I, he—I thought he was going to propose, but I—"

"When?" Dot plopped down next to her.

"Before he shipped out. When he was at Camp Custer, he drove to Detroit one night. Dot, I foolishly I told him about Mary. How hard it was for her to find work and housing for her and her child." She bit back the tears, hating the feeling of helplessness. "I've always been scared that I'd marry a man who would die and leave me. I didn't want a child to raise alone."

Dot offered her a handkerchief. "Like your mother?"

"I wanted security. Mother and I had nothing to call our own. We were like gypsies. Oh, my aunt and uncle couldn't have been better to us. Uncle Franklin became the father William and I never knew."

Esther reached for the extended handkerchief and wiped her eyes. Her mascara inked a dark stain across the white linen like yesterday's newspaper. "Then Buck Briggs came into our lives. He was big as life and full of flirtatious fun, sort of like Eric. Mother didn't accept him nor his shenanigans until he bent his knee to God and accepted the salvation of Jesus. And, well, then he became the Defender of the Weak, a sort of avenging angel against organized crime and crooked politicians and got himself killed." Now that the mask she hid behind was gone, she might as well confess.

"I love Eric so much that I told Mother. But I'm afraid that what happened to Buck might happen to Eric. Mother said not to fret over something I had no control over. She was all for us getting married; that is, until William wrote Mother about Eric, remember?"

"That awful letter about some Italian girl? So I started dating Thomas, hoping I could forget Eric." She closed her eyes, fighting the familiar guilt that heated her skin like sunburn. "I don't love Thomas.

Part of me wishes I could. He's quiet, reserved, has a good stable job, everything I'm looking for in a man. But I can't." Esther slumped forward. "Yesterday, I confessed to him that I was in love with someone else. Dot, he said he wasn't going to give up."

"You did the right thing, telling the truth. Eric's still writing you." The rise in pitch of Dot's voice belied her calm exterior. She only sounded like that when she was upset.

Esther blew her nose. "How can Eric forgive me when I can't forgive myself? How can Thomas forgive me?" She hiccupped, dotting her handkerchief across her tear-drenched face. "The last time I saw Eric, he said his pa was right. That he needed to prove himself. I'm afraid he thinks I'm like his pa, that I can't love him until he's some conquering hero. I tried to write him the truth, that I'd always love him with the love of Jesus." She hiccupped again. "I was afraid for Eric to know I loved him with the marrying kind of love, the enduring, one embodiment kind that Mother talks about." Esther wiped her eyes. "Do you want to know why?"

Dot's moist eyes searched Esther's face. She nodded.

"Part of me feels like, well, Eric might be playing with my feelings like he does with other women. Oh, Dot, what am I going to do?"

Dot knelt, cradling Esther's shoulders, and shook her gently. "Esther Meir, you mean to tell me you, the one who brought me to my Savior Jesus Christ, refuse to lean on Jesus? To accept your Savior's forgiveness and believe He can make all things new again? Remember redeeming love?"

"Huh?" Esther licked the salty tears from her lips, wiped her mascara-drenched face with the handkerchief, and hiccupped. "I— you're right. Dear Dot, when did you become so wise?"

"Not me, the Good Book."

Esther got up, rearranged her skirt, and walked to the grassy knoll near the river before falling to her knees. The water lapped close to her skirt, as if pushing her away. She clasped her hands. "Dear Jesus, forgive me. Show me what to do, what to say when Eric comes home."

Dot wrapped her arms around Esther and knelt beside her.

Esther gave her a sideways look. "I've fallen in love with Eric all over again through his letters. But in all these months Eric never once wrote me that he truly loved me—Oh, he'd write 'love and kisses'—really? Thomas tells me how he can't live without me every time I see him. He proposes practically every day! Maybe Eric's feelings toward me are not strong enough? Maybe he never will propose, Dot."

"What about William? He'd know."

Esther laid her head on Dot's shoulder. "William's not sure. Eric never confides in him about me."

Chapter 32

E ric sat on his stilted lifeguard chair at the tranquil beach resort in Lago di Como and scanned the shoreline and waters. Friday afternoons were usually quiet. He checked his watch. Five p.m. His replacement should show up any time now. He and William were planning a little sightseeing excursion this weekend.

Life had taken a turn for the better in the Engineering Corps. He'd heard good reports that the maps he'd drawn had been accurate and soldiers' lives had been spared.

With the news regarding Hitler's defeat and the bombing of Hiroshima and Nagasaki, the Japanese had surrendered.

Working in an office and lifeguarding made life less strenuous. Living in this fancy resort hotel was a far cry from living in a foxhole, barely alive.

However, Uncle Sam was hesitant to allow his men to return home until they had gone through the necessary health checks—and gained back some of the weight they'd lost.

He took Esther's letter out of the pocket of his swim shorts and lifted it to his nose. He loved the smell of her perfume. The scent had been with him through all his battles, keeping him sane through the toughest fights, as did her little Bible verses. He'd memorized them all.

He especially liked, Be strong in the Lord and put on the whole armor of God. Yes, with God's help, he'd come through the worst without losing any major body parts. He'd managed to keep his wits about him, too, but his pride had taken a beating. Could what William said about Esther being part of the USO and meeting some flyboy be true? She's the one he wanted to bear his name, bear his children. Still, did she love him the way he loved her? Other girls had confessed their love for him, but then they'd drifted off. Or run when the first tough time came.

Had Esther fallen in love with flyboy Thomas?

"Hey, you ready?" William stood alongside Eric's replacement.

Eric gathered his things, climbed down the ladder, and handed the new lifeguard his equipment.

"What's our plan for next weekend?"

"Switzerland." William grinned. "Then the week after, who knows, maybe the States."

es

Eric gripped the rope railing, his stomach lurching in rhythm with the ship's movement on the tide, as he followed William up the gangplank of the *Liberty*. Seagulls colored the blue sky and screeched as if to warn him as GIs crowded forward boarding the ship.

William stood next to him, looking completely at home on the water. "What's the date?"

Eric strolled toward the ship's railing and breathed deeply. "September 27. Why?"

"September 27." William looked over the ship's railing. "Well, I wonder how long it will take this boilerplate special to make the trip Stateside?" He looked around at the soldiers trying to find a place to sit. "They're packing us in like sardines."

Eric's feet slipped on the ship's deck covered in seawater, mud, and debris, all of which made walking difficult. "Looks like the cleaning crew had a day off."

"They probably expect a lot of seasick soldiers before we reach Stateside."

es

Eric lay on a bench that lined the railing, looking up at the stars, trying to fall asleep as the ship crashed through the waves. They'd been on the ship over twenty days now. Soon they'd be home. He debated about asking William if Esther had mentioned that flyboy again. The groans of the men lying on either side of him grew louder, and the smell of vomit hung in the crisp air.

His stomach growled. Because of rough waters, half the food from his mess kit had ended up on the deck. He sat up, seeing the sun peeking over the waves. Shoving his blanket away, he stood and yawned.

William made his way to the ship's rail, breathing in deeply of the salty air. "We've been on this bobbing cork for almost three weeks. We should see the harbor soon."

"I figure it could be today." He peered out across the waves.

"It took seven days to get to Africa. Course they needed us to win a war then."

The waves rose and crested, much like his up and down emotions. Through the early morning mist, Eric envisioned Esther's sassy face. She always ended her letters by writing she loved him with the love of Jesus. Was that the same as personal love between a man and woman?

William looked around the deck. "It'll take a couple of days to get some of these soldiers back on their feet. Did you see the mess down below in the head?"

Eric nodded. "Has Esther written anything more about flyboy?"

"You mean Thomas? You'll have to ask her about that."

Eric searched the horizon, studying the sun's rays that peeked across the foamy waters. The salty breeze hit him in the face like a wrestler's punch, and he tasted brine mingled with the odors of fish and seaweed. "Why didn't you write Esther and tell her not to see that Southerner? I mean, well, I thought she was my gal?"

William rested his arms on the railing and stared at the sunrise. "Do you love my sister, or are you just playing with her feelings like you did with those other dames?"

"I never played with Esther's feelings. I respect her far too much to do a thing like that." Eric squinted at a white spot in the distance. At first, he thought the mist rising from the ocean was playing tricks on his eyes. "I—see the shore line." The rays of the sun swept the gleaming frame of Lady Liberty lifting her torch toward the heavens. The statue rose majestically amidst the ocean's waves, like a lighthouse of refuge, like a beacon of hope.

Nothing had ever looked better.

Eric recalled the inscription at the base of the landmark:

Give me your tired, your poor,
Your huddled masses yearning to breathe free,
The wretched refuse of your teeming shore.
Send these, the homeless, tempest-tost to me,
I lift my lamp beside the golden door!

At that moment the ear-piercing shells, the months of hiding in foxholes enduring the freezing winters, the rain-drenching autumns, and the insect-riddled springs melted away.

"With a lot of help from God Almighty, we did it." William gripped Eric around the shoulders and shook him so hard he could hear his teeth chattering. "We did it."

Soldiers ran to the railing, cheering, waving their hats in the air. "Lady Liberty, we're back. We made it back!" Someone sang the first notes of "America, the Beautiful," and others joined in, tears streaming down their cheeks. "O beautiful for heroes proved in liberating strife Who more than self their country loved, and mercy more than life!" Then they sang the last verse of "The National Anthem." "Praise the power that hath made and preserved us a nation. Then conquer we must, when our cause it is just, And this be our motto—'In God is our trust,' And the star-spangled banner in triumph shall wave O'er the land of the free and the home of the brave."

O'Brien waved his hands in the air, his tanned face wet with tears. "This here old *Liberty* ship may be rickety and not too comfortable, but it brung us here, and I'm mighty glad it did."

Eric bowed his head. He'd left America's shores gullible, thinking he could lick the world. A boy in a man's body, that's what he was, thinking he could beat the Germans with no problem. Yeah, he sure was cocky.

He looked around at the scarred and creased faces, the patched-up arms and legs, knowing every man here had undergone a similar transformation. Their experiences had hardened them, stripped their youth away, and tested their beliefs.

Dick's words echoed in his mind. There was more he needed to do. God had not left him on Earth to sit and gather dust from his memories. Hopefully he'd become a better man who knew the freedom he fought for must be cherished and guarded.

The GI Bill would start him off down the right road. Would he be able to forget the faces of the men he killed? His buddies left lying dead in the foxholes? If there was ever a time he needed to be consoled, it was now.

Chapter 33

Esther rested her hand on the doorknob of her apartment. Thomas's look sliced her heart. Goodbyes were never easy for her. "You will find the right woman someday."

Thomas cut a dashing figure in his Navy dress uniform. He knew it. His jaw tightened to ridged squareness. "I'm looking at the gal who has stolen my heart." He stepped closer, stroking her cheek. "Sure you won't reconsider? You don't know if you and that GI will make a compatible pair—like us."

Esther sidestepped toward the window seat. "I...I want to wait for God to pick my husband out for me." She recalled Eric's letter about when he found her brother and the Bible verse that had comforted him. John 3:8, The wind bloweth where it wishes...so is everyone that is born of the Spirit.

"Well, then you might be waiting a long time."

"Thomas, in the months we have shared, you never could understand my love for God and His Word."

"I doubt I will." Something menacing flickered within his eyes. She couldn't stop the shiver she felt from traveling up her spine. "This God you put such store into allowed thousands of men to die in a senseless war! I'll never forget the horrors of it."

Her heels beat a steady duo on the wooden floor. She rested her hand on the door knob. "I pray God will show you the love He has for you and grant you your heart's desire."

His eyes swept her form approvingly. He didn't seem in the mood to give up.

⁊

Eric jumped off the Harper Street car and gazed at the Kingston Arms Apartments. His wristwatch pointed to ten. He was glad today was Saturday; Esther would be home. He waited outside the building for someone to exit. He smiled at an elderly couple who held the door open for him. "Thank you." He touched the brim of his army cap.

Then he sprung forward, climbed the steps to Esther's apartment two at a time. His thundering boots echoed in his ears.

Outside Esther's apartment, he straightened his tie. A man's, then Esther's voice filtered through the closed door. William said he planned to go to Tiffany's and pick out a ring for Dot, then pick up Dot and head over to the apartment. William thought that would give Eric time to mend some fences. He paused. Maybe he should have called first. He turned, walking down the steps, feeling as if he'd lost his best friend.

Well, what did he expect?

He'd treated Esther terribly. He'd never committed himself. Never said he loved her. Why—she could be engaged or married to that Southern fighter pilot.

Eric balled up his hands. The motto of his 34ᵗʰ Red Bull Division echoed in his ears. Fight soldier—You fought for your country, why not for the woman you love? He stopped. It's now or never. Pounding his way up the stairs, his fist rapped a rat-a-tat message on Esther's door.

⁊

"Eric!" Esther jumped into his outstretched arms, burying her head in his shoulder and sobbed. "Oh, Eric, Eric. Oh, thank you Jesus for bringing Eric home."

His arm closed around her so hard she could feel his ribbons and brass buttons through her dress. She felt his firm muscles, the strength of him, and the tears flowed. She was home. As home as a baby bird would its nest. The solidity of him, the depth, width, and breadth of inner peace, that's what she'd missed most.

Esther's breath caught in her throat as his lips met hers hungrily, as if he couldn't get enough. She drank in the ecstasy of his closeness, of his heart pounding in unison with hers. So different from Thomas.

Yikes, Thomas. "Oh, my!" she murmured. "Eric, I'd like to introduce Thomas Cutter."

Eric swept him with a piercing look. "Oh, right." He cleared his throat, extending his arm. "Nice to see you again, Cutter. See any action your way?"

"Some, banged up my head pretty bad for a spell." He looked from Esther to him. "How about you?"

Eric rocked back on his heels. "Well, I felt like I was in the crossfires of a shooting match more often than I'd like to recall."

Thomas grunted. "Yeah, I can imagine. Well, I'd best be on my way." He took Esther's hand, kissed it. Picking up his coat and cap, he met Eric's gaze. "This gal's a first-class lady, just wanted you to know that. She gave a shell-shocked gent a chance to mend, and if I ever hear you didn't treat her like the genuine lady she is, I'll be back to even the score." He touched the brim of his cap. "Good-bye, Esther." The door closed softly behind him.

"Do I need to know what mine fields I'm crossing here?"

"We were saying our good-byes when you knocked."

Eric fidgeted with the rim of his cap. "Hmm, I was wondering, can you come with me to my parents' house?"

"You haven't been there yet?"

Just then the apartment door opened in a flurry of laughter. "Look who I found at the front door of our apartment," Mother said.

"Look, I'm engaged." Dot held up her left hand.

"William!" Esther ran forward and William caught her in mid-air. "You look great, Sis." He whirled her around the room. "I'm home, and I've got me the most beautiful bride in the world. That is, next to Sis."

"Well, I guess I'd better get a kiss from her before I lose my chance."

Eric gave Dot a kiss on her apple-red cheeks. "Yeah, I can see why you didn't wait to get a ring on her finger. Dot, you've grown lovelier. You've got a glow about you."

"I agree." Esther said. Dot's black velvet pillbox hat perched upon her auburn curls made her large, liquid eyes sparkle. Her cheeks were flushed, and her tailored dress hugged her silhouette like skin.

"I bet everyone could use one of my country breakfasts," Mother said. "I can whip up some eggs and bacon right quick."

William's arm was around Dot's shoulders as they followed their mother into the kitchen. "Mother, make them scrambled, with lots of milk and maybe some cheese. And if you have some green peppers, you can toss those in, too."

"Oh, and don't forget about your biscuits," Dot quipped. "Now that I'm engaged, I don't have to fast anymore."

William peered at her, one eyebrow raised. "Do what?"

"Fast, silly. I needed a little help from God to make sure you proposed and that I could get into this suit."

Ruby laughed. "I suppose you want some of my homemade blackberry jam with that." She turned and looked at Eric. "Eric, you're awful quiet. You staying for breakfast?"

"I don't think so. I need to tell Ma and Pa I'm back."

"I understand."

Esther's heart jumped into her throat. She was foremost in his thoughts. "Excuse me, while I go make myself presentable."

Esther covered her flaming cheeks with her hands, remembering his lips on hers. She stripped off her work dress, then poked her feet through her special-occasions dress. The aqua-blue taffeta hugged her hips and then folded into a generous skirt that reached the middle of her knees. She fastened the cloth-covered buttons running from waist to neck. Brushing her hair, she pinned one side back with a barrette. She applied lipstick, then stared at her reflection in the mirror. "Lord, what if Eric should propose. What do I tell him?"

Did she love Eric enough to forgive him his failings and shortcomings? Did Eric love her as Christ loved the church and gave Himself for it, like Ephesians 5:25 says? Her Aunt Collina's first marriage had ended in a catastrophe. Esther hurried to her bedside table and opened her Bible. "Let love be without dissimulation. Abhor that which is evil; cleave to that which is good." She looked up from her Bible, puzzled. Funny, I've read the Bible from cover to cover, but Romans 12:9 never spoke to me like this before. After several minutes of prayer, she returned to the living room, where Eric waited for her.

"Come and eat, Esther. Eric needs to get to his family."

William looked from her to Eric and smirked. "Sit down, partner."

Her mother set down plates of eggs, sausage, biscuits, and gravy.

"Well, they don't expect me today, and they probably already ate," Eric mumbled.

Esther smiled. Some things about a man never change. She sat next to him, listening to the ping-pong conversation about William and Dot's wedding plans. Too soon for her, Eric pushed away from the table.

"That was delicious, Mrs. Meir. Well, we'd best be off."

Esther's half-eaten eggs stared back at her, asking her the question that had quenched her appetite. Do you love Eric enough to couple your life with his for better or worse if he should ask? Eric's heavy boots echoed on the wooden floor as he walked to the door, each step feeling like nails being pounded into her heart.

"You'd better take your coat, Esther. It looks a little chilly."

Dot nodded. "It is, Mrs. Meir."

Eric helped her into her coat. They descended the stairs with Eric trailing her. As they waited at the bus stop, he said, "Nothing we learned at home prepared us for the horrors we endured. I believe you might have got an inkling of that from flyboy."

"You mean Thomas Cutter?"

"Yeah." He grasped her hand, allowing his to trail up her arms as he assisted her onto the Claremont bus. Her heart beat a pulsating rhythm in her ears. She felt him mount the steps behind her. "We'll have time to talk and get reacquainted during the ride."

Chapter 34

Eric couldn't miss the four gold stars in his parents' front window. They were the largest stars he'd ever seen displayed in a house or store. Each point, decorated with tin, caught the rays of the morning sunlight. In the center of every star was a picture of one of their sons, along with their names.

He looked up at the white framed house with the generous front porch peppered with an assortment of furniture. A wooden swing big enough for four hung from the porch ceiling by chains. Two rockers sat on the opposite side. Nothing had changed.

"Well, are you ready? This is the last time we'll be able to hear ourselves think."

Esther smiled, which caught him off-guard. All the way over here on the bus, she was quiet. He fumed at first, thinking if that's how she felt, she could have flyboy. Only after he cooled down did he realize he didn't want to lose Esther, the love of his life.

As they paused on the sidewalk outside his parents' home, the cold ice he'd wrapped his heart in to keep it safe cracked. Her faithfulness to write when he couldn't, the Scripture verses, her gentle spirit...She was the anchor he needed in his life. The ice had begun to melt. He couldn't blame her. He'd changed, and he told her so as the bus roared down his street. After all, her topsy-turvy emotions were a mirror image of his. The stroll down Mayfield's sidewalk on their way to his parents' house was just what they needed to get rid of the cobwebs of the past years.

"Esther." He grasped her hands in his. "I'm sorry for the way I've acted about Thomas Cutter. I didn't want you to get close to me because I wasn't sure I'd make it back Stateside. I'm a louse to act jealous now. Can you forgive me?"

"Yes." Tears brimmed her eyelids.

His heart felt about to stop. "I love you. I...thought you should know. I'm sorry for all the nightmares I put you through these past years, too."

A tear slipped down one of Esther's cheeks, marring an otherwise perfect complexion. He gently wiped the droplet away.

Before she could reply, the front door jolted open, banging against the white wooden panels. His father bounded down the steps.

Pa had him around the shoulders, his hands shaking with emotion as he patted him on the back.

Eric's mother was behind him, wiping her eyes with her handkerchief. John, Ann Marie, Lee, Mike, and Elizabeth stood behind his mother. His entire family started talking at the same time, each one shoving to get close and hug him. He lost his grip on Esther as his brother wrapped him in a bear hug.

"We were watching for you to drive up."

"We took the Claremont."

They surrounded him with their affection. "Haha, it's good to be home." Turning in circles, he answered every question with a bear hug. The gentle music of Esther's laughter reminded him of that first night at the Vanity. The wedge of ice lodged in his chest melted clean away. Yes, war had changed just about everything, but not his love for Esther.

He slipped his arm through hers. "Bet the only time you've heard so much chatter was during Detroit's Christmas parade."

Eric pulled her into the family circle, presenting her to his parents. "You remember Esther."

Her mother smiled. "How could we forget? Your letters were all about her Bible verses and prayers."

Esther blushed, the prettiest shade of pink Eric had ever seen.

⌒

Esther shifted from one foot to the other, hoping she had not disclosed her nervousness about being the center of their scrutiny.

Eric's father extended his arm toward her. "Those verses helped my boy get home."

"It was all I could do. I mean, God holds the keys to life and death. Pray to Jesus and send scripture to—"

"True." Eric's mother held her handkerchief to her eyes, then buried her head in Eric's shoulder.

Eric walked his mother and Esther to the porch.

Eric's sister Ann Marie glanced at the brick home a stone's throw away. "Ma." Anna followed her eldest daughter's gaze, her smile widening, seeing their neighbor Barbara. Patting Eric on the arm, Ma said, "My last boy's home. They all came back with their arms and legs intact, too. You and the mister want to come over?"

Barbara placed both hands to her ample chest. She wiped reddened eyes with her apron. "I'm glad to see your boy come home safe, Anna. My Anthony was killed during the Normandy invasion, Eric."

Her pale eyes held such pain that Esther ached for her.

Eric intertwined his fingers with Esther's.

"You and Andy come over. We're going to have a little party to celebrate all our boys coming home from the war." Fred shook his index finger. "Now, I'm not going to take kindly if you don't."

The corners of Barbara's lips crept toward a smile. Her mouth moved, but no sound came out. She brushed the tip of her apron across her face. "It is good to celebrate our victory, to leave our sorrow in here." She rested her hand over her heart. "Eric, it does me good to see you well." Her brown hair, peppered with gray, was pinned at the nape of her neck, just like Eric's mother's. "How Anna and I worried over you."

"Our boys did us proud, Barbara," Anna said. "They booted those ruffians out of France and Italy for good."

Barbara headed for her front door. "I'll go and see if I can get my Andy to come. Some time with friends will do him good. He's sad too much." She put a forefinger to her lips. "But don't say I told you." She winked at Esther. "He'll want to meet Eric's girl. I think I hear wedding bells this time."

At Barbara's words, Esther risked a glance at Eric, waiting for his reaction. But he seemed not to have heard and walked through the doorway behind his mother.

The family chattered like magpies at a picnic. Eric's father slapped him on the shoulder. "I got a copy of that speech Winston Churchill gave to your regiment, son. It's right over here. You want to read it?"

"Why should he want to read it, Pa?" Mike paused halfway down the hallway.

"Because he was there, Mike," his father said. "Eric, is Churchill as big as he sounds over the radio?"

"Bigger than life." Eric placed his hand on his brother's shoulder and squeezed. "When he speaks, you can hear a leaf fall from a tree, it's that quiet. That man will go down in the history books someday as one of Britain's greatest men."

"I saw him in the newsreels," Eric's father said.

"He didn't smile much," Eric's mother said. "Did he smile when he gave that speech?" She lifted the mahogany cover from the piano keys, the signal for everyone in the room to wrap up their conversation because Anna would begin the entertainment segment of their party.

"Yeah, he was smiling."

"I bet he was." His father reached for his pipe and tobacco from the top of the piano. "The weight of England was lifted from his shoulders, thanks to you boys."

John took the copy of Churchill's speech that his pa had laid down. He gave a low whistle. "Wow, it says here '...while the Division amassed 517 days of combat, one or more 34th Division units were engaged in actual combat with the enemy for 611 days. The Division was credited with more combat days than any division in the Theater.'" John looked up. "That's more than any other US Army Division stationed in Europe during World War II."

Eric avoided everyone's eyes. He was the center of Pa's and everyone else's attention, and he didn't care for it. Esther understood.

Elizabeth clasped Eric's sleeve and rested her finger on the patch. "What does that mean, Eric?"

"He was part of the 135th Infantry Regiment, in a rifle company. They were the first ones to go into enemy territory." Francis pointed to Eric's coat sleeve and read. "To the Last Man."

"Yeah, well, it came down to that too often to remember," Eric mumbled. "What will it be, Ma? Some of our old favorite hymns?"

The front door opened.

"Hey, look, our neighbors have stopped in." Fred motioned Barbara and Andy around the piano. "You're just in time for some singing."

"What happened to your buddies?" Elizabeth asked.

"They died," John said. "Eric's company was in front, ahead of the tanks, guns, and heavy artillery."

Anna stopped thumbing through her songbook. "How many boys came back from your original company?"

Esther recalled what Eric wrote about how Tommy recited the Soldier's Prayer that last morning of his life…let me die thy friend, thy soldier still. Esther could just imagine what Eric was going through remembering Tommy's last words. Eric leaned down and took a sip from his coffee cup and muttered, "Shadow of death. Yeah, death is a shadow. Just like Psalm 23 says." His piercing eyes fell onto their neighbors. "Life's never over. Nah, they're not dead. They were promoted to heaven. And they'll come again when Jesus returns to clean out all the bullies for good." He nodded toward their neighbors. "God will be there, too, for the next war."

Fred looked at him, his eyes glassy, and started to speak.

"It's over, Pa, and we won because of guys like Anthony, Tommy, and Captain Kimble." Eric cupped his hands around his mouth and whooped out a war cry, and everyone joined in.

"Now that we're warmed up, let's sing until we're hoarse and can't talk. Afterwards, what about some football?"

"Haven't you had enough fighting to last a lifetime?" Ann Marie huffed, placing her hands on her hips.

Eric seized his older sister around the waist and danced her around the room. "Never. Attack, attack, attack. We gotta keep those bullies of the world in their places."

Chapter 35

Eric rubbed a hand along the dust-covered Ford coupe. He opened the front passenger door. Esther slipped in. He ran around the car to the driver side. Esther slid closer next to him. The motor rumbled loudly, and he raised his voice an octave. "I plan to get my old job back. Of course, I'll be pretty busy going to school. I need to finish my engineering degree now that I've got the GI Bill. I think I'll enroll in U of D. They have a good engineering program there." He steered the car out of the driveway and toward Maywood.

When they stopped at a red light, he glanced at her. Esther's hands rested demurely in her lap. *She's gorgeous.* "I know no one thinks I can do this but me. But someday I'll have my own engineering and manufacturing company."

He reached out, and Esther laced her fingers in his. "I believe you, Eric."

"You do? I'll work for some engineering company for a while. Save up a good chunk of change before I start my own business. It'll be hard going. Everything will have to go back into the company for a while. Then, I'll need to get hitched and start a family."

Esther blushed, looked away, and removed her hand from his. "Oh?"

"Do you plan to get married?"

Esther moved a fraction of an inch away on the leather upholstery. "Of course, I want to get married. What woman doesn't?"

"Then you looking for some Southern guy?"

"Thomas and I are friends. He stopped by because he was leaving for Tennessee and wanted to say one last good-bye. That's when you—" Her voice broke.

"Ah, yes, I remember now."

"Every letter you wrote practically pushed me into Thomas's arms." She turned her gaze from the window to him. "You made me believe all you felt for me was friendship. By the way, how is that little Italian girl you met? You ever hear from her?"

Eric's breakfast lurched as if he were out on high seas in the *Liberty* again. "So, William told you about that Italian gal, huh?"

She frowned and looked out her passenger window.

Eric cleared his throat. He'd put his foot in his mouth that time. "I couldn't get my mind off you the whole time I was in Italy, and that's the truth. Believe me, Esther, I loved you so much that I didn't want to hurt you by breaking your heart with promises I didn't know I could keep."

Leaving the city, Eric laid his foot on the accelerator. Soon the landscape changed from houses to rolling green hills, majestic maples, and elm trees lining the dirt roads to Roxy Stables. That place had become their refuge. That was the place to take Esther.

"Apache missed you," Esther said.

"Did you ride him much?"

"Some. I was careful not to go too fast, due to his extremely hard mouth."

The hum of the tires running through the gravel driveway of Roxy's drowned their conversation. Eric rolled to a stop in front of the stable.

Esther packed the bread sacks loaded with sandwiches and cookies his ma had given them.

He quirked his chin toward the open fields. "There's still enough daylight to ride out to our favorite spot and have a picnic. You game?"

"I have some clothes where I keep my grooming tools for Magic."

Eric had an extra pair of cowboy boots in his car. The rest of his clothes were fine to ride in. He saddled up the horses. Hearing a noise, he looked up. There stood Esther dressed in a pair of tan riding breeches that complemented her shapely legs. Her red turtleneck sweater highlighted her dark locks and tanned complexion to perfection. Eric whistled. "You're gorgeous! So, when do want to get hitched?"

Esther stopped. Her face aflame. She rushed toward her horse.

He gripped Apache's bridle. Cool it, soldier. One more mistake like this morning's, and Esther will hightail her way to Tennessee after Mr. Perfect.

⁓

Esther cantered down the lane alongside Eric. Green, red, yellow, and orange leaves arched over the bridle path like a scene in a medieval knight tale. All that was missing were the armor and swords. She didn't slow her horse until they were at their favorite spot overlooking a babbling brook and spring-fed pond.

"I forgot how beautiful Michigan's falls are." Eric inhaled deeply, his chest filling out the folds in his jacket. "I don't remember the colors being this vibrant or the air so crisp."

The landscape had captured his attention. What was so different about him? He'd filled out in his shoulders, but his face was leaner. His clothes didn't quite fit him the same either. Definitely leaner, his cheek bones were more defined. There was no pudginess anywhere, not even on his face. Not that he was anything but fit before the war.

Now there were deeper crevasses around his mouth that emphasized his strong, square jaw. His eyes had changed most. There was nothing youthful left. No boyish twinkle, no jesting smirk. That would change, if she had anything to say on the matter.

Still, there was something else. His face had a strong, impregnable look to it with shadowed lines beneath his eyes, like he'd seen death too many times. She shivered.

Eric sidled his horse next to hers. "I envied John. I can't believe I'm admitting this, but I was jealous of my older brother." A muscle moved along his jaw. "I couldn't understand why I had to be the one born colorblind. Why not him? I wanted to be the one to learn how to fly a plane. I felt plenty sorry for myself in those cold, damp foxholes."

They dismounted and Eric tied their horses to a nearby tree.

Esther's riding boots sank in the soft banks of the pond. Its tranquil calmness soothed her nerves, and she drank in the aroma of a nearby apple tree. "Whenever it was possible, I'd come here to read your letters. Beneath that apple tree." She pointed to the spot showing signs of wear. "Sometimes I had to scrape the snow away, and then I reread your letters, over and over again."

He gestured to a spot beneath the tree.

"It was hard to picture your world, that world of death, pain, and misery, when the world I sat in was peaceful."

He didn't respond. His head was down and she couldn't see his facial features. He kept twirling a three-leaf clover between his thumb and forefinger. She hesitated, recalling her Aunt Collina's words. Never rush forward into a matrimonial decision. Your heart is the last thing you should listen to. Remember Proverbs 28:26, "He that trusteth in his own heart is a fool: but whoso walketh wisely, he shall be delivered."

He sighed. "I hated killing. But it was kill or be killed."

She remembered what he wrote about Tommy and Captain Kimble. "Eric, I feel we need to pray." She clasped his hand in hers. "God, we realize that we have sinned. Because You tell us in Romans 3:23 that 'all have sinned, and come short of the glory of God.' Thank You for sending Jesus to pay the penalty for our sins. We turn away from our sins and ask You to renew our lives. Amen."

Eric pocketed the three-leaf clover, his smile conciliatory. "Father, Son, and Holy Spirit, if one of us brothers had to be in a foxhole, I'm glad it was me." His eyes delved into the innermost regions of her soul. "Remember John 3:8?"

A breeze ruffled her hair and stirred the potent aroma of fresh air, snapdragons, and apples. "'The wind bloweth where it listeth, and thou hearest the sound thereof, but canst not tell whence it cometh, and whither it goeth.'"

He touched a stray tendril of hair. They strolled toward the lake.

"Every time I felt the wind on my face, I thought of that. Every time I was ready to give up, the wind would come and I remembered how much God loved me. 'For God so loved the world, that he gave his only begotten Son, that whosoever believeth in him should not perish, but have everlasting life.'"

"For God sent not his Son into the world to condemn the world; but that the world through him might be saved." Esther felt the peace of God and the answer she was looking for. Eric and she were kindred spirits in their love for God and His Son.

"During the battle of Anzio, I lost hope. Oh, I put on a good front for William and the others, but I was ready to quit. Then the mule came up with kettles of hot soup, and the quartermaster handed me a bunch of letters. Yours was in there. You wrote Romans 8:38–39 'I am persuaded, that neither death, nor life…shall be able to separate us from the love of God, which is in Christ Jesus our Lord.' It was as if God knew—He knew I needed that to hold onto."

"Oh, Eric." She fell into his waiting embrace. He wrapped his arms around her and they stood gazing across the pond.

"When you face death day after day, you realize how unimportant your life is." Eric turned her to face him. A breeze swept the trees, causing the leaves to rustle. "The wind blows free, and so are we. There were times I wondered if we would overcome Hitler and if I'd be around to know. At Cassino, I didn't understand why I was alive and the best of the infantry had died. Why was I spared?"

"I thank God He granted you a little longer on Earth."

"I believe God wants me to make a positive difference to the people in my life. I could never bring them to the Lord like you can, but I can give them security." His eyes searched her face. "Together we'll make a good team. I was always seeking my earthly father's acceptance when I should have kept my eyes on my heavenly Father's guidance. You showed me that."

Esther's tears streamed down her face like that stream a few feet away, but she didn't care. "God had to correct me, too. I can't believe how shallow and vain I was. I had in my mind what type of life I wanted, and I looked to God like I would a fairy godfather."

He chucked her under the chin. "That night when I found William, I felt God telling me that He loved me unconditionally. I really felt the Holy Spirit's presence."

"When you give your heart to Jesus, your destiny is no longer yours."

She sniffed and fished in her pockets for a hanky. She didn't have one and sniffed again.

He reached into his pocket and produced the needed handkerchief, the one she'd given him the day he left for boot camp. She smiled at the Scripture reference her mother had embroidered on the hankie. "If you have faith as a grain of mustard seed." The threads looked a little worse for wear. She blew her nose and blinked.

"Love is very much like the wind, Esther. You can't change its course."

"Especially when it's the heart-wrenching type of love between an obstinate man and a willful woman. Mother says that first comes romance, then comes commitment. The unromantic labor of self-denial. That kind of unselfish love and sacrifice that Jesus did on the cross. Not that I plan to hang on one for you."

Her wet eyelashes created a veil that made Eric's face look hazy. She swiped her eyes. Now she could see not just the handsome former soldier standing next to her. She saw God's plan for marriage and love, through Scripture, and through Eric's love for her.

His strong arms enveloped her. "You know I heard Ma's neighbor say we could be the greatest generation since the American Revolution. Ha! That's a laugh. This nation has survived because of what our parents taught us, because of everyday families who had faith in the one true God and His Son, Christ Jesus. It was this generation's moment to put to practice what we'd been taught."

Eric's coarse Army coat felt like sandpaper to her moist cheek, as rough as his emotions and as hard as his convictions. "Shushan's legacy from Esther 9:2 was left by my grandfather: 'And no man could withstand them; for the fear of them had fallen upon all people.'"

"Exactly. Israel was a nation of Jews. We are a nation of Christians." He kissed her cheek. "You're as much a part of your grandfather's legacy as he."

"I am?" Yes! I am and I pray my children will be, too. I didn't realize, but now I see that God carried me through my fears.

"And as long as Americans keep their faith and trust in God and follow His teachings laid out in the Good Book, we will be an indivisible nation where 'no one could make a stand against them.' Second Chronicles 7:14

means more to me than ever now. Humility, prayer, and turning from wickedness, the stuff of which we fought a grueling four years against— God help us to heal our land and keep our eyes on You."

When you meet the right man, you'll have no trouble following. Mother was right. "You never asked me how many children I wanted." Not waiting for his reply, she said, "I'd like a half dozen."

"Why so many?"

"Your mother. Anna is so full of fun, and she's never too tired to laugh. I want to be like that when I grow old." Esther wrapped her arms around his neck. "Children are a blessing from the Lord, and I want your quiver to be full. And I believe in the sanctity of marriage."

The twinkle was back in Eric's eyes. "You mean, fidelity and 'til death do us part,' that stuff?"

"Exactly. No more robbers' dances."

"The former playboy no longer exists. Christ has given me a new purpose." His voice was but a rumble in his chest. "Besides, I haven't been able to think of another woman since you waltzed into my life."

"I'm not planning on being the one left behind. I hated it when I thought you might not return." She kissed his cheek and walked toward the pond until her boots made impressions in the sand. She bent down, picked up a pebble, and threw it in the water. "I plan on seeing our children raised with families of their own. When our work at raising them is over, I want to leave for heaven first."

Eric drew her to him. "Look, we have a lot of living to do first. Now when do you want to begin?"

He lowered to one knee and kissed her hand as though she were royalty. "Esther, I've been down in that valley of death, and that couldn't separate me from my loving Jesus or my faithful Esther. That night at the Vanity I met God's destiny for me, to love our Lord and you with every breath I take. So why don't we get hitched?"

She laughed. "I thought you were kidding with me back at the stables. How romantic. 'Let's get hitched?'"

"Let me hear you say yes first, then I'll show you how romantic I can get." His silhouette was aflame with the sunset illuminated by the pond and the autumn colors of red, orange, and gold maples. She felt as if a rainbow of faith, hope, and love encircled them. "Yes, Eric, I will get hitched to you. You are my true love and will be forever until death does part us."

"My darling!" He swept her into his arms and danced her around the grassy knoll, the sunset drenching them in glowing light. "Did You hear that, Lord? She loves me enough to spend her life with me…and has finally admitted it. Yes…and we plan to hitch our lives to one of Your heavenly stars!"

Author's Note

Harry S. Truman once said: "There is nothing new in the world except the history you do not know."

Waltz with Destiny was inspired by the notes, the scraps of pictures, and the worn pocket Bible my dad carried close to his heart marching up the boot of Italy.

Dad was an avid history buff, and upon his death I found numerous magazine articles, notes, and newspaper clippings frayed and brown with age. Family members gave me letters that my dad wrote and prayers he carried with him in Italy. My greatest treasure came in a folder tucked away that had pictures of the Italian mountainside, and two pictures of my mom. On the back of these pictures, scribbled in Dad's handwriting, were the dates of his battles, parades, and stays in the hospital that added to the colorful backdrop of this novel.

The trip I shared with my dad to Carlisle, Pennsylvania, to see Gettysburg with his World War II infantry division gave me *The 34th Infantry Division*, published by Information and Educational Section, compiled by members of the 34th Infantry Division; *Dogfaces Who Smiled Through Tears: The 34th Red Bull Infantry Division* by Homer R. Ankrum; and *The Battle for Cassino* by Janusz Piekalkiewicz.

At the Gettysburg National Military Park and new museum displayed the US Army Heritage and Education Center. At a special ceremony, a commemorative brick was laid to honor the 34th Infantry Africa/Italy Campaign. The German captives often referred to the 34th

307

as the thundering Red Bulls.

Growing up in the Great Depression taught Dad the value of a dollar. Fighting the Germans in Italy taught him the value of life and that prayer was the channel to Jesus. He learned this by elbowing his way through the minefields, machine gun fire, and living in foxholes. When a buddy died, it was his time. His favorite words in describing his war experiences were: "You'll never meet an atheist in a foxhole."

Always the life of the party, Dad and Mom could waltz with the best of them. Mom gave the credit to her leading partner. Dad's last prayer was that his sons and grandsons would find a partner like he did—one who could waltz with best of them and follow their lead, supporting them through life's decisions and hardships.

CATHERINE ULRICH BRAKEFIELD

Catherine is an ardent receiver of Christ's rejuvenating love, as well as a hopeless romantic and patriot. She skillfully intertwines these elements into her writing as the author of *Wilted Dandelions, Swept into Destiny, Destiny's Whirwind, Destiny of Heart,* and *Waltz with Destiny* inspirational historical romances; and *Images of America, The Lapeer Area.* Her most recent history book is *Images of America, Eastern Lapeer County.* Catherine, former staff writer for *Michigan Traveler Magazine,* has freelanced for numerous publications. Her short stories have been published in Guidepost Books *Extraordinary Answers to Prayers, Unexpected Answers* and *Desires of Your Heart*; Baker Books, Revell, *The Dog Next Door, Horse of my Heart, Second-Change Dogs,* and *Horse of my Dreams* scheduled for Fall 2019; CrossRiver Media Group, *The Benefit Package,* and Bethany House, *Jesus Talked to Me Today.* She spent three weeks driving across the western part of the United States, meeting her extended family of Americans. This trip inspired her inspirational historical romance *Wilted Dandelions.*

Catherine enjoys horseback riding, swimming, camping, and traveling the byroads across America. She lives in Michigan with her husband, Edward, of forty years, and her Arabian horses. Her children grown and married, she and Edward are the blessed recipients of two handsome grandsons and two beautiful granddaughters.

www.CatherineUlrichBrakefield.com
www.Facebook.com/CatherineUlrichBrakefield
www.Twitter.com/CUBrakefield

If you enjoyed this book, will you consider sharing it with others?

- Please mention the book on Facebook, Twitter, Pinterest, or your blog.

- Recommend this book to your small group, book club, and workplace.

- Head over to Facebook.com/CrossRiverMedia, 'Like' the page and post a comment as to what you enjoyed the most.

- Pick up a copy for someone you know who would be challenged or encouraged by this message.

- Write a review on Amazon.com, BN.com, or Goodreads. com.

- To learn about our latest releases subscribe to our newsletter at www.CrossRiverMedia.com.

FIND MORE GREAT FICTION AT CROSSRIVERMEDIA.COM

SWEPT INTO DESTINY

Catherine Ulrich Brakefield

As the battle between North and South rages, Maggie Gatlan is forced to make a difficult decision. She must choose between her love for the South and her growing feelings for the hardworking and handsome Union solder, Ben McConnell. Was Ben right? Had this Irish immigrant perceived the truth of what God had predestined for America?

DESTINY'S WHIRLWIND

Catherine Ulrich Brakefield

Collina McConnell is thrust from adolescence to adulthood as she promises her dying father she will manage their estate. But her father dies before disclosing the mystery behind his legacy for Shushan. Dashing Rough Rider Franklin Long offers his help, and suddenly ollina's heart has a will of its own. Does he feel the same for her? War is declared, and he leaves for the Cuban shoreline. He holds the key to her heart, but will he return?

DESTINY OF HEART

Catherine Ulrich Brakefield

As 1917 arrives, Ruby McConnell Meir and her husband leave home and family for the Colorado prairies. They hope the climate will cure Stephen's mysterious illness. Back home, Collina battles to save not only Shushan, but her own life as well. Franklin Long lost what money couldn't buy. Is it too late to make right his failings? Each yearns for contentment, but life has other plans. Will their faith see them through?

WILTED DANDELIONS

Catherine Ulrich Brakefield

Hostile Native Americans, raging rivers, and treacherous trails are nothing compared to marrying a man she doesn not know. Can husband wife overcome the challenges of a marriage of convenience and eiscover a true and lasting love?

22918374R00176